About the author

Lucy Saxon is a cosplayer, book-lover, con-goer and all-round nerdgirl. Her first novel, *Take Back the Skies*, was published when she was just nineteen. She gets a lot of her best writing done in the dead of night and sometimes wakes up in the morning with keyboard prints on her face. When she's not writing she's playing video games, walking her dog or yelling at fabric until it behaves. She spends part of each year wrangling horses on a ranch in Arkansas. Most of the time though, she lives in Hertfordshire with her parents and her brother.

THE CITY
BLEEDS
GOLD

LUCY SAXON

BLOOMSBURY

LONDON OXFORD NEW YORK NEW DELHI SYDNEY

Bloomsbury Publishing, London, Oxford, New York, New Delhi and Sydney

First published in Great Britain in March 2017 by Bloomsbury Publishing Plc
50 Bedford Square, London WC1B 3DP

www.bloomsbury.com

BLOOMSBURY is a registered trademark of Bloomsbury Publishing Plc

Text copyright © L.A. Saxon 2017
Illustrations copyright © Jeff Nentrup 2014

The moral rights of the author and illustrator have been asserted

A CIP catalogue record for this book is available from the British Library

ISBN 978 1 4088 4773 2

Typeset by Integra Software Services Pvt. Ltd.
Printed and bound in Great Britain by CPI Group (UK) Ltd, Croydon CR0 4YY

1 3 5 7 9 10 8 6 4 2

Books by Lucy Saxon

Take Back the Skies
The Almost King

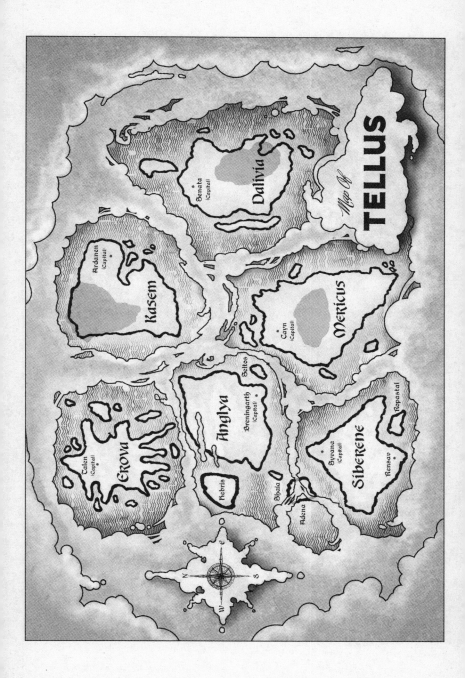

Map Of

TELLUS

Dallvia

Senata
(Capital)

Kasem

Ardanen
(Capital)

Mericus

Cayn
(Capital)

Erova

Calon
(Capital)

Anglya

Dreningarth
(Capital)

Beltos

Febris

Shala

Adena

Siberene

Syvana
(Capital)

Kensau

Rapastal

N
E
S
W

1

It was well past dark, not that anyone would know it by the activity in the city centre. Every lamp at every street corner shone brightly, and the noise from all the people still about was deafening. The blond-haired teen wandering through it all with his hands in his pockets was unsurprised to hear the sound of squalling sprogs irritated at being kept awake so late. It was a far cry from the deserted late-night lower city he was used to – the air was thick with anticipation and the sharp tang of bleach as the city went through its annual pre-festival cleaning.

Everywhere he looked, crowds of people in olive-green work uniforms were scrubbing and sweeping and dusting every inch of stone and metal in the lower city until it was pristine, ready for the most important event of the year. Soon, he mused, the troupers and merchants would arrive and set up their stalls, and then the tourists would appear, undoing all the hard work of making the city gleam. The only time the lower city ever got any kind of attention, and it would be gone in the blink of an eye.

The Festival of the Goddess began every year on the summer solstice and lasted for five hectic days of feasting, dancing and – in many cases – debauchery. Everyone in Erova who was able came to the royal city of Talen to praise the Goddess for keeping them healthy and prosperous over the past year, and to gain her favour for the upcoming harvest. They needed a good harvest now more than ever; a lot was riding on this year's festival. The weather hadn't been stellar over the recent months – too dry when rain was needed, and a far colder winter than Erova was used to – and if the murmurings from the outland farmers were anything to go by, they'd need nothing short of a Goddess-given miracle to have enough food to feed all of Erova once the Anglyan government had taken its ever-increasing share.

As he walked, the teen's hazel eyes were sharp beneath his messy fringe, taking in that which most would overlook. His pace was slow but purposeful, drawing eyes to his movements – in part due to him being almost a head taller than the rest of the crowd. He caught his name whispered a few times, and smirked to himself; people always thought they were being so subtle in their recognition. He made eye contact with several people, each of them giving him a brief nod of deference before quickly and carefully getting back to their work. He would never get used to having this effect on people.

'Daniel!' He looked up at the call of his name, the smile not coming as quickly as it should have in return for the blinding one bestowed upon him. Emilie's light brown hair bounced in its perfect curls as she hurried towards him, not hesitating to lean up and peck him on the lips. 'I was wondering where you had got to! You're missing all the fun, come on!' Without waiting for a response, she slid her hand down to take his, dragging him in the direction of a small courtyard not too far from the river. He'd heard that the troupers might be causing trouble and had been heading there anyway, but he wasn't really in the mood for distractions. He'd had a long day.

'So where is this fun I'm missing, exactly?' he asked lightly, earning an eye-roll from the girl at his side.

'Oh, don't start! Look, isn't it beautiful?' She directed his attention to the lower courtyard, which they could see beyond a cracked stone railing. Obviously some troupers had arrived early; a shimmering bronze tent had been erected in the centre of the stone square, a bright blue pennant flying from the central pole. Acrobats, then. 'Imagine how incredible everything will look once the festival is all set up! Oh, I just can't wait – it's going to be spectacular!' she gushed, sliding her hand into the crook of his arm and leaning against his shoulder.

He allowed it, but made no move to bring her closer. His eyes had landed on two men in work uniforms lurking around the back of the shining tent, shadowed by the structure. One man was rail-thin with wide, desperate eyes and trembling hands clenched tight around a leather money pouch. His companion was taller, broader, holding a small glass bottle that flashed green in the light. Recognising the gold insignia on the bottle, Daniel grimaced. He hadn't realised the Meyers brothers were working for Diora now. They'd been dangerous enough by themselves, selling all manner of illegal substances, but with that kind of backing Daniel would have to think carefully about his next step in getting them under control. If they were still selling when the festival rolled around, the Goddess only knew what kind of trouble it would cause.

It was things like this that made it hard for Daniel to truly enjoy festival time. He'd always loved it as a child – the lights, the parade, the food and the dancing were the pinnacle of excitement for a young boy. But the older he grew, the more difficult his life became around festival time, and it had begun to tarnish his outlook. People were more daring in times of celebration, and it wore him down trying to keep track of them all.

Shaking his head, Daniel turned to the honey-skinned girl at his side, offering a pleasant smile. 'The festival is still almost two weeks away, Em,' he reminded her lightly. 'Plenty of time to stare at tents. I was working.' He still was working, she just didn't know it.

'You work too much,' Emilie retorted, head briefly resting on his arm before she pulled away. 'Take a break, it's late. And I know you're done for the day – you said so earlier. Even Adamas has managed to find time away from the Boss to come out and see the tents.' Sure enough, when Daniel looked around he could see Emilie's older brother standing with the rest of her friends in the courtyard, grinning at something one of the girls had said. It surprised him; Adamas was usually far too busy to spend time with his sister. That changed things.

He sighed, though a smile tugged at his lips. 'Fine,' he agreed. Emilie beamed, taking his hand once more and leading him towards the rest of her friends.

'Aha!' Adamas crowed by way of greeting. 'The infamous Daniel Novak, deeming us worthy of his presence.' His voice was teasing but his eyes were cold, mocking. Daniel forced an even smile in return.

'Em insisted,' he replied. 'Apparently I work too much.'

Adamas barked out a laugh. 'You and me both, kid.'

Daniel bristled; he was only two years younger than Adamas, and was both taller and broader at the shoulders – certainly not a 'kid'.

'At least my work keeps food on the table,' Adams continued. 'You ever gonna get a real job? I'm sure the Boss could find something for you, now you're starting to get a bit of a reputation.'

Daniel resisted the urge to scoff. He had more of a reputation than most of Diora's men, including Adamas, who apparently assumed Daniel had gained that reputation through dealing with anything deemed too petty for Diora to be involved with – and most of the lower city believed it too. But his stomach turned at the thought of working for Diora. He'd spent the last three years working to bring the man down.

'I'm managing all right with my work as it is, thanks,' Daniel assured the man somewhat sharply, then winced. He took a deep breath, mentally reminding himself that he had to play nice; arguing with Adamas would only get him noticed. The longer Diora thought that Daniel wasn't worth worrying about the easier it would be for Daniel to get his work done without interference. 'But I'll keep the offer in mind.'

'Can you boys stop talking about work for ten minutes?' Emilie cut in, her lips pursed in irritation. She wound her arm through Daniel's, and he tensed. 'All we want to do is enjoy festival time, and it's hard to do that with you two being so boring.'

'Sorry, Em,' Adamas said. 'The Boss has been giving me so much more work lately, it's hard to go off duty. It's difficult for him when there are so few people he trusts as much as he does me.' He twisted the gold ring on his middle finger – the mark of Diora's men – and Daniel's lip curled slightly. Now he remembered why he didn't spend much time with Adamas in person. It was much better to hear about him through Emilie, when he could coax her into bragging about the things he needed information on without having to endure the man's astonishing ego. If he had his way, he wouldn't spend much time with either of them, but Adamas was Diora's third in command, and Daniel's best source of information on the Boss's plans. With Adamas's unwitting help, he might one day find Diora and get rid of him so he could never hurt anyone again. Emilie didn't care how he really felt about her; as long as half the lower city knew her as Daniel Novak's girlfriend, she was happy.

Under Emilie's scolding gaze the conversation turned back to the festival, and Daniel let the rest of her friends talk around him, preferring to listen. Daniel Novak made his work in secrets, and luckily, most people tended to underestimate what constituted a secret.

The whole group's conversation paused at the loud chimes that rung out through the city, and he counted them with a frown. 'I need to get going,' he declared.

'Oh, but you've barely been here an hour!' Emilie protested, bottom lip forming a pout. He leaned down to kiss her cheek.

'I'll see you in a couple of days,' he promised. He moved to step back, but Emilie's hand reached for his jacket collar before he could get too far. She pulled him down into a firmer kiss, lingering enough for a man across the street to wolf whistle at them. Daniel flushed – he hated it when Emilie made a scene. Unfortunately, it was her favourite thing to do.

'I look forward to it.' Emilie's painted lips curled in an attempt at being coy. It fell short, however, and he merely nodded, heading on his way.

Daniel followed the well-lit streets through several twists and turns, up and down endless stone staircases, before slipping into a dark side alley and climbing up on to an overhead walkway, a cool breeze ruffling his hair.

It was always joked that there was never more than ten feet of flat land in Talen at any one time; the whole city was made up of slopes and stairways and bridges over narrow rivers and streams. Daniel loved it; it made sneaking around infinitely more interesting, and it made the city breathtakingly beautiful. He'd only ever seen pictures of the other cities in Tellus, but none of them compared.

With pale yellow stone buildings and neatly paved pathways, and parks and courtyards never more than a ten-minute walk from one another, Talen truly was stunning – the Golden City of Tellus. Daniel only hoped it would stay that way. All over the world cracks were forming in Anglya's carefully built empire. There was word that Mericus was preparing to make a bid for independence and might force Anglya out of its borders. Erova had no need for independence yet – its monarchs were strong, and they had no quarrel with Anglya. But all that would change if the harvest was poor and they didn't meet their side of the trade agreements. Anglya was quick to punish these days, and Daniel dreaded to think what might happen should the Anglyans get involved in Erova's business.

Crossing the city at roof height was something he did with hardly a thought, leaping and rolling on instinct, his feet pounding rhythmically on the slates. No one noticed him flying from rooftop to rooftop, scaling buildings to get ever higher without a moment of hesitation. He'd been exploring the city from above for years, and the routes were so familiar to him now that he could clear his mind and lose himself in the motion of his arms and legs, watching for handholds in brick walls and noting where his previous holds had worn away or broken off. As his blood pumped faster with every step his stress melted away, a grin coming unbidden to his lips. Everything was simpler when he was in motion.

Slowing down a little in order to swing hand over hand across the decorative struts above the bridge to the upper city, Daniel breathed in the fresh air with a smile; twenty feet above the ground, he could almost forget he was in the most crowded city in Erova. Performing a tricky twist mid-air to leap from the bridge to the nearest walkway without having to drop to street level, he continued on his way, soft-soled leather boots digging into the small cracks and dips in the stone.

As soon as he was within the bounds of the upper city, it was like he'd stepped into a whole new world; the buildings were larger and newer, gleaming without the help of a cleaning crew. Decorative steel and bronze trimming on the roofs and windows made Daniel's journey infinitely easier here. Flower baskets hung from almost every corner of the quiet well-lit streets, filling the air with a sweet scent; a far cry from the damp-river smell that permeated most of the lower city. The upper city didn't need a special cleaning crew as it was already regularly maintained.

Taller buildings were no problem for Daniel. He swung from one of the higher walkways on to the roof of a nearby building, scaled its stone facade to the top and jumped across to the next building. A loose tile on the roof had him sliding towards the edge, but without missing a beat he slung an arm around a chimney stack and propelled himself across to the next roof.

It was a while before he climbed down, dropping to the pavement below. Picking up his pace, a spring in his step, he hurried along a quiet residential street until he came to a familiar dark-brown door. Digging his key from his trouser pocket, he unlocked the door and went inside. He didn't bother calling out to his father straight away, but instead headed towards the basement stairs and padded down in socked feet.

'Evening, Father,' he said fondly, dropping the rougher voice he used as Daniel in favour of his natural upper-city accent. The older man was sitting at his workbench, goggles covering his eyes as steady hands worked a soldering iron. Pausing in his work, the thin mechanic raised his goggles to sit on his salt-and-pepper hair, his glasses still over his eyes, and turned to his son. His smile became a critical frown and his thick brows furrowed.

'I'm not talking to you while you look like that. We've been through this,' he declared, returning to his work with his goggles still raised.

'Goggles, Da,' Daniel reminded him as he walked out of the workshop and turned left into his bedroom. Shutting the door, he shed his jacket and dropped on to his bed, reaching beneath it for the large wooden box he kept there. Flipping the lid, he dug out a cloth, dampening it in the bowl of water that rested on his desk. As he wiped the cloth over his bared forearms the skin darkened several shades and the cloth turned a peachy colour. Daniel skimmed his hairline with blunted fingernails, pulled the wavy blond hair off, then tugged at the netted wig cap to reveal dark brown locks that hung straight to his chin.

A quick wipe over his face with the damp cloth turned it the same tawny colour as the rest of his skin. Finally, he held an eyelid open, removing the near-invisible film over his eye and revealing the true dark-green colour. When both lenses were removed and stored in their liquid-filled cases, he turned to the mirror above his desk, a smile breaking free at the sight of his natural face. He ran a hand through his hair to get it back into place, checking his throat and jawline for excess make-up. Satisfied, he returned to the workshop, clearing his throat to gain his father's attention.

'There you are, Noah!' Evander enthused, greeting his son by his true name. 'Much better. Come, come, sit,' he insisted, gesturing to the chair at the desk adjacent to his workbench; Noah's desk. The dark-haired teen obediently moved to sit, sliding open the top drawer and pulling away the false bottom to grab a battered black notebook. 'Good day?'

'Quiet,' Noah replied, cracking his neck and letting his shoulders slump. Being Daniel Novak was always stressful during festival time, this year more than ever. 'Everyone's mostly staying out of trouble. For now, at least.' He didn't doubt that would change as the festival grew closer. With so many country folk and outlanders in the city, Diora never could resist the many opportunities to swindle and steal and profit from human naivety.

'Oh, I don't know,' Evander mused with a hum, paintbrush between his teeth muffling his words. 'Maybe Daniel's reputation is finally enough to keep the troublemakers at bay.' Noah sighed, resting his elbow on the desk. He knew where this conversation was leading. 'This year might be Daniel's last.'

'Da, I know you don't approve of Daniel, but he can't stop until the city is safe. You know that,' Noah implored, no longer finding it odd to talk about his alter ego as a separate person. He'd been splitting his time between Noah and Daniel for over three years, and was now used to keeping them apart in his head.

'So you say,' Evander muttered skeptically, lips pursed as he painted. Noah bit back a sigh; no matter how much he tried, he couldn't get his father to understand how important Daniel was. Without Daniel, there would be nothing to stop Diora from having the entire lower city under his thumb.

'What are you working on?' A knowing look in his father's brown eyes let him know he wasn't off the hook yet, but Evander obligingly turned to let his son get a better look at the mask he was painting. It was equal parts porcelain and metal, with carefully painted gears melding with real ones so seamlessly you could hardly tell which was which. Noah was always impressed with his father's work. While Evander made most of his money from fine-detail mechanical work, he was a craftsman at heart, and an incredible artist. The pair only spent two or three months of the year making masks for the festival, but it was easily their favourite work, though Evander had also been working on a secret project lately, which was absorbing him more and more.

'This beauty is for one of the noblemen from Coamar,' Evander said. 'He was very specific in his instruction.' Noah snorted; the men from Coamar always were. Lording over the biggest of the Erovan Isles often gave them a sense of self-importance far greater than was bearable. A common problem among nobles, Noah found.

Straightening up, he turned back to his own desk, digging out a pen and flipping open his notebook to the next blank page. He'd almost filled the book, and it was messy with near-loose pages and splotches of black ink among his neat, cramped handwriting. The notebook was the most valuable thing he owned. Or, rather, the most valuable thing *Daniel* owned. In it was everything he needed to bring down Diora's gang. Almost everything. He just needed the whereabouts of Diora himself, and then he could finally put a stop to the man's control.

Discovering the truth about Diora's men had mostly been an accident – Daniel had started out as a way for

Noah to wear his own mask and be all the things he wasn't: bold and daring, brave and mysterious, and able to explore the lower city he was so often warned away from. He'd enjoyed climbing the older buildings in that half of the city, and soon became caught up in people's lives, their secrets. And when he'd stumbled across a man with a gold ring on his middle finger making a drug exchange in the dead of night, there was no going back; Daniel was here to stay. Gold rings were the symbol of Diora's men, the gang of 'protectors' supposedly helping the citizens of the lower city, the people the guards never bothered with.

Curiosity sparked, the then-fifteen-year-old stalked the men and women enforcing Diora's word, and soon realised that they were behind all the crimes Diora was lauded for having supposedly solved – black market sales, violence, theft. Diora's gang were taking a small fee in exchange for their 'help', and had made a very profitable business out of fear and deceit. Daniel had spent most of the last three years sneaking about, gathering information. All of it went in his notebook, ready for the day he could find Diora and get rid of him, dismantling his stronghold and freeing lower Talen from the corrupt reign they didn't even realise they were under.

He made himself available to those in need, asking for nothing in return and making it clear he worked alone. He was careful, and only ever called the guards in when it was absolutely necessary. Daniel hadn't expected people to rely so much on his help. But now his reputation was so exaggerated that people seemed to think he was *always* around, like some sort of omnipotent shadow, and he couldn't deny there was a part of him that liked playing the hero.

'Can you get back to your real job now?' Evander asked when Noah had finished writing in his notebook. He sighed, a smile at his lips, and reached into the box of blank festival masks beside his desk, pulling out the first one his hand met. It was a fully porcelain mask, clearly made for a woman's face, with unusually short sides and several small holes at the edges and top for him to glue feathers once it was painted.

He flicked through the large binder propped against the wall until he came to his sketch of a beautiful feathered mask. Reaching for his deep sea-green pigment and a complementary royal purple, Noah got to work. It was easy to lose himself in the delicate methodical brushstrokes as he painted an array of feathers on the mask.

'I've got a box of these for you to take over to the palace tomorrow, if you're not busy,' Evander murmured, breaking the comfortable silence between them.

'You mean if I'm not Daniel,' Noah corrected. Evander had been trying to get him to give up Daniel for the better part of a year, claiming Diora wasn't his responsibility. He didn't understand how bad it was down there; he never went to the lower city, except for the odd repair job. No one from their area went to the lower city unless they had to. 'I'm heading over in the morning anyway, so I'll drop it by Damien's office.'

'Excellent,' Evander said, setting his finished mask on the drying rack with several others. 'I'm off to bed. You should be too.'

'As soon as I finish this mask, Da,' Noah promised, brush not faltering when the older man ruffled his hair gently.

'Goodnight, lad. I'll be working on some of our other orders tomorrow. Will you be around later to keep going on the masks?' Other orders meant mechanical work – their *actual* work. Noah thought for a moment.

'I'll try to be.'

Evander left his son alone in the workshop, heading upstairs to his bedroom. Noah turned back to his mask. As much as he liked festival time, he would be glad when it was all over. The festival meant having thousands of unfamiliar people in his city, and Daniel worked on overdrive to keep everything in order. All that, combined with his growing duties to Crysta . . . he was finding it impossible to be everywhere he was needed.

2

Noah was up early the next morning, dressed in dark-blue trousers and jacket with a matching waistcoat over his white shirt, the suit perfectly tailored and finished with subtle silver thread — far finer clothes than Daniel wore. Evander was already in the workshop, up to his elbows in the mechanisms of his latest project. Noah still didn't understand what his father was building; it was the one project the older man wouldn't allow him to touch. 'I'll see you for dinner?' Evander asked without lifting his head.

Noah hoisted the box of finished masks into his arms, shrugging non-committally. 'Probably, but I'll see how things go with Crysta,' he replied. 'Don't forget about lunch, or I'll have to send Ms Reyes over to feed you.' Marie Reyes, who lived in the house opposite theirs, had been pining for his father for years. Not that Evander noticed; since the death of Noah's mother ten years ago his only love was his work — and Noah. In fact, most things seemed to have ceased existing for him after Alina's death.

Cradling the box of masks carefully, Noah jogged up the stairs and left the house, leaving the door unlocked in case Ms Reyes did need to drop in. His spirits light and a faint smile curling at his lips, he walked the familiar route through the market towards the central courtyard. His smile faltered at the sight of the market stalls, still open but looking rather emptier than he was used to – a far cry from the overflowing stalls of years past. The harvest would change that, he hoped. Crysta had been running herself ragged to make this year's festival the best it had ever been. If it all ran smoothly the Goddess would reward them tenfold. Noah was sure of it.

He turned the corner to the courtyard. The enormous royal palace sat pride of place, surrounded by tall gilded fencing topped with lethal-looking spikes. At least three times the size of any other building in Talen, it was Erova's pride and joy. It had been built hundreds of years ago and yet the white stone walls were as flawless as if they'd been erected only days before.

Noah headed for the guard station at the very front of the palace, just to the left of the entry gate. A large Erovan flag flew from the slanted roof, its embroidered leaping fish glittering in the sun, but there was barely any breeze and the green and bronze fabric hung still as Noah entered the building.

'Captain Conti is up at the palace, but you're welcome to leave the masks here, sir,' one of the junior guards responded when Noah asked.

'Thanks. I'll catch up with him,' he replied, setting the box down and heading through the back door. Out in the palace courtyard Noah raced across the expanse of gleaming paved stone until he reached the smaller side door used for personal visitors. 'Morning, Jonas,' he greeted the guard, earning a grin in return.

'Morning, Master Hansen,' Jonas called cheerfully.

Noah stepped through the door into the antechamber. Allowing the maid to take his jacket, he continued through to the palace's huge entrance hall, where several awaiting servants bowed at his entry.

'Good morning, Master Hansen. She's in the music room. Would you care to be escorted there?' the nearest servant asked politely, but Noah waved him off.

'No, no, I'm actually here for Captain Conti, but thank you for the offer,' he replied, ever warm to the service staff.

'Very well, sir. The captain was in the small ballroom, last I checked. Good luck, sir.' She winked cheekily at him and Noah snorted. He'd need it.

With a nod of thanks, he made for the small ballroom, forcing himself not to get sidetracked by the faint music coming from upstairs. He would see Crysta after he and Damien were finished.

As promised, the captain was in the ballroom when Noah arrived, half his uniform abandoned in the corner, standing on a large padded mat in the centre of the room. He gave a shark-like smile.

'Morning, Noah. I thought we'd do some close-combat training today. I've been running nothing but shooting drills and surveillance for the last week in order to prepare for the festival, so I could do with a good old-fashioned fist fight.'

Cursing under his breath, Noah dropped his satchel. 'You wanted an excuse to take your frustration out on an easy target, you mean,' he said wryly. Damien chuckled.

'Don't sell yourself short, you can hold your own well enough!'

'Against the cadets, maybe, but we both know who comes out on top here,' Noah replied without malice, removing his boots. At least once a week for the last eight months Damien took time out of his busy schedule to train Noah in just about every form of combat he could manage. Everything the king thought he should know.

Shedding his shirt, waistcoat and shoes so his attire matched his friend's, Noah squared his shoulders. 'All right. Do your worst.'

The shark-like smile returned, and Noah's heart sank.

Twenty minutes later, gasping for breath, he glared half-heartedly at his friend, who looked smug even though his skin was flushed and sweaty, undershirt abandoned long ago. Noah had made him work for the victory, at least. 'That makes it six–four to me, I believe,' Damien declared, hopping to his feet and offering Noah a hand.

'Yeah, yeah, no need to rub it in,' Noah grumbled, wincing once he was back on his feet. 'Storms, man, use a punching bag next time you need to vent – I'll be black and blue till the festival at this rate!'

'Hush. You're fine,' Damien insisted with a roll of his eyes, running a hand through sweat-damp hair. 'Doing a lot better than I expected, actually. It's been a while since we went hand-to-hand. Good work there.'

Inwardly, Noah preened. It had taken a long time and a lot of bruises to get to a level that Damien deemed praise-worthy. 'Are you done beating me up, or did you want one more round?' he teased. Damien rubbed a towel over his face, shaking his head and throwing a second towel at Noah.

'We can call it a day. Don't want to leave you feeling too fragile, after all.' He jostled Noah's shoulder playfully. 'Crysta's got too much planned for you this week. Besides, I don't know if your poor ego can take another defeat.'

'I'm out of practice!' Noah argued. 'I've been stuck in the workshop painting masks for the last six weeks.'

'Excuses, excuses.' Damien shook his head mock-sadly. He dropped into a stretch, and Noah copied the movement, hissing at the ache in his muscles. 'Gods, though, I can't wait to get back to normal. This festival's been even worse for security threats than usual, what with everything going on.'

Finishing the warm-down routine, Noah helped Damien drag the mat over to the side of the room. 'Are you busy for the rest of the day?' Noah asked, rifling through his satchel for a fresh undershirt. 'You're welcome to join us, though I can't say for sure what we're doing.'

'Settling performer contracts, I'm told,' Damien supplied, buttoning his uniform shirt to his throat. 'So, no, I'm afraid I'm a very, very busy man.' Noah gave him a disparaging look, and Damien laughed. 'No, really, I've got a full schedule all day. So many of the nobles are bringing their own personal security with them, I want to get my men as prepared as possible before those idiots come in and disrupt things. Plus there's staff checks to be run, the parade route needs to be checked, and, of course, His Majesty returns home tomorrow, so the shipyard needs clearing . . . Storms, I hate my job sometimes.'

Noah winced. He often forgot that his friend was still the youngest guard captain in Erovan history. Damien did so well at his job, and seemed to have adulthood figured out far more than Noah did, it was hard to believe he struggled with anything.

'I suppose I'd better let you get back to work, then,' he sighed. 'And surrender myself to Crysta's enormous pile of festival work.' He made a face, which Damien mimicked.

'I hate to say it,' the captain teased, slinging a companionable arm over Noah's shoulders, 'but you brought this upon yourself. Come on, I'll escort you up there.'

Noah could have made the journey to the music room with his eyes closed – it was Crysta's favourite room in the palace – but he wasn't supposed to see her unchaperoned, and Damien took his duties as honorary big brother very seriously.

Nudging the door open, the pair looked in silently from the doorway. Crysta Octavian, crown princess of Erova, and her younger sister, Rosa, spun around the room in an effortless waltz, their skirts swishing at their ankles. Crysta was leading, as usual. Their piano tutor sat at the bench, fingers flying over the keys, and Rosa's ever-present handmaid, Lena, was sitting in the corner, watching in awe. With beaming smiles on their faces, the princesses didn't seem to notice anything but each other and the music. Crysta loved to dance.

The song came to a close and the girls slid to a halt, giggling as they curtseyed to one another. For sisters, they were vastly dissimilar – Rosa was taller and thinner, fey in appearance and rarely spoke above a whisper, if she even spoke at all. Crysta was the opposite, small in stature but with a far larger personality, always ready to speak her mind.

Yet they both shared the same ink-black hair and misty grey eyes that ran through the entire Octavian line, their faces too alike to mark them anything but siblings.

Crysta started so much she almost fell over when Noah and Damien began to clap. 'Noah!' she exclaimed, face lighting up. 'How long were you watching?' She dropped Rosa's hands, rushing towards him with light feet. His hands settled on her waist, balancing her as she leaned up to press her lips to his. Crysta was a full foot shorter than him, and it never failed to make him smile when she had to stand on her toes.

'Long enough,' he replied, stepping further into the room.

'Yes, Cryssie, it's good to see you too – I'm wonderful, thanks for asking,' Damien said loudly, though Crysta's gaze didn't break from Noah's face. 'Oh, honestly, you two are disgusting,' he muttered, shaking his head with a fond smile.

'I saw you at breakfast, Damien – I didn't think your mood would have changed so much since then,' Crysta said, finally tearing herself away from Noah. She didn't go far, though, twining her fingers with his.

Noah smiled to himself, his heart still giving the same little skip it had the first time he'd laid eyes on her. He didn't think he'd ever get used to being allowed to kiss her or hold her hand so easily.

'How was your training?' the princess asked Damien.

'Terrible. I think I'm bleeding,' he groused dramatically. 'Your brute of a boyfriend roughed me up something good.'

'That's what I like to hear. You show him, Noah.' Crysta's voice was full of pride, and she patted his arm affectionately.

'No sympathy around here!' Damien turned imploring eyes on Rosa, who giggled quietly.

'You'll heal,' she assured him. Her voice was soft but the humour was evident, as it always was around Damien. He doted endlessly on both sisters, and was one of the few people who could get Rosa to properly relax and laugh. Unlike Noah. For the first year of Noah's courtship of Crysta, the younger Octavian sibling had barely said three words to him. She was much more comfortable with him now, but it still wouldn't surprise him if she, like plenty of others, thought him too low-born for the future queen. Many people disliked the prospect of him marrying Crysta, preferring the idea of some young lord or even a foreign prince. In the eyes of most, he was Crysta's last childish indulgence before she grew up and took a proper nobleman as her husband.

Noah counted himself lucky that Erova was relatively peaceful under Anglyan law. That peace could be disrupted by marrying a foreigner into the royal family, and so King Leon was definitely set on his eldest daughter marrying an Erovan native. The king had got over most of his qualms about that person being Noah, so now Noah just had to convince the rest of the country that he was good enough for their future queen.

'So, hard at work were we, ladies?' Damien drawled, smirking. Crysta's cheeks flushed.

'It *is* work! We're preparing for the festival.' Both men looked skeptical but Crysta held her ground. 'Rosa and I shall have to dance with so many noblemen, and since *someone* loathes dancing I hardly ever get to practise.'

'I don't loathe dancing!' Noah defended. 'I'm terrible at it. There's a difference. I don't want to break your toes this close to the festival.' Damien failed to cover his laugh with a cough, and Crysta merely huffed.

'All the more reason to practise, then.' She stepped closer to him, stroking his cheek and fixing him with the full force of her pleading grey eyes. Noah's mouth became dry; the longer they were together, the more she seemed determined to test his resolve in keeping to the rules of their courtship. 'Please, Noah. Dance with me a while, I'm so tired of leading. Or should I just ask Damien instead?'

'I'm always up for a dance, Cryssie,' Damien offered. 'I've got time for a quick waltz before I need to get to work.'

Crysta beamed at him, leaving Noah feeling like he'd let her down. He stepped back to watch the pair take to the floor. Rosa quietly approached her piano tutor, then replaced him at the bench, long fingers resting delicately on the ivory keys. Damien took Crysta in hold and the music began.

It was a good thing Noah wasn't a jealous person. The captain of the guard was an attractive man from a family of excellent standing, and the age difference wasn't so great that he was too old for Crysta. Noah knew all too well how beautiful Crysta was; her hourglass figure was envied by almost every girl in Erova, and her braided black hair was always immaculate. Combined with her sweet dimpled smile and fiery personality, she was the prize jewel in Erova's crown. By all logic they would be a perfect match, and Noah knew the prospect had crossed the king's mind more than once. He thanked his stars daily that Crysta had rejected the idea of making a political marriage.

Still, they looked beautiful together, gliding smoothly across the floor with the grace of those who had taken up dancing lessons almost as soon as they could walk. Damien often tried to distance himself from his noble birthright, but at times like this it was obvious how he'd been raised.

One dance turned into two, which would have become three had Crysta not sneezed abruptly, causing Rosa to collapse into giggles and stop playing. 'I believe that's my cue to leave,' Damien declared with a frown, checking the clock on the wall. 'The festival waits for no man, and time is running ever short. Noah, behave yourself in my absence,' he warned lightly, a twinkle in his caramel eyes. 'And give the lady a dance, for the Goddess' sake. Rather you trip over your feet now in the privacy of the palace than at the festival in front of all of Talen.'

Bidding the trio goodbye, the guard captain left the ballroom, and Noah glanced at his girlfriend. 'Damien said something about performer contracts needing to be taken care of today?' he said, watching as annoyance crossed Crysta's face.

'Yes. They were supposed to be Father's job, but with his unexpected trip away he passed them on to us.' She emphasised the last word, sliding an arm around his waist.

'He's determined to involve me in the preparations as much as possible, isn't he?' Noah said. King Leon was set on making sure Noah was shouldering an equal burden in this year's festival. Last year he'd been too busy trying to find any legitimate reason to call off Noah's courtship of Crysta in favour of a man with far higher standing. He'd finally warmed to the idea of Noah becoming part of the family, but Noah was sure he was being tested now.

'He's preparing you for the future,' Crysta replied knowingly, a faint flush to her olive-skinned face. Noah kissed her before the conversation could continue much further. They both knew the king and queen were expecting a proposal from him any day now, but he had yet to work up the nerve. He couldn't commit to marrying Crysta until his work as Daniel was done for good, and he had no idea when that would be. Whenever Diora was gone, he supposed.

'One dance,' Noah relented, loath to ruin the small bit of fun Crysta found among the stressful festival schedule. Besides, Damien had a point. If he was going to embarrass himself, he'd much rather do so in private. 'But if I step on your feet, you can't say you weren't warned.'

'You're really a lot better than you used to be, you know,' Rosa piped up from the piano, and Noah smiled at her earnest compliment.

'I appreciate your sweet, sweet lies,' he called back. Settling one hand on Crysta's hip, the other clasping hers, Noah took a deep breath, praying to the Goddess for grace. Of all the things he'd had to learn during this courtship, dancing was quite possibly the most problematic.

3

One dance turned out to be all they had time for anyway. Before the song could finish there was a knock on the door and a servant entered with a hasty bow. 'I'm sorry to interrupt, Your Highness,' he said, addressing Crysta, 'but your mother has just received word that Lord Silva and his family are to arrive this afternoon, and I'm afraid you and Master Hansen are the only ones available to go down to the shipyard and greet them.'

Noah saw Crysta frown, while Rosa ducked her head, her hair falling like a curtain across her face. Rosa was far less busy than Crysta, but would never offer to go to the shipyard by herself. Especially not for a family like the Silvas.

'They're awfully early. I thought they were supposed to arrive in three days!' Noah said indignantly. He and Crysta had organised the arrivals schedule just last week, as a favour to King Leon. For the Silvas to decide to change it to suit themselves . . . it was frustrating. But typical of the Silva family; none of them were particularly considerate to the needs of others. They held the region of Denas, the largest mainland region in Erova, and believed that owning more land than anyone else gave them higher status than anyone but the king himself.

'So did I,' Crysta muttered, letting out a quiet sigh. 'I suppose that's my evening sorted, then. You don't have to come if you don't want to, Noah — I know you weren't planning on staying for dinner.'

'Of course I'm coming,' he said without hesitation. He didn't want Crysta meeting the Silvas by herself. Fabian Silva, the family's youngest son, was an arrogant little toad who had been desperately looking for a wife for far too long. Last time they'd met Noah and Fabian had almost come to blows over some of the perverse and downright insulting things the young noble had said to or about Crysta, and recently the lordling had had the cheek to ask Noah to find some 'better' gemstones to set into the eyes of the disturbing snake-faced mask he'd commissioned for this year's festival.

'I'll just head home to pick up some things and meet you at the tram station. I still have some masks to work on.'

'The tram will leave at quarter past, sir,' the servant said.

'Then I'll be there on the hour,' Noah confirmed to Crysta. 'Rain check on those contracts?'

'We can't really afford to wait,' Crysta said, grimacing. 'But if I'm out this evening, I'll need to shift a couple of meetings to this afternoon.' She paused, lips pursed, before slowly turning to her sister at the piano. 'Rosie, you know I wouldn't normally ask —'

'I can't do your contracts,' Rosa said. 'All those numbers make my head spin, I'll only get them wrong.'

'Please, Rosa. I don't ask you for much, especially not around festival time, but you're going to have to take on more responsibility sooner or later. I need to be able to trust you to take care of things for me.'

Noah watched, feeling awkward, as the two princesses stood locked in a staring match. Crysta's expression grew more and more annoyed until Rosa finally broke. 'Fine,' the younger Octavian sulked. 'You always give me the worst duties.' Noah was surprised that Crysta hadn't lost her temper. She was right; Rosa had to grow up. Sometimes it was hard to believe Rosa was already sixteen.

Crysta turned back to Noah, and he couldn't help but find the fire in her eyes captivating. 'Rosa can handle it,' he assured her quietly, giving the younger princess a brief smile. 'Everything will get done. Just breathe.' With this year's festival being so important, and the potential for the harvest to turn sour so easily, Noah knew Crysta felt more responsible than ever for making sure it went without a hitch. As the eldest princess – the future queen of Erova – she'd be the one blamed for incurring the Goddess' wrath if anything went wrong.

'I hope you're right,' she muttered with a frown, rocking up on her toes to kiss him. 'I'll see you after lunch.' When he stepped back the palace servant at the door smiled at him.

'I'll escort you out, Master Hansen.' It wasn't an offer. Far too used to being shepherded about to suit Crysta's schedule, Noah followed, already adjusting his mental to-do list to account for the excursion.

4

Noah was early to meet Crysta, though his satchel was full of the mask work he should have been doing that day. He was running behind with the orders enough as it was, and he couldn't expect his father to shoulder all the work. He leaned against the railing on the platform edge, watching the palace servants ready the forest-green tram carriage for a royal excursion. Many of them had their jackets off and their shirtsleeves rolled to their elbows as they worked in the sun, and Noah was glad for the awning overhead shading the platform.

Mind drifting to the designs he had yet to complete, running through construction steps to keep him occupied, he almost missed the sound of footsteps on the paving stones. A smile crossed his lips, and as he turned to see Crysta approaching down the steps from the back of the palace, escorted by two guards and her handmaid, Ana, Noah found himself lost for words. She looked effortlessly beautiful in a silk blouse and skirt and a short-sleeved jacket over her shoulders to ward off the chill. Her hair was pinned up in an elegant bun, a few loose strands curled into ringlets. He could hardly believe that of all people, Crysta – the gorgeous, intelligent heir to the throne – had chosen *him*. And he still hadn't married her yet – never would if he didn't get his life back in order. Gods, he was a fool sometimes.

It took a moment for him to wipe the dumbstruck look off his face. 'I like your hair – I hope it's not for the Silvas.' He winked at her and Crysta scoffed.

'Hardly. It's a test run for the parade; I need to see how well this fares if I open the tram windows. I don't want to go about looking windswept the entire parade like I did last year.'

'Well, it looks beautiful, if that helps,' Noah commented, reaching to take her hand. 'Come on, let's get this over with. Are we expecting any more people?' It seemed a small group for a trip beyond the safety of the upper city, but then they weren't going to be there very long. He hoped not, anyway.

'No, sir, it's just us,' one of the guards confirmed, stepping towards the waiting tram carriage and opening the door. 'The captain sends his apologies, but he's unable to join us.' Noah nodded his understanding; having the entire festival's security on your shoulders was no small feat.

Following close behind Crysta as they boarded the tram, Noah waited patiently for the guards to check the carriage and deem it safe for them to sit down. He chose a seat at the table in the back corner, giving Crysta an apologetic smile. 'I really need to get these masks done,' he told her, setting his satchel on the table. 'So I'm probably going to be fairly absorbed for most of the journey.'

Far from being annoyed, Crysta's face lit up, her eyes eager as she sat opposite him. 'Whose mask is it?'

Noah pulled a shallow wooden box from his satchel, handing it to Crysta, and then dug around for his sketchbook. She flipped the latch and opened the box, letting out a soft gasp. A gentle finger brushed over the polished bronze metal of the mask, intrigue on Crysta's face. It was bare at the moment, but Noah planned to change that. 'Damien's, actually,' he confessed. 'Don't tell him I left it this late.' Usually the masks for personal friends were some of the first Noah made, but he'd been so busy recently he'd had to prioritise. Business came first, his father said.

The tram rumbled quietly as the engine warmed up and the wheels began to move, sending it down the tracks with a faint plume of purple tyrium smoke in its wake. Ana reached up to open a window, letting the wind in to try its best at ruffling Crysta's hair, but the princess didn't seem to notice. Her focus was now on the contents of his sketchbook. 'I can't let you look at that,' he said, shaking his head at her with a smile. 'Damien's mask isn't the only one I have sketches for in here.'

Crysta's grin grew mischievous. 'Is mine in there?' she asked, though she already knew the answer. She'd been begging to see her mask design for weeks, but Noah was keeping it secret. Hers was special, after all. 'Can I see it? Just a little peek? The festival isn't that far away!'

'Absolutely not,' he insisted, opening the book to the design of Damien's mask. It wasn't too extravagant, the man preferring an understated design, but the full-face mask was still very much suited to the guard captain, its geometric filigree pattern seeming to have more dimensions the longer you looked at it, playing with the way the light reflected off different thicknesses of metal. There was no colour other than the natural hue of the metal, as Damien insisted his job as a guard was to blend in rather than stand out, but it would still captivate and intrigue people, as befitted a man of his standing. Noah didn't get prideful about many things, but his work was definitely one of them. 'I'm not letting you ruin your surprise.'

Crysta pouted playfully, but settled down to watch as he delicately lifted the mask from its cushioned box. She tilted her head, getting a better angle to look at the sketch Noah had made for the design. 'It's going to be exquisite,' she declared with quiet confidence. 'Damien will love it.'

Noah flushed, ducking his head as he unrolled the leather pack holding his engraving tools. 'I won't be offended if you go and sit by the window,' he said. 'This is hardly exciting to watch.'

'Don't be ridiculous.' Crysta waved him off, perched on the edge of her seat. 'You sit and watch me dance or play violin all the time – I *never* get to watch you do what you love.' She'd only been in his workshop a few times, and only in fleeting visits.

'That – that's different,' he started, biting his tongue before he could finish his sentence. He watched her do those things because she was beautiful when she was enjoying herself. All he was doing here was working.

Still, it looked like Crysta had no intention of moving, so Noah got to work, trying not to feel self-conscious as he turned his attention to the mask. Within minutes, though, his mind had cleared to nothing but himself and his art, everything narrowed down to the repetitive movement of engraving tool against metal, etching smooth lines and curves into the shining surface. His eyes moved only to double-check the sketch in reference, the rest of the world disappearing around him. Making masks was freeing for him; at least when he wasn't under so much pressure.

Despite the rocking of the tram as it sped through the upper city, Noah's hand was completely steady, the intricate filigree design slowly unfolding. He had worked in worse conditions.

He finally looked up when he had to change tools, cheeks heating when he realised how completely he'd zoned out. Crysta leaned against the back of the seat opposite, hair still perfectly in place despite the open window, chin propped on her hand and her gaze fixed on Noah, a soft smile tugging at her lips. A glance out of the window told him they'd already crossed the river into the lower city – had he really been working that long?

As they hit a winding section of track the tram slowed down, Noah watching the blurs of colour become recognisable entities once more. He froze, doing a double take at one in particular – hurrying down a narrow side street, briefcase in hand and gold ring glinting on his finger, was Adamas. Noah's heart skipped a beat as he watched the man turn at the sound of the tram rattling past. For the barest of moments their eyes met. It was over in a blink, but it was enough to send Noah's pulse skyrocketing; surely Adamas wouldn't recognise him. He wasn't Daniel, and it wasn't like the man had got a long look at him. Still, it made him uneasy, and he moved away from the window. As Daniel's reputation grew so did the likelihood of his path crossing with Noah's in the worst of ways.

The smell of burning tyrium in the air grew stronger the closer they got to the shipyard, and it was almost over-whelming when they crossed over the river into the shipyard itself. Shipyard was a bit of a misnomer; the mechanical heart of Erova was a small city within itself, complete with pubs and hotels and shops, and a whole resi-dential area for its workers. There was almost no need ever to cross the river into the main parts of Talen.

Knowing their journey was coming to an end, Noah wiped down Damien's mask with a soft cloth and set it carefully back in its box, packing away his work things. The part of the shipyard dedicated to skyships was rather small, tucked away at the very edge of the city limits. They had no need of a larger area as they hardly ever had visitors by air. Erova wasn't the most welcoming of places to outsiders – through both its weather and its people – and most of the outlanders travelled by tram or horse.

They drew to a halt at the end of the tracks and their guards disembarked first, checking the way was clear for Crysta. The trio stuck close as the princess stepped out of the tram carriage, Noah at her side, his eyes alert for any signs of trouble.

'The Silva ship is about to arrive, my lady,' the most senior ranked of the guards told her as she tucked her arm into Noah's. 'Would you prefer to wait inside while it docks?'

'No, the weather is fair enough, thank you,' Crysta replied with a smile.

A gleaming, clearly privately owned skyship cut through the sparse clouds above, aiming for the empty space in front of Noah and Crysta. The Silva family crest flew from the top of the mast, and everything from the support struts to the sail itself was shining silver. They really weren't subtle. Most of the nobles from the outlands didn't even own a skyship, having no need for one. But, of course, the Silvas had to make it as obvious as possible that they had the money for a skyship advanced enough to manage the dead zone over Talen without any problems. Noah was surprised they hadn't waited to arrive until more nobles were in the city, to show off even more.

His attention firmly on the overly extravagant machine, Noah almost missed the woman standing near a shipping container, arms folded over her chest as she watched the royal contingency. It wasn't the innocent gaze of someone intrigued by the royal family; she looked attentive, expectant. The flash of gold at her fingers made the hairs rise on the back of his neck – of course Diora had a presence in the shipyard. The man had eyes everywhere. Pulse picking up, Noah kept his head down, not wanting to risk even the slightest chance of a connection being made between Daniel Novak and Noah Hansen. Though for all he knew Adamas had already put it together and was running to Diora even now. It just took one person to notice their similarities. His disguise only worked because he never had to use it in front of people who knew his true face. Plenty who knew Noah would recognise Daniel, he was sure.

His arm slid protectively around Crysta's waist as they took several steps backwards, giving the ship room to land without it blowing them off their feet. 'Here goes nothing, then,' he murmured, trying to project an air of calm, not wanting Crysta to question his sudden anxiety. The princess laughed quietly.

'Let's try and make it as quick as possible, shall we?' she said under her breath, plastering a sweet smile on her face as the trapdoor was thrown open and a silver-clad servant emerged, stepping aside to let his employers pass. First on deck was, of course, Lord Philippe Silva, the head of the family. A rather rotund man, Noah was surprised he fitted through the trapdoor. Behind him was his wife, Lady Helena Silva, her grey-streaked dark hair scraped back from her face in a tight bun, matching the pinched expression she wore constantly.

Noah could never remember which of the two eldest sons was which; identical twins, Argento and Aeris, absolutely despised each other. No one had recorded which of them was the firstborn at the occasion, everyone far too busy making sure Lady Silva delivered both babies safely, and as such the two had to share everything, right down to the title they would eventually inherit when their father passed. They had both brought their wives, and their hordes of brats, who spilled out on to the deck with cheers of freedom.

Behind the two families was Oscar, the third eldest son, and his wife and two children. Oscar was probably the most manageable of the Silva family, content with the fact that he would never have a title of his own. Finally, Fabian Silva stepped out, his black hair slicked back as always, his beady eyes immediately landing on Crysta in a way that made Noah's skin crawl.

'Lord Silva,' Crysta greeted, the warmth in her voice very much forced. 'It is a pleasure to see you and your family. I trust your journey went well?' The portly man wobbled down the gangplank, dropping into a short bow when he was in front of the princess, taking her hand and bringing it to his lips.

'Well enough, my dear princess, though there is little peace with seven children in a skyship for three hours,' he remarked with a disparaging look towards his grandchildren. As much as Noah disliked the man, he almost found himself sympathising; he wouldn't want to spend three minutes in a ship with those hellions, let alone three hours.

'I'm sure the children will enjoy the space of the city,' Crysta replied. 'I fear many of our troupers have yet to arrive, considering how much time we have until the festival begins, but I'm sure there is plenty to keep them occupied until more come.'

'So long as I'm not the one who has to take them, that sounds like a wonderful idea, Your Highness,' Lady Silva said, offering the princess a curtsey. Noah wasn't surprised that neither of them greeted him. They had been among the more vocal protesters when King Leon had first consented to him courting Crysta, and they had initially refused to attend the festival last year when Crysta requested Noah sit with her at the head table. When the king and queen had accepted their refusal graciously and proceeded to continue to organise the festival as if nothing had changed, the Lord and Lady Silva had quickly changed their minds.

'Lord Silva, Lady Silva,' Noah murmured, inclining his head to the couple. He tried not to smirk as they were obliged to bow and curtsey to him, only a fraction less than they would to Crysta. He had to admit, he got more joy than he probably should out of forcing nobles to treat him respectfully.

'Mr Hansen,' Lord Silva grunted. Crysta went on to greet the rest of the family, and Noah's jaw clenched at Fabian's salacious gaze over Crysta's form when he went to kiss her hand.

'My lady,' the younger Silva drawled, his nasal voice as irritating as ever. 'You look even lovelier than you did last year. Time is turning you into a fine young woman.'

'Thank you, Mr Silva,' Crysta responded somewhat awkwardly. Noah rested a hand on her shoulder, squeezing gently, reminding her of his presence. 'Shall we take the tram back up to the palace? I'm afraid Mother is otherwise engaged, but I have arranged dinner for us all before you are escorted to your lodgings for the festival.'

'That sounds wonderful,' the wife of one of the twins said with a smile, as her hand curled firmly in the collar of her eldest son's jacket to stop him running off. As Noah offered his arm to Crysta he glanced back towards the shipping container, but the woman was gone. Still unable to shake the feeling of being watched, he led the way back to the tram carriage, the slightest frown on his face. His two lives were drawing ever closer together as the festival approached, and it made him nervous.

5

Dinner was, in short, a nightmare. The seven Silva brats wouldn't stop running about the dining hall and taunting each other, barely paying attention to their food, unless it was to smear it on a sibling or cousin's face. Noah was surprised at their unruliness; the eldest of the children was almost Rosa's age, and he was still running about just as much as his six-year-old cousin.

Fabian Silva spent the entire meal alternating between flirting with Crysta, flirting with Rosa, and making disparaging remarks about Noah. Noah was sure he only had the confidence to do so because the monarchs were absent and Lord and Lady Silva were far too preoccupied with feeling insulted by the fact that Queen Sofie hadn't dropped everything in her schedule to welcome them.

Even Damien, who usually kept quiet at court meals, spoke up in the girls' defence several times, shooting Noah sympathetic looks across the table every time one of them had to interrupt Fabian before he could say something truly deplorable.

Noah was glad of the man's company; the captain of the guard often ate with the royal family, both to ensure that a guard was always present and because since the passing of his father they were the closest thing to family he had. He was of noble enough blood that even the Silvas couldn't complain. Especially not when they were so busy commenting on Noah's lack of nobility. As far as Noah was concerned, the more allies he and Crysta had around the table, the better.

Crysta was trying her hardest to keep the meal on track and the conversation polite, though Noah could tell she was losing her patience.

'And how are things in Denas?' she queried, directing her question to Lord Silva, interrupting him mid-rant. 'Our reports say your people are doing well, but obviously to hear from you personally will be much more reassuring.'

The reports said that Lord Silva was raising taxes unreasonably again and making an enemy of himself, but Crysta could hardly say that to his face.

'We're doing a darn sight better than plenty of other places, but that's still terrible compared to years past,' Lord Silva grumbled, scratching at his bristly moustache. 'We've lost almost half our livestock to disease, and the crops just haven't been coming through like they usually do. Not to mention that lout DeCosta trying to claim my land for his own region's farms. But do not fear, Princess, there's enough money in this family to keep things running smoothly until next year; hopefully by then things will begin to brighten, Goddess willing. You and your sister had better pray until your pretty little lips are raw.'

Crysta's eyes widened in shock at his words, and Noah's expression grew dark when Fabian's gaze dropped to the lips in question. Out of the corner of his eye he saw Damien's hand clench, the other dropping to his empty holster. It was impolite to have weapons at the table, as tempting as it sometimes was.

'I don't believe that's an appropriate thing to say to a princess, Lord Silva,' Noah said tightly, warning clear in his tone.

'And I don't believe you're in any position to lecture me on propriety, *Mr* Hansen,' Silva retorted with a sneer, emphasising Noah's lack of title. 'I'm just reminding the girl what's at stake here.'

'I am not a *girl*, Lord Silva, but your future queen, and you would do well to remember it,' Crysta said icily, though her smile was as sweet as ever. 'And I assure you, Rosa and I are well aware of our duties.'

'If you were truly aware of your duties, my dear, you would drop that common mechanic and allow someone of higher standing to court you,' Fabian piped up, his oily tone making Noah flush with anger. Crysta's gaze hardened, and she fixed her stormy eyes on the youngest Silva.

'If you have a problem with my choice of partner, Mr Silva, I suggest you take it up with my father. If I were not making a favourable match, you can be sure he would have put a stop to things by now.' She was using her 'I will be queen and you will not disobey me' voice, and it made Noah smirk to himself.

'We can only hope that your younger sister has a little more sense in her,' Lady Silva mused conversationally, though her eyes were mocking as she glanced at Noah, then at Rosa. 'You're pretty enough to have any of the men of the court; it would do you well to make the best choice available.' Both sisters flinched as if slapped, and Noah felt his metaphorical hackles rise. The Silvas would be sorely disappointed if they were expecting Rosa to care much about the social standing of any husband she may have to take. Perhaps that was why they'd arrived so early, to try and get their bid for a betrothal contract in before anyone else arrived. Rosa was sixteen, after all; old enough to wed.

'And you would consider your youngest son – a man who would hold no title nor land of his own, I might add – to be that best choice?' Noah asked evenly, knowing that any of his companions would be reprimanded if they were to ask the same thing. He was disliked by half the court anyway, and the king would never scold him for standing up for the honour of either of the princesses. 'Forgive me, my lady, but Rosa has free choice of a husband, just as Crysta does, and I don't believe it's in your best interests to make any sort of insinuation that you might want to influence her choice.' Lady Silva opened her mouth, but closed it again as soon as her husband placed a hand on her arm.

'We meant no offence,' Lord Silva said, looking like it was causing him physical pain to apologise for his words. 'It is a very difficult time for everyone, and you can understand the court merely being concerned whether our monarchs are truly making the best decisions for our glorious country.'

'As I said before, if you have any problem with my decisions or those of my family, do feel free to take your concerns to Father.' Crysta's voice was perfectly cordial, and Lord Silva's expression implied that he would rather be tossed into the Stormlands than dare tell King Leon Octavian that he thought the princess needed to choose a better husband.

After that the meal continued in tense silence, finally coming to a close as several servants appeared to escort the Silva family to their hotel. When the doors shut behind them, Rosa allowed herself to shudder. 'And so it has begun,' she murmured, a frown at her brow. 'How I long for the days when I was too young for the noblemen to eye me in such a way.'

'If you need me to blacken their eyes so it's difficult for them to look at you so, you only have to ask,' Noah offered with a grin, drawing a quiet giggle from the girl. Damien attempted to look disapproving, but his heart wasn't in it; he too looked like he'd love to give Fabian Silva a few bruises.

'Rosa, how did you get on with the contracts?' Crysta asked, and Noah groaned under his breath. She could hardly go five minutes without thinking about the festival!

'I managed about half of them,' the younger princess replied. She seemed to be mostly over her sulk at being forced to take on some of Crysta's work; arguments never lasted long between the two sisters. 'I tried my best, but . . . there's an awful lot. Even with Lena helping. I don't know how you do it all so quickly.'

'Don't worry about it,' Crysta assured. 'I'll finish it all off tonight before bed.'

'You mean you're actually planning to sleep tonight?' Noah remarked drily, earning a dirty look.

'Very funny.'

'He's only concerned, Crysta,' Damien cut in. 'You have been working awfully hard recently.' Noah gave him a brief, grateful smile for the support, but Crysta huffed.

'I'm just doing what needs to be done,' she said. 'There's hardly *any* time left before the festival!' Noah reached and took her hand, squeezing it gently. Dining with the Silvas had left her with an even shorter fuse than usual, and he was waiting for the moment she cracked. The festival usually caused her stress, but this year there was far more pressure on her than ever before – to please the Goddess, to take a husband, to prepare herself to take the crown and lead the country; it seemed that reaching the end of her teenage years was bringing a whole host of brand new demands. Noah could hardly keep up as a bystander, and was astonished that Crysta handled it all so gracefully.

'Why don't you take the night off, Cryssie?' Rosa said quietly, using her childhood nickname for her sister. She only did that when she desperately wanted Crysta to agree to something. 'I'll finish off the contracts, I promise. Relax a little, you deserve it.' She smiled hesitantly at the older girl, grey eyes pleading with her to accept the respite. Crysta bit her lip, then sighed, nodding.

'If you really don't mind,' she relented.

'I don't mind at all,' Rosa assured, only half lying. Perhaps she wasn't so immature after all. Noah smiled at her in thanks, then checked the time.

'I had best leave,' he declared. 'Father will be expecting me back soon.' And he had business as Daniel that evening.

'But you finished your masks on the tram! Surely he can't have more work for you already?' Crysta protested.

'I thought you might want to stay a while longer, seeing as I suddenly find myself with no duties this evening.'

Noah sighed; any other day he would love an opportunity like that, but he couldn't miss this meeting. 'I finished some of my masks,' he corrected, 'I still have more back at the workshop. Besides, I think he said we had a new order come in for our regular work that needs to be filled.' The lie felt sour as it crossed his lips. His guilt doubled as Crysta's expression became crestfallen. This meeting had better be worth it.

'Well, I wouldn't want to upset your father. I'll walk you down,' she offered, sliding her arm through his. He bid the rest of his companions goodbye, promising to see them all in the morning, and the pair left the dining room. Ana followed them as she was expected to do, but hung back when they reached the entrance hall to give them some semblance of privacy. Crysta turned to Noah, wrapping her arms around his neck and reaching up for a kiss. 'I'll see you tomorrow?'

'Bright and early, for whatever festival duties I can help with,' he confirmed. Crysta made a face and he snorted. 'Try and relax just a little bit this evening, please? Rosa was right, you deserve it. You don't want to make yourself ill over this festival.'

'I just need everything to be perfect,' she murmured, looking tired. 'The Goddess isn't favouring us at the moment; if the festival doesn't change that, Erova will struggle, and people will want someone to blame. That usually means Mother and Father. At least if I'm the one organising everything, and praying to the Goddess for prosperity, then

'I'm the only one at fault.' Noah cupped her cheek, meeting her gaze.

'No one can blame you for the will of the Goddess,' he insisted, his thumb stroking her silk-soft skin. 'And if they do, they're idiots. The festival is going to be wonderful, and the Goddess will bestow favour upon us for the next year and several more to come.'

'I suppose I'm being a little overdramatic about things,' Crysta confessed. He kissed her, winking.

'You said it, not me,' he replied teasingly. 'I had better get going. Have a good evening, my love.'

Crysta pulled him into one last lingering kiss, then stepped back to allow him to leave through the antechamber. With a brief wave over his shoulder Noah jogged across the palace courtyard towards the guard station.

It didn't take him long to get home, taking a shortcut across several walkways and the long roof in a row of terraced houses. Heading straight down to the workshop, he found his father at his desk, and Noah wondered if the man had actually moved at any point in the day. 'Have you eaten?' he asked, sinking down in his own chair.

Evander started, looking up from the mask he was painting. 'What? Oh, is that the time?' He looked surprised, glancing up at the clock.

Noah sighed. 'Go on upstairs and make yourself some food, Da. The masks can wait,' he urged gently, smiling at his father's sheepish expression. When Evander was gone and Noah could hear the clattering of pots and pans from the kitchen upstairs, he reached into the bottom drawer of his work desk, rifling under several mask sketches and mechanics blueprints to find a small wooden box. Setting it on the desk, he flipped the catch, staring at the piece of jewellery inside. It was quite possibly his favourite of all the things he'd ever created, the intricate metalwork having taken him weeks of working with a magnifying glass.

It was a ring made from a single piece of bronze that coiled round the finger three times, studded with tiny emeralds and decorated with flowers around the outside, roses and chrysanthemums, Crysta's favourites, twining across the coils of bronze. Engraved around the inner edge was Noah's favourite part of the Erovan marriage vows – *Our souls flow together like the rivers flow to sea.* It was simple on the surface, but infinitely detailed when you looked closer. Crysta would love it, he hoped. If he ever worked up the nerve to actually give it to her. He just had to find Diora first. Once he had finally shut down Diora's gang for good, then Daniel would have no reason to continue pretending to date Emilie, less need to spend time as Daniel, and there would be nothing to stop him marrying Crysta.

'After the festival,' he murmured to himself, shutting the box and storing it away safely.

6

That night was possibly the most important meeting Daniel had ever had – and having done most of the detailed engraving on Damien's mask during the tram journey, he didn't have even the most feeble of excuses to stay at home. Noah almost missed the days when Daniel was a welcome respite from the stresses of his true life. Now there was far more at stake, especially if he was discovered. Still, he hadn't lost sight of why he was doing all this in the first place; people needed him, and he couldn't ignore that. He could barely walk for tripping over the intertwining threads of his double life, but it would be worth it in the end. It had to be.

Daniel's soft-soled boots were soundless on the tiled roof as he crept through the lower city, heading for the shipyard. Emilie had told him weeks ago about a meeting Adamas and a couple of his friends had been discussing, at which Diora himself would be present, and Daniel had been planning for it ever since. Diora hardly ever conducted business in person, preferring to hole himself away and send his men out in his stead.

Daniel grinned to himself as he climbed – tonight he might finally get somewhere. Despite all his efforts, he'd never come this close to Diora before. His guilt warred with his excitement, the thrill he could never quite shake at the prospect of sneaking around unseen, just another shadow in the lower city. It was moments like this that made him wonder how he could ever give Daniel up. He'd have to, eventually.

The meeting was going to take place in one of the warehouses on the city side of the river. He hadn't thought Diora's reach extended as far as the shipyard; there were too many guards stationed there, and the community was too tight-knit. But after what Noah had seen when he was out with Crysta he could no longer be sure.

Checking the address he'd written on a scrap of paper, he glanced at the roof in front of him. This was definitely the place. The warehouse was a long, low brick building with several small windows along the highest part of the wall, the back wall of the building mostly taken up by a large mechanical door.

The three-foot gap between where he was standing and the roof of the warehouse was an easy jump. Once across, Daniel dropped into a crouch at the edge of the roof to inspect the windows. The building was old, the brick somewhat crumbling and the window frames chipped, and it didn't surprise him in the slightest to see one of the window locks had rusted through. Perfect.

He lowered himself over the edge and gave the lock a swift, solid kick, which broke the seal enough for him to wrench the window open and climb inside. The metal gallery running along three of the walls looked precarious, but there were enough dusty, heavy-looking crates on it for him to be sure it could hold his weight. Dropping down as silently as he could, he closed the window behind him, checking the pocket watch in his jacket. The meeting was set to begin any minute now.

He settled behind a pile of crates, his view of the warehouse floor below fairly clear. It was evident the building hadn't been in use for a while, and certainly not for anything legitimate. Everything was covered in a thick layer of dust, and most of the lights didn't seem to work. There was no one around yet, so he pulled his notebook and pen from his bag and waited. Years ago he wouldn't have been able to do all this silently – too excited, too nervous to sit still – but he'd learned a lot in his years as Daniel, including how to wait patiently.

He checked his watch again, feeling like an age had passed as he sat in the cramped space. It had been five minutes. His pulse picked up, sweat gathering at the small of his back as the seconds ticked by, past the point the meeting was supposed to start. He glanced around, trying to spot any signs of movement. What if this was it? What if he'd been set up, caught in his own arrogance? Adamas wasn't too bright, to be sure, but he could have purposely arranged that conversation knowing Emilie was listening and that Daniel would eventually get the information. Had he finally become a big enough problem for Diora to want to take care of?

He froze when he heard the low, loud creak of the loading doors being opened.

'Hurry up, hurry up, he'll be here any minute!' the man who stepped inside hissed, beckoning at two more people carrying a large crate between them. Obviously they were here to sell something to Diora. What was in the crate was anyone's guess. The man leading the operation was short and balding, his suit ill-fitting on his scrawny frame. His companions, a man and a woman, were fairly nondescript, the kind of people who could slip into the background without causing a second thought. Brown hair, average height, no unusual features. Perfect for work of a shadier nature. 'Just set it down there.' The pair deposited their crate off to the side, letting out a sigh of relief. Whatever they were carrying seemed to be heavy.

'You said ten, right?' the woman asked, checking her pocket watch. 'He's late.' As soon as she spoke the front door of the warehouse swung open, and Daniel could hear his heartbeat thumping in his ears. This was it. He would finally get to see what Diora looked like.

'I am exactly to schedule, thank you,' a deep voice declared. The man who stepped into the warehouse reminded Daniel of several of the more distasteful lords he'd met: well-groomed, well-dressed, and with an air of self-importance that he immediately disliked. Entering closely behind him was Adamas, dressed all in black and looking like the cat that got the cream, chest puffed out and head held high. Daniel was surprised to see him; was Adamas not only in Diora's inner circle but also his trusted bodyguard? Shaking off the thought, he focused on Diora.

He was clearly lower city – his plain grey trousers and matching jacket were nice, but they weren't upper-city-nice – but he strode into the warehouse like a lord to his manor. When he turned, Daniel was able to get a proper look at him. He was so *young*. Older than Daniel, but much younger than he'd expected a man like Diora to be. His jet-black hair was cut close to his head, his clean-shaven jaw strong and square, and the look in his brown eyes was that of a man who would rather be anywhere else. Daniel could understand why the balding man stepped back as Diora approached; Diora looked almost as tall as Daniel himself, and was broad-shouldered and heavily muscled under his grey jacket.

'M–Mr Diora, sir?' the balding man stuttered, making the tall man laugh softly.

'Not quite,' he said. Daniel frowned. 'I am his second in command. You are Mr Lambert?'

Daniel swore softly; Diora had bailed! He'd come so close, but the luck of the Goddess was against him. For a second he debated leaving immediately – he'd lied to Crysta for *this*? – but he couldn't allow his disappointment to turn into frustration just yet; the situation wasn't a total loss. He now knew what Diora's right-hand man looked like, after all. If anyone was likely to lead him to Diora himself, it was this man – with a little unknowing help from Adamas.

Scrawling down Lambert's name in his notebook for future reference, Daniel stayed where he was, watching Lambert practically trip over himself in his haste to shake the man's hand. Adamas didn't offer a greeting, but stood silent and intimidating at his colleague's shoulder. 'Not a problem, not a problem, Mr Diora is a busy man,' he babbled. 'Yes, yes, I'm Lambert. What do I call you, then, sir?'

'You don't,' the man replied flatly, causing Lambert to falter. 'Do you have the goods or not?'

'Yes, of course, everything is right here!' Lambert patted the top of the crate he'd brought with him, chuckling nervously. 'Samples of everything Mr Diora requested. The rest is ready to be brought in as soon as the deal is made – I've got a friend at the tram station in Casora.'

Daniel's frown deepened; the only business in Casora was agricultural. What could these people be bringing in from there?

'I hope not *quite* ready to go. We won't need it for a few weeks at least,' Diora's second stated, reaching for the bolt on the crate. Flipping the lid, he peered in. Daniel wished the angle were better. It was too far away for him to properly see what was inside. Whatever it was, it seemed to be exactly what Diora's second was expecting, for he hummed in approval. Reaching in, the tall man pulled out . . . a marrow?

He took a knife from his pocket, deftly slicing the vegetable in half. It was decently sized, much more so than most of the food currently available in the lower city. 'Good,' he murmured, setting the two halves of marrow back in the crate. Next he took out a vine of tomatoes, followed by a small melon and what looked like a bag of rice. He held them out to Adamas, who made vague noises of approval. 'And you'll have all this in the quantities we discussed, ready and waiting?'

'Yes, sir,' Lambert confirmed. 'As soon as it looks like those little princesses didn't pray hard enough and the deliveries to the city get smaller and smaller, we'll be ready to swoop in with an abundance of food, feeding Lower Talen, where the monarchs cannot, and making Mr Diora a pretty penny in the process. The king won't be able to do a thing about it, not without looking like he wants his people to starve! Even the upper city will want Mr Diora's business.' He sounded overjoyed at being able to serve Diora in such a way. Daniel's eyes widened in shock. Erova was a big country when you counted all the islands under its law, and it was supposed to be the land of plenty, supplying food to half of Tellus. But as Anglya got more and more greedy, there was less for the people of Erova. If the weather meant a poor harvest, and Anglya refused to reduce their demands, the people of Talen – especially those in the lower city and shipyard – would struggle to survive.

Because of this deliveries to Talen were closely regulated, making sure every single grain was accounted for. If Diora suddenly brought in shipments of food, would it look like the royal family had been stockpiling, purposely holding back food from their subjects? The people of the lower city trusted Diora. Even if the king discovered Diora's illegal business, he couldn't step in without looking like the villain for taking food away from the starving. Diora would be untouchable, and Talen could fall into chaos – the lower and upper cities at war over rations. Goddess only knew what would happen.

Daniel listened intently as Diora's second negotiated with Lambert over the price and quantities of the produce, as well as the first delivery dates – just weeks from now, once the harvest allocations had been made, when it would be obvious that Talen would struggle. There was even mention of interfering with the usual food deliveries should the harvest be a success, to make it look like the festival hadn't worked. All blame would be shouldered by the princesses, as ambassadors to the Goddess herself.

Daniel wrote down every piece of relevant information. Diora had a hand in drugs, weapons, human trafficking, every sin you could think of in the city, and yet it was crates full of vegetables that might bring down the monarchy.

As the meeting began to wind down Daniel shifted, preparing to sneak out of the warehouse and follow Diora's second — this was the biggest lead he'd had in months, and he didn't want to waste the opportunity. Crouching low behind the crates, he peered through a gap to watch the mysterious man leave with Adamas at his heels, expecting Lambert and his colleagues to follow swiftly after. He cursed silently when the trio made no move to exit, lifting the crate of food back on to a trolley and murmuring to each other too quietly for Daniel to hear. He couldn't leave without them seeing him; Diora's second would be long gone.

Finally, the warehouse fell silent, but with his urgency gone Daniel waited several long minutes before heaving himself to his feet. 'Storms,' he muttered, heading for the window he'd entered through. He didn't know whether to be elated or furious. How on Tellus would he find Diora's second now?

Talen was a compact city — if he spent more time as Daniel and kept his eyes open, eventually they would cross paths again, if he was fortunate. At least he knew who to look out for. But with the festival drawing ever closer, and Noah's responsibilities growing by the day, he would need the Goddess' own luck to succeed.

7

Noah was glad to be back at the palace early the next day. He was frustrated that Diora's whereabouts were still a mystery, and was in need of the distraction of his other life while he waited to pick up the second's trail once more. 'Good morning, ladies,' he said as Lena opened the door to the living room of Crysta's suite, where the princesses were having breakfast; Ana wasn't present, but Rosa's handmaid was rarely far from her mistress. His escort stood to attention just inside the door, prepared to chaperone for as long as Noah was with the princesses. Crysta smiled at Noah, but her expression didn't reach her eyes. He frowned. 'What's wrong?'

'Father returned home this morning. Apparently the schedule has changed, and instead of Mother doing all the outland blessings herself, she and I are to divide and conquer, for time's sake. I leave tonight, but I'll be back in time for the court dinner.'

Noah's frown deepened. Every year before the festival the queen travelled to each of the outland regions and islands to bless those who couldn't be present in Talen for the celebrations. Crysta wasn't supposed to start accompanying her until she was married.

He forced his brow to clear. 'I shall sit right here and pine every second you are away,' he declared, deadpan, heading over to join her on the sofa.

Crysta giggled, shooting him a scolding look, her pale grey eyes amused. 'No one has the time for you to do that,' she teased lightly, leaning in for a kiss.

Noah reached to pull her closer, but let his hand drop, remembering the other people in the room.

'You have work to do. How long can you spare to be with me today?'

'Considering you leave tonight? I have all day,' Noah replied without hesitation. If Crysta was going to be gone for several days he would have plenty of time in which to be Daniel. He was supposed to be meeting Emilie that evening, but he would make it up to her later. 'But do you have the time to spare for me?' Knowing Crysta, she had done a small mountain of work the night before, and given herself an even bigger mountain of work as a result.

They were interrupted by a knock on the door and Noah's chaperone hurried to open it, revealing the queen already dressed and ready for the day. 'Oh, Noah, when did you get here?' she asked, surprised.

'Not long ago, m'lady,' he replied. 'I woke early and thought I may as well see what Crysta was up to. A good thing I did, too; she's just informed me of your departure this evening. I'd hate to have only found out this afternoon.'

'It is a rather abrupt change in plans,' Sofie agreed, perching on the arm of Rosa's chair. 'But in light of that, I have a request for the three of you. Four, if Damien isn't busy.'

'We can send for him, if you need us to,' Crysta said, eyeing her mother curiously.

'I need you to go down into the city this morning and greet some of the troupers who have arrived already, so Rosa doesn't have to see all of them alone.' Rosa looked startled at Sofie's words, but held her head high.

'I can do it, Mother. It was to become my duty alone soon enough, anyway,' she added with a glance at Crysta and Noah, who blushed in unison. Greeting the troupers was a job for royal children – when Crysta married she would no longer be considered such, and then Rosa would have to go by herself.

'I know, dearest, but it'll be easier on you to do the first few with company,' Sofie said with a smile, setting a hand on her youngest daughter's shoulder. 'It shouldn't take long, only five or six tents are up so far.'

'So long as I'm back with plenty of time to pack for this evening, I don't see why not,' Crysta reasoned, shrugging and flashing Noah an apologetic smile. 'Noah?'

'I'm free,' he said. If it was the only way to spend time with Crysta before her trip he would have to make the most of it.

'Excellent! Do stop at the guard station and see if Damien is free to go with you. If not, take two other guards, but I would feel much safer if it were Damien,' she told them. 'I'll leave you to finish your breakfast, then.' Smiling once more at the trio, the queen left her daughter's chambers, and the two princesses resumed eating.

Crysta rolled her eyes as Noah leaned over to steal a slice of apple from her plate, eating it with a playful smirk. 'If you're hungry, we can have breakfast brought up for you,' she said.

'Oh, no, I've already eaten,' he assured, his smirk widening as he stole another slice, just to be irritating. Crysta huffed and Rosa giggled quietly, sharing an amused look with her handmaid.

When Rosa finished her breakfast she excused herself to get dressed, and Ana returned to help Crysta do the same shortly after, leaving Noah in the living room.

Several minutes later, Crysta stepped out of her bedroom wearing a simple green silk sleeveless tunic and loose bronze-coloured trousers.

'How do I look?' she asked, giving an obliging twirl, the tiny beads decorating her tunic sparkling in the light.

'Radiant, as always,' Noah said with a grin, catching her hand and nudging her into another spin, before pulling her back to his chest. She smiled up at him, raising an eyebrow.

'Someone's in a good mood,' she noted in amusement. Noah winked at her, looping her arm through his.

'It's a beautiful day, and I'm spending time with a beautiful woman. Hard not to be.' Crysta flushed at his words, making his grin widen.

With Ana following them, the pair left Crysta's suite and made for the entrance hall, finding Rosa and Lena already waiting. The two girls were standing close together, talking quietly, and immediately jumped apart when Noah and Crysta arrived, Lena placing her hands behind her back, waiting for instruction.

'Let's just hope Damien isn't too busy today,' Rosa murmured, allowing Crysta to lead the way through the side exit to the palace courtyard. The guards on patrol duty stopped to salute as they passed, and Crysta and Rosa greeted each of them with a smile. When they reached the guard station everyone inside scrambled to stand to attention.

'At ease,' Crysta insisted, though several of them remained upright, barely switching to parade rest. 'We came to see Captain Conti.' Damien smiled at them from across the room and headed towards them.

'How can I help you, ladies?' he asked cheerfully.

'Mother has asked us to go down to the city and greet the troupers who have already arrived,' Crysta explained. 'We were hoping you might be free to accompany us. And also provide us with a map of which tents have been set up.' Damien grinned at the prospect of a couple of hours wandering the city with his friends.

'For you, Your Highness, I am always free.' He turned to a nearby desk, rifling through a stack of papers for a document Noah recognised as the festival tent map; Crysta had spent hours finalising it. 'Though I would feel much safer bringing someone else along too. Lieutenant Salo?' At his call a tall woman with coffee-brown hair in a neat bun offered him a salute.

'Sir?'

'You're free to accompany us on a little morning excursion, are you not?' She nodded. 'Excellent. With us, Noah, and your handmaids, that should be plenty. Shall we?' he asked Crysta, who smiled in affirmation, allowing the captain to lead the way into the main courtyard. Salo walked at the rear of the group, concentration in her expression.

'So we're off to greet troupers, are we?' Damien asked, falling into step between Crysta and Rosa, with Noah on Crysta's other side. 'Why so early?'

'I'm going with Mother to the outlands tonight, so she wanted me to escort Rosa before leaving her to do the rest alone,' Crysta said.

'Well, you're in luck, there aren't that many tents set up yet.' Damien unrolled the map, pausing to allow the girls and Noah to look at it. 'Three in the upper, three in the lower, nice and simple.' Noah's light heart suddenly turned to ice; he'd completely forgotten about the tents in the lower city. He'd watched them go up, he should have remembered. Storms, what if he bumped into someone he knew? He usually avoided spending time in the lower city as Noah for that very reason, but it was too late to make an excuse now.

The first tent they arrived at was in the upper city. It was full of acrobats, setting up their trapeze bars and safety net. They all stopped what they were doing when the princesses entered, immediately falling into bows and curtseys.

'Your Highnesses!' said a man whose elaborately embroidered green tailcoat marked him as the troupe master. He dropped into a bow so low he let it turn into a forward roll, drawing laughs of delight from the two girls. 'What a wonderful surprise! Had we known you were coming, we would have prepared a show.'

'Please don't worry, sir,' Crysta said. 'I'm sure my sister and I will see your troupe perform during the festival, and I have no doubt it will be spectacular. Blessings on you and your company – may the Goddess smile upon you.' The troupe master bowed low again, thanks in his eyes.

'I would ask the Goddess to smile upon you and yours in return, but I do believe you already have the Goddess' smile, dear princess,' he returned solemnly, making Crysta laugh once more.

'You flatter me, sir. Are you well? And your troupe, is everything to their liking?' Some pieces of equipment, especially for the acrobatic troupes, were too cumbersome to travel with, and it was the royal family's duty to make sure that each troupe was lent whatever they needed upon arrival in Talen.

Crysta's conversation with the troupe master was easy. Rosa sighed quietly, her shoulder bumping Noah's as she moved closer to him. 'How does she do it so effortlessly?' she muttered under her breath.

'Necessity ... and lots of practice,' he replied, offering her a supportive smile. With Crysta set to take the crown and all the responsibilities that came with it, Rosa had been somewhat babied, allowed to stand back while her sister did most of the talking. Noah was even guilty of it himself sometimes, but the younger princess was so shy he felt awful forcing her out of her comfort zone. She couldn't avoid things forever, he supposed. 'You'll get there, Rosie,' he said, slinging an arm around her shoulders and squeezing briefly. 'Crysta will help.'

At the next tent Crysta made sure to get Rosa a little more involved, bringing her into the conversation with a bright smile. Luckily the owners of the tent were a friendly husband and wife from the small island of Lalia, selling beautiful hand-woven tapestries in all shapes and sizes, and they were delighted to have the princesses visiting. They welcomed the group warmly, even insisting the princesses each pick out a tapestry as a gift, and Rosa was happy to discuss the artistry for several minutes unaided by her sister. Noah joined in where he could, keeping one eye on Crysta as she roamed the tent, even though Damien was at her side. Still, he couldn't resist the rare opportunity to talk about art with those who understood it as he did.

They didn't stay long at the third tent. It was jet black and full of curiosities, jars containing odd, coloured liquids and what looked like fossilised animals, with a dark curtain shielding the rest of the tent from those not brave enough to enter. The tent owner was a strange grey-haired man with hardly any teeth, and while he was perfectly polite, the contents of his tent unnerved both girls – it unnerved Noah too, if he was honest – so after a swift blessing they took their leave and turned towards the bridge to the lower city. Noah tensed as he walked, keeping his eyes peeled. There were plenty of people he recognised, but he couldn't see anyone who knew Daniel well enough to identify him and Noah as the same person.

Crysta slipped her arm through his, and Noah noticed both Damien and Lieutenant Salo shuffle in closer, shoulders tight and eyes far more alert than they had been in the upper city. The lower city loved the royal family as much as the rest of Talen, but the same could not be said about the guards. They were lucky it was nearing festival time; it was the only time of year the two halves of the city came together in goodwill.

'All three tents are close by, so we should be done fairly quickly,' Damien said, looking at his map and leading the way to the first tent. A small troupe of dancers was inside, all girls around Rosa's age. Very excited to have both princesses visit them, they insisted on putting on a short performance. It always amused Noah how much outlanders practically fell over themselves when faced with royalty – the princesses particularly seemed to have a special spot in the nation's heart.

After blessing the troupe and thanking them for their performance, the group moved on to the tent Noah had been dreading – the tent of acrobats Emilie had shown him when they had first set up a couple of nights ago. What if Emilie was in the courtyard, or any of her friends? They had known Daniel for years; if anyone was going to recognise him, it was them.

'Are you all right?' Crysta asked quietly as they walked, eyeing him in concern.

'What? Yes, of course, why wouldn't I be?' he replied, trying to stay as calm as possible. Crysta frowned slightly.

'You seem . . . anxious.' He winced mentally; was it that obvious?

'I'm fine,' he assured her, managing a smile. 'I just . . . something doesn't feel right,' he lied. 'It's probably nothing.' Crysta's eyes lingered on him for a long moment, clearly not believing him, before they turned the corner to reach the tent in the courtyard. Noah's eyes immediately scanned the area, and he had to stop himself from letting out a breath of relief when he didn't see Emilie or any of her usual crowd. He could only hope it stayed that way.

The acrobats were all set up and practising when they entered, but like every troupe they'd greeted that morning they stopped what they were doing, hurrying to bow and curtsey. Crysta stepped forward, giving the obligatory blessing and asking the troupe master how they were faring. Noah kept his gaze low, his hair falling forward just enough to shadow his features; some of the acrobats might have seen him when he was with Emilie.

'We should take the rest of the day off,' he said as he ducked his head to whisper in Crysta's ear, making it even harder for anyone to see his face as he stood behind her, his arms linked around her waist. 'We can head back to the upper city and have Damien make some excuse. Or he could come with us, pretend we're on official business, and we'll bring Rosie too. Your mother won't be expecting you back for a while yet.' He felt her shiver as his lips brushed the shell of her ear, unaware of the tension in his frame, his eyes alert as the acrobats set up for their impromptu show.

'I have to pack,' Crysta protested, though her heart wasn't in it, her body curving into Noah's embrace. 'And the festival plans –'

'I'll do them while you're gone,' Noah said. He lowered his voice, not above using seduction to get Crysta to relax. And if it got them out of the lower city quicker, he wouldn't complain. 'Please, love. Just a few hours, we'll be back after lunch.'

Crysta bit her lip, the only visible tell that she wasn't completely engrossed in the performance. She was very good at keeping a straight face, after years of important events with Noah and Damien making jokes and comments only she could hear. 'I'll think about it,' she said eventually. Noah grinned. From Crysta, that was almost a yes.

The show was brief, but the group were sure to praise the troupers for their talent. The troupe master flushed, bowing in response. 'Just doing our jobs, Your Highnesses,' he said. 'We've all got to do our bit, y'know. Especially this year. What they've been saying about the harvest . . .'

Noah felt Crysta's wince, though her smile didn't falter. 'There's no need to worry about the harvest,' she placated, her words forced. 'The festival will secure the Goddess' favour, and we'll have another prosperous year.'

'Well, like he said,' one of the acrobats interjected, standing at his troupe master's side, 'we've *all* got to do our bit.' This was said with a pointed stare at the two princesses, and Noah bristled on their behalf. He opened his mouth to argue, but then a ripple of tent fabric caught his eye.

His heart dropped to his stomach. In through the back entrance of the tent stepped Eric, one of Emilie's friends, chatting companionably with a female acrobat. He didn't seem to have noticed the princesses, but Noah doubted it would stay that way for long.

He should have known coming to the lower city was a bad idea! Eric had seen Daniel enough times over the years that Noah wouldn't put it past him to make the connection. He had to leave, fast.

'I need some air,' he muttered under his breath, barely pausing to kiss Crysta's cheek before hurrying out of the tent from the front, praying whatever business Eric had didn't bring him in contact with the princesses. He heard Crysta call his name but ignored it, confident that she wouldn't excuse herself until she'd appropriately welcomed the acrobats – and no doubt had a few curt words with the troupe master and the acrobat for their insinuations about her duties.

Standing alone outside the tent Noah tapped his foot anxiously, waiting for someone to leap out and shout his other name. He didn't like being at a standstill in the most exposed courtyard in the lower city, but he couldn't leave without Crysta and the others. He felt like every eye in the courtyard was on him, and it made his skin itch.

Thankfully, it wasn't long before his companions emerged from the tent, Crysta rushing to his side with concern on her face. 'What was that all about?' she asked quietly, reaching up to place a hand against his clammy forehead. 'Are you well?'

'Fine,' he said, grasping her hand and squeezing it in assurance. 'I just needed some air, but I'm fine now.' Behind Crysta he could see Damien and the others, keeping their distance but looking worried. 'The last tent is over here, right?' He started to walk, but Crysta held him back.

'Yes, but – Noah, are you sure you're OK?' Her brow was furrowed, and he pressed a kiss to the centre of it, trying to force himself to behave normally. He'd give himself away in a heartbeat if he didn't calm down!

'Don't worry yourself, love, I'm fine,' he said again. 'I just want to get this over with, then we can go to lunch.' Some time with Crysta away from royal duties was just what he needed. 'Have some fun, before such things are temporarily outlawed,' he added wryly. Once the other nobles arrived and the festival truly began they wouldn't have anything resembling 'fun' for a while. The girls couldn't even properly enjoy the festival itself, owing to their prayer duties.

'I haven't agreed to it yet,' Crysta pointed out, but he merely grinned, tugging her by the hand in the direction of the final tent. The sooner they were out of the lower city, the better.

'But you were going to,' he teased, pushing away his anxiety. Crysta mustn't suspect anything. 'You love me. You can't resist me. And you *definitely* can't resist me offering lunch at Livana's.' Crysta's favourite little restaurant near Stanos Park was somewhere she didn't get to visit that often, especially not without a full guard contingency, but every now and then she and Noah managed to sneak away for a meal there. Sometimes with company, sometimes without. They liked to pretend that no one knew they went there, but Leon and Sofie had eyes and ears everywhere.

Noah caught Crysta's gaze, seeing her resolve waver.

'We'll discuss this after we've finished our duties,' she said eventually, letting him lead the way out of the courtyard. He caught Rosa and Damien exchanging a bemused look, and the tension in his shoulders began to recede. Being in the lower city was fine. He could handle it. Nothing bad would happen.

Noah didn't truly relax until they were over the bridge to the upper city, duties successfully completed. Damien and Salo relaxed too, Damien linking arms with Rosa as they walked. Salo stayed back with the two handmaids, letting the four have some impression of privacy. Damien was probably just as worked off his feet as Crysta, but in different ways, and it doubled Noah's resolve to persuade his friends into skipping out on their responsibilities for an afternoon. They were still young enough to get away with it without too much of a reprimand, though that wouldn't last much longer.

'So, Livana's?' he suggested with a grin.

Crysta sighed. 'Oh, go on, then. It would take a stronger woman than me to say no to those cream cakes. Damien? Rosa?'

'As tempting as it sounds, I'm afraid I've got drills to run with the festival team all afternoon. Your safety being vital to the country and all that,' Damien said wryly, giving Crysta a wink. 'Another time, perhaps?'

'Hmm. Acceptable excuse, I suppose,' she relented. 'Little sister?'

'What, and be the odd one out sitting between you and Noah making eyes at each other across the table?' Rosa asked with a laugh. 'No thank you.'

'Lena would be there. You wouldn't be the odd one out,' Noah volunteered. Rosa's smile faltered for the barest moment, and when she laughed again it sounded ever so slightly forced.

'Lena would be stood behind my chair waiting for me to need something – it's hardly the same. No, I'll leave you two to your lunch date. Besides, *someone* has to cover for you both with Mother and Father. Go, have fun. I'll see you at dinner.'

'Oh, thank you Rosie!' Crysta said, breaking away from Noah to hug her sister. 'I owe you one.'

'One of many,' Rosa teased, giving them a fond look.

'Thanks, Rosa.' Noah kissed her cheek somewhat apologetically; him dragging Crysta into the city would no doubt mean more work for Rosa. At least he'd be around to help her later in the week when Crysta was gone.

'Look after her,' Damien said, clapping Noah on the shoulder. 'And if Their Majesties ask, I sent Lieutenant Salo along as your guard.' Salo snorted, giving her superior an amused look.

The other four soon left, leaving Noah, Crysta and Ana in the courtyard. Noah turned to his girlfriend, his breath catching in his throat at the excited sparkle in her eyes. Grinning, he sketched a bow and offered her an arm. 'Shall we?'

Crysta beamed, taking his arm and rocking up on her toes to kiss his cheek. 'We shall.'

8

Not wanting to waste a single moment of their freedom, Noah led Crysta through several of his favourite shortcuts, those that didn't involve climbing or jumping – he'd been informed countless times that such things were improper for a princess to do in public. Without the usual royal fanfare accompanying them they were easily overlooked; no one expected to see the princess and her suitor out for a stroll in the city, especially not at this time of year. A few people did a double take upon passing them, but Crysta kept walking and merely turned her smile on them, the one that made her cheeks dimple and even the most iron of spines bend to her will.

'You know, sometimes,' Crysta began, looking up at Noah as she walked, 'you have ideas that aren't entirely terrible.'

'Only sometimes?' he asked laughingly. He almost missed a step as she turned the full force of that smile upon him. Two and a half years, and it still made his heart race just as much as it had the first time he'd met her in a hallway of the palace, his arms weighed down by the festival masks he'd been delivering on his father's behalf. He'd been besotted since day one.

'Occasionally. Though Father may kill you when he discovers you and I went out unguarded in public, especially this close to the festival. So many nobles around – they're bound to start talking.'

'They're already talking.' Noah waved off her concerns, stopping on the street corner to pull her up into a kiss. The rush from successfully avoiding Eric's notice was still coursing through him, and he couldn't bring himself to care about what the court might say about his behaviour. Half of them hated him on principle, anyway. 'They've done nothing *but* talk since I began courting you. Let them, I say. It doesn't matter.'

Crysta sighed, suddenly serious. 'It will if they call into question our courtship. There's still no ring on my hand, and should they insist that you've broken courtship rules they can –'

Noah cut her off, pressing a gentle finger to her lips and offering a reassuring smile. It was hard to forget their troubles when Crysta insisted on being so *sensible* about things. 'Ana's with us,' he said eventually, gesturing to the handmaid three paces behind. 'We're chaperoned. And there's nothing in the courtship rules that says I can't do this.' One hand on her shoulder, the other cupping her face, Noah kissed her as firmly as he dared in such a public place. Crysta leaned into the embrace without hesitation, her lips soft against his.

'Let's pretend the court doesn't exist, just for the afternoon.' He saw the brightly coloured awning of Livana's, and could already smell the delicious aromas wafting from the restaurant; fresh-baked bread and sweet honeyed cakes and perfectly grilled steak combining to attract hungry customers. His stomach growled in anticipation.

'If only that could be true,' Crysta sighed wistfully, letting Noah lead her towards the restaurant.

The waiter looked surprised to see them, and quickly ushered them to Crysta's favoured table in the back corner. Noah took the seat against the wall, giving him full view of the restaurant. Ana stood off to the side, hands clasped in front of her and eyes alert.

They placed their order without even needing to look at the menu. 'Remember the first time we came here?' Crysta said suddenly, a small smile on her face at the memory.

'How could I forget?' It was their first official date, once the courtship papers had been signed. Before that, Noah had been limited to making up excuses to visit the palace under the guise of work for his father, seeking out Crysta immediately while all the residents of the palace pretended they weren't aware of what was going on between the pair. When he'd finally plucked up the courage to ask to court her – and when, to his surprise, her parents agreed – he bribed thirteen-year-old Rosa with sweets in order to get the name of Crysta's favourite restaurant. 'It was one of the most terrifying experiences of my life.'

Crysta giggled. 'It wasn't *that* bad.' He levelled a flat look at her and she snorted. 'OK. Maybe it was a little.' Damien had offered to chaperone them, bringing four of his most intimidating guards as backup, and spent the entire evening standing directly behind Crysta's chair, glaring daggers at him. Noah hadn't even been brave enough to hold Crysta's hand, for fear his would be cut off. 'And look, Damien warmed to you eventually.' The captain had only just been appointed then, so Noah had comforted himself with the thought that Damien hadn't wanted to let the king and queen doubt their trust in him. He knew better by now, of course.

'There's protective, and then there's that,' Noah retorted drily. 'I spent the whole week certain he was going to kidnap me in the night and have me killed.'

'Oh, hush,' Crysta scolded, unable to quell her laughter. 'You survived, didn't you? Everything my family has thrown at you, you've survived. They were just testing your commitment.' Her eyes met his, the implication hanging heavy between them, until they were interrupted by the arrival of several plates of food. Most of it was finger food – crackers piled high with cheeses and roasted vegetables, small cubes of seasoned meat with a honey sauce, seafood wrapped in salad leaves – but in the centre of the table the waiter placed a bowl of rich beef and vegetable stew, along with a plate of bread to accompany it. All Crysta's favourites, which Noah was happy to share.

The moment broken, he shuffled his chair slightly closer to Crysta's side of the round table, his thoughts drifting involuntarily to the ring in his desk drawer. His commitment was no longer in question; his maturity, on the other hand, and his ability to step up to the role Crysta needed him to play . . . these were still under scrutiny.

As they ate Noah started to let his guard down, watching the line of Crysta's shoulders ease as she let all the stress of the festival wash away. He was so captivated by her that he almost didn't notice when a familiar figure entered the restaurant; it was only Ana tensing fractionally at Crysta's side that prompted him to look up. His heart sank.

'Don't look now, but I fear we're about to have a rather unwelcome intrusion,' Noah muttered, wishing there was some way to shield their table from view. Unfortunately they had no such luck, and just as Crysta glanced surreptitiously towards the door Fabian Silva's gaze turned in their direction. The noble's face lit up in a cruel smirk, and Noah heard Crysta make the smallest noise of discontent. There was nowhere for them to hide as the dark-haired man made a beeline towards them, squeezing between tables and ignoring the waiting staff who tried to offer him a seat.

'Princess Crysta! What a surprise. I would have thought you'd be far too busy to leave the palace at this current time,' Silva said by way of greeting, resting a hand on Crysta's shoulder. Noah caught her shudder before she could restrain it, and he glared at the man's hand, willing it to somehow detach from his body.

'Rosa insisted on taking over some of my duties, to practise for when she will very likely inherit them next year. Thanks to her, Noah and I managed to get time to ourselves this afternoon.' When Crysta mentioned Rosa inheriting her duties Fabian's eyes dropped to her left hand in a brief moment of panic, and in that same moment Noah wished Crysta *did* have a ring there, just to see the look on the man's face.

'How accommodating of Princess Rosa. Yet I notice there is no guard accompanying you? Not even your *friend* the captain.'

'Noah has been training with Captain Conti and the rest of the guard, and Father deems him more than competent to have my safety in hand,' she told him, one dark eyebrow rising, daring him to comment. Fabian Silva was never one to back down from a dare.

'No guard, and only a handmaid to chaperone?' he remarked, eyeing Ana disparagingly. 'I'm sure your safety is not the only thing Hansen has *in hand*.'

Crysta gasped, and Noah's chair scraped against the tiles as he jumped to his feet, knuckles white with anger. Before he could act, he heard a throat being cleared.

'Sir, I'm afraid I'm going to have to ask you to leave.' It was Theo, one of the restaurant's waiters, a mountain of a man. He towered over Silva, eyes hard. 'The princess and Mr Hansen come here for privacy, and we pride ourselves on being able to provide it. I cannot allow you to disturb their meal further.' His voice carried through the near silent restaurant, every patron in the room turning to watch. Fabian's face purpled indignantly and he glared at the enormous man.

'How dare you speak to me that way! Don't you know who I am?' he exclaimed, puffing out his chest. He was about as effective as a kitten against a wolf.

Theo looked him up and down. 'No, actually,' he admitted, and Noah snorted. 'But you're bothering the princess. Leave now, or I shall make you.' Looking around, Fabian seemed to realise he was outmatched.

'Fine,' he bit out, turning back to the table, venom in his gaze. 'I look forward to seeing both of you at the welcoming lunch.' With that, he turned on his heel and stalked out of the restaurant, leaving an uneasy silence in his wake.

'Your Highness, sir, I'm so very sorry about the intrusion,' Theo apologised hurriedly. 'I hope this does not reflect poorly on our restaurant.'

'It's not your fault, Theo, honestly,' Crysta insisted. 'You weren't to know Mr Silva would be so rude.'

'Still, I can't apologise enough. I'll leave you to your meal. Please don't hesitate to ask if you require anything.' Ducking a quick bow, Theo left them alone, and Noah sank back into his chair. He was still shaking with rage.

'Crysta —'

'Don't,' she cut him off, eyes flashing like steel. 'Just . . . don't. Don't let that *vile* man ruin our day. We haven't even had dessert yet.'

Noah let the subject lie, but Fabian's words echoed in his mind throughout the afternoon. He was only saying what many of the nobles were thinking . . . everyone was calling Crysta's morals into question, her dedication to both her country and to the boundaries of courtship. All because Noah couldn't untangle his life enough to fully dedicate it to her. It couldn't go on much longer; there was only so much the Octavians would put up with before something had to give. He had to hurry and find Diora's second so he could start pulling at the thread that would unravel Diora's empire.

Despite Fabian's intrusion, the pair managed to enjoy the rest of their meal, and when they finally left the restaurant it was late enough that Crysta began to feel guilty about having been absent for so long. Noah relented, walking with her back to the palace; several hours of Crysta's company was more than he'd expected, and she really did need to pack for her trip.

Rosa was nowhere to be found when they returned, but there was a stack of paperwork on Crysta's coffee table, all filled out in the younger princess's neat handwriting. Noah grabbed a pen and took responsibility for the remaining stack, calling out to Crysta for her input as needed, while she and Ana debated which outfits to pack.

Crysta occasionally emerged from her bedroom wearing one beautiful gown after another to ask for his opinion. As his hand began to cramp from writing, he started at the sound of a knock at the door. 'Come in!' he called, setting his pen aside. The door opened and a servant edged nervously into the room. He looked around, frowning at seeing Noah alone. 'She's in the bedroom,' Noah supplied drily. The young man flushed scarlet, making Noah chuckle. '*Packing.*' Noah craned his neck in the direction of the bedroom door. 'Crysta! Message for you!'

There was a rustle of fabric and Crysta emerged, dressed in the same clothes she'd been wearing earlier. The servant bowed low, his cheeks still glowing in embarrassment.

'Forgive me for interrupting, Your Highness, but your father has requested your presence in his office immediately. Uh, both of your presences,' he said, giving a quick glance at Noah. Noah's heart sank; Leon must have learned of their little excursion. He feared he had Fabian Silva to thank for that, and who knew what else the man had said.

From the look on Crysta's face she shared his concerns. 'Let's go and see what Father wants, then,' she said, sighing.

Noah's stomach churned with guilt as they were escorted to the king's office, feeling a little like he was walking to his own execution. Scenes of angry crowds accusing Crysta of enraging the Goddess flashed through his mind. 'Don't make that face,' Crysta murmured, squeezing his hand.

They reached Leon's office and the servant left to return to his duties. Crysta knocked before opening the door, entering with trepidation. Noah followed, his hand still in hers. The least they could do was present a united front.

'Ah, good. I was wondering if you two would be back for dinner,' Leon remarked, eyeing the pair coolly. Noah winced. They were *definitely* in trouble.

'I hear you had a rather interesting afternoon.'

'Father, please,' Crysta cut in hurriedly, stepping closer to his desk. 'We didn't mean to cause any worry, I just wanted a break.'

'I persuaded you to take a break, you mean,' Noah corrected, shooting her a pointed look – he wasn't going to let her take the heat for this. 'It was my idea, sir, I dragged Crysta into it. She shouldn't get into trouble for my actions.'

'It's nice to see you're so eager to fall on your own sword for my daughter,' Leon drawled, amusement on his face. 'I'm afraid the rumour mill has been running riot, thanks to a certain Fabian Silva, and while I've been assuring anyone who asks that you two had my permission to be out together, I'd like to know exactly what I gave permission for.'

It took a minute for the man's words to make sense in Noah's head – he was siding with them, no questions asked? No scolding for their recklessness, or disapproval of Noah's behaviour around the princess?

Crysta gave her father a matter-of-fact report on the afternoon's events. 'It really wasn't anything to worry over.

At least, it wouldn't have been, had Silva not got himself involved.'

'Well,' Leon said, leaning back in his chair. 'That is a far cry from what the rumour mill's saying.' Noah winced, certain he didn't want to know. 'There's nothing to be done now, at any rate. In future, please do be more careful. I can't begrudge you the odd lunch in peace, but . . . remember what's at stake, Crysta. All eyes are on you, more so now than ever. Everyone who loves you knows that the pair of you are behaving, but should the Goddess not be swayed by our efforts at the festival . . . people will look for the cause of her displeasure, and a princess not sticking to courtship agreements is an easy target.'

Crysta's cheeks were flushed with anger, her eyes stormy. 'The festival won't fail,' she insisted. 'I won't let it.' But Noah had to admit that Leon had a point, and it made him burn with shame. He'd been childish, enjoying the feeling of irritating the nobles and showing how little their opinions mattered to him. But this wasn't a game, and his actions would only harm Crysta's reputation. The Octavians had done so much for him, and all he was doing was causing them trouble. He had to stop playing around.

'I know you won't, love,' Leon said soothingly to his daughter. 'I truly didn't bring you here to lecture you on propriety. I wanted to check you had the details for all your travel arrangements, and to make sure Noah is also aware. Unfortunately, Damien cannot guard you personally as he'll be with your mother, but he has assured me his second is up to the job, as well as the usual contingency of guards. You'll be heading out to Casora together to do their blessing tonight, and then you'll travel down to Forezza while your mother makes for Stenia. Then each of you will circle round in opposite directions, until you meet in Denas and return home. It's going to be a lot of travelling with very few breaks, but I'm afraid we left things a little late this year.' He paused, brow furrowing. 'Crysta, my darling, I want you to be careful in the outlands. The outlanders . . . they know the signs of a good harvest, and it's not looking promising. There are mutterings, and while it's early days, you know how easy it is for crowds to get riled up.'

Crysta's face hardened, and she nodded. 'I can handle it, Father, don't worry.' She looked confident, but the king's words still made Noah nervous. He didn't like the thought of Crysta so far away from him, in the midst of a potentially dangerous situation. They were so sheltered in Talen, so cut off from the rest of the country, in their own little bubble of court drama and silly gossip – the outlands were a whole other world, and they were even more superstitious than the inlanders. They would definitely blame any sign of the Goddess' ill will on Crysta.

It was growing late by the time Noah bid Crysta good-bye, reluctantly leaving her to a mostly packed suitcase and a long list of travel arrangements. He should have been home hours ago, but he'd wanted as much time with her as possible before he lost her for three days.

Heading down the main staircase Noah was surprised when his name was called, and he turned to see Leon outside his office. 'Might I have a word before you leave, if you're not in a hurry?' the king asked. Noah couldn't decline. Stomach churning apprehensively, he followed him into his office, pulling the door shut behind him. Leon's personal office was surprisingly welcoming, unlike the public office where he conducted meetings, The tall shelves lining the walls were stuffed with books and trinkets from his travels, and the entire Octavian family smiled down at Noah from a family portrait on the wall behind the desk.

'Is everything all right?' he asked, a frown on his face. Had he done something wrong?

'Don't worry, you can relax,' the dark-haired man assured him, smiling. 'I merely wanted to speak with you without my daughter present. I love her, and admire her independence, but . . . some things must be discussed among men, I'm sure you understand.' Suddenly, Noah had a very clear idea of where the conversation was leading.

'Sir, I —' he started, but fell silent when Leon cleared his throat.

'I have been receiving marriage proposals and betrothal contracts for both my daughters since before they were born, as is to be expected with girls of royal blood. I ignored all those sent before the age of sixteen — I would not give my daughters away before they were old enough to make the decision for themselves. And then, of course, Crysta met you, and the courtship began despite my . . . initial protests.' He coughed awkwardly, and a fleeting smile crossed Noah's lips as he remembered being chased from the palace by Damien and a horde of guards.

'Everyone is aware of your courtship, and yet I still receive these proposals. More so now, with comments that your courtship has been going on for an unusually long time without an engagement.' Noah held back a sigh; would the Goddess give him no peace?

'Despite how insistent Crysta has always been about proving herself worthy of being queen in her own right before taking a husband?' he returned wryly. 'I'm not sure my pride could stand a rejection on that scale.' It was a weak excuse and he could tell Leon didn't buy it, but he couldn't let him know about Daniel.

The king's eyebrows rose. 'You and I both know my daughter has more than proven herself up to the task. Believe me, Noah, I am now well aware that you are the best person for my daughter. But you must understand that I'm running out of good reasons to decline these proposals. Lord Brunner is very insistent on creating a match between Crysta and his eldest son, Marc.'

Noah growled under his breath at the thought of Marc Brunner courting Crysta.

'Your courtship claim may have been enough a year or so ago, but Crysta will be twenty in the coming year, and a three-year courtship does not suggest any permanence. With everything going on – including the threat of Anglyan interference hanging over our heads – Crysta cannot afford to stay unmarried much longer. You know how this family operates; we rule as a partnership, we always have. She cannot be queen without a king by her side, and our people are uneasy enough about the future without questioning the strength of their monarchy. And if you are not ready I will be forced to look elsewhere.'

Noah wasn't an idiot, he could parse the man's true meaning; allowing Noah to court her for so long, when he was a nobody in the eyes of the court, was making Crysta look childish and irresponsible. It made her seem like she was dodging her responsibilities. And it was nothing Noah hadn't heard before.

'Are you telling me to propose to your daughter?' Noah asked flatly.

'If I were to do that, my boy, you would only ignore me,' he replied knowingly. 'If only because you are now comfortable enough to stand up to me. All I'm asking is that you consider it, and talk it over with Crysta. It's for the good of Erova.'

'I understand, sir. I will discuss it with Crysta,' Noah relented. 'But I won't pressure her into a decision she isn't ready to make.'

'Crysta is aware that her duty to her country comes before personal preference. I'm sure she will see sense,' Leon insisted. 'Perhaps I shall talk with Rosa about Marc Brunner; it would please the country if I at least made an attempt at a strategic match for one of my daughters, since you have stolen the heart of the other.' Noah chuckled, keeping his expression neutral, not wanting to betray his wince at the prospect of talking arranged marriages with Rosa. It would be the poor girl's worst nightmare to be married to a stranger.

'Maybe during this festival Rosa will choose a man under her own power,' Noah mused, though he highly doubted it. Rosa would never take a husband of her own free will.

'One can only hope,' Leon agreed, falling silent for several moments, lost in thought.

Noah coughed politely and the king's attention returned. 'Gods, it's getting late, I should let you get back to your father. Just . . . think things over, won't you?'

Noah nodded and offered him a brief bow before leaving the office, his brain swirling with thoughts.

Crysta would be furious that her father had taken Noah aside to talk to him about marriage. But he did have a point; a courtship claim was fine at the age of sixteen, but now Crysta was nineteen it wasn't enough. He knew without a doubt that he wanted to marry her, and had known for more than two years . . . but things weren't that simple. There was Daniel to consider. The moment he married Crysta he would be expected to move into the palace, and he would officially become part of the royal family. He would have official duties and it would be impossible for him to roam the lower city in disguise. He couldn't commit to a life within the court until the lower city was safe.

The clock was ticking, and Noah's two lives were beginning to pull apart at the seams before he could do anything to salvage them. Kill Diora. Propose to Crysta. He could not do one without the other, and the window in which he could do either was growing ever smaller.

9

Deciding that Crysta's absence would give him the perfect opportunity to tidy up his life, Noah dug out his notebook almost as soon as he got home, preparing for a long night wearing Daniel's face. His father was in the workshop with the door closed, and Noah didn't disturb him as he left, not wanting another lecture about his life choices.

'This had better get some results,' he murmured to himself, his tone deeper and rougher than his natural voice as he slipped into his other persona. If he didn't find Diora's second soon, he would have problems.

It was easy for him to reach the lower city without being noticed, only allowing people to see him when he reached an acceptable distance from the upper city. He made it look as if he were coming from the shipyard; a different location from the last time he'd turned up, just to keep people guessing. No one knew where Daniel lived, who he lived with, or anything at all. Even Emilie, counting herself among a privileged few, hardly knew much more about him than his name.

The further he walked into the lower city the more crowded it grew. The ever-present cleaning crews had just about finished making it look decent – the grime had been washed off the buildings and the litter picked up off the streets. Daniel hardly recognised it in the build-up to the festival – it looked almost like the upper city in some places, all the parts the outlanders were likely to see. He imagined what it would be like when Diora was gone, when the guards were free to walk within the lower city and keep it in order. Would it be this clean all year round?

More tents had started setting up since he'd been there that morning, and were steadily crowding the courtyard. Each tent flew a different coloured pennant from its top: blue for acrobats and circus performers, red for dancers and musicians, green for merchants, purple for curiosities, and yellow for everything else.

Daniel wandered the streets surrounding the courtyard, making sure to hit his usual places, where he knew underhand dealings were likely to happen. Especially at this hour; all the worst sorts of people came out in the dark. Hanging from his fingertips in the shadows of a walkway, he heard a man planning to replace a merchant's wares with fakes once his tent was set up. Back on level ground he pulled his notebook from his satchel and scrawled down the details.

'Mr Novak, sir.' Daniel looked up suddenly; the speaker was a man with sandy blond hair and a beard threaded with red, dressed in a slightly tattered brown suit. Daniel recognised him as Jon Bauer, one of the men he'd caught selling black market goods several months back. He wasn't one of Diora's men, but he did a few favours for him every now and then, often without realising. 'What brings you to my neck of the woods this fine evening?'

'Just keeping an eye out,' Daniel replied vaguely. 'And you?'

'Out for a walk, sir – hoping to see you, as it happens,' the man replied, his tone deferential despite the fact that he was several decades older than Daniel. 'Friend of mine said he heard a couple of the cleaning crew on Sempar Street planning to approach some of the girls in that new dance troupe that just set up round there. Said they want more than a performance, if you catch my meaning.'

Daniel's blood ran cold. Incidences of assault skyrocketed during festival time; that and pickpocketing. Anything easy to get away with in a busy crowd. Few would notice if a dancer or two went missing for a couple of hours in all the chaos.

'Thank you. I'll make sure to look into it.'

Bauer looked relieved at having unburdened himself of the information, and quickly scarpered once Daniel turned to leave, heading for Sempar Street. Things like this were what made him come to the lower city night after night. If he wasn't around, who would people turn to? The guards cared – of course they did – but a man like Bauer would never have told his story to a guard.

Gritting his teeth and picking up his pace, Daniel focused on the task at hand. He had three and a half days before Crysta would be home. Three and a half days he would need to spend mostly as Daniel; probably the last he would have until the festival began, other than a few hours here and there. He had better make the most of things. Starting with putting the fear of the Goddess herself into that cleaning crew if they even *thought* about touching any of the dancers without their consent. Then, of course, on to Diora's mystery right-hand man. He was determined to get to the bottom of things as quickly as possible; the sooner he could get rid of Diora, the sooner he could start properly cleaning up the lower city, and the sooner Daniel could disappear for good.

Walking away from Sempar Street, fists clenched, Daniel was confident the cleaning crew would treat any and all dancers they might come across with the utmost respect. He grimaced at the blood on his knuckles – he hadn't meant to break that man's nose, but he'd just been so *obnoxious*. There weren't many people who were still willing to pick a fight with Daniel Novak, and after that little show the number would be even smaller.

Heading back towards the centre of the lower city, Daniel was tempted to climb up to rooftop level and run to his next destination. But it would benefit him far more to stay on the streets. If one of Emilie's friends saw him around, word would no doubt get back to her and she'd appear. Of all his avenues of gathering information on Diora's second she was probably his best bet.

Walking briskly through one of the narrower streets of the lower city, he stopped in his tracks at the sound of hurried footsteps on the cobbled ground. He turned to see a woman running towards him, tears streaming from her eyes. His heart skipped a beat; he knew this woman. Or rather, Noah did. She wore the green and bronze livery of a palace servant, and he was almost certain she worked in the kitchens. What if she recognised him? It wasn't fully dark yet, and she was coming right towards him; there were no shadows for him to hide in. He just had to trust that his make-up and wig were enough.

'Mr Novak! Mr Novak, sir, please!' she called, skidding to a halt in front of him. 'Sir, it's my daughter. Please, you have to help me.'

'What's happened?' he asked, pulse racing. He could only hope that the woman would be too upset to think about where she'd seen his face before.

She reached for his hand, tugging at him to follow her. 'My daughter, sir, her boyfriend, he's got an awful temper! He –'

Daniel cut her off with a grim expression, getting the picture. 'Show me the way.' He picked up his pace and the woman broke into a run, leading him down a side alley towards one of the residential areas.

Daniel heard the screams before anything else. Several people were standing in their doorways, silent as the man's muffled shouting rang out from what must be the woman's house. None of them were making a move to help. 'He's in there, sir,' the woman told him, gesturing to the open front door. 'Please, help her, he says he's gonna kill her!' Daniel didn't waste any time, letting go of her hand and striding through the door, following the sound of yelling to an upstairs bedroom. The door was locked, but when he forced it open with a swift kick he saw a young woman cowering in the corner of the room, face bruised and bloody as she sobbed. The man standing over her was broad-shouldered, his head shaven. Disgust curled in Daniel's gut at the sight of a gold ring on his right middle finger. Of course.

'Don't you touch her!' Daniel roared, interrupting the man before he could land another blow.

He turned, an ugly expression twisting his face. '*Novak*,' he hissed, taking a step towards Daniel – a step away from the woman. 'What the raging storms are you doing here? It's none of your business.'

'You're committing a crime – it's everyone's business,' Daniel replied sharply, walking further into the room. He was taller than the man – he was taller than most people – and that seemed to make the bully falter for a second. 'Give me one good reason why I shouldn't throw you out of that window,' Daniel said menacingly.

'Lying cow deserved it! Told me she didn't have money for an investment for the Boss, then I find out it's because she's been giving it all to her bloody mother! She should be thinking of our future, not that stupid old woman! Her mother doesn't need it, not with that fancy job scrubbing the king's silverware.' He turned back to glare at his girlfriend whimpering in the corner. 'Selfish brat needed to be shown what her real priorities should be.'

Daniel felt something snap inside him, his rage bubbling over; everything that had angered him in the last few days, all his pent-up frustration and the restrained urge to punch Fabian Silva in the face came spilling out in that moment, the impulse he had only begun to awaken when he confronted the men in Sempar Street. For the second time that evening Daniel got blood on his knuckles, fist swinging clean into the man's nose with a sickening crack. In two long strides he had him pinned up against the wall by his throat as if he weighed little more than a child. 'All right,' he growled, ignoring the blood streaming down the man's face. 'Here's what's gonna happen. When I let you go, you're gonna walk yourself down those stairs, out of this house and back to whatever pitiful hole you crawled out of. You'll leave this woman alone, and her family, and never darken their door again. And if anyone comes to me and tells me you've been bothering her, then the anger your "Boss" will have at you having tarnished his reputation will be *nothing* compared to what you'll get from me.'

His wild expression and increasingly tight grip made the man buckle at the knees. Daniel looked him dead in the eye. 'We clear?'

The man opened his mouth, but the only sound that came out was a squeak. He nodded hastily, and Daniel released him. 'One more thing,' he said, reaching out to grab his collar before he could get too far. The man gulped, using a sleeve to staunch his free-flowing nosebleed. 'You will pay back any money you owe this family by the start of the festival. Or I'll come and wring every last copper out of you myself.'

Nodding furiously, the man wriggled out of his grip and fled from the room. Daniel immediately turned to the woman on the floor, who by this point was crying silently, blood still trickling from the cut on her head. 'Are you all right?' he asked softly, crouching at her side. Gone was the storm-faced avenging angel that was the Daniel Novak people in the lower city told awe-filled stories about. The Daniel Novak that was everything Noah hated about himself, everything he couldn't contain and everything Crysta could never discover. In his place was the Daniel

Novak who took time out of his work to help lost children find their parents; who had joined in the reconstruction when half the plaza had burned down. That was the Daniel Novak he wanted to be, but unfortunately the two often came hand in hand.

'I – I'm fine, sir. T-thank you, I . . . he would've – I'd be dead if you hadn't showed up,' she stuttered, wiping at her face.

'Thank your mother,' he told her, pulling a handkerchief from his pocket and pressing it to her wound. She took it from him, and he helped her to her feet.

'I thought he was a good man,' she sniffed, unable to stop the tears. 'I mean, he wore the gold ring, so he had to be, I thought.'

In that moment Daniel hated Diora more than ever, for taking those men and women who were quick to turn to anger and violence and making them a symbol of protection and all that was good. Sure, the majority of Diora's gang were just as corrupt as their master, but some of them likely had no idea what their boss really stood for.

'Wearing the ring doesn't always mean they'll have the values to go with it,' Daniel pointed out gently. The woman snorted, raising a dark eyebrow at him.

'I know that now, don't I?'

They were interrupted by the woman's mother appearing in the doorway, gasping at the sight of her daughter. She rushed forward, hugging the young woman tightly, before turning to Daniel. 'Thank you, Mr Novak, sir. I don't know what we'd do without you. I can never thank you enough!'

She grasped his hand in both of hers, squeezing tightly. 'You saved my little girl! This family will be forever in your debt.'

Daniel forced a smile and awkwardly reclaimed his hand. After a second he reached into his satchel, digging into his money purse for a few coins. 'This should cover getting the door fixed,' he said, pressing the coins into the woman's hands. She looked back at the door, which was hanging off one hinge and now had no lock to speak of, and laughed.

'The door? Don't be daft, sir, you saved my girl's life!' She tried to give the money back but he refused to take it.

'No, I insist. I can spare it.'

'Goddess bless you, sir,' the woman said emphatically, shaking his hand once more. Looking up at his face, she paused. 'Excuse me, but – are you ever up at the palace, sir?'

Daniel's stomach turned to lead. 'Never set foot in the place, ma'am. But you've no doubt seen me around the lower city plenty. Perhaps you've seen me at temple a time or two.'

'Yes, of course,' she said, and he let out a silent sigh of relief. Still, he was eager to leave.

'Do you need me to call for a medic?'

'We'll be fine,' she insisted, waving him off.

Accepting their gushing thanks again, Daniel managed to excuse himself, jogging down the stairs and out of the front door. The man was long gone, but there were still several people watching from houses nearby. They started clapping when he appeared, and he ducked his head, a flush rising to his cheeks beneath the heavy stage make-up. Still, he couldn't help standing a little taller, his step lighter as he headed back the way he came.

Even if he married Crysta and became king he'd never be respected enough among the nobles to affect them like that. In the lower city Daniel Novak was far more valued than the guards, than the king, than even Diora to some people. Daniel Novak mattered in a way that Noah Hansen never could. And while he knew it was selfish, he wasn't entirely ready to let go.

With nothing but a face to go on, Diora's second wasn't the most reliable lead in the world, but Daniel had worked with less. The lower city was big, almost as big as the upper city, but the majority of it was housing and factories; the areas in which people congregated were few and far between. It was easy enough to find a specific person just through waiting in certain spots and keeping an eye on the crowds for a few days. Provided, of course, the person he was looking for went outside more than once in a blue moon. The fact that Daniel had never seen this man before the other night suggested he didn't leave Diora's side often, and he was very good at staying hidden when he did.

Sighing to himself, Daniel decided on a different approach – he didn't have time to just wait around and hope fortune found him. He turned for a walkway that would set him on the path to Emilie's house. Hoisting himself up on to a low stone wall, he then jumped and gripped the overhang of a nearby roof, scrambling up on to the building with ease. The city was much easier to cross from above, and no one ever raised their eyes above street level. The air was warm even in the evening, and he stripped off his jacket as he ran, stuffing it into his satchel before climbing even higher.

Hopping over a few walls on the way and taking a flying leap across a narrow canal, he followed the familiar route to Emilie's part of the lower city, not too worried about staying out of sight. It wouldn't be odd for Daniel to be seen visiting his girlfriend's house – and if anyone was likely to tell him the name of Diora's second it was her.

Instead of approaching the front door, he snuck around the back of the small building Emilie lived in, peering through the window into the kitchen. He liked to try and avoid her mother at all costs, else he'd end up getting a twenty-minute lecture on how he should be treating her daughter.

Sure enough, the woman was sitting at the kitchen table sewing a tear in a shirtsleeve with a look of concentration on her face. Daniel backed away from the window, using the drainpipe to shimmy up towards the window sill of Emilie's bedroom, a journey he'd made only a couple of times in the past. He'd never entered her room, merely tapped at her window to let her know he was around. He didn't want the implications that would come with being in her private room.

To Daniel's surprise, the room was empty, and he cursed to himself. There went his plan. Perched awkwardly on the sill, he waited for a few minutes, just in case she'd stepped out for a moment. When it became clear Emilie wasn't home he cursed again, reaching into his satchel for a pen and a page from his notebook.

Emilie,

I stopped by, but you weren't home. If you're free to meet tomorrow, I'll be around the main courtyard all evening. Wait for me at seven on the bench by the Goddess fountain, I'll find you.

Daniel

Folding the note over and writing her name on the front, he slid open the window just enough to push the note through, watching it settle on her dressing table.

Disheartened at the jammed gear in his perfect little plan, Daniel wandered back across the lower city, his eyes scouring the streets and tension building in his neck and shoulders. He wished he had the luxury of time, enough to carefully and methodically plan how to find Diora's second and track down Diora himself. But the festival was fast approaching, and soon it would be too late to stop Diora from flooding the black market with food. All he had to depend on now was luck, and it wasn't enough.

Half an hour later he was tucked away in an alcove high above one of the larger courtyards in the north of the lower city, watching the small swarm of people below him. Despite the late hour a new tent had arrived and was in the process of being set up, groups of heavily muscled men lifting large boxes and pieces of equipment while dancers and acrobats carried endless garment bags back and forth. Daniel didn't pay much attention to them, keeping an eye on the rest of the courtyard. Just maybe, his luck would change.

10

Daniel's back ached, his eyes were sore from the coloured lenses, and his face and arms felt sticky with make-up. He sat up groggily, body stiff from sleeping on cold stone; how long had he been asleep? He cursed as a glance at his watch showed it was mid-morning. He hadn't meant to stay up there much past midnight, but obviously his exhaustion had got the better of him.

He despised sleeping in his disguise, and the night had been completely wasted; he had seen neither hide nor hair of Diora's second. The new troupe setting up had some very interesting-looking substances in their belongings, but that was just another thing for the long list of problems he was going to have to sort out. At least he'd managed to leave a message for Emilie to meet him in the evening.

Even for festival time, things were getting a little out of hand – or perhaps he was now less able to deal with them alongside everything else he had on his plate. With so much of Noah's time devoted to helping Crysta, and almost all of Daniel's spent hunting down leads on Diora, he'd started to lose his previously iron hold on the petty crime network of the lower city. More than once he'd been tempted to send an anonymous tip-off to Damien and get the guards involved. He couldn't, though; bringing guards into the lower city right now would only be adding fuel to the fire. But if Daniel could get Diora out of the way, he could work on the guards being welcome again in the lower city – only then would it be safe to let Daniel disappear.

He winced at the pain in his muscles. Picking up his satchel, he began to walk gingerly home. Back in the upper city, he vaulted on to the nearest roof and picked up his pace as his muscles loosened, glancing warily at the greying clouds on the horizon. Talen was a dead zone, except further south where the skyship port was located, and to have storms so visible already didn't bode well for the festival. There was no place for the gods of sea and sky in Erova, especially not at that time of year.

Slipping into the house, Daniel had just one desire in his head. He walked downstairs and straight to the bathroom. The thought of a hot shower, of washing away the make-up caking his skin, made his failure just about bearable.

He felt a hundred times more human when he stepped out of the shower, wrapping a towel around his waist and pushing his soaked hair back from his forehead. With the shower off, he suddenly realised he could hear a female voice in the hall outside. He edged closer to the door.

'Are you sure you can't come out, just for an hour or two? It's been an awfully long time since I've seen you out and about, and the city is looking rather lovely with the decorations going up.' The voice was unmistakably Marie's – the woman from across the street – and a rueful smile crossed Noah's lips. When would she learn that she needed to be a little more blunt if she wanted his father to realise she was trying to ask him on a date?

'I'm sorry, Ms Reyes, but I have far too much work to do. I appreciate you bringing lunch for me, but I'm afraid I need to finish another batch of masks before the evening. Another time, perhaps?' Evander's tone betrayed that he wasn't entirely paying attention to the conversation. Noah could picture it; Marie hanging around the workshop doorway, Evander not even looking up from his work. He did feel sorry for her; all she'd done wrong was set her sights on a man in love with a ghost.

'Yes, I suppose,' Marie sighed. 'Good luck with your work, and I shall see you another time.' Noah heard footsteps on the stairs, signalling the end of the conversation, and he went back to getting dressed. Emerging from the bathroom, he turned towards the open workshop, his eyebrows rising at the sight of what the room had become in his absence. It looked like his father's mysterious project was progressing very quickly, and it seemed he was beginning to piece it all together. There were still several smaller parts around the older man's half of the room, but in the corner was a shape that was almost humanoid, nearly as tall as Evander, with exposed gears and wiring. It had what appeared to be legs, but no arms or head, and it was clear it still needed a lot of work. What on Tellus was the man creating?

'What in the name of the Goddess is that supposed to be?' Noah remarked, eyeing the machine with incredulity.

'Not finished yet, that's what it is. Now, would you care to tell me where you were last night? Or, rather, where

101

Daniel was?' Noah winced at the expression on his father's face.

'In an alcove in Albia Park,' he replied hesitantly. Evander tutted in disapproval, but didn't outright scold him. 'Are you ever going to let Marie take you out?' Noah asked, quickly changing the subject. Evander blinked, looking perplexed.

'Excuse me?' he asked, and Noah laughed.

'You're joking, right? That woman has been trying for a date with you for years.' The greying man looked startled, glancing at the doorway Marie had left through minutes before, then he returned to his project with misty eyes.

'If it's been years, surely she would have given up by now?' he muttered. 'You're being ridiculous, lad. She's just being friendly, making sure I've not lost my senses so much that I forget to eat. Since my son is too busy gallivanting around the lower city dressed as a commoner to even sleep in his own bed.' The jibe was sharp, and Noah bit his tongue before an equally barbed retort could escape.

'I have to get as much done as possible before the festival,' he replied calmly. 'As do you, or have you forgotten the pile of masks that still need your attention?' They always split the orders evenly between them, based on who had drawn the preferred design for each mask. Noah was much further down his list than his father, even taking into account all his time as Daniel. Evander had been spending far too much time on his mystery project. 'The festival has a deadline, your project does not.'

Evander frowned, turning to the sketchbook of mask designs lying ignored on his desk, and the list pinned to the wall of the ones he had to complete. 'I'll get them done,' he assured Noah confidently. 'Now, are you here for the day, or just for a change of clothes?'

'Here until after lunch,' Noah replied. 'Then I need to head up to the palace for a while. Crysta's in the outlands for the rest of the week, and I promised I'd help Rosa with some of the festival preparations while she's away. I fear Rosa might have a meltdown if left to do it all by herself.'

'Well, that's better than nothing, I suppose,' Evander remarked, eyeing his son carefully. 'Perhaps you should stick with Rosa while Crysta's away, take on some of the responsibility that's due to be yours anyway. Let the lower city cope without you for a while.'

'They can't cope without me!' he retorted. Evander looked taken aback, and Noah forced himself to calm down. 'At least until I can make it a safe place for the guards again.' He needed to learn as much as he could about Diora's second before it was too late.

'You mean you're finally going to invite the guards back into Daniel's domain?' Evander asked with raised eyebrows, his tone wry. In the years since he'd started going after Diora as Daniel, Noah had often insisted that the lower city didn't need guards when they had him – that the guards needed to focus on the upper city problems. He knew better now; the lower city was too big for one man alone, and Daniel couldn't last forever.

'It's not Daniel's domain,' he insisted. 'It's Diora's. And that's the problem.'

Evander fixed him with an unreadable look, his gaze making Noah feel like a child who had just been scolded.

But he didn't say anything for a long time, and eventually Noah looked away. 'I'm going to work on some masks,' he said, turning towards his own desk, forcibly ending the conversation. He didn't want to hear his father's opinions on Daniel's ego – opinions that usually hit a little too close to the mark.

Uncomfortable with the tension in the workshop, Noah only stayed long enough to catch up on some of his more pressing mask commissions before he was back out, this time heading for the palace. Rosa wasn't expecting him, but he doubted she'd mind as soon as he offered to help with the festival work.

Passing through the guard station on his way in, the place seeming oddly bereft with both Damien and his second away. Noah waved in greeting to the guard at the palace door. 'Good afternoon! I'm here to see Princess Rosa, if she's around?'

'Of course, sir! She should be in her suite. I'll have someone escort you up,' the guard replied cheerfully, stepping aside to let Noah enter. He gestured to a nearby servant, beckoning her closer, and after a few murmured words the girl turned to Noah with a polite smile.

'Follow me, sir.'

Despite being very familiar with the path to Rosa's suite – it was on the same floor as Crysta's – Noah let himself be led. He knocked on the ornate door to Rosa's room. The servant stood politely by, not leaving him despite having done her job. Noah might have earned the trust of the royal family but he was still a long way off being free to roam the palace unsupervised. After a few moments the door opened and Lena's wide eyes met him. 'Master Noah!' she exclaimed in shock. 'I'm sorry, I wasn't told you were visiting today.'

'Oh, it's fine, this is an unplanned visit,' he assured her. 'So if Rosa is too busy or unwilling, it's no trouble, I'll head back home. I just thought she might like some company, with both Crysta and Damien out of the palace. And perhaps a hand with the paperwork?' Rosa didn't know that he'd promised Crysta he'd help her, and he was happy to keep it that way. He didn't want to cause an argument between the sisters if Rosa took it to mean Crysta didn't think she could cope alone.

'Storms, you must be desperate to win the family over, if you're willingly subjecting yourself to all that without Crysta around.' Rosa appeared behind her handmaid, a tentative smile on her face.

'You mean I haven't won you over already?' he mock gasped, making her giggle quietly.

'If I say no will you do the final seating arrangements for me?' she asked hopefully. She laid a gentle hand on Lena's shoulder, prompting the older girl to move aside so Noah could enter. The servant didn't follow him in, clearly deeming Lena an acceptable chaperone.

Rosa's living room was very similar to Crysta's, though where the elder sister had hers decorated in rich earthy tones, Rosa's room was a pretty sky blue, accented with silver furnishings and dark wood. The scent of flowers filled the room, and Noah spotted a bouquet on the mantle.

'Gods, no! Crysta had to do those last year and they were torture,' he said with a shudder. 'I will, however, split them with you. And anything else you might have left to work on. Da's taken over the workshop with some bizarre project of his, so I find myself at a bit of a loose end without Crysta around.' He didn't have to meet Emilie until later, and he wasn't going to get any further in his hunt for Diora's second without her. Not on the timeline he had to work to, anyway.

'And here I thought you were joking about pining every second she's away,' Rosa teased. 'Come in, come in. I apologise for the slight mess, but I wasn't expecting company.' If Rosa thought her room was a mess, Noah would never allow her to see the workshop. Or his room, for that matter.

He took a seat on a part of the sofa that wasn't covered in papers, and Lena shut the door. He didn't often spend time alone with Rosa – or time at the palace outside of Crysta's company – but he pushed past the slight awkwardness with a smile that he hoped didn't look forced. 'Those are pretty,' he said, gesturing to the flowers. 'The noble boys trying to win your favour already?'

'What? Oh!' Rosa realised where he was pointing and she ducked her head, long hair falling across her eyes. 'No, no, Lena picked them for me, from the palace garden. To brighten the room.' When she looked up, she met her handmaid's eyes and pink rose in both their faces.

'Well, Lena, you have excellent taste,' he complimented, earning a quick curtsey. 'Shall we get on with this, then?' He reached for the large folded piece of paper he recognised as the court dinner seating arrangements; arguably the most important document of the lot. The court dinner was the main chance for nobles to make business deals and secure alliances before the festival, as it was bad luck to discuss business once the festival itself began and all attention was focused on praising the Goddess. In making the seating arrangements, the monarchs aimed to group together the nobles who they wanted to make deals with each other, and avoid any less desirable pairings in the mix. It was a difficult task, and not one Rosa should have to do alone. 'Rosie,' he said, patting the sofa beside him. 'I'll let you in on a little secret. Seating arrangements are probably the worst duty to get stuck with, but there is one great thing about being in charge of them.'

Rosa raised an eyebrow at him, curling her feet up underneath her with an amused look. 'And I'm sure you're going to tell me what it is.'

'The only positive thing about setting the seating arrangements,' Noah continued, grinning, 'is that you get to choose all the people you dislike. And you get to seat them *as far away from you as physically possible*.' Rosa looked at him, a slow smile creeping across her lips.

'Lena,' she said suddenly, turning to her handmaid. 'Would you please bring tea for Noah and me? And some pastries, if the kitchens have any left.' She looked back to Noah, some of the shyness leaving her gaze. 'Between the two of us, I might actually get this finished in time.'

'I'll make sure of it,' he promised. 'And then after, perhaps, we could spend some time in the music room? I know I'm not as good a partner as Damien or Crysta, but . . . before long, the palace will be too full of guests for you to play undisturbed, and I'd be happy to accompany you if you wish.' Crysta's absence was a perfect chance for him to try and get to know Rosa properly, to prove he was serious about becoming part of the family. Throughout the courtship he had done what he often did when unsure of how to proceed: he followed Crysta's lead. Treating Rosa as a sister was easy when Crysta was there, but he wanted her to truly believe it. He wanted her to *want* him in the family. And if piano duets and seating arrangements were the answer, then he was happy to oblige.

'Let's get this out of the way first,' Rosa said eventually, holding up the seating plan, 'before we start planning our freedom.' Noah chuckled, happy to leave it at that and get to work. It was a start, if nothing else.

It probably would have been a lot easier had Noah been able to keep his mind on the task at hand, instead of letting his thoughts drift to Daniel's business. He couldn't get his mind off the subject of Diora's second, no matter how hard he tried to focus on seating arrangements and opening ceremony performance orders and the multitude of other things Crysta had left them to deal with.

'Maybe we should take a break?'

Noah snapped back to attention, giving Rosa an apologetic smile. One of her dark eyebrows was arched, her arms folded over her chest.

'I'm sorry, Rosie. My thoughts were elsewhere for a second.'

'Try half the afternoon,' she corrected ruefully, setting a stack of papers on the table. 'Don't get me wrong, I appreciate the help, but we would probably get this all done a lot faster if you would actually, y'know, *help*.' Noah flushed; she had a point. 'What's bothering you, if I might ask? Perhaps I can be of aid.'

'It's nothing,' Noah insisted. 'Work stuff.' He really had to be more careful. Usually he was good at keeping Daniel's business separate in his head. The last thing he wanted was to let something slip in front of one of the royal family.

'If you – if you need to go home and work on masks,' Rosa began hesitantly, 'I can finish all this by myself. I have a couple of days until Crysta returns.' Despite her offer she didn't sound confident, and Noah shook his head.

'No, no, it's nothing that urgent. Just . . . you know how it gets, this time of year,' he said with a smile that was more of a grimace. Rosa nodded sympathetically.

'Have an eclair,' she said eventually, gesturing to the plate of pastries that Noah had yet to touch.

He sighed but did as she bid, reaching for one of the delicious-looking cream-filled pastries, while Rosa selected a cinnamon-dusted pastry swirl for herself, resting it on a napkin on the arm of the sofa and glancing at her hand-maid. Lena was in the armchair, having spent the last couple of hours focused on her embroidery and pretending she wasn't listening, given away only by the occasional smile tugging at her lips when Rosa's complaints became overly theatrical.

'Lena, would you like a pastry?' Rosa offered softly, causing the dark-haired girl to look up, startled.

'Pardon? Oh, no, ma'am, I couldn't, they were brought for you and Master Hansen,' she insisted, earning a pointed look from her charge.

'Don't be silly. If Noah and I eat all of them by ourselves we shan't fit into our festival clothes. Join us, please.' Lena's eyes flicked warily to Noah, and the young princess huffed.

'It's just Noah, he won't tell. *Please*, Lena.' Rosa's mercury gaze fixed earnestly on her companion until Lena's posture slumped, a reluctant smile crossing her face.

'Very well. If you insist.'

'I do,' Rosa agreed imperiously, handing her an apple strudel without a second's hesitation over choosing the pastry. Noah smiled around a mouthful of eclair, leaning back into the sofa cushions and returning to his paperwork.

11

Noah left the palace that evening satisfied that for now at least one of his responsibilities was out of the way. Despite the slow start, he and Rosa together had managed to get through almost everything on Crysta's list; the only things remaining were ones that Rosa could easily handle by herself. One task down, only about a hundred more to go.

He stopped at home just long enough to change into Daniel, avoiding the workshop as he did so. The less he interacted with his father at this point, the better.

To his relief, Emilie was waiting alone where he had asked her to meet him, her pocket watch in hand as she stood with one hand on her hip, clearly annoyed at his lateness. He hadn't seen her for more than twenty minutes at a time recently, as she'd been so busy working for her mother and getting ready for the festival, and only sought him out when she needed the status boost that came from being Daniel Novak's girlfriend. It was hard for him to feel bad about dating her to get information on Adamas and Diora when she was only dating him for the notoriety that came with his reputation. The guilt regarding Crysta, however, was a whole other story.

He kissed her chastely in greeting and allowed her to loop her arm through his, but he didn't even attempt to look enthusiastic as they set off towards the nearest merchant's tent. Emilie led the way, taking him through some of the busiest parts of the lower city. With only a week left until the festival it was even more crowded than usual. Several people greeted them as they walked, and Emilie's smile grew with each one, her grip on Daniel's arm tightening.

'I thought I saw your brother in Colta Square the other day,' he lied evenly. 'He hasn't been around much lately, has he?'

Emilie glanced at him in surprise at the odd change in conversation. 'He's been awfully busy,' she told him. 'With *work.*' The emphasis placed on the word could only mean one thing: Diora's work, rather than his actual job as a bartender. Daniel nodded sympathetically.

'Aren't we all at this time of year?' he mused. 'I've been run ragged trying to stop the Meyers brothers from setting up their still again before the festival begins.' He hadn't, actually – one conversation had been enough to strike the fear of the gods into the brothers' hearts – but the easiest way to get information from Emilie was to offer a story of his own experience, and she would immediately try and top it with one of her own. Or, in this case, one of her brother's.

'Adamas has barely been home all week,' she started, as Daniel had known she would. 'The Boss has had him conducting meetings all over the place, doing all sorts of business. He was up all night not long ago, watching out for a train full of contraband some lowlifes were planning to sell at the festival, trying to stop them before they could start spreading it around.'

Daniel didn't doubt the train full of contraband was one of Diora's, and Adamas was only watching it to make sure the guards didn't get there first. Emilie was oblivious to her brother's true work, and Daniel wanted to keep it that way.

'But he says the Boss has been so pleased with his work lately that he's giving him a bonus soon,' Emilie continued, barely stopping for breath. 'Adamas promised to buy me a new dress for the festival with it. What colour do you think I should choose?'

'Uh –' was all Daniel managed to say before Emilie carried on talking, pondering aloud the possible options for her dress.

'Of course, it would be easier to choose a dress colour if I had my mask already!' she added, squeezing Daniel's arm pointedly. He grimaced; she'd been dropping not too subtle hints about him buying her a mask for weeks. Gifting a mask to someone else, unless they were a family member, was considered a sign of romantic intent. Needless to say, she was waiting for her gift. She'd done the same thing the year before, and refused to speak to him for a week when he hadn't bought her anything. It wasn't good for her image if he couldn't commit to her enough to buy her a mask.

'Perhaps Adamas's bonus will be big enough to buy your dress *and* a mask to go with it,' he suggested, trying desperately to steer the conversation back on track. 'Like you said, he's been so busy recently. Surely whatever he's been doing is enough – he's practically the Boss's right-hand man now!'

Everyone in the lower city was careful not to say Diora's name aloud in public, simply referring to him as the Boss.

Emilie laughed, leaning into his shoulder. 'Don't be silly, I can't have Adamas buy my mask, he's got no taste! Dark blue, perhaps – ooh, or red! I look pretty in red, don't you think?'

'You look pretty in any colour,' Daniel said obediently, watching Emilie's smile grow. 'And if he hasn't the taste to pick your mask, how has he got the taste to buy you a dress?'

'Because I'll pick the dress. He'll just pay for it,' she told him with a roll of her eyes. 'If I'm lucky, he'll let me pick out shoes too. He does owe me, after all – he had the boys over for poker at the house the night before last, can you believe it? He has his own damn apartment for that, but apparently there was something wrong with it that day. I think he didn't want Laurent to see the pigsty he calls a home. Trying to impress him.'

Daniel's step faltered for the barest second – that was a name he hadn't heard before. Who was Laurent? He thought he'd heard about all Adamas's friends; it had to be someone he worked with if he'd never been to his apartment. 'I didn't think Laurent was the type to join in poker night,' he remarked nonchalantly. Letting Emilie assume he knew far more than he did was a tried and true method of gaining knowledge.

'He's not usually. But he can't spend every waking minute at the Boss's side, and to be honest, I think he was swayed by the chance to win big. He needs all the money he can get nowadays.' Emilie tugged on his arm, a secretive smile

114

on her face as she leaned up to whisper in his ear. 'Don't tell anyone, but Adamas thinks Laurent's going to move on soon. He reckons he's just waiting for a pay cheque big enough to get a place in Tanza before he'll pass on his duties. I don't blame him; Gemina is no place for a man in his position to be living, don't you think?'

Pulse racing, Daniel tried to play it calm, though he was sure he was on the right track now. It was all about saying the right thing to lead Emilie where he wanted without her going off track again. 'Oh, definitely,' he agreed without hesitation. 'But do you really think he's ready to go?'

'It wouldn't surprise me,' Emilie said frankly. 'He's got other concerns now, and the Boss keeps him so busy he can hardly stand it. And he's been taking Adamas out with him on business more and more lately; I bet he's training him up to take over.' She giggled, grinning wickedly up at Daniel. 'Then Adamas really *will* be the right-hand man. Think of how many dresses I could buy with that sort of a bonus!'

Bingo.

Daniel laughed, dropping a kiss to Emilie's hair to hide his triumphant smile – she didn't know it, but she'd just helped him astronomically. At last, he had a name to go with the face of Diora's second, and a location too! Goddess bless Emilie's need to gossip. 'Somehow I think your priorities might not match with your brother's,' he said playfully.

'Nonsense. Adamas loves to spoil me,' she pointed out with a smug grin. Suddenly, Emilie stopped walking, turning her head towards one of the nearby fabric stalls. 'Oh, look, there's Clara and Eric, and Simon!' Sure enough, her friends were by the stall, Clara holding up a bolt of brightly patterned green fabric for the boys' opinion. Emilie turned back to Daniel, her face falling. 'Look at us! First time we've been alone in weeks, and we spent the whole bloody time talking about the Boss and my brother.' She looked annoyed, but not at Daniel.

'Sorry. We could pretend we didn't see them,' he said, though it was insincere.

'No, no, I promised Clara I'd shop with her,' Emilie sighed. 'Never mind.' Leaning up to peck him on the cheek, she took him by the hand and led him towards her friends.

Daniel allowed himself to be urged from stall to stall, occasionally having to give his opinion on something Emilie was considering buying. Her friends didn't really talk to him that much – he always got the impression they were never really sure why or how he'd ended up in their group, but were too intimidated by him to question it and put up with him for Emilie's sake. That was fine by him.

'Oh, look at this!' she squealed, dragging him over to an open-fronted tent full to bursting with festival masks. They were pretty enough – obviously nowhere near a match for the ones he and his father made, or even the ones for sale in the upper city – and decorated fairly simply in bright colours and bold designs. Some of them even featured jewels or metal parts, but those weren't cheap. 'Aren't they lovely?' Emilie's hand reached up towards a dark green mask with silver detailing that looked like storm winds around the eyes. She glanced back over her shoulder at Daniel, her gaze somewhat pointed behind her sweet expression. 'If I don't get one soon I'll never find a good dress to match!'

'Time's running out,' Daniel agreed evenly, turning away as her face fell. He looked through some of the other masks, ignoring each time Emilie paused at a particularly eye-catching – and particularly expensive – one, shooting him a look that turned sourer as he continued to feign obliviousness. They were beginning to draw attention, and not just from their friends; the merchant was watching them with thinly veiled amusement in her eyes as she directed Emilie to some of the most expensive masks on offer. Did she really think he had the money for these sorts of things?

Eventually, Emilie gave up trying to get her point across subtly, throwing her hands up with a huff of annoyance, her skirt flaring as she turned on her heel and left the tent with a thunderous expression. Several faces turned to Daniel, clearly waiting for his response. He merely stuck his hands in his pockets, turning back to the dark red, full-face mask he was examining. The craftsmanship wasn't terrible, for a lower city merchant.

'You're going to lose her, you know.' The quiet voice startled him, and he looked down to see Emilie's friend Clara at his side, a disapproving look on her dark-skinned face. 'If you don't get a little more serious about things, she won't wait around forever.' Daniel hummed, not paying much attention to her words. It wasn't like he had any intention of marrying Emilie. He was close enough to finding Diora now; maybe it would be better for both of them if she got frustrated and left him, rather than him having to break up with her. But it wouldn't be fair to Emilie to be needlessly rude. She might be using him as much as he was using her, but she still deserved a little courtesy.

Under Clara's steely gaze he followed the path Emilie had taken out of the tent, seeing her sitting on a wrought-iron bench nearby, trying valiantly not to cry. By the faint tracks of black make-up at the corners of her eyes she'd shed at least a few tears before composing herself. Approaching tentatively, he gave the girl an apologetic smile, waiting for a nod of permission before sitting beside her. 'You're not going to buy me a mask, are you?' she asked knowingly, voice hollow. Daniel ran a hand through his hair then shook his head.

'No, I'm not. I don't do commitment, Emilie.'

'But . . . it's been years, I thought . . . never mind. I was clearly being foolish.' Her tone was hard, and it made Daniel wince. Silence fell between them, only broken by her occasional sniffles as she continued to pull herself together. 'That's new,' she said suddenly, reaching for his hand and pulling it into her lap. Daniel frowned in confusion before his gaze landed on the object in question. He silently cursed himself. He was still wearing Noah's watch! How had he been so stupid? 'It's nice too. Much nicer than what you usually wear.'

'It was a gift,' he said nonchalantly, pulling his hand away and tugging his sleeve down. He wasn't technically lying; Crysta had given him the watch on his last birthday. 'Why don't we go and watch the decorations go up in the main courtyard?' he said, to change the subject and hopefully cheer her up. 'Leave Clara and the others to their shopping. The lights are being strung today, and I know you love watching them turn on for the first time.' There were always incredible displays of lights in all sorts of colours hung around the main courtyard, some even creating pictures when lit.

She blinked, surprised. After a heartbeat, a hesitant smile crossed her features. 'I'd like that a lot.' Daniel smiled back, leaning in to press a brief kiss to her forehead, then looped his arm through hers. Emilie deserved to be treated well, whatever her motives for seeing him.

They reached the main courtyard to the sight of teams of olive-clad men on ladders, stringing up endless yards of lighting on every conceivable surface. Trees, tent poles, the eaves of buildings, newscast screens, lamp posts; nothing went untouched. He and Emilie leaned on the railing to look down on the park, and her hand twined with his. 'They're really outdoing themselves this year,' she mused, watching as a set of blue and silver lights sprang to life, forming the image of several fish leaping from water across one wall of the clock tower. It was already sunset, and Daniel was amazed at how fast the time had flown.

'It's going to be a good festival this year,' he declared. 'If everyone can manage to stay out of trouble for more than ten minutes at a time.' Emilie laughed. She was several inches taller than Crysta, and her head was gently resting against his shoulder. The contact gave him a squirming feeling of guilt. He pushed the feeling away – Daniel and Noah were not one and the same, and could not be held to each other's responsibilities – but shifted to make it uncomfortable for Emilie to remain in her position, forcing her to straighten up. He didn't know why he was so discomfited by the girl's affection all of a sudden. He'd been able to separate his relationship with Emilie and his relationship with Crysta in his own mind for years. Perhaps it was all the talk of engagements and marriages.

'Oh, we should cross the bridge!' Emilie urged, tugging on his arm, her gaze on the bridge over the river that would take them to the upper city. It was already festooned with green and bronze ribbons wound through the steel struts, and the lights hanging from the top made the fabric shimmer. 'I bet the upper city looks incredible already!'

'If you want to go to the upper city, go with Clara and Eric,' Daniel told her. 'I don't do upper city.'

'Oh, *please*, Daniel. Just for twenty minutes. I want to see the main courtyard.' Daniel shook his head. He was safe in his disguise in the lower city, where most people had never seen Noah Hansen from more than thirty feet away. But if Daniel went into the upper city and bumped into someone who knew Noah personally, there was no way his facade would hold up.

He opened his mouth to refuse once more, but the words died in his throat; Emilie's eyes were wide and pleading, and still slightly red. He'd already upset her plenty that evening, and she *had* just given him the most important piece of information he needed. 'I'll go on the bridge,' he relented. 'But that's it.'

Emilie squealed excitedly, hugging him around the waist. 'Thank you! We won't be long, I promise.' Not wanting to risk him changing his mind, she grabbed his hand and ran for the bridge, joining the steady stream of people crossing to see the upper city lights. Daniel directed her towards the bridge railing, leaning against it to look into the upper city courtyard. 'Oh, it's so beautiful,' Emilie breathed in awe.

Daniel had to agree with her; the upper city never failed to astonish with its light shows. It was one of Crysta's favourite parts of the festival too. At that thought, his stomach turned.

He was distracted from his guilt by the sight of a small skyship on the horizon, most likely coming from the outlands in the North. It was circling around the dead zone of Talen before landing in the port further South. The ship was gleaming bronze, and when he squinted he could just about make out the Dupont family crest.

'The first ships are arriving,' Emilie murmured. 'Looks like the party may be kicking off earlier than usual this year.' Daniel's brow furrowed; what were noblemen doing arriving while Sofie and Crysta were still in the outlands? The Silvas arriving early was one thing, but more noble families turning up so soon? There was supposed to be a day between the monarchs returning and the court members arriving, to give them a chance to rest before their obligations as hosts. He felt sorry for Leon and Rosa, having to dine with the early arrivals on their own. Poor Rosa would have no choice but to attempt conversation.

'I should get going,' Daniel declared, glancing up at the clock tower. 'I have meetings.' Emilie sighed, forlorn. 'Come on, let's get back to Clara and the others. I don't want you wandering about in the dark alone. Not with so many strangers in the city.' He'd experienced first-hand what happened to people late at night during festival time.

They found Clara and the rest of Emilie's friends several tents down from the merchant with the masks, watching a troupe of performers set up their trapeze equipment. Clara was flirting heavily with a rather muscular performer in a tight green unitard, his sable skin oiled and gleaming, enhancing his physique. She looked at Daniel with an irritated glance when he interrupted. 'I need to go,' he told her. 'Emilie is going to stay with you.' Clara eyed him with distaste, then looked back at her acrobat, a smirk at her lips.

'Of course she is. Off you go, Daniel. Em, I'd like to introduce you to Milo. He's an *acrobat*, isn't that incredible?' Emilie's cheeks reddened at the heated glance Milo gave her upon introduction. Clara's resulting expression was triumphant as her dark blue eyes flicked to Daniel, but the complete lack of reaction on his face made her scowl. Clara would have to do better than that to make him jealous. He didn't mind if Emilie turned her attentions to Milo the acrobat. He rather wished she would, though he suspected Milo didn't have enough status for her to be interested, Emilie was definitely determined to marry upwards.

Daniel slipped away without saying goodbye as Emilie and Milo began chatting. He darted through the gathering crowds, crossing the bridge into the upper city and immediately hitting the walkways and rooftops. He discarded the idea of going to Gemina so late at night; he needed a plan before he could hunt down the mysterious Laurent. With Laurent would come Diora, and with Diora would come freedom from the double life he'd trapped himself in. Freedom to marry Crysta and get on with his life – *Noah's* life. Finally.

'Oh, Goddess, grant me strength to do the right thing,' he murmured as he passed the smallest of the three temples in the city, pressing a kiss to his fingers and placing them on the statue of the Goddess in the temple courtyard.

12

Noah rose at dawn, despite going to bed late and lying sleepless well into the early morning as he ran through his responsibilities. After nearly a full day as Daniel, his own sanity demanded he return to Noah's less complicated life for a while. Besides, there was mask work to be done. But Evander was still locked in the workshop when Noah made breakfast, ignoring his son's calls of concern and offers of food. Noah sighed to himself, giving up and going to dress for the day. He couldn't work on masks if he wasn't allowed in the workshop, so to the palace it was.

With the festival now only days away, the streets were teeming with people and tents and market stalls, everyone ready to begin the celebrations. It was always strange for Noah, seeing both the public preparation and the far more private preparation the royal family went through. While the majority of Erova saw the five-day festival as an excuse to dance and drink, it was a different story for the monarchs. Crysta and Rosa would both spend the entire period between the opening and closing ceremonies in a private room in the palace, deep in prayer to the Goddess. While that happened, the king and queen would have their work cut out for them entertaining the nobles and keeping everything under control throughout the city. Long gone were the days when the entire country would dedicate themselves to prayer during the festival; people were getting selfish, forgetting the origin of it all. Perhaps that was why the Goddess was beginning to favour them less and less.

Shaking his head to himself, Noah dropped down to street level as he reached the palace, for once taking to the rooftops without Daniel's disguise in order to avoid the crush of people. Heading to the guard station, he paused just inside the door. The atmosphere in the small building was tense, guards hurrying from desk to desk and speaking in low tones, their expressions serious. Only a couple of guards looked up as Noah entered, but one approached him swiftly.

'Mr Hansen.'

It was Lieutenant Salo, her hair beginning to escape from its bun and her brow furrowed. 'We weren't expecting you. I'm afraid His Majesty – actually, he could probably do with your presence.'

'What's happened?' Noah asked, alarmed. 'Is something happening in the city? Or –' his stomach turned to lead as another thought occurred, '– in the outlands? Is Crysta OK?'

Salo squeezed his shoulder briefly. 'She's fine. But Felix's last message was . . . not all that positive. The outlanders are being difficult. We're supposed to be turning away any visitors until the king allows it, but I can't see him turning you away, sir.' Far from being reassuring, her words only served to make Noah more anxious. Felix, Damien's second in command, was Crysta's personal guard for the trip. If he was worried, that was definitely cause for concern. Salo frowned at Noah, looking grim. 'Go on, head through. I'm sure someone will give you further explanation. But if you'll excuse me, sir, I need to get back to work.'

Noah nodded. 'Yes, of course. Thank you,' he added belatedly, realising she was technically defying orders by letting him through. Not wanting to risk any of the other guards being slightly more rule abiding, Noah slipped through the door at the other end of the building, hurrying through the palace courtyard. The guard at the door seemed surprised to see him, but let him through with a curt nod.

Noah nodded back and set off for Leon's office. He had no escort and didn't pass anyone on the way up. It made him uneasy; usually there were at least a few staff about. He knocked on the door and waited for permission to enter. 'Sir?' he greeted hesitantly as he nudged the door open and saw King Leon sitting at his desk, with a guard he vaguely recognised at his side. The king's eyebrows rose and he shook his head with a wry smile.

'I should have known you'd get involved. Who summoned you?'

'No one, sir,' Noah replied, edging further into the room once it was clear he wouldn't be sent away. 'I was on my way over to see if I could be of any help with the festival preparations, and as soon as I got to the guard station, well …' Even a blind man could have sensed there was something amiss there. 'Is Crysta OK?'

Leon's smile widened slightly at Noah's concern, and he leaned back in his chair. 'She is unharmed,' he confirmed.

The knot in Noah's gut loosened a fraction. 'She and Felix are still on schedule, and so far it has all gone smoothly. However, Crysta and her mother will be uniting in Denas late this afternoon for the final outlands blessing, and there has been . . . talk. The outlanders are unhappy with the harvest prospects and are looking for somewhere to point the finger. Up until now, things have gone to plan, but with the pair of them travelling together, Felix fears there will be some form of disruption once they reach Arevona.'

'But you can't cancel the blessing,' Noah finished for him. If the monarchs skipped an entire region, there would *definitely* be disruptions. Especially in Denas – their capital city of Arevona was almost as big as Talen itself, and with the Silvas owning the region they would never forgive the slight.

'Quite. But it would be just as insulting to send in armed guards with no due reason. And, unfortunately, rumours and hearsay are not considered due reason,' Leon said, brow furrowed in thought. 'My initial reaction is to send the guards and smooth any ruffled feathers later on, but that is me acting as a husband and a father, not as a king.'

'I'll go,' Noah blurted, the words out of his mouth before he'd even thought it through. But it made sense. 'I know I'm not a guard, but Damien's been teaching me well, and I value Crysta's safety more than anything. I wouldn't let her or Sofie get hurt in any way.' He flushed, realising how he sounded. 'Not that I'm a substitute for sending a guard team, of course, but . . . a slightly more discreet option.'

Leon's lips pursed in consideration, and Noah tried not to squirm under the man's gaze. Going to Denas right now was appalling timing, but if there was even the slightest chance of Crysta being in danger Noah wanted to be there. And if it all went well they'd be back by morning anyway.

'You know, I think that might actually work,' Leon said eventually, glancing up at the guard by his side. 'You've seen Noah train, do you think he's up to the task?'

'I believe so, sir,' the guard said slowly, nodding. 'He's a quick study. And, well, there's no one we could find who'd pay more attention to the princess and her surroundings.' He smirked, and Noah felt his cheeks redden.

'Sending anyone else would make the outlanders nervous,' Noah reasoned, 'but for the princess's suitor to come for a visit – bringing a guard or two to chaperone, of course – to observe the blessing as a step to becoming more involved in the festival proceedings . . . and I can always say I was pining too much to wait until tomorrow,' he added with a grin.

Leon chuckled. 'No one would bat an eyelash,' he said. 'After all, the kingdom is expecting a proposal from said suitor any day now, and the city of Arevona is supposed to be the most romantic place in Erova . . .' Noah was sure that if his blush wasn't noticeable before, it definitely was now; his entire face was on fire at the king's words, and it took him a moment to find his tongue.

'Sir, with all respect, we spoke about that – I can't just, that is to say –' Both Leon and his guard laughed at Noah's stuttered attempt at a response.

Leon shook his head. 'I am very aware of your feelings on the matter, and of Crysta's. But should the urge overtake you . . . there are worse places to propose than by the ocean,' he finished slyly, before growing serious once more. 'Thank you, Noah, for helping me avoid what could have been a messy situation. Tensions are running high this year, and I dread to think of my wife and daughter in the midst of it all with very few reinforcements. No doubt, Goddess willing, we will have worried over nothing. But rather safe than sorry.'

'I want them safe just as much as you do, sir,' Noah said. 'Now if I might be excused to pack? What time will I need to leave?'

'I'll tell them to have the train ready to leave at noon. That should get you to Denas before Crysta arrives, to settle yourself in. I'll have word sent ahead to Felix and Damien, so they know to expect you. Are you sure your father can spare you so close to the festival?'

Noah grimaced; there were more unfinished masks than he'd like this close to the festival, but he could manage. For Crysta, he'd forgo sleep for the next few days if he had to, just to get it all done. 'Not a problem,' he confirmed. With his father locked in his workshop all day, he might not even notice him missing.

'Excellent,' Leon declared with a nod, reaching across the desk to shake Noah's hand. 'Safe travels, then, lad, and I'll see you tomorrow.'

'Thank you, sir.' Despite the unfortunate situation Noah found himself with a spring in his step as he left the office; it had been almost six months since he'd last left Talen, and he was excited about seeing Crysta. His mind cast back to the ring box sitting in his desk drawer, and he bit his lip; King Leon was right. Denas' capital city, situated on the northern coast of Erova, was indeed a very romantic city. Surely it couldn't hurt to have the ring with him, just in case.

Noah boarded the train at the palace at noon, satchel full of unfinished masks to keep him occupied on the journey. He wished he could bring Daniel's notebook – five uninterrupted hours would be perfect to work through the mess of notes and start untangling Diora's web – but he couldn't risk it with two guards inside the carriage with him.

As they travelled further out of Talen, Noah found himself drawn away from his work and towards the train window. It always amazed him to see how very different the world became when he passed the city's borders – acres and acres of nothing but open fields, broken by the occasional village or small town. There was just so much *space* everywhere. Everything in the North was far flatter than Talen, and the pale buildings sprawled out without a care for how much space they occupied, bleeding into rolling green hills with their neat wooden fences to keep the livestock in. Noah had never seen so many cows in his life.

Looking at all the space dedicated to agriculture, it was hard for him to believe that they were facing rationing. Everything looked so lush and green and vibrant, and he spotted a few farmers already out reaping their early crops. But even Noah, who had very little knowledge of farming, could see the signs; shorter stalks and sparser trees, the livestock a touch skinnier than they should be, fields with large patches of bare, dry earth. If the Goddess did not answer the princess's call, if things got much worse . . . there would hardly be anything left once the Anglyans got their greedy hands on their share.

Giving up on his work entirely, Noah settled in the seat with the best view, ignoring the knowing smiles of the guards watching him. They were drawing closer to their destination, only twenty minutes or so away by his count, and he didn't want to miss his first glimpse of the ocean.

Before he knew it they were slowing down, ready to pass through the border of Arevona. The city was beautiful to look at, built on an incline and stretching right out to the pebble beach of the northern coast, buildings in off-white stone grouped close together, all with flat roofs that made Noah itch to climb them. This far out the wind was far stronger, and the city couldn't get away with the tall spires and narrower buildings that Talen favoured. He grinned to himself at the sight of children playing in the surf, taking advantage of the nationwide holiday. Just because they couldn't attend the celebration in Talen didn't mean they couldn't create their own.

Indeed, the city was already decorated for the occasion, festooned in banners of green and bronze, lights hung all over waiting to be turned on when it grew dark enough. It was nowhere near the grandeur of Talen, of course, but it had its own charm. Noah got to his feet as the train rolled to a gentle halt in the station at Arevona. When the doors opened he found himself greeted by three servants dressed in the livery of the Silva family, as well as a couple of the family's personal guards, and a woman around Sofie's age with dark skin and brown hair almost to her waist.

'Lady Santel,' Noah greeted cheerfully, offering the woman a bow. As Lord Silva's younger sister, this year she was in charge of the Silva property with the rest of the family out of the region. He had first met her at last year's festival, and found that she seemed to have avoided whatever genes made her brother so awful. 'It's a pleasure to see you.'

'The pleasure is all mine, Mr Hansen,' Lady Santel replied, returning his gesture with a quick curtsey. 'And please, do call me Felicity.'

'Then you must call me Noah,' he insisted in return.

'I must say, when the king wrote ahead to say you would be joining us I was somewhat surprised.'

'Well, I believe His Majesty grew bored of me roaming the palace looking like a puppy without an owner,' Noah joked, shrugging on his jacket as they walked along the platform. It was colder in Arevona than it had been in Talen, thanks to the coastal winds. 'I find I hardly know what to do with myself when Princess Crysta is away.' It would be very insulting for him to admit that he'd come as extra protection for Crysta and her mother, so he was happy to play up the image of the lovesick young man.

'Ah, young love,' Felicity teased, giving him a knowing look. 'I'm sure Her Highness will be delighted to see you when she arrives. Which won't be long, actually; the boats are due to dock in about twenty minutes. If you'd like, I can escort you back to the manor to wait for her there?'

'I'd much rather wait at the docks, if it's not too much trouble,' Noah requested politely, giving his most charming smile. 'Crysta doesn't know I'm here, and I'd like to surprise her as soon as I can.' Felicity giggled, linking her arm with his.

'No problem at all, it's not far to walk from here. Your escorts are welcome, of course,' she added with a glance at his two guards. With the guards seemingly unarmed and in their regular uniforms it looked like the king had sent along extra chaperones to protect his daughter's virtue. Exactly as they wanted it to appear. If Felix's hunch was correct, any trouble would happen as soon as Crysta and Sofie arrived, and Noah wanted to be there to protect them as soon as they reached the city. The pair would be docking at around the same time, so there would only be one journey back to the manor. The sooner Crysta and Sofie were safe inside, the better.

As they walked Noah was happy to converse with Felicity, though he tried to remain alert to the people around him. He had guards, at least, and it wouldn't do him well to look too suspicious. But it was plain for him to see that Felix's unease was warranted; while the city seemed cheerful enough on the surface, Noah could feel the tension brewing. All the instincts he'd honed as Daniel were blaring alarms in his head, his eyes darting from person to person warily. They whispered among themselves, sending distrustful looks at Noah and Felicity. He dreaded to think what it would be like when the royals arrived.

Felicity had been right in saying the docks weren't far, and Noah's breath caught in his throat as they reached the little shipyard. It was vastly different to the kind he was used to; here narrow wooden walkways reached out into the water, anchored by steel posts for people to tie their boats to. Living in the city, he'd only seen the ocean a handful of times, and it still made him speechless. 'Beautiful, isn't it?'

Felicity mused. Noah couldn't help but agree. He loved Talen, but the outlands definitely had their charms.

The sun was beginning to set on the horizon, turning the water a glowing gold-purple, and Noah saw the two royal boats in silhouette as they approached, their flags rippling in the sea breeze. His heart raced at the prospect of seeing Crysta, all thoughts of potential danger flying from his mind. 'We can go closer if you'd like,' Felicity offered, already heading for the concrete steps down to the water-front. Noah's eyes stayed fixed on the two boats drawing closer, unsure which contained the princess; they were identical, and the only people on deck were the crews.

It wasn't until both boats were docked that anyone emerged from the cabins – Felix and Damien first, followed by their respective charges, and then their handmaids. Noah froze at the sight of Crysta, looking radiant in a deep-blue tunic and trousers, her skin darkened a shade or two from her time spent in the sun. It took her a minute to spot him, but she almost fell overboard when she did, her face lighting up. It was only with Felix's assistance that she managed to gracefully disembark, at which point she sprinted forward, throwing her arms around Noah's shoulders. He went with the motion, lifting her clean off her feet and spinning her around, his lips pressing to hers as if she were the last drop of water in the desert. 'Noah,' she breathed, one hand on his chest as she regained her balance. 'What are you doing here?'

'Surprise,' he replied playfully, tucking a strand of hair behind her ear and letting his knuckle brush her cheek. 'Your father sent me. He wanted me to be knowledgeable on all aspects of your festival duties, for the future.' He wouldn't tell her the real reason, not even when they were in private. She didn't need any more stress.

Her gaze burned into his, making his skin tingle and a familiar heat squirm in his belly, before they both remembered where they were. Crysta's cheeks reddened and she stepped away, offering their audience an apologetic nod. 'I'm so sorry,' she blurted, looking mortified as she realised how she'd acted in front of them. Noah also blushed when he saw Sofie watching them, an amused smile on her lips. Her eyes were knowing as they met Noah's, and she nodded once; she knew exactly why he was here. That didn't surprise him – Leon didn't keep secrets from his wife.

'Your Majesty,' Noah greeted, offering Sofie a quick bow. 'Forgive my intrusion into your time with your daughter.'

'Nonsense, Noah, you're always welcome,' Sofie insisted, squeezing his shoulder with a smile. The pair exchanged greetings with Felicity while Noah moved to embrace Damien briefly, glad to see his friend.

'Good to have you here,' Damien murmured, his face serious. 'If we're going to have trouble anywhere, it will be here.' Denas was probably the region with the most precarious relations with the monarchy, mostly due to Lord Silva's enormous ego.

'Shall we head to the manor?' Felicity suggested brightly. 'It's not long until the blessing, and I'm sure you would all like to eat and rest before the ceremony.' She began to lead the way, Sofie at her side, and Noah twined his fingers with Crysta's as they followed.

Though it wasn't far, the distance to the Silvas' mansion felt near endless as the citizens of Arevona quickly realised they had royal company. No one made any overt moves, but there were crowds of people lingering in the streets watching, fists clenched and mouths set in scowls. Noah squeezed Crysta's hand tighter, glad to see they had almost arrived. At least they'd be safe inside until the blessing.

13

They ate dinner quickly, the blessing drawing ever closer. As soon as the meal was over the two royals were whisked away by their handmaids to prepare. Noah took the chance to retire to the room he was sharing with Damien, which was on one side of Crysta and Sofie's suite, while Felix and the two guards Noah had brought took the room on the other side.

Damien followed him, sinking down on to his bed with a sigh. 'Storms, I'm glad you're here,' the captain of the guard remarked. 'The situation has been getting more and more volatile with every place we've visited, and I'm exhausted. Everyone seems to think the royals don't care about them any more, since they squeezed all the blessings into such a tight schedule. This last one might be the final straw for some.'

Noah grimaced. He could hardly believe it had reached this point, where the arrival of a monarch in the outlands was looked on as anything other than a happy occasion. What was Erova coming to, that one poor harvest made people so quick to turn? They were better than that, surely!

Reaching for his bag, Damien rummaged around for his dress uniform. 'You should get changed, we don't have long.' There was a knock on the door as Damien shrugged on his new shirt. 'Probably Felix. Come in!' he called. His eyebrows shot up when the door opened and Crysta slipped into the room. She was dressed in a beautiful sea-green silk gown for the blessing, but her hair was down and she wore no make-up.

'Not Felix, then.'

Crysta's eyes zeroed in on Damien's bare chest, exposed by his unbuttoned shirt, and she flushed. 'Sorry to disturb you,' she started, but Damien waved her off, swiftly doing up his buttons, unabashed.

'Nonsense, you're never a disturbance. It's good to see you well.' She beamed at Damien, then Noah pulled her into a tight hug, kissing the top of her head. 'Should I leave you two alone?' Damien's eyes twinkled with mirth, and Noah shot his friend a look.

'And leave the Princess Crysta unchaperoned?' he retorted mockingly. 'What kind of guard captain are you?'

Damien snorted, then looked serious. 'I'm going to go talk to Felix about the arrangements for tonight. I'd guess you've got about five minutes before you both need to finish getting ready,' he said before ducking outside to leave them alone.

Crysta leaned up for a long kiss. Noah pulled her close, silk slipping between his fingers. Her shoulders were bare, and he couldn't resist drawing his fingers across her back, feeling sparks skitter across his skin wherever they touched. 'I've missed you,' Crysta murmured against his lips, one of her hands in his hair. 'Three days is far, far too long to be without your company.'

'My thoughts exactly.' Noah let his forehead press against hers, eyes closed. 'How has it been? Has there been any trouble?'

'Nothing Felix couldn't handle,' Crysta assured him. 'But if this festival fails, if the Goddess doesn't answer my call . . . even in Talen I might not be safe.'

Noah held her tighter. 'I won't let that happen,' he insisted quietly. 'As long as I'm around, you will always be safe. And this festival will be an enormous success, just you wait.'

Crysta sighed, letting her head fall against his shoulder. 'Oh, Noah. I wish I had your optimism.' He smiled, lips pressing to her temple.

'Yes, well. One of us has to be positive.' With the threat of Diora inciting a riot, Noah couldn't afford to be anything less. The harvest would be good, and there would be no reason for people to seek out black market food, and Daniel would break Diora's hold on the lower city for good. In Noah's eyes, there could be no other outcome.

Glancing at the clock on the wall, Crysta reluctantly pulled away. 'I need to get my hair done,' she declared sadly. 'If I take any longer, Mother will wonder where I am, and she won't be pleased to see me in here alone with you.'

Noah smirked, pulling her down into a brief kiss. 'We can't have your mother displeased,' he agreed. 'Go. I'll see you later.' Soon the blessings would be over and they'd be heading home. The quicker they were back in Talen, the better.

With the number of blessings Crysta must have been part of in the last three days Noah was amazed at her enthusiasm. She was exhausted, but she still put a bright smile on her face when the Santels gathered everyone to take them across to the central courtyard. Sticking close to Crysta, Noah kept one eye on Damien for instruction.

There were crowds all along the street as expected, but they were kept well back from the carriage by officials, and he could tell that not everyone was there just to see the monarchs. The curtains shielding the carriage windows were only half drawn, and he could hear the faint murmurs of discontent within the crowds as the carriage passed them. Damien, back straight and hand ready to grab his gun at any moment, pursed his lips and edged closer to the queen. They couldn't close the window, or draw the curtain further for fear of offending the people of Arevona.

Crysta was doing a valiant job of pretending she couldn't hear the slurs from the crowd, and Noah wondered if she'd been lying about how well her travels had been going. Her only tells were the tension in her shoulders and the hand clenched at her side.

The carriage rolled to a halt, and Damien disembarked first, holding the door open for the others. Noah stepped down close behind Crysta, eyeing the crowd with trepidation. Every entrance to the courtyard had been barricaded, but that didn't stop the outlanders gathering at the barriers, watching. Plenty of them looked cheerful, dressed in vibrant clothing and ready to celebrate the blessing. But others were sour-faced, muttering under their breath or outright shouting above the crowd.

The open space had been transformed into an enormous banquet hall beneath the stars, much as the palace courtyard would be for the opening ceremony. Long tables were set up, with a head table for the monarchs and their entourage.

Ignoring the tension in the air, Sofie turned to the crowd at the barricade with a smile on her face. 'Thank you all for inviting us to your city,' she greeted cheerfully, facing the less than thrilled people without fear. 'My daughter and I are honoured to be here to perform the blessing in preparation for the upcoming Festival of the Goddess.'

'What's the point?' a man yelled from deep within the crowd. 'It's too late to change the fact that the Goddess hates you!' Several people chipped in their agreements, and Noah saw Crysta wince slightly.

'I think we'd best get seated,' Lord Santel murmured, offering Sofie an arm to escort her in. The queen sighed quietly but nodded, allowing him to lead her across the courtyard towards the head table. Noah did the same with Crysta, walking between two of the long tables. They were already full of people, including members of the extended Silva family, city officials and other important citizens of Denas. It was surprising to Noah how different the assembled guests looked compared with the dignitaries back home. Talen's upper class wouldn't be seen dead in the same festival outfit twice, but here he could see plenty of patched dresses, faded coats and worn jacket elbows that spoke of many years of wear. Talen really was a world away from the outlands.

Having never been to a blessing before, Noah was content to follow Crysta's lead, taking a seat at her side. So far it seemed to be much the same as any court dinner, but once everyone was settled Sofie got to her feet and a hush fell over the crowd. 'Today we have gathered to show our appreciation for the Goddess who protects us and nurtures our land, and to ask her blessing for the harvest before us. We ask her to protect our crops and make them fruitful; to keep our livestock from harm and our seas abundant. We ask for shelter from the gods of sea and sky, for security in their never-ending battle of the storms. The Goddess has given us this land, and we have tended it the best we can, caring for it as we care for her.' She took a deep breath, setting a hand on Crysta's shoulder. 'The princess will now offer the prayer to the Goddess, as a daughter of the crown and ward of the Goddess herself.'

Crysta stood, glancing down at Noah for the briefest of moments, and when she spoke her voice travelled clearly throughout the courtyard. Despite the crowd's displeasure at their arrival, there was not a single sound other than Crysta's words. They were happy to yell at the monarchs all they wanted, but when it came down to it no one wanted to risk angering the Goddess.

Noah had heard Crysta rehearse the blessing prayer a dozen or more times before she'd left, and it was easy to let the words wash over him as his gaze travelled over the crowd. Everyone looked hopeful, desperate for the Goddess to hear their call and fill their fields with life. For all the differences between Talen and the outlands, that was one thing they had in common. The entire country was precarious right now, both dreading and hopeful for the upcoming harvest. Only time would tell, and he hoped it told of good things.

After the prayer came the meal, showing the Goddess the product of her efforts and allowing her to appreciate the food symbolically through Crysta and Sofie. Crysta settled back in her chair, taking a drink of water after speaking for so long, and Noah briefly placed a hand on her knee. 'Well done,' he murmured, making her smile as she leaned into him.

Before he knew it the last plates were being cleared and they were standing up, ready to be escorted back to the Silva manor for the evening. Crysta slid her arm through his, sending a wistful look in the direction of the ocean. 'I wish we had more time here,' she said quietly. 'I've seen nothing but beaches in the last few days, and yet I find myself wanting to visit one more now that you're here.'

Noah, who had been to the beach only a few times, but never with Crysta at his side, couldn't help but agree. A thought popped into his head, and a smile quirked his lips. 'When we get in, change into something more casual — trousers, if you've got them — and meet me on the balcony as soon as you can get away. Tell your mother you wish to retire early; you know she'll be up all night gossiping with Lady Santel, if Damien lets her.'

Crysta eyed him, intrigued. 'What about the guards?'

Noah winked, squeezing her hand. 'You leave them to me.'

14

They returned to the Silva manor just as it was growing dark, and when Lady Santel offered the parlour for drinks, it was all too easy for Noah to direct the conversation towards court gossip and let Sofie and Felicity take over. Quietly excusing himself for the night, he gave Crysta a quick wink, bidding goodnight to the assembled group. He felt Damien's eyes on his back as he left the room, and prayed that his friend wouldn't be too suspicious.

With the relative success of the blessing – no riots, no injuries, and everyone having left the table well fed and happy – the guards were more relaxed that evening. Noah smiled at Felix on his way past. The man was standing guard at the base of the stairs, back straight and showing no signs of tiredness. 'The other two turned in for the night?' Noah queried, and the guard shook his head.

'They're swapping shifts on the front door all night. I don't expect anything, not with how well it's all gone so far, but better safe than sorry,' Felix replied. 'Have a good night, sir.'

'You too, Felix,' Noah said, carrying on his way. If Felix was on stairway duty it would make things significantly easier. Instead of heading to his bedroom, Noah turned towards the door to the balcony on the floor above, stepping out into the cool evening air. He leaned against the balcony's stone railing, gazing out across the skyline as he waited for Crysta. The sun was fully set by now, the festival lights a riot of colour. With the blessing done, the citizens were having their own pre-festival celebration, music blaring from several points around the city. Perfect for what Noah had planned; with all that activity, they would very likely go unnoticed.

He waited only fifteen minutes or so before the balcony door creaked open behind him. Noah tensed for a moment, only to relax as Crysta eased the door shut behind her. She'd changed into loose, dark-blue trousers and a match-ing sleeveless tunic, her jacket slung over her arm. 'You were right. Mother is so busy chatting she barely noticed me leaving. I don't know whether I'll get back to my room with the same success, though — Felix will be guarding the suite once Mother retires for the night.'

'I'll take care of that,' Noah promised, already thinking of a few options. 'Don't worry.' Crysta eyed him skeptically but didn't argue, stepping forward on light feet to kiss him.

'All right, then, Mr Mysterious,' she said teasingly. 'What's your grand plan for the evening?'

'Put your jacket on,' Noah instructed, leaning out over the railing to check a couple of things. He didn't doubt his own ability to make the climb down, but he wasn't going by himself this time.

Crysta buttoned the jacket all the way up, then raised an eyebrow expectantly. Noah merely grinned. 'Do you trust me?' He took her hands, pulling her close.

'You know I do.' There wasn't a hint of hesitation, and he kissed her nose, warmth bubbling in his chest at her certainty. 'Why do I feel like you're about to test that?'

He laughed, dropping her hands. 'Because you know me far, far too well.' Noah turned around, offering her his back. 'Climb on.'

'I beg your pardon?' She sounded utterly scandalised, and when Noah glanced over his shoulder her face was bright red in the low light.

'Climb on,' he repeated patiently. 'I need to give you a piggyback if this is going to work.'

'That is so undignified.'

'But you're going to do it anyway.'

'Well, *obviously*,' Crysta responded, rolling her eyes at him. 'I'm far too curious now.'

Noah easily managed to get her securely on his back, her arms wrapped around his shoulders. 'I need you to hold on tight, and trust that I know what I'm doing.'

'Well, doesn't that fill me with confidence,' she muttered drily. 'If you drop me, I'll have Damien shoot you.'

'Noted.' Without delay, Noah climbed up and over the balcony railing, Crysta letting out a squeak of alarm as they stood on the edge.

'What are you *doing?*' she hissed, her fingers in a white-knuckled grip at his lapel. 'If someone sees us —'

'They won't see us,' he promised. Aware that the extra weight could throw off his balance, he twisted around to face outwards, his eyes on the roof of the building next door, ten feet below them. 'You might want to close your eyes. And please don't scream.'

He didn't give her a chance to argue, pushing off the edge and jumping towards the roof, feeling Crysta nearly choke him on the way down. He managed to land steadily, dropping into a crouch so low his knees almost hit the ground. Reaching up with one hand, he squeezed her forearm. 'That wasn't so bad, was it?'

'I'm going to kill you,' she declared flatly. 'When we get down from here, I am going to *strangle* you.'

'If you don't ease up, you might do so a little earlier than intended,' he warned her, urging her arms to loosen up around his throat. 'I promise that was the worst part.' He'd never done something like this before with Crysta. He'd shown her some of his shortcuts in Talen, and had even encouraged her to try and climb a few of the easier ones with him, but he'd never taken her along for the ride.

Making sure she was holding on tight, he jogged to the edge of the roof and lowered himself down, his feet easily reaching the window ledge below. It was an absurdly easy wall to climb down, as he assured her multiple times on the way, and within a minute he was setting his feet on the dark paved street and helping Crysta find her feet. Her legs were shaking, her face pale, but her bright eyes told a different story. Noah pulled her into a secure embrace. 'Don't tell me you didn't enjoy that,' he teased.

'That was terrifying,' she declared as her lips curved in a reluctant smile.

'That's not a no,' he returned with a wink. She could claim fear all she liked, but he'd heard her exhilarated laughter. 'It's all done, anyway,' he assured her. 'You were brilliant.'

'No it's not,' she retorted. 'We still need to get back.'

'That's a problem for later,' he replied brightly. 'Come on, we don't have much time.' They had an early morning to catch the train home, and they couldn't waste a second of their freedom.

Crysta's hand securely in his, Noah led the way down the street and around a corner, following signposts and the sharp smell of the ocean. No one recognised them in the low evening light, too busy with their own revelry, and he found an opening that led to a small empty stretch of pebbled beach. The sea roared as it washed against the shore, the coastal breeze blowing Crysta's hair about her face. Feeling her shiver slightly, Noah wound an arm around her shoulders, tucking her into his side.

She sighed quietly, sinking into his embrace. 'We could get into so much trouble if we're caught.'

'We won't get caught,' he insisted confidently. 'Come on.' He released her and bent down to slip off his boots, rolling his trousers up to mid-shin. Crysta kicked off her shoes and he helped her do the same. Noah's throat went dry as he knelt in front of her. The engagement ring was practically burning a hole in his pocket, but he couldn't bring himself to do anything about it. Not just yet.

He led the way closer to the water, the pebbles uncomfortable beneath his feet. Crysta gasped when the tide came up over her toes, colder than both of them expected, and it made him laugh. 'I wish you'd been with me this entire trip,' she mused, reaching down to tangle their fingers together.

'Maybe next year,' he replied unthinkingly, and they both froze. The only way Noah would be able to accompany

Crysta for the entire blessing trip would be if they were married. Anything else would be improper. 'If you . . . want to, that is,' he added hesitantly, unable to meet her eyes.

Crysta pulled him closer, forcing their gazes to meet. 'A year is a long time, Noah,' she murmured. 'Plenty can happen in twelve months.' Her lips curved in a tentative smile, the tension between them palpable.

Noah swallowed thickly, his heartbeat pounding in his ears. Unable to help himself, he tightened his arm around her waist and lifted her off the ground in his haste to kiss her. She responded easily, gripping his collar to steady herself as he took control of the kiss, his entire body burning with the need to get closer, his pulse wild at the feel of her lips parting against his, chasing the faint taste of salt from the sea air. He could count on one hand the times they'd kissed like that, but there on that beach, truly alone with each other for perhaps the first time, he couldn't stop even if he wanted to.

Crysta pulled away, her cheeks glowing red in the light of the moon. But she was smiling, eyes bright, fingers caressing his jaw. She looked like the Goddess herself, ethereally beautiful, untouchable to Noah's mere mortal hands. And yet there he was, holding her tight, able to kiss her as many times as he wanted. Storms, he'd never loved her more.

'Next year,' he repeated breathlessly. She nodded, grinning.

'Next year.'

That was that, then. A timeline. A promise. There was no going back now.

★ ★ ★

148

In the couple of hours the pair spent alone together, skipping stones and walking through the shallows, exchanging kisses as often as they liked, it felt to Noah like something had changed in their relationship. The ring was still in his pocket, but he was one step closer to actually giving it to Crysta. He'd get there, when the time was right.

When they wandered back to find their shoes, their trousers were damp from the knees down, and Crysta walked with Noah's jacket draped around her shoulders to fend off the night's chill. Everyone at the Silva manor would probably be in bed, except the guards.

Despite Crysta's skepticism, it was easy enough for Noah to climb up to the balcony with her holding on to his back. But not so easy to get past Felix, who was guarding the door to the monarchs' suite, oblivious to the fact that one of his charges was not inside. Noah gave Crysta a quick smile. 'I can do this,' he assured her confidently, hopping up on to the balcony railing. 'Just give me a second.'

Not waiting for her response, he dropped down below the balcony, swinging on to a nearby window sill. A glance inside confirmed that it was the room he shared with Damien; the guard captain was fast asleep in bed, his blanket half kicked to the floor. Noah eased his way across to the next window, hurriedly continuing on when he realised it was Sofie's room and not Crysta's. Finally, he found her window, and with a quick jiggle of a wire under the frame and a tug, he had it wide open. Being Daniel was hard work, but his skills had *so* many other uses.

Climbing back up to the balcony, he offered Crysta his most charming grin, gesturing to his back. 'Last time, I 'promise,' he assured her, happy to let her pretend she hadn't enjoyed it.

'Thank the Goddess for that,' she said, playing along and obediently climbing on to his back. Noah headed straight for Crysta's window, ducking inside and helping her to step down.

'Safe and sound in your room, with no one the wiser,' he declared in a whisper, pleased with himself. 'And now I'm afraid I must do the same.' He jumped up on to the window sill, one hand braced on the frame. Reaching out, Crysta halted him for a moment, pulling him into one last kiss.

'Thank you for this,' she breathed, smiling against his mouth. 'It was just what I needed.'

Noah grinned at her as he reluctantly pulled away. 'Happy to be of service, my love. Sweet dreams.' Before he could be tempted away from returning to his room like a respectable suitor, he hoisted himself out of Crysta's bedroom window and traversed the wall to his own, feeling light as air. He was grinning like a fool as he opened the window, trying to stay as quiet as possible so as not to wake Damien.

'You're a state, Hansen.' Noah froze at the muttered words, one foot on the ground while the other was braced on the window frame. Damien was lying in bed with one eye open, his gaze travelling over Noah's dampened trousers, untucked shirt and wind-blown hair. 'And you seem to have lost your jacket. Dare I ask what you and Crysta have been doing?'

Noah flushed at the innuendo in the older man's tone, shooting him a look as he stripped off his shirt. 'Nothing that would break the courtship agreement,' he retorted. 'We just went down to the beach for a while. I never get to see the ocean.' Taking his wash bag into the bathroom, he missed Damien's reply, and raised an eyebrow upon his return. 'What was that, sorry?'

'I said, you're going to get yourself in trouble one of these days,' he repeated tiredly. 'You can't just abscond with the future queen whenever you feel like it.'

Noah grinned, shrugging his shoulders. 'For now, I can. Eventually I won't have to.' Reminded by his own words, he picked up the trousers he'd hung over the end of the bed to dry off, reaching into the pocket to palm the ring. He tried to get it back in his bag without Damien spotting it, but the guard was far too observant for that.

'Shouldn't that be on her finger?'

Noah froze, looking up, ring still in his hand. Damien stared back, his expression frustratingly unreadable. 'Not yet. I, uh, think I'll save it for after the festival; she's got enough going on at the moment.'

'If you keep making excuses you'll never get there,' Damien pointed out. 'It's pretty, though. She'll like it, if she ever sees it.' That was probably the best blessing he'd get from the man who was the closest thing Crysta had to a brother. Noah beamed, setting the ring securely back in its box.

'She will see it. Soon,' he promised. Damien didn't understand; he didn't know what Noah had to do before he could take that step. What Daniel had to do. 'She'll see it when the time is right. And if you spoil the surprise, I'll put nothing but glitter and lace on your mask.'

Damien barked out a laugh, reaching for his blanket and rolling on to his side. 'Just go to sleep. It's a long day tomorrow.'

Noticing that Damien had said nothing about promising to keep his secret, Noah scowled to himself, settling into bed. He'd get there eventually. When his work was done.

15

The train journey home was entirely unremarkable, if you ignored Noah's nervous squirming under Sofie's gaze. He was sure that the queen somehow knew about his little excursion with Crysta the night before, though she hadn't said anything. Perhaps she was waiting to murder him in private.

The rolling green hills of the outlands eventually made way for the familiar haphazard stone sprawl of Talen. When they arrived at the palace the king was there to greet them, kissing his wife and hugging his daughter tightly. He shook Noah's hand, though he raised an eyebrow pointedly after a quick look at Crysta's finger.

Still, he didn't raise the topic as he led them back inside. 'There are rather more guests than we had when you left, I'm afraid,' Leon told them quietly, arm in arm with Sofie. 'But so far everything has been running smoothly. Everyone seems fairly happy to get out and enjoy the festival tents, so we shouldn't have too many problems – at least, not until the court dinner.' Even Noah made a face at that. The court dinner the next day would include the heads of every noble family in Erova, as well as the monarchs – and Noah, as

Crysta's suitor. It was quite possibly the most excruciatingly painful part of the entire festival, with no purpose other than business negotiations disguised as friendly conversation.

As they entered the palace Sofie beckoned her daughter to follow her through to her office. 'No rest for the wicked, I'm afraid. There's lots to do before the festival. You're welcome to join us, Noah,' she added. Not willing to leave Crysta and spend the rest of the day working on masks just yet, he agreed, though excused himself to freshen up first.

Parting from the women and turning to the nearest bathroom, Noah splashed water on his face, trying to wake himself up. He hadn't kept Crysta out all that late, not compared to some of the late nights he'd had as Daniel, but five hours of the rhythmic train motion was incredibly soporific.

Exiting the bathroom, Noah made for the marble stair-case, hurrying up multiple floors towards Sofie's private office. As he started down the corridor he was surprised to find Rosa standing there. Her eyes narrowed venomously when she saw him. Noah took a step back, unused to such hostility from her. They'd parted on good terms, hadn't they?

'Rosa? Is everything all right?'

Rosa moved closer, her dark hair curtaining her face as always. 'I saw you,' she declared. 'You were wearing a wig and make-up, but I knew it was you. With that common girl, the night before you left, on the bridge to the lower city. You were holding her hand and kissing her.'

Noah's stomach turned to lead, and he could feel the colour drain from his face. He'd been found out. 'Don't be ridiculous, what –'

'Don't lie to me,' Rosa hissed. 'Even if I hadn't recognised you in that disguise, I'd know the watch you wore anywhere. I spent days helping Crysta pick it out.'

Biting back a curse, Noah hung his head. The stupid watch. 'It's not what it looked like,' he started, but Rosa interrupted with a harsh shaky laugh.

'So you aren't cheating on my sister with that girl?' she questioned, arms folded over her chest. Noah opened his mouth to argue, but shut it again almost immediately. He couldn't deny her accusations; she was technically right. Though he had never seen it that way; Emilie was just part of his cover as Daniel. He couldn't expect Rosa to understand that, though.

'That's what I thought,' Rosa snapped. 'And I truly believed you were a decent sort. Crysta loves you w-with everything she has, and th-this is how you repay her?' Rosa's stutter, which usually only arose when she was incredibly emotional, was creeping through, and it made Noah's guilt double for upsetting her.

'I love her just as much in return!' he insisted. 'If you'd just let me explain – Emilie means nothing to me, it's all just to keep up appearances, it always has been.'

'Always?' Rosa asked incredulously. 'H-how long has this been g-going on?'

'That's not important,' Noah urged, not wanting to admit the truth. 'Please, Rosa, I have a good reason, just let me explain.'

'You think I w-want to listen to your excuses? You're lucky I didn't tell Father while you were away, but I'm t-telling Cryssie as soon as she's done with M-Mother,' she said, trembling despite her firm stance and defiant eyes.

'You can't,' Noah blurted, eyes widening in panic. If Rosa told Crysta about Emilie, about Daniel, everything would be ruined.

'Why not? It–it's what you deserve,' she retorted, flinching when he took a step closer to her. Noah took a deep breath, hating what he was about to do. He forced a stony expression on his face, meeting Rosa's gaze dead on, trying not to look as desperate as he felt.

'You might have this secret of mine, but I have one of yours too,' he told her, regret gnawing at his gut at what he was about to say. Rosa would never forgive him for this, but he had no other choice. 'You're not the only one around here who's seen things other people have missed.'

Rosa paled a fraction, the only visible sign that he was on to something. Noah ploughed on, hating himself with every word that came out. 'I know about Lena, Rosie. I've known since it began.'

'I–I don't – there's not – you must be mistaken,' Rosa stuttered out, taking a step back.

'We both know I'm not. There's a difference between an attentive handmaid and . . . more. The way she's always with you – right by your side when she should be standing in the corner – the amount of time you spend in your room with her. I see how you look at each other, the hand-holding when you think no one's watching. Storms, Rosa, she brings flowers for your room and you order her favourite pastries even though you hate them. That's not how someone treats a handmaid.'

'So we're friends,' Rosa defended, 'there's nothing wrong with that.'

156

'You kiss all your friends on the lips, then, do you?' Noah retorted smoothly, watching Rosa freeze. 'You really should be more careful about that. The library is rarely as private as you think it is.' He'd only seen it once, months and months ago, but it had been enough to confirm things for him. He'd been happy to let the two girls be, but desperate times called for desperate measures. 'You know it can't go on forever, Rosie. Your father is already looking at marriage contracts, since Crysta clearly isn't going to make a political match.'

'That's none of your business.' Rosa's voice wavered, her hands shaking at her sides. Noah's heart raced. He wanted to apologise, to bundle the girl in a hug and beg forgiveness, to assure her that everything would be fine. She didn't deserve this. But she'd left him no choice; it was for Crysta's sake.

'If you're going to make my private life your business, you can be sure I'll make yours mine,' he said evenly. 'If your father remains oblivious, if Crysta and your mother remain oblivious, then when you're matched to some nobleman and sent to live on his estate, no one will think twice of your request to take your handmaid with you. But if I tell them, if I tell everyone that you and Lena are . . . intimate? She'll be sent away, Rosa. You'll never see her again.'

'You're despicable,' she breathed, horrified. Noah nodded briefly in acknowledgement, and it took all his skill to keep his shame and self-loathing from his face as he stepped closer to the terrified girl.

'Pretend you never saw me in the lower city. Allow me to sort out my own business, and don't breathe a word to anyone. It'll all be over soon enough, and I can't let you ruin it. There's more going on here than you know. And the last thing I want is to hurt Crysta. I promise. You're almost family, Rosie, and I don't want to hurt you either, but if you won't allow me to have my secrets, then I'm afraid I must return the favour.'

'You are no family of mine,' Rosa spat, voice clear and stutter-free in her vehemence. 'And with any luck, you never will be. Crysta deserves better than you.'

Noah shut his eyes for a moment. 'That may be so,' he admitted, 'but do we have an agreement?'

'Do I have a choice?' the girl asked in response, eyes filled with tears. Noah merely stared at her. 'We have an agreement. But you're a bastard, and I hope my sister finds out on her own and stabs you through the heart.'

'My lady?' The quiet voice startled both of them into taking a step back, and Noah's head whipped round to see Lena at the top of the stairs, eyeing Rosa in concern. Who did they think they were fooling? It was easy to see the love in Lena's amber eyes was not that of a servant towards her mistress. The girl was good at going unnoticed, he supposed; it was her job, after all.

'The seamstress is here, she wants to do a final fitting on your dress for the opening ceremony. And then it is time for lunch, you've hardly eaten all day.'

'Right,' Rosa called, looking over Noah's shoulder to meet the older girl's eyes. 'I'll be there in a minute.' She stared at him, shaking her head. 'I hope the Goddess strikes you dead where you stand.' With that, she walked past him to join her handmaid at the stairs, heading down to her room.

Noah took a deep breath, running a hand through his hair to hide his shaking fingers. What had he done?

Noah knocked on Sofie's door, smiling as best he could at the two women inside. They were leaning over the desk, and Crysta grinned at him, beckoning him to join them. Discreetly wiping his clammy palms on his trousers, he took her hand. Crysta mustn't suspect that anything was amiss. 'What's left to take care of, then?'

'Everything,' Crysta sighed melodramatically, making Sofie laugh.

'Not quite *everything*,' the queen assured him. 'But this is really the only time we have left to get the last of the minutiae done. There are still the vendor contracts for the festival, the expense forms, the itineraries for the noble families who requested them ... not to mention all the decoration that has yet to be put up. Soon the city will be full to bursting, and we'll all be so busy we won't have time to sit and discuss arrangements.'

Crysta sighed, leaning into Noah as his arms moved to her waist. 'I know, but I was so hoping for some free time before getting back to business. I suppose I should know not to expect as much by now,' she mused wryly. She paused, looking up at Noah with a frown. 'Are you well? You look a little pale.'

He blinked; clearly he wasn't as good at faking composure as he thought. Opening his mouth to assure her he was fine, he faltered at the concern in her eyes. If she only knew ... would she still look at him in such a way? 'Actually, I am feeling a little unwell,' he admitted. 'But I'm sure it will pass. If you need me, I am yours to command.'

Crysta leaned up on her toes to press the back of her hand to Noah's forehead, her frown deepening. 'Don't be ridiculous, you must go home and rest. You'll be no good to anyone if you're sick in bed through the whole festival!'

'She's right,' Sofie cut in. 'Go home, Noah, let your dear father take care of you for a change. Being cooped up in this office won't do you any good.'

'Are you sure?' Noah asked, only for Sofie to roll her eyes at him.

'We managed this festival just fine before you came into the picture, and I'm sure we can continue to do so without you for a day. It won't take three of us to draft a polite refusal to King Brandon's travel request, and after that it's nothing but rehearsals and frivolities.'

'Travel request? Another one?' Crysta said, incredulous. 'But he has no right to be at the festival!' The Festival of the Goddess was sacred to the Erovan people, and those not of the country by birth or marriage weren't allowed to participate. Even the king of Mericus was not an exception to the rule, though he seemed unable to grasp that.

'I know, but he wants you to marry his son,' Sofie murmured non-committally, tapping glossy painted nails on the desk.

'I am not available to be wed,' Crysta said indignantly, but Sofie wasn't fazed.

'Until Noah puts a ring on your finger and a contract is signed, you are,' she retorted, far less subtle about things than her husband. She was unafraid to tell Noah outright – as she had done on multiple occasions – that he needed to hurry up and propose to her daughter.

'Mother!' Crysta exclaimed, scandalised. 'We talked about this, there is no rush.'

'You're a princess, my dear, there is always a rush.' Sofie's eyes landed on Noah, who felt like every inch of him was being scrutinised. The queen had always terrified him a little, even after he grew to know her. 'Noah is aware of his duties to you, as you are aware of your duties to your country.' The words, so soon after his confrontation with Rosa, made Noah feel sick to his stomach. 'And right now, Noah's duty to you is to keep himself healthy for the festival, so he's going to go home now. Aren't you, dear?' While her voice was sweet and motherly, her eyes dared him to argue.

'Yes, of course,' he relented. Crysta pressed a kiss to his cheek, squeezing his hand.

'Rest well, and I'll see you tomorrow for the dinner.'

Noah offered her a half-smile, kissing her temple. All he needed was a distraction from worrying about Rosa, and an end to his problems in the lower city. Unfortunately, Crysta couldn't help with either. Daniel, however, was the perfect solution – for once.

16

Noah spent the walk home chasing thoughts around his head, the bright colours and music of the festival preparations around him doing little to lift his black mood, and he was glad to reach the solitude of his bedroom when he got home. Leaving his bag on his bed and rolling his shirtsleeves to his elbows, he went through to the workshop, finding his father once again working on his project instead of the masks.

'Welcome home, lad!' Evander greeted brightly, not looking up from his soldering iron. 'How was your little trip to the outlands?'

Noah ignored him in his sour mood, almost tearing through paper with his pen as he crossed out the masks he had already completed on his list.

'What did that list ever do to you?' Evander remarked lightly, and Noah whipped his head up to glare at the older man. 'Now, now, no need for that. I wasn't the one to upset you, was I?' There was a hint of reprimand to his father's tone, reminding Noah that he was eighteen and too old to be throwing tantrums. The green-eyed teen sighed. His guilt sat like a stone in his stomach.

'No, you've done nothing wrong, Da. Sorry. Don't worry about me.'

'There's an impossible request if ever I heard one,' he replied, lifting his goggles off his head and turning his chair to eye his son through his spectacles. 'Come on, let an old man attempt to ease your troubles. What's wrong, lad? Did something happen while you were gone? Is it Crysta?'

'No. Yes. Sort of.' Noah sighed, head in his hands. 'Rosa knows about Daniel. And, more importantly, about Emilie. She saw me kissing Emilie the other day, on the bridge.' Evander's lips pursed, but he didn't look surprised. Noah would bet the man had been expecting this to happen far sooner. 'She threatened to tell Crysta, and I . . . I threatened to reveal a secret of hers.' It sounded even worse when spoken out loud. Evander's usually kind gaze grew stony, and he sat up straighter in his chair.

'I thought I taught you more respect for people than that, Noah Sebastien.' Noah winced. 'Can you blame her for looking out for her sister?'

There was a long silence, Noah's blood pounding loudly in his ears as his cheeks burned with shame. Evander set his screwdriver down, his full attention on his son for once. 'I have let you get away with far more than most parents would, and no doubt there's plenty more that I don't even know about. But you're not fifteen any more, Noah, and while Daniel has done some admirable work, the lower city survived without him before, and they will do so again.'

'They need me,' Noah argued, though he knew his father was not finished speaking. 'Until Diora is gone, they need protection. They need Daniel.'

Evander shuffled his chair closer, reaching out to place a hand over his son's. 'One of your best friends is the captain of the guard, and if you were truly doing that work for the people of the lower city, you would ask him to assign more guards to the troubled areas. That's what they need. I think, if you look deep down, you can admit that being Daniel isn't really about helping people.'

Noah swallowed thickly, his eyes fixed on the floor and stinging with the urge to cry. Yes, he could admit his father was right. He felt good as Daniel; he felt important, mysterious, *older*. He felt like a heroic vigilante, with everyone in the lower city knowing his name. At least, he had before. Now all Daniel gave him was a sickening feeling of guilt. 'What do I do, Da?' he asked, his voice hoarse with emotion.

'I can't make that decision for you, son. But look at your options – with a man's eyes, not a child's. Daniel is beginning to hurt as many people as he's helping, and you have responsibilities now that you didn't have before. You need to decide on your priorities for yourself.'

'I can't lose Crysta,' Noah insisted without hesitation, shaking his head. Evander squeezed his hand once more.

'Then I think you know what you have to do.' The man sighed, leaning back and scratching at his stubbled cheek. 'If I had paid less attention to my mechanical creations and looked more to my greatest creation of all, I could have stopped all this before it got out of hand,' he said sadly.

'You remember how stubborn I was at fifteen, Da,' Noah pointed out with a faint rueful smile. Evander snorted, lips quirking.

'What do you mean, at fifteen? You're just as stubborn now, you're just quieter about it.' He stood, bending down to kiss his son's chocolate-brown hair. 'I'm going to go make some tea and put lunch on. Take some time to have a think. The next week will be chaos enough, and you need a calm mind before you deal with it.' Noah nodded, then went to his bedroom while his father continued upstairs.

Shutting the door behind him, Noah crossed the room in two strides and sank down on to the bed. Kicking off his boots, he leaned his back to the wall, letting his head thud almost painfully against the plaster. Storms, he was a mess. He'd lied to himself, convinced himself Daniel was necessary, insisted that people wouldn't be able to cope without him. All along, the only one he wasn't sure would cope without Daniel was himself.

His gaze landed on his desk, on the dark wooden frame perched in the corner. Inside was a full-colour painting of Noah's mother, her eyes bright and her cheeks glowing, like they had been before her illness had turned them dull and lifeless. She was beautiful. Evander had painted the portrait for his wife's birthday when Noah was a baby, and after her death the artwork had migrated to Noah's room. Evander found it too painful to look at her face these days, whereas Noah was forever worried he'd start forgetting it. What would she think of him now, in such a mess, having treated the people in his life with such disregard? All he'd wanted was to make himself someone she would be proud of, and he hadn't even been able to do that properly.

But who would he be without Daniel? 'I guess I'll have to find out,' he breathed to himself, squaring his jaw. Daniel needed to go.

Reaching beneath his bed, he pulled out the box that contained his disguise, feeling the impulsive urge to throw the blasted blond wig in the fireplace. But he didn't. Daniel couldn't just disappear spontaneously. He had to do this right.

He had enough information to go on to achieve his goal, if he stepped up his game. He hadn't been trying as hard as he might have to find Laurent, he could admit that. But that wasn't going to cut it any more.

'I swear to all the gods of Tellus, by the end of this year's festival Daniel will be no more,' he vowed, staring at the small carving of the Goddess on his shelf. It was no doubt a trick of the light, but he could have sworn he saw the figure smile for the briefest moment. He really was going mad.

A lunch of soup and tea was waiting for him when he came into the kitchen, and several slices of crusty buttered bread on a plate in the centre of the table. Evander had already sat down, and he gave his son a concerned look as he joined him. Noah went to sit, then paused; there were three bowls on the table, three sets of cutlery. He sighed, chest tightening for a moment. 'Da, you've done it again,' he murmured, reaching for one of the empty bowls. Evander blinked, confused, then his cheeks flushed when he realised what Noah was referring to.

'We — we could be having company,' he sputtered.

Noah merely raised an eyebrow at him. 'We *never* have company, Da.' Putting the third place setting back in the cupboard, he finally sat down to his own meal. Evander didn't do it all that often any more, but even after ten years he still sometimes automatically set the table for his late wife to join them, and every single time was like a knife to the heart for Noah.

Trying to push past the awkwardness that had settled, Evander cleared his throat. 'So we're four masks short, and they need to be done by tomorrow evening.' It was Noah's turn to look abashed; he'd been so neglectful of his mask orders this year. 'No, no, it's as much my fault as it is yours,' Evander insisted. 'We've both been . . . preoccupied. But we have work to do, lad.'

As much as Noah wanted to put on Daniel's face and run to the lower city to end things as soon as possible, he couldn't leave his father to pick up the slack. Not now he'd decided to be more responsible. Diora could wait a few more hours; his father needed him.

'That's that, then. We're ready for the festival,' Noah declared as the last feather was glued in place and the final mask was put on the rack to dry.

Evander let out a snort. 'Oh, if only it were that easy,' he said. 'I've still got to get them to their owners. I suppose you're off out?' Noah had kept Daniel's notebook open on his desk beside the masks as he worked, flicking through it at every free moment spent waiting for glue to dry or metal to cool, a plan slowly forming in his mind.

'I'll try not to wake you on my way in. It'll be a late one,' Noah warned.

'Be safe,' Evander called after his son, and Noah waved behind him to acknowledge it, heading back to his room to begin the process of becoming Daniel.

As he changed, Noah smiled at the thought of no longer having to put on his disguise. A few more days and he'd never have to deal with the wig or contacts, no longer have to manage his time to the minute in order to switch between the two without raising suspicion. Daniel had once been his source of true freedom, but the identity had trapped him more and more as time went on, and Noah realised that he was now desperate for it to end.

Double-checking he hadn't left any trace of Noah on his person, Daniel grabbed his satchel. He had a long night ahead of him, and several even longer days – the more he could get done tonight, the better.

'Don't forget to eat dinner, Da!' he called into the workshop on his way up the stairs, not expecting a response. Just as he was about to reach for the unlocked door, the handle began to turn. He quickly jumped back, wide-eyed. With no time to think, he opened the coat cupboard and threw himself into it, shutting the door. No one could see him leaving the house as Daniel.

'Mr Hansen! Mr Hansen, are you free?' It was Marie, her heeled shoes clicking on the wooden floor. Daniel allowed himself a half-smile. He wasn't the only one with relationship problems. When the corridor was silent, Marie's faint voice drifting up from the basement, Daniel snuck from the cupboard and out of the front door, silent as a mouse. It was windy outside, the sky full of clouds as the sun set, and he crossed his fingers for good weather until the end of the festival. After that, they'd welcome all the rain they could get.

Finding Emilie wasn't hard, but Daniel was disheartened that she wasn't alone. He should have expected as much; she never went anywhere without at least three of her friends. They were in a street just off the main courtyard, the space full to bursting with tents of all shapes, colours and sizes, their pennants flying proudly. Music played loudly, lanterns with coloured flames twinkled from every tree and lamp post, and people laughed and chattered as they walked, taking in the sights and sounds. Just as Daniel arrived, Emilie, Clara, Eric and Simon were coming out of a yellow-flagged tent with looks of amazement on their faces.

'That was incredible! I wonder how he does it,' Clara gushed, and the two boys laughed.

'Magic, of course,' Simon teased. Daniel moved closer, and the four stopped in their tracks.

'Daniel,' Eric greeted, surprised. 'Didn't know you were coming out today.'

'It was a last-minute change of plans,' he replied, gaze fixed on Emilie. 'Em, could I talk to you for a moment? In private?' His original plan had been to spend a little time with her first, so as not to ruin her evening completely, but at the look on her face he realised it would be far crueller to pretend that everything was fine.

'Yes, of course,' Emilie agreed, sounding perplexed. She hitched her handbag further up her shoulder, and when she leaned up for a kiss he turned his head at the last moment, her lips landing on his cheek instead. 'Is everything all right?'

'Come on, it's quieter up on the plaza,' he urged, taking her hand. While it was still fairly crowded, it was markedly quieter than the street below, and he led her over to the corner, where they could have a little privacy.

'Daniel, what's wrong? You're making me nervous,' Emilie said softly, once they were away from the crowd.

Daniel dropped her hand and turned to lean on the railing, letting out a long breath as he looked over at the street full of happy and laughing people. Storms, he wished his life could be as carefree and simple as theirs.

'This isn't easy for me to say, Em,' he started, wondering how to word things delicately. 'And it's nothing you've done. This is all my problem, my fault . . . I can't be the man you want me to be. We need to stop seeing each other.' Her face had crumpled at his first sentence, and she watched him speak with an expectant look on her face; she knew what was coming. 'I don't love you, and you don't love me; it's just not enough any more. And I . . . I'm leaving soon.' Her eyes widened, shimmering with the threat of tears.

'What? Where are you going?'

'Mericus, at least for a while,' he replied, going with the story he'd thought up. If Daniel was out of the country, no one would be looking for him. 'I have family over there, and they're having some trouble. I need to go and be with them, and I won't be coming back to Talen. I'm sorry, Emilie.' Her breath hitched and the first tear fell, leading the way for several more in quick succession.

'You couldn't have waited until after the festival to tell me?' she said accusingly, and he gave her an apologetic smile.

'I need to leave before the festival starts.' He had far too much to do during the festival to spend time as Daniel, and afterwards would be too late. 'I truly am sorry, Em. I never meant to hurt you.' She laughed at that, the sound cold.

'That's what all the boys say,' she replied drily. Stepping closer, she took his hand, squeezing it briefly. 'The only

170

reason I didn't love you was because you never let me,' she told him, her voice quiet. 'I played my part, sure, but . . . I would've been happy for things to change, to be more real.' She paused, shaking her head with a reluctant smile. 'My mother always told me you were nothing but trouble, but I doubt she'll be pleased to have been proved right.' Standing on her toes, she pressed a soft kiss to his cheek, one hand on his shoulder. 'Goodbye, Daniel. Good luck in Mericus.'

'Goodbye, Emilie. May you find a man more worth your time than I,' he replied. Tears sliding down her cheeks and smearing her make-up, Emilie turned away from him and walked towards the steps, heading back to her friends. Daniel watched her go with his elbows on the railing, then he let out a sigh. The dirty work had only just begun.

17

Gemina, a small area squeezed in at the edge of the lower city, was definitely not the kind of place Daniel expected a man like Diora's second to live. It wasn't the slums by any means, but the area was cramped and overpopulated, the people virtually stacked on top of each other in their narrow brick houses. It was a great place to go unnoticed, he supposed; with so many people coming and going, and so many streets you could only find if you already knew how to reach them, it would be easy to be almost invisible to most people. Unluckily for Laurent, Daniel wasn't most people.

But before he went looking for Laurent he had some business to take care of. Finding Diora wasn't Daniel's only work, after all, and there were some who wouldn't be too keen to play nice once he was gone.

Stopping at a pub near the bridge between Gemina and the lower city, he caught the eye of the owner behind the bar. The man's skin paled three shades upon spotting him. 'Mr Novak, sir!' the portly man greeted, his bald head already beginning to sweat nervously. 'What can I do for you?'

'You can talk to me for a minute, Gabriel. In the back, where we'll have some privacy.' Gabriel didn't hesitate, lifting the bar top for Daniel to step behind and heading for the door to the pub's small back room. He had first met Gabriel when he'd discovered the man was using the upstairs floor of his pub as a brothel. Daniel had quickly put a stop to it, only threatening to call in the guards once before the man closed up shop, and he was now running his pub in a completely legal manner; or so he claimed. Daniel was fairly certain that the upstairs floor was no longer full of women, but he'd recently heard whispers that it was being used for some nefarious new purpose.

Gabriel shut the door behind them, eyeing him warily. 'I'll make this quick,' Daniel said, hands in his pockets. 'I've got plenty of other places to be this afternoon. I'm done playing around. I've been letting things slide all over the city for long enough, and it stops now.'

Gabriel gaped for a moment. 'I – I beg your pardon, sir?'

'You know what I mean,' Daniel snapped. 'Everything you've got going on upstairs? It stops now. The lower city needs a full clean-up, and it starts here. I'm not moving on until it's done.'

'Moving on, sir? You're leaving?'

Daniel nodded sharply.

'Well, that is a shame, a mighty shame. May I ask, sir, why you're telling me this specifically?' A vein in Gabriel's throat jumped nervously, and it made Daniel grin for a second before his jaw tightened. This was exactly the feeling his father had accused him of being addicted to.

'You're a popular man, Gabriel. You seem to know a fair few people around here, many of whom I've had . . . dealings with in the past. I need you to get the word out to anyone you think needs to hear it. Anyone wanting to come clean and square away their debts needs to talk to me before the first day of the festival. Part with me on good terms. Those who don't . . . they'll very much wish they had. I have friends in all sorts of places, many of whom owe me favours.' He smirked darkly, watching Gabriel flinch. 'There's a reason I have this reputation, Gabriel. I'd advise you and your friends not to test it.' Daniel folded his arms over his chest, straightening up to his full height and towering over the landlord. He was very good at looking terrifying if he needed to, and he had learned a long time ago the effective intimidation tactic of letting people fill in the blanks.

'Yes, yes, of course,' Gabriel stuttered. One hand moved towards his jacket pocket, fingers shaking. 'Just what sort of debt are we talking about here?'

'I'm not interested in money, Gabriel,' he said, waving him off. 'That hasn't changed. All I want is for people to clean up their acts. If they come to me before I get to them, I'll let them off lightly. But if I have to seek them out? Their lives will not be worth living. I'm a busy man, and I don't like having my time wasted. So you can tell your acquaintances that if they wish to risk the assumption that I don't know what they're up to . . . on their own heads be it.'

'Of course, Mr Novak, of course. I can get the word out,' Gabriel babbled. Daniel nodded in satisfaction; that should take care of most of the lawbreakers outside of Diora's control. The rest he could sort out through other methods.

'Excellent, thank you, Gabriel. And, of course, in your support of my efforts to clean this place up, I should hope

you don't mind me putting on a little show.' Without waiting for a response, Daniel turned towards a door he knew
led to the upstairs level of the pub.

'I don't sell the product, sir!' Gabriel blurted, face turning
red. 'I'd never get into that. I just give people a quiet spot to
smoke it. Better than them doing it on the streets, or around
their kids, right?'

'Then *you* don't have anything to worry about, then,'
Daniel retorted. Wrenching the door open, he strode up
the stairs, snorting in disgust when he reached the upper
level. The place was a mess, broken armchairs and piles of
blankets scattered all around, and the strong smell of drug
smoke infusing the room. Spotting a dark wood cabinet
with a padlock on the door, he crossed the room and broke
the padlock off with one swift kick. When he pulled open
the door he was unsurprised to see several large glass jars of
green crystals, as well as a stack of pipes and matchboxes. He
turned to Gabriel, who flushed an alarming shade of purple.

'Well, you see, sir – I can explain – I'm just holding it – I
didn't want any trouble –' Shaking his head at the man's
stuttered excuses, Daniel reached in to grab the jars, carefully stacking them in his long arms.

'Don't worry, Gabriel!' he said mock cheerfully. 'Once
I'm done, you won't have any trouble at all!' Turning on his
heel, careful not to drop any of the jars, he made his way
back downstairs and through the pub, startling the patrons.
Kicking the front door open, he stepped into the street,
curious people flooding out behind him. The sight of
Daniel Novak with his arms full of illegal drugs was definitely enough to draw a crowd.

He strode across the street towards a narrow bridge over one of the branches of the main river. Stopping on the bridge, he carefully deposited his collection of jars at his feet, then picked one up and popped the lid. Looking over at Gabriel, he smirked at the man's pale face and bugged eyes, though the landlord didn't make any move to stop him. He wasn't nearly brave enough for that.

Watched intently by at least fifty people, Daniel calmly upended the jar out over the bridge rail, watching the crystals pour out into the water below. Gabriel howled like he'd been wounded, but Daniel ignored him, eyes on his task. Not water soluble by any means, the crystals were carried away by the current in a swirl of glittering green. When the jar was empty he picked up the next one and continued. 'Sir, that's – that's half my life savings, that is!' Gabriel protested.

Daniel didn't falter. 'Then you should've thought a little more wisely about what you chose to invest in,' he argued simply. 'I told you. I'm done playing around. Clean up now while you have the chance, or I will do it for you.' He looked around, meeting the gaze of several people in the crowd. 'That goes for everyone.' He raised his voice, making sure they could all hear him. The news would spread through the lower city within hours. 'This ends now. I'm coming for everyone – anyone who isn't playing by the rules. Come to me first, or you can be sure you'll regret it.'

When the last jar was empty, the green crystals dispersing downstream and out of the reach of anyone who might want to try and salvage them, Daniel walked away, shoving the empty jars into Gabriel's hands as he passed him.

'Thank you for your time, Gabriel. I appreciate your co-operation.'

With that, he kept walking, turning to the steps that would lead to his next destination. Reports of his actions would be all over the lower city before the end of the night; that should do quite nicely in spreading his message and getting people to start turning themselves in. Now he had to start working on his other problem.

It had barely been a few hours since Daniel had warned Gabriel of his impending departure, and already half the petty criminals of the lower city had approached him, promising to clean up their act.

Jumping down from the roof of an old library on to a spindly walkway that crossed an offshoot stream of the river, he kept his eyes peeled for any sign of Laurent. Daniel didn't come out this far East very often, and wasn't completely sure of the shortcuts. People in Gemina tended to keep to themselves and stay out of trouble, or at least conduct their trouble elsewhere. Or perhaps it was Laurent's presence that kept everyone in line.

There was a courtyard not far from the stream, the closest thing to a park that Gemina had. Several young children played with a ball on a patch of grass, and a group of schoolgirls sat cross-legged under the gazebo, chatting to each other with wide smiles on their faces. It made Daniel grin to himself, glad to see people so carefree when he felt like all the troubles of the world were weighing him down.

He hadn't managed to find out exactly where in Gemina Laurent lived, but it was a small place. Pretty much everyone who lived in the area had to come through the courtyard at some point in their journey home. One of the residential buildings overlooking the courtyard had an inconspicuous balcony, and Daniel climbed up there with ease, perching on the small platform several storeys up. It was the only place where he could stay for a long period of time without drawing attention; no one thought twice about a man sitting on a balcony, but a man crouching in a very visible alcove would be cause for suspicion.

He was just starting to wonder if the day would be a bust, the sun mostly set on the horizon, when he caught sight of a broad figure with short black hair. Laurent was dressed unobtrusively in all black, briefcase in hand, crossing the courtyard like any other man on his way home from a long day at work. Daniel didn't hesitate to jump into action. He climbed over the railing on the balcony to stretch across and grab a nearby window sill, then pulled himself on to a cracked stone ledge. Hopping down on to the roof of the building beside it, he kept his eyes on Laurent's head, tracking his every move.

As Laurent approached the door of a modest-looking house and pushed it open without knocking, Daniel climbed down to street level; he could see nothing of use from up high. Making a mental note of the street for future reference, he edged closer, his stomach tense.

Getting as close as he dared to the house, he peered through the window into a homely looking kitchen. It was small, the counters cluttered, and he could see a woman at the stove with an apron around her waist. Her back was to the window, but she turned at a sound from the hallway. Daniel's eyes widened a fraction; strapped to her chest in a pink fabric sling was a baby with a mop of dark hair. As he watched, Laurent stepped into the kitchen, his face transformed by a tender grin. He bent to kiss the baby's forehead, then his wife's lips, pulling her close without squashing the baby. His wife was laughing, one hand straightening his collar affectionately. This was a far cry from the arrogant man he'd seen in the warehouse.

Daniel pulled away from the window. For the first time, doubt began to creep into his mind about his master plan. Not once had he stopped to think about what kind of lives Diora's men led. Whether they had families, people depending on them. It was hard to reconcile the image he had in his mind – ruthless, cold-hearted people with nothing but greed and lust for power motivating them – with what he saw in that kitchen. He'd been naive to believe things would be so black and white. Being Daniel should have taught him that more than anything.

Of course, he wasn't going to leave them to break the law just because they might have kids, but . . . what if Diora himself had a family? If he had children who depended on him and loved him as much as Daniel loved his own father . . . could he really take that man's life?

But the people who Diora – and Laurent – had hurt might have children too. No, Diora had to be stopped, even if there was a cost.

He watched for as long as he dared, his shaky morals making his unease grow as he observed the family go about their evening like any other. When Laurent's wife cracked the window open, allowing him to overhear their conversation – including Laurent promising to stay at home until nine the next day to fix a leak in the bathroom before work – Daniel figured there wasn't much point in lingering. Laurent wasn't going anywhere before morning, and it was clear his wife had no idea what he truly did for a living. Turning away from the small house, he retreated into the shadows, lips pursed in contemplation. This was not what he'd expected.

Thoughts weighing heavily on his mind, Daniel made his way back towards the centre of the lower city, trying to concentrate on anything other than what he'd just seen. It helped that every now and then, someone would approach him while he walked, assuring him vehemently that they were going to clean up their act. Several people he had never seen before were among them, and it made him smirk; being thought omnipotent had its benefits.

As he'd expected, the only ones not running scared were those who knew the truth behind the city's seedier businesses. Those in the know trusted Diora to keep the guards out of the lower city and off their backs – more fool them, when Daniel was finished.

Ready to call it a night, he began to make his way to one of the bridges to the upper city. He couldn't help but catch snatches of conversation, mostly about the festival or plans for the evening. It was his instinct, both in the lower city as Daniel and surrounded by the court as Noah, to pay attention to as much as he could, never sure where the next vital piece of information would come from. Still, sometimes he just wanted to turn that instinct off and remain oblivious for a while, lost in his own thoughts. The only person he'd ever found who could quiet this in him was Crysta.

Balancing effortlessly on top of a narrow archway between two buildings, his instinct flared like an alarm in his mind as he heard the one word he could never ignore.

'... the princess is far too well guarded – you'll be killed!'

'Not if I do this right,' a low, nasal voice replied insistently. Daniel froze, dropping down into a crouch. The speakers were in the alley below the archway, unaware of who was above them, and he didn't dare look over the edge in case either of them saw him. Both voices were male, talking quietly.

'Besides, it's not your job to tell me what I'm capable of doing. All you need to do is supply me with the means to do it.' He had the neat, curt accent of a member of the court – Talen or outland noble, Daniel couldn't quite tell at such a quiet tone.

'Fine, fine. I agreed to take the job and I will. And at this much money, I can't really say no. But I'm warning you, if you get caught and incriminate me in any way there will be no place on Tellus where you can hide. The Goddess herself won't save you then. We clear?' Daniel wished he could peer over and get a look at the two men, but he couldn't risk it. He knew this archway – it was barely stable and the last thing he needed was for it to crumble beneath him and dump him right in the centre of this transaction.

'Clear as glass,' the nobleman assured. His voice was muffled, like he was covering his face with some sort of cloth or hood. But he sounded achingly familiar. Noah had probably dined with this man multiple times; but what did he want with Crysta? 'You have nothing to worry about. I know what I'm doing.'

The lower city man snorted, his opinion obvious. 'Don't see why you can't just go about things the normal way, like the rest of your lot.'

'You don't think I've tried that?' the nobleman snapped. 'This is my last resort. To get what I truly want, the princess needs to die.'

Daniel's heart turned to ice. He slowed his breathing and crouched lower, cheek pressed against the rough stone as he listened intently. He couldn't miss a word of this conversation.

'I can get you what you need,' the man from the lower city confirmed, though he sounded somewhat reluctant. 'When do you want it by?'

'As quickly as possible. I want to make a scene. The opening ceremony should be dramatic enough, I think.' The nobleman chuckled, the sound sending shivers down Daniel's spine. Eyes wide in alarm, he silently begged the men to say something more; a name, a place, anything he could use. What was it the nobleman needed? A weapon, perhaps? Or an assassin for the job, if he didn't want to get his hands dirty? The conversation was so frustratingly vague it made Daniel want to swear.

'If you insist,' the lower city man sighed. 'I'll send a messenger when everything is ready.'

'I'll have the money ready and waiting,' the nobleman replied curtly. 'Pleasure doing business with you. I'll pass on a good word to your *boss* for this, don't you worry.' The emphasis on the word made Daniel's stomach clench.

'All the trouble I'm going to, you'd bloody better,' the other man grumbled. 'Now go, before someone catches you straying so far from home.'

At the sound of footsteps, Daniel lay flat on his belly against the stone archway and risked looking down at the men below him. They were both dressed in black with hoods over their heads. Scrambling to his feet as soundlessly as possible, he hurried to find a better vantage point to get a look at either man's face before they left. Clinging to a rough stone wall and edging his feet along the decorative moulding, he craned his neck, trying to get the perfect angle. He caught the slightest glimpse of dark hair beneath one of the hoods, before a piece of stone broke off beneath his right foot, and only his quick reflexes saved him from plummeting twenty feet to the ground. Now hanging off a drainpipe, pulse racing, he hauled himself up, cursing quietly into the night. Neither man was in sight. He sprinted across rooftops and over walkways, trying desperately to catch another glimpse of the nobleman, but he was nowhere to be found. After about ten minutes Daniel admitted defeat. He'd lost him.

Leaning back against a railing, he growled in frustration, hands clenched and trembling at his sides. As if his original goal of finding Diora and dismantling his network wasn't enough, he now had a second goal: to protect Crysta from whoever it was threatening her life.

He let out a deep breath, trying to steady his racing heart and ease the nausea that was about to overcome him. He had no idea where to begin looking for whichever nobleman had been under the bridge, but one thing was certain: he had a *lot* of work to do. Lives depended on it, Crysta's first and foremost. If the threat to Crysta was the Goddess' idea of punishing him for how he had treated her charge, she had quite the warped sense of justice.

18

Laurent left his house at nine the next day, and by noon Daniel had followed him over what felt like half the lower city, but not once had the man met with someone Daniel didn't recognise. However, while the search for Diora was coming up empty, it hadn't been a completely fruitless endeavour; Tor Virtan was a pharmacy owner, and though Daniel knew of him their paths had never crossed. Hearing him greet Laurent as he entered his shop, Daniel instantly pinned him as the lower city man he'd heard speaking with the mysterious nobleman the night before. It made sense; Virtan had quite the reputation among certain circles for being a master at mixing up just about anything you could need. Medicines, yes, but also poisons, sleeping draughts and a plethora of other drugs. Poison – the thought sending ice through his veins – would be an easy way for someone to kill Crysta in the chaos of the opening ceremony banquet.

In the distance Daniel heard the bells in the clock tower begin to ring, prompting him to check his watch. His heart stopped. He'd promised Crysta he'd be at the palace in plenty of time for the court dinner that evening, and the affectionately named 'lordling lunch' beforehand. With a muttered curse, he tore himself away from his quarry and raced towards the upper city. Laurent would have to wait.

As tempting as it was to continue his hunt, and as much as he quailed at the idea of seeing Rosa, Noah owed it to Crysta to be by her side. She was expected to attend the festival events held for the reigning nobles, as was her right as future queen, and preside over those for their children, to maintain strong ties with the future generation of nobles. The lordling lunch wasn't entirely compulsory for Noah, but he had promised to attend in solidarity. The court dinner, however, was a different matter – though he would have preferred to avoid the company of the nobles, the fact that he was even invited was an honour he couldn't turn down, especially as he hadn't been allowed to attend last year. He couldn't let Crysta down.

Damien wasn't in the guard station when Noah arrived, and he was escorted inside the palace as usual. Crysta was upstairs in one of the old ballrooms, and as Noah entered, keen to get the dinner over with as soon as possible now that Daniel's work had doubled, he saw that she and Damien were both wearing white fencing garb, their masks on as their foils flashed rapidly, each trying to score a point against the other.

Noah sat on the bench against the wall as the pair fought, not wanting to disturb them. He forced down his annoyance at having left the lower city earlier than needed, though he was glad Crysta was still getting the chance to do things she enjoyed. Not that she'd admit to it; as with dancing, she claimed fencing was a useful way to prepare for the festival, in case anything were to happen.

A fierce protectiveness rose in him as he watched her, his mind stuck on the prospect of someone harming her. Perhaps he should tell Damien. But he didn't want Crysta to find out; she had enough to think about with the festival, not to mention her suspicion once he admitted to being in an obscure part of the lower city in the dead of night. No, it was best if she remained oblivious for now.

They were done after a few minutes, Crysta's dark braid tumbling down to her waist as she removed her mask, an exhilarated smile on her flushed face. 'Another victory to you, but I shall best you next time,' she vowed, making Damien chuckle as he removed his mask, tucking it under one arm.

'I look forward to it,' he replied. 'Afternoon, Noah. I'd offer you some practice, but I'm already late for patrol.'

'Of course. I'm sorry, I didn't mean to keep you,' Crysta apologised. 'Thank you for the lesson.'

He flashed them a grin. 'I'll see you both at the court dinner.' Squeezing Noah's shoulder, the captain left the ballroom, and Crysta hung up her mask, having to stretch to reach the hook.

'I'm sorry to leave you when you've only just arrived,' she said, 'but I have to shower and change to meet with my parents and some of the nobles before lunch. Apparently I'm expected to be in two places at once these days.'

Noah grimaced, noticing the dark circles beneath Crysta's eyes. 'Have you actually taken a break at any point since we got back?' If there was anyone busier than he was this year, it was Crysta, and he hated watching her run herself ragged.

'I just did,' she replied breezily, sighing at the look on Noah's face. 'There will be time for a break after the festival. Besides, I can't imagine you've had any free time either.'

For a moment Noah worried that she somehow knew about his double life, before he realised she was referring to the mask work. 'Father and I finished,' he assured her, 'and he's all but banished me from the workshop while he works on some new project of his.'

Tucking a stray lock of hair behind her ear, Noah kissed her temple, holding back the need to pull her in close, which arose at the thought he might lose her. He couldn't let on that anything was amiss until he had more information. 'Go on, go and get ready for your meeting – I'll see you at the lordling lunch.' Giving in to temptation, Noah wrapped his arms around her waist, tilting his head to kiss her. Crysta allowed it quite happily, but there was a frown on her face when they parted.

'Are you well?' she asked, concern in her voice. 'You're acting . . . odd.'

Noah forced himself to relax, offering up an easy smile. 'I'm fine,' he assured her. 'I just feel like I've hardly seen you all week.' Crysta's face turned sympathetic and she kissed his cheek.

'It'll all be over soon.' Her words were meant to be soothing, but they only made him more uneasy.

'Now, I really must go. Stay out of trouble,' she added playfully, squeezing his hand before darting out of the room.

Alone in the ballroom, Noah bit his lip thoughtfully as he remembered something his father had said earlier. Might Rosa be willing to forgive him if he explained himself? He didn't really have much to lose, in any case.

Leaving the ballroom, he bypassed Rosa's room – it would be far too obvious a place for her to be with so many nobles around; she'd never get any peace. Instead he headed to the top floor, nodding in greeting to those he passed. It was odd, having so many nobles in the palace; he was used to it being near empty, as there were rarely more than two or three visiting noble families at a time. He had to be on his best behaviour at every moment, just in case someone was watching him.

The top-floor library door was closed but unlocked when he reached it, and he wasn't surprised to find Rosa in there, sharing a leather sofa with her handmaid, Rosa reading comfortably and Lena repairing a pair of torn breeches. The fact that servant and mistress were even sitting on the same sofa said a lot about their relationship.

Both girls looked up at his entrance, and Rosa's face immediately turned stony. Lena lowered her gaze before she could meet his, but Noah didn't miss the way she shuffled slightly closer to Rosa, hand reaching out a fraction, ready to comfort or protect if the need arose. 'Ladies,' he greeted evenly.

'What are you doing in here?' Rosa asked, voice like ice as her eyes trailed him across the room.

'Looking for you, actually. I was hoping I might have a word?' He kept his posture and tone as unthreatening as possible, praying Rosa would hear him out.

'I don't want to hear anything *you* have to say,' Rosa retorted sharply. 'So get out.'

'Please, Rosie.' Noah was begging and he knew it, but he had little room for pride these days. 'I *am* sorry for what I've done to you, and Lena. But I couldn't find any other way. I still can't. You may not understand it, but I'm trying to help people, down in the lower city. What I do there – it's bigger than Emilie, it's bigger than Crysta, it's far bigger than you could even *begin* to understand. Everything I've done has been for the right reasons, even if they look wrong to you.'

Rosa surveyed him for a long moment, incredulity in her gaze. 'You really believe that, don't you?' she scoffed. 'Whatever you've dreamed up to stop yourself feeling guilty about this, I don't care. Soon my sister will realise just how cruel a man you are, Noah Hansen. Then you will be out of our lives for good.'

Noah sighed, turning to meet Rosa's gaze. 'I am not a cruel man,' he insisted wearily. 'And I truly regret having to blackmail you into silence. Your business should be your own. But what I'm trying to achieve is too important to risk you destroying it now. I love Crysta, but she is impulsive; she won't want to hear another word from my mouth once you tell her of . . . she won't want to hear the truth.'

As he spoke Rosa stood up, and Lena followed without hesitation. The younger Octavian sister glared at him, stalking towards the door. 'The difference is that my secret will not break hearts.'

'Are you so sure about that?' Noah called after her. Rosa paused, her hand clenching just shy of the doorknob. She faltered for only a moment, then swept out of the room with tense shoulders, while Lena hung back in the doorway. As she looked up at Noah, her eyes darkened in hatred.

'You may be a master, sir, and I only a servant,' she began, voice shaking, 'but you would do well to remember which of us has easy access to the kitchens.' The handmaid was clearly trying her best be threatening, despite her ingrained urge to respect the masters of the house.

'I am very aware of that, Lena,' Noah replied, serious. He wouldn't anger her even more by seeming to laugh off her threat. 'But I only ask you to be aware in turn that I am not the enemy. I'm not trying to hurt anyone, I just need you both to keep my secret until it's no longer relevant.'

'You're asking Rosa to betray her own sister, sir. Would you ask that of Princess Crysta?' Lena glanced towards the half-open door, behind which Rosa was no doubt waiting for her. 'Just something to think about, sir.' With that, she left, and Noah was alone in the library.

19

Noah tried to occupy himself with one of the books on the library shelves, but when he found himself reading the same page for fifteen minutes he knew it was a lost cause. Rosa's words were echoing in his mind, combined with the venomous look on her face as she'd left the room.

Giving up on the book entirely, he decided to go and see if Crysta was ready for lunch.

He knocked on the door to her suite, not waiting for a response before slipping in discreetly. 'Crysta, are you decent?' he called, making himself comfortable on her sofa.

'And just what are *you* doing here? Without an escort, no less?' Crysta surveyed Noah with her hands on her hips, standing in the doorway to her bedroom.

Noah offered up his most charming grin. 'I got bored.' His eyes swept over her body, encased in deep-grey satin, her hair up in an elaborate braid that was no doubt of Ana's doing. Crysta looked every inch the future queen, and Noah was a little embarrassed to admit how attractive he found her when she held herself with such regal arrogance, as if she was ready to take on an army. His feelings must have shown in his gaze, as she blushed and shot a scolding look his way.

'You're lucky I'm ready to go,' she said, rounding the sofa and perching on his knee for a minute. Noah almost forgot about Ana, watching from the doorway with exasperation on her face. 'Lunch?' Crysta said, bouncing to her feet and tugging on his hand.

'Of course. Lead the way, my lady.' He could only hope they'd left it late enough that most of the nobles had already eaten.

Unsurprisingly, the pair of them together seemed to draw attention, and they were stopped several times on their way downstairs. Crysta did most of the talking, greeting those she had not yet welcomed, inquiring politely after spouses and children and townships. Noah had a reputation among the court for being the silent type, and he was loath to break it.

Turning into the hall set aside for the lordling lunch, Noah was hit with a wave of noise, and his hand tightened in Crysta's momentarily.

'Oh, we missed the start,' she sighed. 'I wonder what bout they're on now.' She urged him forward, eyeing the score-board set up along one wall.

In the centre of the room, surrounded by countless tables, was a raised platform with a fencing strip marked off – half the entertainment of the lordling lunch each year was watching the young lords and ladies compete. It was all friendly, vying for nothing more than bragging rights, but some took it more seriously than others. All around them people cheered for their favoured competitor, egging them on or heckling their opponent.

Looking at the pair currently facing off, he saw the matching family crests on the breast pockets of their fencing jackets – the Callis twins from Galian. That was one fight Noah wouldn't want to get in the middle of.

He and Crysta were quickly called over by a group of nobles from the Eastern outlands and islands, sitting at a table near the back of the hall. They were far enough away that the commotion of the fencing wouldn't interrupt their conversation too much.

'Dear lady, it would be an honour if you deigned to eat with us,' one of the young men said by way of greeting, raising his voice to be heard over the shouts as one of the Callis brothers got in a good hit. His name was Stefan Tamm, Noah remembered.

'The honour is all ours,' Crysta replied, the picture of politeness as she pointedly reminded the group of Noah's presence. The pair took two free seats at the table, and barely had to blink before servants were placing plates of steaming food in front of them. 'How have you all been enjoying your stay so far?'

'Talen is as lovely as it is every year,' gushed Kaya, a girl a year younger than Crysta, whose father owned the far-flung island of Furna. 'And the festival looks as though it will be even more spectacular than it has been in previous years.'

The hall erupted into applause as the twins' bout ended, the pair shaking hands and vacating the strip for the next duo. The fencing had started as just a bit of fun, something to keep the younger nobles occupied as their parents prepared for the court dinner, and to help foster friendship among the future generations. It had grown over the years to become one of the most anticipated events of the festival for many of the nobles. Every arrogant lordling was eager to hop up on the platform and prove their skills. Noah could see Rosa across the room, hardly paying any attention to the event, surrounded by some of the quieter girls her age. On the table behind her sat Fabian Silva and several of his compatriots, and Noah's skin crawled at the way the man watched the younger princess.

Glancing around the dining hall, Noah took careful note of who sat where. If you wanted to predict the future of Erova, you merely had to watch its younger members of the nobility. The adults were set in their ways, associating with those who could benefit them most, or with those they had been allied with for decades. The teenagers, however, were more likely to branch out when left to their own devices.

The heirs to the regions of Fatia and Spiago, whose fathers hated each other with a passion, were sitting quite happily beside one another, joking and laughing with a girl Noah was sure came from Halema. It warmed his heart to see friendships made in a place where so much importance was placed on business relationships.

Noah growled loud enough to stop several people mid-word as he overheard Darius Segal, clearly thinking Noah wasn't paying attention, telling one of his friends in a hushed tone that there was probably something wrong with Crysta for her father to have given her to the first 'scruffy little nobody' to raise an interest.

'I think we're done here, my love,' he said to Crysta, his hand almost crushing her fingers beneath the table. By the look on her face she too had heard Segal's words, but it wasn't worth causing a scene over. Leon had given them instruction years ago; words could be ignored but actions could not.

'What, you're not staying to see the winner?' Stefan asked with a frown as he gestured to the platform, oblivious to Noah's irritation.

'Noah's right,' Crysta said lightly, 'it's about time we went back to prepare for the court dinner this evening.' Several people around their table flinched. Only the heads of families and the royals were to be present at the court dinner. It clearly stung several of the more arrogant lordlings and ladies that Noah was considered important enough to attend yet they weren't allowed.

The two kept up their unaffected air until they were back in Crysta's suite, with Ana the only other person present. As soon as the door was shut, Crysta's shoulders slumped and she let out a long sigh, turning to bury her face in Noah's chest. He wrapped his arms around her, dropping a kiss to the top of her head.

'Sometimes I wonder if my parents had to go through similar trials when they were my age . . . and then I remember,' she murmured, making him grin. Crysta's mother was the daughter of the Lord of Reyenne, and her betrothal to Leon was about as perfect an example of a strategic match as you could possibly get. By the time they were Crysta's age, they were already married and Sofie was pregnant.

'Give it two weeks, and the nobles will all be gone,' Noah reassured her. 'We can handle it.' If everything went to plan, it would be the last festival during which people would question Noah and Crysta's relationship. Next year, he was sure, it would be too late for them to do anything about it. 'Now come, we need to get ready for dinner.'

The court dinner would last most of the evening and continue well into the night, allowing deals to be made and conversation to flow freely. There would be entertainment from Talen's own troupers, and Noah hoped it would be enough to keep him occupied.

He went to a separate chamber in Crysta's suite of rooms to get dressed, his suit already waiting for him and a servant there to help him dress. Noah would have preferred to dress by himself, but knew it was rude to refuse the offer. He had yet to see Crysta's dress for the dinner – or indeed any of her festival outfits – and so the sight of the dark red tailcoat laid out for him, adorned with silver buttons and brocade, made him grin. She looked stunning in red.

Noah dressed carefully with the servant's help, then combed his hair, tying it back to keep it out of his face. The servant assisting him applied some make-up to his cheeks and forehead, insistent when Noah tried to refuse. Finally, he was deemed fit to leave.

Knocking on the door that connected his room to Crysta's suite, he waited for Ana to allow him entry. At the sight of his girlfriend Noah's jaw dropped. Her dress was a bright ruby red, its bodice and hem decorated with intricate silver embroidery to look like the stars themselves had been sewn into the fabric. It had short sleeves, leaving the honey-coloured skin of her arms bare but for the fingerless lace glovelettes. While many women of her height might have preferred to wear high heels, Crysta proudly proclaimed her small stature, her silver shoes having only a low heel.

'How do I look?' she asked, holding her arms out to display the dress properly. Noah took several moments to respond.

'Like the Goddess herself,' he replied, taking another moment to find his voice.

'That's blasphemous,' she said, laughing.

'It is only the truth, I swear it.'

That drew another of her beautiful laughs, and she crossed the distance between them to kiss him.

Ana poured them tea while they waited for the summons to dinner, Crysta reclaiming her place on Noah's knee. He worried about her creasing her beautiful dress, but she waved off his concern, pointing out that most dresses were designed for sitting down in.

A knock on the door startled them, as it was a little early for them to go down to dinner yet. Ana opened it to reveal Rosa already dressed and ready. Noah's stomach lurched.

The younger princess looked surprised to see him there. 'Crysta. I didn't expect Noah to be with you,' she said in greeting, slipping into the room with Lena a stride behind her as always. Rosa looked like a creature from a myth, dressed all in pale gold, like a ray of light that would disappear if you tried to catch it, but her anxious expression gave Noah a firm suspicion of her reason for visiting her sister so close to the dinner.

'He got ready in the other room; his usual quarters are occupied,' Crysta explained as she stood up. 'Rosa, you look wonderful. Was there something you wanted?' Rosa stiffened, glancing at Noah, then shook her head.

'No, no. I was hoping to talk to you in private, but . . . it can wait.'

Noah's shoulders tensed; she wasn't thinking of telling Crysta, was she? Even after he'd threatened to tell her parents about Lena?

'If you're sure,' Crysta replied doubtfully. 'Noah won't mind leaving if it's urgent, will you?'

'Not at all,' he said, though his eyes flashed a warning at Rosa.

She swallowed, then shook her head. 'No, no, it isn't important.' As if on cue, there was another knock on the door, and a servant called through that it was time for him to escort them to dinner. Noah held his arm out to Crysta with a short bow, then offered his other arm to Rosa. She looked about to refuse, but then reluctantly took it. With the servant in front and Lena and Ana walking several steps behind, the trio went down to the dining hall. Noah kept his head high, trying not to let Rosa's tense face and calculating gaze worry him unduly. So long as he held her secret, she wouldn't betray him.

As was custom, the members of the royal family were the last to be seated at the dinner, so the dining hall was full by the time Noah and the two princesses entered. The room was a breathtaking riot of colour, green and bronze most prevalent of all. Swathes of fabric were draped from the ceiling, and the tables were dotted with bright flowers and intricately crafted bronze animal statues.

The chatter quieted almost instantly at their arrival, and Noah kept his gaze focused on the empty chair waiting for him, concentrating on looking nonchalant and not tripping over the skirts of either of the princesses. The tall gilded bronze chairs at the head of the table were empty; Leon and Sofie had yet to arrive. Rosa sat on the left of her parents' places, with Damien on her other side, and Crysta and Noah took the two chairs on the right.

Noah pulled Crysta's chair out for her before seating himself on her right, next to an older man with a rather large bald patch. He was the Lord of the Southwestern island of Tablis, and Noah sent up a silent prayer of thanks that his input to the seating arrangements had stuck. Lord Tarik Romano was one of the few noblemen who actually liked Noah and didn't object to his courtship of Crysta. The less Noah had to concentrate on not strangling irritating noblemen, the more he could focus on everyone around him and glean information about Crysta's potential assassin.

When the two princesses were seated comfortably, the sound of a trumpet pierced the silence, followed by the master of ceremony's booming voice. 'Please rise for His Majesty Leon Maximilian Octavian and Her Majesty Sofie Julienna Octavian, King and Queen of Erova.' Everyone in the room jumped to their feet with a scrape of chair legs on tiles, except for Crysta and Rosa, who were expected to remain seated. The king and queen were mesmerising as they entered the dining hall, dressed in their country's colours of green and bronze.

Only once the monarchs were seated was everyone else allowed to take their seats again. Noah relaxed a little at the beaming smile on Sofie's face. Unlike the rest of her family, she adored all the formal dinners and dances and court events that surrounded the festival, and even the trade negotiations. It worked out well for Leon; his wife was happy to take over the organisation of such things and told him where to be and when to be there. Noah wished he could be so lucky; he and Crysta hated these occasions with equal measure, and would probably be flipping coins to decide who got which duty when it was their responsibility to organise them.

'Thank you all for coming,' Leon greeted, his voice loud in the hush of the dining hall. 'We look forward to hosting you and your kin, and hope you enjoy what is sure to be another glorious Festival of the Goddess. May she herself bless your lands and families, and may we all walk away from this festival with prosperity in our pockets.' A cheer went up at his words, and the king's smile widened. 'Before we begin what I don't doubt will be a fantastic meal, we have some entertainment for you all. Miss Grace Bonet is perhaps the most talented pianist in all of Talen, and she has consented to play for us this evening.'

A woman in a long blue dress entered the hall to much applause, and sat down at the piano in the corner. But as much as Noah wanted to listen to her play, conversation in the hall started almost before she'd even set her fingers on the keys. There was much business to be discussed.

Knowing what was expected of him, Noah responded to idle questions from Lord Romano and his wife, making pleasant small talk while he listened to as many conversations as he possibly could. It was at times like this that his experience as Daniel came in handy; he could glean far more information by playing strong and silent than he could by trying to charm it out of people. He just wished everything he'd learned from being Daniel was quite so harmless.

Desperate to pin down the familiar accent he'd heard discussing Crysta's murder the night before, he paid close attention to everyone's voices, as well as the words they were speaking. It was hard when he could barely hear himself think, but he wasn't likely to get another chance to hear all the nobles talking before the festival itself, and by then it would be too late. He was worryingly low on both useful information and time. He already had plans for Daniel later, as soon as he could get away after the dinner.

Noah's eyes flickered towards Rosa, who was as silent as always, her hands folded in her lap. Damien seemed to be attempting to coax her into conversation, but to no avail, and the captain shot a despairing look at Noah, who raised an eyebrow in response. Damien should know better than to try and get Rosa to chat with so many people around.

As if feeling his gaze upon her, she raised her eyes, giving him a dirty look. With a discreet hand signal Sofie prompted the meal to begin, and immediately the hall hushed as a swarm of serving staff appeared from the wings with plates containing fresh green leaves and some sort of tiny roast bird. It was small but beautifully presented, and considering the meal was to be seven courses, it didn't need to be much bigger.

The king and queen took their first bites before the sound of cutlery clinking filled the hall. Noah clenched his knife and fork tight, focusing on his meal and the voices of the people around him, still hoping to pinpoint the assassin. Of course, it was entirely possible the man wasn't even in attendance. Many noblemen weren't lords, after all.

The next four courses followed without any problems, and Noah was starting to relax. But just as he was tucking into a four-layer chocolate and raspberry cake things started to go downhill.

'So when are we going to hear wedding bells from your one, then, Your Majesty?' Noah's ears pricked up at the conversation topic and he looked for the speaker, finding a man in his fifties whose blond hair suggested he was from one of the Eastern regions. He was smirking, giving Crysta a look that was pure lechery.

'In due time, I'm sure,' Leon replied, chuckling. 'You know how my daughter is, she won't make any decision without thinking it through thoroughly.'

'Perhaps she should think a little harder,' Rosa muttered under her breath, quiet enough that the only ones to hear her were Damien, her parents, Crysta and Noah. The hairs on the back of Noah's neck stood on end, and he eyed the girl warily. Leon, still focused on the man who had asked him the question, pretended he hadn't heard, but Sofie was sending her younger daughter a scolding glance.

'I suppose with a face like that, you can sit around thinking as long as you like and that boy of yours won't stray,' the man remarked with a grin, winking at Crysta. Noah's hand tightened on her shoulder. Rosa coughed pointedly and Noah glared at her, making sure she could see his gaze move to Lena against the back wall, his meaning clear.

'Hold your tongue, Karl, and be aware that it is my daughter you're speaking of,' Leon said, warmth gone from his tone. The blond man's eyes widened, and he shook his head, gesturing apologetically and nearly knocking over his wine glass.

'I meant no offence, sire, of course. I merely meant that the princess is pretty enough that the lad won't get bored while she makes her mind up.' Noah winced at the expression on Crysta's face at the man's words. He stroked her shoulder soothingly with one finger while he practically held her in her seat, fearful that she might jump across the table to choke the man with his own napkin.

'You'd think so, wouldn't you?' Rosa said, a little more loudly, making Crysta's brow furrow.

'Rosa,' Noah murmured in warning. The girl paled, but took a deep breath that looked uncomfortable considering how tightly her corset was laced.

She glared back at him. 'No, Noah. I won't let you *control* me.'

'You mean the same way you're controlling me?' he hissed under his breath, making her smirk.

'Except I'm not. Not yet, am I? You have the upper hand in this,' she said, her voice shaky despite the look of steel in her eyes. 'But not for long.'

'Noah, what's she talking about?' Crysta queried under her breath. Before Noah could make up an excuse Rosa got to her feet, a look of determination on her face, her hands clenched at her sides so hard her knuckles were white.

'The longer I stay quiet the more likely it becomes that someone else will find out, Noah, and that someone might not be so *gracious* as to keep it to themselves,' she spat at him. Noah's eyes went wide. She was going to tell it all. Emilie, Daniel, everything. He was finished.

'Rosa, no, we can settle this in private,' he insisted. 'You're making a scene.' She laughed, the sound harsh.

'Storms forbid I make a scene,' she said sarcastically, shaking her head. 'You know the thing about secrets, Noah? As soon as someone knows them, they're not secrets any longer.'

His heart pounded in his chest as Rosa turned to the assembled lords and ladies, her shoulders squared. The hall was dead silent. Even the man with the harp had stopped playing to stare at Rosa incredulously.

'There's something I've been hiding,' the younger princess announced. 'Something I've not told anyone because I was worried about the consequences of revealing it. Worried about hurting people. But over the past few days, I've realised something. Shrouding yourself in lies will only cause pain in the long run, especially to those who deserve the truth. So I'm going to do something I should have done long before now.'

'Rosa, don't,' Noah urged. The black-haired girl glared at him, fists clenched even tighter.

'Do not dare to reprimand me when it's your fault I'm in this position,' she hissed under her breath. Crysta sent him a look of confusion at her sister's words, but quickly looked back to Rosa as she cleared her throat. The entire room waited with bated breath for the princess to speak, wondering what she was about to reveal.

'I'm in love with my handmaid.'

Noah blinked, stunned. Wait, *what*??

20

The silence after Rosa's words was even more deafening than the silence before them. Still stunned, Noah couldn't take his eyes off the young princess.

'Her name is Lena, and she has served me for two years now. And I have been completely, utterly, unchangeably in love with her for almost every second of it.'

Rosa glanced over her shoulder to where Lena was standing and smiled at the dumbstruck look on the other girl's face before turning back to her audience. 'I didn't understand it myself, at first. I was too young to have heard anything about relationships of those sorts. I thought . . . I thought I was broken, that there was something wrong with me. I denied it, I raged at Lena, at myself, at the entire world around me. But soon I learned that there was nothing wrong with me; I was different, not broken. And Lena . . . Lena loves me back, just as much.

'I always knew it would be my duty to marry for politics. I had accepted that, even more so when Crysta met Noah. But then I thought to myself, why should Crysta get all the luck? If anything, she, as the older sister, should be the one to marry for duty. After the initial protest, no one seemed to complain about Noah, and suddenly everything was down to me. But . . . Father, Mother,' she said and turned to her parents, a pleading look on her face, close to tears. 'I cannot change the way I am, and I would not want to. Lena makes me happy, and I in turn make her happy, something you told me was vital in a loving relationship. Why must I marry a man I will have no feelings towards, in order to bring peace between our regions. Are we not already at peace?

'There are no family feuds to settle or bruised egos to soothe. We do not need to tie our family to foreign royalty, and why should we tie those here to our family in marriage when they are already so dear to us? Erova is a strong country, a proud country. We are a Goddess-blessed country. We let Anglya believe they rule us, but truly we rule ourselves. We are a country of bounty, of promise, and of *freedom*. But . . . where is my freedom, if I am to be forced to marry for the sake of increasing *trade routes*? True freedom is being allowed to love without boundaries, without judgement, and without force. And I believe that Erova is a country of true freedom.' Her voice was strong as she spoke, more fierce and vehement than Noah had ever heard from Rosa – than *anyone* had ever heard from Rosa. He was still reeling from the fact that she had revealed her own secret rather than his. What did she have to gain from outing herself like that?

Freedom.

'Rosa, I . . .' Leon breathed, looking completely floored by his daughter's words.

She smiled sadly at the grey-eyed man. 'You don't need to say anything, Father. I think . . . I think I've said it all. And now I think I'd best excuse myself. My apologies for disturbing your meal.' The wind seemed to be well and truly gone from her sails and she was visibly trembling. Not waiting for permission from either of her parents, the girl turned and ran for the door. Lena chased after her, and the next thing Noah knew, Crysta was doing the same.

'Rosa, wait!' she exclaimed, hurrying after her sister, skirt flaring in her wake. Noah knew he should stay, should attempt to help Leon and Sofie call some sort of order to the shambles that the dinner had become, but Crysta was more important. There was nothing to stop Rosa from telling his secret now. He couldn't leave them alone together.

Noah ran upstairs to Rosa's suite, knocking once and not waiting for a response before entering. Rosa was sitting on the sofa by the fireplace, tears streaming down her cheeks as Lena stroked her hair and held her hand, and Crysta stood leaning on the back of the chair opposite, staring at her sister with a look of helplessness on her face. All three of them whipped round to look at him as he entered.

'Get out,' Rosa hissed, eyes red-rimmed. 'Have you no decency? Get out!' Noah held up his hands, opening his mouth to placate her, but there was another knock on the door and Damien entered hurriedly, his face panicked.

'Thank the Goddess, you're all in here,' he said, clearly having just run up the stairs. 'Rosa, what on Tellus?'

'You do know we don't care, Rosie?' Crysta soothed at the same time Damien spoke. 'All of us, we only want what's best for you. Mother and Father won't care so long as you're happy.'

'You have no power over me now,' the youngest princess declared with her eyes fixed on Noah, not even acknowledging Damien's entry or Crysta's words. 'The whole court knows my secret, and it no doubt won't be long before half of Talen knows too. I don't care any more. I meant what I said in there; Erova is too strong to be felled by something as ludicrously simple as a girl loving another girl. People will move on. But you now have nothing to barter with, do you?' Her expression turned icy as she smiled at him.

'Rosa, don't, please, you don't know what you're doing,' he started.

'Noah's been cheating on Crysta,' she announced, speaking over him. The entire room went silent, and Noah felt like he'd been physically struck as Crysta flinched, looking at him warily.

'W–what?' she breathed, stunned.

'Crysta, I can explain –'

'He's been putting on a disguise and seeing a girl in the lower city. Emilie, did you say her name was?' Noah's shoulders slumped, and it seemed to be all the sign Crysta needed. She let out a choked sob, shaking her head.

'No, he wouldn't do that, you must be mistaken.'

'I saw it with my own eyes. He had on a wig and make-up, but I'd know Noah anywhere, and he was kissing that girl, watching the lights go up in the main courtyard with her. And from what he said when I confronted him about it, it's been going on for a while. I told you from the start, Cryssie, he's not good enough for you. You should've listened to me when you first started courting. But even I was starting to trust him, until I saw them together.'

Crysta looked up at Noah, betrayal in her tear-filled eyes. 'Is it true?'

'I can explain, Rosa's got it all wrong. Emilie wasn't like that.' Crysta's sob cut him off, and she reached up to smack him hard across the face, the family ring on her finger cutting his cheek enough to draw blood.

'*Gods*. Damien, take him. I don't want him here, I don't even want to *look* at him right now. Storms, I can't believe I trusted you. I *loved you*, for the Goddess' sake!' Though Damien looked shocked, he did as ordered, grabbing Noah and forcing his arms behind his back.

'No, wait! Crysta, just let me explain!' Noah pleaded, voice cracking.

'I don't want to hear it!' she shouted in reply. 'This is over, Noah. *Storms*, I can't believe you would do this, after everything! I never want to see your face again. If any of the guards catch him trying to get in here, I want him arrested. Is that clear, Damien?'

'Yes, Your Highness,' Damien replied dutifully, tightening his grip on Noah's arms as he struggled. 'Come on, Noah. You need to leave.' With that, he began to drag him from the room, barely paying attention to his attempts to break free. The last thing Noah saw before he was forced from the room was Crysta turning to Rosa with tears in her eyes, looking utterly broken.

Noah struggled all the way to the palace gates as Damien dragged him out through a small side entrance and towards the guard station. 'Damien, stop! I can explain myself if someone would just *listen* to me!' he said desperately. Damien's pace didn't falter.

'If what Princess Rosa says is true, then none of us want to listen to you right now. Or ever, in fact.'

The guard station was nearly empty when they entered, almost everyone busy inside the palace or out in the city. Damien didn't stop; he was heading for the front door to throw Noah out on the street. Noah grabbed at the edge of a desk, forcing the captain to stop. The older man whirled round angrily. 'What do you want me to say, Noah? We trusted you! All of us, despite our better judgement, let you into the palace, into the lives of Crysta and the rest of the Octavians, because you and Crysta seemed so in love. And now I find out that you've been lying to all of us, you've broken Crysta's heart, and from what Rosa implied you've been *blackmailing* her? Those girls are like sisters to me, and you've walked all over them. You're just lucky I haven't slit your throat yet, but I swear to the gods, if I see you anywhere near the palace or either of the girls again, you won't be quite so fortunate.'

Damien's face was grim, his intense stare assuring Noah that he had every intention of carrying out his threat if he stepped out of line.

'I won't give up this easily,' Noah vowed. 'I love Crysta. I've made some bad choices, but they don't affect my feelings for her. I'll find a way to get her to listen to me.'

'You've been one of my closest friends for over two years now, Noah, so I'm only going to say this once. If you value Crysta's heart and your own skin even in the slightest, you'll leave her alone. It's the best thing for everyone involved.' Damien reached out to grab him by the collar of his tailcoat, his other hand prying Noah's off the desk in order to drag him through the door of the guard station. Damien shoved him down the steps and Noah landed on his knees on the paving stones so hard he saw black spots.

'Damien, you can't, I need to warn you –' his shout was cut off as Damien slammed the door of the station. After a brief moment Noah heard the lock click. He let out a curse, ripping the tie from his hair where it was already coming loose, fist slamming the ground in frustration. He had to talk to Crysta, to convince her to hear him out. He needed to tell Damien about what he'd heard the other night! The festival was approaching fast and he still didn't know who the assassin was or exactly when he would strike.

Dragging himself to his feet as his knees seared with pain, Noah moved to lean against the palace gates, staring up at the window to the dining hall he'd been in barely fifteen minutes ago. 'Damien, come on!' he shouted at the guard station. 'You know me better than this. You know I wouldn't do this without good reason. Damien, let me in!' There was no response, and with a sound of despair Noah let himself sink to the ground, head in his hands, back against the palace gates. Storms, how had he managed to mess everything up so spectacularly?

Resolving not to give up, he settled down against the gates, huddling into his tailcoat for warmth. It wasn't a particularly cold night, but the sun was almost fully set and the wind was beginning to pick up. Still, he'd slept in worse places as Daniel. Maybe if he stayed out long enough, Damien would take pity on him and let him inside to explain. It was his best shot.

21

The sun had long since set and the city was in darkness. Noah sat outside the palace gates, right beside the guard station. He had dozed off once or twice, but had still managed to catch Damien checking on him several times before he finally headed home far later than usual. Noah had pleaded with the captain to listen to the truth, but Damien cut him off, insisting he didn't want to hear it.

Noah's heart ached as he remembered the look on Crysta's face when she'd banished him from the palace; betrayal, hurt, disbelief. He hated himself for making her feel like that, but he would fix it. He would make up for his mistakes, face them like he should have done long ago.

With a sharp breath of pain, Noah pulled himself to his feet, his knees still throbbing. Checking his watch, he grimaced at seeing it was almost three in the morning. Maybe he should make the most of being awake at such an ungodly hour; he wasn't going to get any sleep, anyway.

He wasn't surprised to find the house silent; his father would have gone to bed hours ago. He'd long since stopped waiting for Noah to get home before locking up for the night. His body pulsing with adrenalin, Noah hurried down the stairs to his room. He paused outside the closed work-shop door with a frown, testing the handle. It was locked. 'Da, what are you up to?' Noah muttered to himself, shaking his head. He could only hope his father hadn't decided to sleep in the workshop again. What on Tellus was this project that was taking up so much of his time?

With everything else he had to take care of, his father's sleeping habits would have to wait. Continuing on to his room, he eased the door shut and got to work, digging out the box containing Daniel's disguise. It never took long for him to change identities these days.

He looked over himself in the mirror, easily able to see his true face under the disguise; no wonder Rosa had known it was him. When he'd first created the disguise, he hadn't worried about ensuring he looked markedly different from his true self; he hadn't ever expected to meet anyone in the lower city who knew him as Noah. Evander had taught him about the subtleties of the human face so he could better understand mask design. The poor man had probably never anticipated what his son might do with the knowledge.

Not wanting to waste any more precious time, Daniel grabbed his satchel and ran upstairs. He skidded to a halt in the hallway, eyes catching on the bronze statue of the Goddess in a small alcove in the wall. Above it was an engraved sign, identical to the one hanging above their front door – '*Hansen & Son mechanics; we fix even the unfix-able, and create the unimaginable*'. Daniel smiled to himself briefly, touching his fingers to his lips and then to the Goddess' left shoulder.

'Please,' he breathed into the hallway, silent but for the mechanical tick of several household objects. 'Grant me the ability to fix this mess.' Even if the Goddess hated him for what he'd done to Crysta, he was currently the only person looking for the princess's assassin. Surely that was reason enough to receive divine assistance?

Daniel's destination was clear in his mind; with the court dinner out of the way, he was free to head straight to Tor Virtan's pharmacy. He had at least two hours until the sun even thought about rising, and despite the ache in his knees and the tickle in his brain reminding him that he had yet to properly sleep, he was ready to use those two hours to the fullest.

The pharmacy was identifiable by the purple heart painted on its sign, and Daniel jumped to land on the building's roof, rolling to cushion the blow. Then he gripped the narrow ledge around the edge of the roof and swung himself over the side, using drainpipes and window sills to ease his descent. His soft-soled leather boots barely made a sound as they touched the ground in the alley behind the building. Daniel approached the back door, pulling a pair of thin tools from his satchel. Picking the lock was child's play.

Creeping inside the pharmacy, he found himself in the darkened stockroom, staring at shelves and shelves of bottles and packets and boxes of medicine. It was well stocked, that was for sure. No wonder Virtan was able to create poisons and illegal drugs without suspicion. His eyes trailed carefully over the walls and floors, looking for some kind of crack or partition that might give way to a secret door. There had to be one; the building was far bigger on the outside than it appeared on the inside. Virtan must prepare his illegal substances somewhere here. With any luck, it was something that would help him kill two birds with one stone – Diora had to know about the plans to kill Crysta. Nothing that big would happen under his nose without him being aware. If Daniel could find some kind of proof to confirm the connection, and then get the rest of the information from Diora himself once he found him . . . it was a long shot, but Daniel didn't have time for much else.

Eventually, he found it. Half blocked by a workbench on wheels, the door was the same colour as the walls and blended in almost seamlessly. But Daniel's eyes were good, even in the dark. He quickly crossed to move the workbench, wincing at the squeak of the wheels as he pushed it aside just enough to open the door. He hoped the sound wasn't loud enough to carry upstairs.

The door now exposed, its lock nothing more than a narrow groove in the surface, Daniel set to work picking it. This one took a little longer than the entrance lock, but it opened eventually. He nudged the creaky door open and, slipping inside, shut it behind him before reaching for the light switch.

With the lights on he could see that the room was a laboratory of sorts. There were several bottles and beakers of unidentified chemicals, with all kinds of equipment for mixing and decanting. He would bet any amount of money that the substances in those bottles weren't for medicinal purposes.

Opposite a tall glass-fronted shelf full of boxes and bottles was a rickety dark wood desk, its drawers overflowing with papers, the desktop itself stacked high with even more. Daniel made a beeline for it, groaning under his breath at the mess. How on Tellus was he going to find any useful information in that chaos? 'Well, here goes nothing,' he murmured, reaching for the first pile of papers on the desk. Most of them seemed to be covered in scrawled equations and formulae, and he ignored them, knowing he wouldn't understand them even if he had days to figure them out. In among all the chemical gibberish were several common names for various poisons, which he definitely recognised. He was now more certain than ever that the assassin planned to poison his beloved.

This made his heart clench painfully. An endless number of nobles could poison Crysta's food, or shoot a poisoned dart at her neck.

He was only slightly comforted by the fact that he'd been responsible for designing the princess's mask for the opening ceremony and festival ball; there was no way any type of dart was going to touch her neck in that. He prayed that the king would make her wear some sort of shoulder armour. She had plenty that wouldn't look out of place with a dress, and a dart would bounce harmlessly off the layers of tightly woven fabric. Her food, however . . . he couldn't protect that.

He thought of the immense number of new kitchen staff brought in for the festival, and his stomach turned. The accent of the assassin didn't sound like that of a cook or servant, but he couldn't be certain, and the background checks on the newly hired staff only went so far. Any one of them could be capable of slipping something into Crysta's evening meal.

Snapping out of that particular thought before it spiralled out of control, he focused on Virtan's papers, skim-reading as quickly and efficiently as he could. He only had half an idea of what he was looking for, but as his sharp eyes spotted Diora's name, his breath caught.

My good friend,
I must thank you for your help in the personal matters we spoke of. I have been searching for a solution to this pesky problem for quite a while now and you have given me the means with which to solve it. You have worked far more swiftly than I had anticipated, for which I am grateful. Rest assured I will pass on a message to our mutual friend Diora, telling him how well you have served me. You shall be richly rewarded. After all, I will have much more influence in his eyes should my venture succeed.

I will no doubt speak with you soon, once I have completed my task.

The letter was dated that day, written in a neat hand that Daniel was sure he'd seen before. He read the short missive a second time, his heart turning to lead. While there was no signature on the letter, no mark of who it might have come from, it was enough to confirm that Diora and Virtan were friends. And the timing of the letter made it entirely likely that the 'personal matter' discussed in the letter was the supply of the poison intended to kill Crysta.

Daniel's mind cast back to Laurent opening the crate of food in the warehouse, and a frown crossed his face; Diora was already planning bigger and more far-reaching things for after the festival, extending his empire past the lower city. Perhaps killing Crysta was all part of that, making the monarchy even more unstable under the threat of a poor harvest. It would certainly upset the Goddess enough to deny them fruitful crops, to kill her eldest daughter during an event designed to praise her. What if the whole thing was just another one of Diora's schemes, controlling his men like puppets in order to stay blameless?

Still, Daniel wasn't entirely convinced. He only had one shot at this, and he didn't want to make any mistakes. He put the letter back where he found it on the desk, careful to make sure everything looked undisturbed. It wouldn't do to give himself away by being sloppy. Deciding to dig a little deeper, he tugged open the desk drawers. They were full to bursting with order forms, recipes, experiment notes and all sorts of other notes that made his head spin. But somewhere in that mess was information on the man planning to take Crysta's life, and Daniel would quite happily sift through five times as much paper in order to find that information.

Going through Virtan's desk was a special kind of hell, but eventually he found a blue-bound ledger with half the pages falling out, buried beneath a pile of order forms. He let out a quiet sound of triumph when he opened it and saw plenty of names scribbled down beside the orders for drugs and poisons he recognised as being illegal. The ledger dated back at least two years, and he flicked forward to the most recent pages, looking for something that might give him more information. Virtan did a lot of deals; there were twenty lined up for the past two weeks alone.

Trailing a finger down those dated the day before, Daniel froze. Right there was an order for velora, an incredibly lethal poison. The number in the 'price paid' section of the ledger made him let out a low whistle; who on Tellus could afford that?

Following the line across to the client name, Daniel's heart skipped a beat. *A. Laine.* He knew that surname, and now he remembered where he knew that handwriting too. Adamas. Any doubt that Diora was behind the whole scheme flew out of Daniel's mind – Adamas didn't have access to that kind of money by himself, but if he was working at Diora's behest . . .

Finally, it felt like he was getting somewhere, though one thing still confused him; the man in the alley with Virtan the night before. Daniel liked to think he knew Adamas's voice fairly well after dating his sister for so long, and that had not been Adamas's voice. Perhaps he had sent a messenger on his behalf, or Diora had more than one of his men working on this together. It could all be solved with a quick visit to Adamas's apartment.

Looking through the ledger, Daniel was surprised to see that Adamas wasn't the only one ordering velora; his gaze landed on another order, made only the day before Adamas's, for roughly the same amount. It was a small dose, but with velora that was all you needed. Without the proper antidote administered within ten minutes of the poison entering your bloodstream, you'd be dead.

The second order had no name attached to it – it looked like even Virtan didn't know the names of some of the shady characters he dealt with. It made Daniel frown. Could this second dose be for a different purpose, or did Diora have a back-up plan somewhere? The idea sent shivers down Daniel's spine. He was barely able to track down one assassin, let alone two.

Doing a quick check through the last pages of the ledger, he confirmed that those two orders were the only promising leads. Nothing else was even half as deadly, not in the last week or two.

Checking his watch, he bit his lip; he'd been in there for over an hour already. With no idea what time Virtan opened his business, Daniel needed to get out, and quickly.

As tempted as he was to rip out the page from the ledger to show to Damien, he knew it would be a glaringly obvious giveaway when Virtan went to check his ledger, and the page didn't actually link back to Crysta in any way. It was alarming enough that the man was selling lethal substances, but without evidence to prove that those substances were going to be used to kill the princess, Daniel had little more than nothing.

Burying the ledger back beneath the pile of forms, he shut the desk drawer and turned away. He paused, frowning contemplatively. It couldn't hurt to tamper with the man's merchandise just a little bit, could it? Changing course to the workbench, Daniel picked one of the full vials at random, uncorking it and pouring a little into each of the beakers and bottles on the worktop. Several of them changed colour, while others began to fizz violently, and one even melted through its container and began dripping over the worktop. Smirking, Daniel set the vial back in its place, careful to make sure it merely looked like an upset in the chemistry rather than active sabotage, though the work-top and everything on it was very clearly ruined.

Not wanting to linger any longer, he left the back room of the pharmacy through the same door he'd entered, the street barely lit by the tip of the rising sun. His adrenalin rush could only get him so far, and after everything he'd been through in the last twenty-four hours his body was beginning to tire, limbs feeling sluggish and heavy. His bruised knees ached, but he forced himself up on to a walk-way and began to run, heading in the direction of Adamas's apartment. He didn't have time to sleep, not with Crysta's life on the line.

22

As the sun slowly crested the rooftops, the early risers of the lower city began their days, and Daniel was no longer alone in the streets. Knowing that Adamas definitely wasn't the type to rise with the sun, Daniel took his time, stopping for a few conversations along the way. Things were changing since he'd announced his intention to leave, and it looked to be for the better. Perhaps after the festival things would be calm enough for him to approach Damien about reintroducing the guard patrols down there – providing Damien ever wanted to speak to him again.

When he arrived at Adamas's apartment there was a light on in the front window, and Daniel peered in. Adamas lived alone, he knew that much, but he could easily have company. Emilie could be there, for all he knew. However, it looked like he was in luck. Adamas was the only person in the small living room, dressed in an undershirt and rumpled grey trousers. He had a book in his hands which he didn't really seem to be reading, and a glass of some sort of amber liquor on the table. There was a possibility that other people were elsewhere in the apartment but, looking at the man's unkempt state, Daniel doubted it. It was early in the day for

Adamas to be drinking. Perhaps guilt was finally catching up with him.

Squaring his shoulders, Daniel left the window and stood in front of the door, bringing the brass knocker down sharply three times. He waited, eyes straight ahead, willing his face to look as intimidating as possible. Adamas was broader than him, but Daniel had a few inches of height in his favour.

The door swung open, Adamas glaring at the interruption. He did a double take upon seeing who was standing on his doorstep. 'Novak,' he spat, making Daniel smirk to himself. 'What in the Goddess' name do you want at this hour?'

'May I come in?' Daniel asked with false courtesy, barging his way past the man and into the hallway. Adamas spluttered, face contorted with anger.

'You have no right to force your way into my house!' he started, but Daniel cut him off by slamming the door in his wake.

'And *you* have no right to take the life of an innocent.' Adamas gaped, the colour draining from his cheeks. He surged forward, pinning Daniel to the wall by the shoulders.

'What have you heard, you little brat?' he growled, his face so close to Daniel's that he could smell his alcohol-tainted breath.

'Enough. I saw you, speaking with Tor Virtan. What would your dear sister say if she knew what you were planning?'

'You can't prove anything with eavesdropping!' Adamas argued, shoving Daniel harder against the wall. 'And how dare you talk about my sister like you actually give a damn about her!'

Daniel glared, reaching up and pushing back, nearly sending the man flying in his tipsy state. He would not let this piece of filth push him around. He'd played nice with Adamas for years, wanting him to let his guard down enough to give him the information he needed, wanting to stay in Emilie's good books and off Diora's hit list. He didn't need that any more.

'No, but that letter you wrote in thanks will do quite nicely as evidence. Now tell me, what would Diora have to gain from your plan? You seem to be quite sure he'll thank you for it.'

Adamas laughed sharply. 'What *won't* he gain? That second of his is far too soft! Getting cold feet every bloody ten minutes, wanting to shut down some of the more dangerous investments for good. With me in his place, the Boss could double his reach, triple it even! All it takes is just a little prick of a needle and no one will ever know. This time tomorrow I'll be getting a promotion.'

Daniel's brain stuttered to a halt at the man's words. Diora's second? He was planning on killing *Laurent*? 'You want to kill Laurent, and you think Diora will let you replace him, just like that?' he asked, trying to come across like he'd known that was Adamas's plan all along.

'I'm next in line, and if I do this right he'll never know I was behind Laurent's sad, untimely demise,' Adamas replied with a vicious grin. 'Who's going to stop me? A brat like you? Don't make me laugh! I know you, Novak; you're all bark and no bite.'

For a moment, Daniel was tempted to leave him to it. But he replayed Adamas's words in his mind; if Laurent truly was getting cold feet, trying to bail on Diora's work, he would be far easier to convince into letting Diora's empire fall than if Adamas was at the helm.

Besides, he couldn't help but remember the sight of Laurent with his family, the small child in his wife's arms. How could he stand back and let Adamas kill the man in cold blood? If the Goddess was counting his sins, he definitely needed to even the scales a bit, especially after the last few days.

'See, that's where you're wrong,' Daniel said, taking a step forward and pulling himself up to his full height, gaze boring straight into the man's eyes. 'You might not think I have the power to stop you. After all, calling the guards is a bit late once you've already killed a man, correct?' He took another step, backing Adamas into the same wall he'd had Daniel pinned against moments ago. 'But I have much more in my repertoire than just calling the guards, my friend, and I can assure you that my bite is very much worse than my bark. I may only be around for another few days, but that is more than enough time to make some house calls, and I'm fairly certain I know the right people to visit to make your life rather difficult.'

Adamas didn't move. 'What are you going to do, tell the Boss?' he mocked, though his voice shook just a fraction.

'For starters,' Daniel replied. 'And I'm sure Laurent's friends will be fascinated. And Emilie would no doubt like to hear about what you really get up to, since she does so *enjoy* talking about your work.' Adamas's eyes narrowed, but Daniel merely smirked. He wasn't above taking cheap shots – not now.

'I don't need to be in the city to make your life hell, Adamas. You won't be able to hide from me, if you go through with your plan. Everywhere you go, everything you do, every time you stop to take a bloody piss, someone will be watching you on my behalf. And one day, one of those people will do to you what you're planning to do to Laurent. But you won't know who, and you won't know when.' His voice was low, almost a whisper, but Adamas was hooked on every word, eyes wide with fear. The stink exuding from the man changed abruptly, and Daniel grimaced at the realisation that Adamas had wet himself. That was a first.

'It'll be too late,' Adamas croaked, visibly trembling. 'Laurent will be dead.'

'But so will you, and so will Diora, and none of it will be worth it in the end. So I think it's in everyone's best interests if you go and get me whatever you bought from Virtan, and let me take it with me as I leave. Don't you think?' Daniel asked smoothly, his heartbeat surprisingly normal, all things considered. He should have felt awful, should have felt very wrong threatening this man until he soiled himself, but all he could feel was a sense of satisfaction. This in itself was a clear sign that he needed to rid himself of Daniel as quickly as possible, and never look back. But not *quite* yet.

'How do you know I won't kill him by some other means?' The retort was feeble at best, and Daniel's smirk widened.

'Because you're a coward. That's what poisoning is, isn't it? The coward's method of murder. Not brave enough to look someone in the eye as you take their life.' He folded his arms over his chest. 'Now go get it.'

He didn't need to ask again, Adamas jumping to life and running into the living room, where he pulled out a small metal chest. Taking a key from a chain around his neck, he unlocked the chest and grabbed a small brown paper bag. There were a few other things in the chest, but the lid slammed shut before Daniel could get a proper look, and Adamas locked it, thrusting the bag in his direction. 'I paid good money for that,' he grumbled as Daniel pocketed the bag. The teen rolled his eyes.

'One more thing, Adamas. If I were looking to talk to Diora, where might I find him?'

Adamas snorted. 'You really think I'd give up that sort of information? Men have been killed for less.'

'The thing is, though,' Daniel drawled, 'I will find Diora sooner or later. I know where Laurent lives, and eventually I'll get the information I need. If you don't help me out here, and I find him myself . . . who's to stop me sharing with him that you were in fact plotting to poison Laurent in order to take his place? I'm sure Diora would be very interested to hear how one of his most trusted men was going to betray him.'

Any colour that might have been left in Adamas's face drained rapidly at Daniel's words. He shook his head. 'He wouldn't believe you,' he insisted. 'He knows I'd never hurt him, he knows I'm loyal.'

'Does he? Because killing another man he trusts – trusts more than you, I'd say – doesn't sound like loyalty to me.' Daniel folded his arms, and Adamas glared at him viciously.

'Not if I get to him first. He'd never take your word over mine.'

Daniel's smirk widened. 'Oh, I was hoping you'd say that.' Without giving him a chance to react, he struck. Springing forward, he grabbed him by the shoulder and spun him around, reaching into his pocket in one smooth movement as his other hand brought his wrists together. Before Adamas knew what was happening, there was a flash of metal and Daniel had him handcuffed securely to the steel lamp brace above his head. Adamas's eyes were wide in alarm, and the cuffs rattled as he pulled against them. But Daniel was familiar with the structure of these light fittings, having repaired more than a few for work purposes – he wasn't going anywhere.

'You can't do this!' Adamas roared, rapidly sobering up in his panic. 'Let me go!'

'Tell me where Diora is,' Daniel said, stepping back as Adamas tried to kick out at him.

'Will you let me go if I do?'

'Tell me,' Daniel repeated, twisting Adamas's arm against the pull of the handcuffs, making him cry out in pain.

'All right, all right! He's in Petria, on Caria Street! You won't miss it when you get there, it's the biggest house on the street. But you'll be dead before you can get in.'

'You underestimate me,' Daniel said dismissively. Finally, he was getting somewhere! 'I'll be needing this, as well,' he added, reaching up to force the man's gold ring off his finger and slipping it into his pocket.

'Hey, you said you'd let me go if I told!' Adamas said, rattling his handcuffs emphatically. Daniel's lips curled at the edges, an eyebrow rising.

'Did I?' He chuckled. 'Don't worry, I'm sure someone will come by soon. If you're lucky. Now, I believe we're done here. Keep your eyes open, and your mouth shut. You never know who might be watching.'

He turned on his heel, ignoring the man cursing as he slipped out of the house, brushing his clammy palms against his trousers. Finally out of sight, tucked away in a little-used alley, he let out a long breath, leaning against the cold stone wall as the mentality of Daniel receded, leaving him shaking and horrified at what he had done – at who he had been. The residue of Daniel's power trip left him feeling wrung out and dirty, even after the tremors subsided. It was necessary, sometimes – men like Adamas only understood one thing, and that was force – but storms, he would be glad never to have to do that again.

He pushed away from the wall, flipping his hood up and vaulting over a railing on to the level below. He needed to rest. His lack of sleep was starting to show, and he couldn't afford to make mistakes. Then, finally, it would be time to meet Diora.

23

Noah hadn't intended to sleep very long, but his body clearly had other ideas; when he woke up it was dark outside, and the clock on his wall declared it to be almost eleven. He swore, jumping out of bed and rifling through his wardrobe for black clothing. He'd wasted most of the day!

He had to admit, though, that he felt refreshed from the sleep, and it gave him a chance to try and see Crysta before he went to the house on Caria Street. Adamas's words about Diora's guards killing him before he could even get through the front door had stuck in his mind. If he was going to go after Diora, he might not come out of it alive. He needed to at least try to warn Crysta that she was in danger.

Aware that he was running out of time, Noah grabbed his jacket and left the house, shutting the door silently behind him. Not once did he see or hear anything from his father; he was beginning to wonder if the man was OK, locked in the workshop for days on end. Had he emerged for food at any point? Had he slept? Not that Noah could see, but he hadn't exactly been the most attentive son recently. He called out to his father that he was heading out for a while, but there was no response. He'd pick the lock in the morning if the door was still locked, just to check on him. For now, he had to get to the palace.

The pre-festival celebrations were still going strong in the city, but the streets near the palace were quiet. The perimeter guards stood to attention at their posts, eyes drooping; it was nearing the end of their shift. Noah stayed well out of their sight, heading closer to the guard station.

The nearest guard to the building was about ten feet away, and it was almost too easy for him to creep up to the front of the building without being spotted. He would have been worried about the safety of the palace's inhabitants, but he knew the majority of intruders wouldn't be able to pull off what he was about to do. No one else had his combination of skill, inside knowledge and drive.

Picking up his pace as he drew within a few strides of the side wall of the imposing stone building, Noah counted down from three in his head, on the last count jumping up and reaching with outstretched arms for the lowest window sill, fingers scrabbling for purchase. He'd never been more glad of his height as he made it without too much of a problem, tucking his legs up to dig his leather-clad toes into a groove between the stones, then holding himself flush to the building. From there it was a slow climb upwards, and he eventually managed to perch on the window sill he'd been hanging from. Closing his eyes and slowing his breathing, Noah braced himself to continue upwards. He had to climb even further to make it over the top of the gates without eviscerating himself, and he could feel his heart hammering against his ribs so hard he thought they'd split as he hung from a window sill directly above the sharp

231

metal. He didn't linger, continuing his climb until he was safely within the palace gates. Then he began the careful manoeuvre downwards. Shimmying down the drainpipe, it was only a short drop to the ground, and Noah was as silent as a ghost as he landed on the paved courtyard. Now for the hard part of his little late-night excursion – the palace itself.

The courtyard was dark and silent as Noah hurried through, and as he crept around to the side of the building he could count on one hand the number of illuminated windows. He let out a relieved breath when he saw Crysta's bedroom window wasn't one of them. She was sleeping; good.

The palace was smooth-cut stone, hardly worn by age and storms, and Noah eyed it incredulously. He couldn't believe he was contemplating doing this. Crysta's window was four storeys up a sheer face of rock, and as his eyes scanned for hand and footholds he came up woefully short. It was an entirely likely possibility that he would fall and break his neck before he could even reach Crysta's room. 'This is a terrible idea,' he murmured to himself as he gritted his teeth and wiped his hands on his jacket front, reaching up for the nearest groove that looked even vaguely like a handhold. His palms were sweaty, making it harder to hold on, and he wished he'd had the forethought to bring some chalk dust along. It had been a long time since he'd needed to chalk his hands to climb a building, but he'd never attempted a building quite like the palace before.

His hand slipped, and he barely remembered not to shout out a curse as he scrabbled at the wall for a new hold. His pulse was racing faster now, his breathing shallow and quick, and he leaned into the wall to hang for a minute or two while he tried to calm himself. He didn't want to look down to find out how high up he was. He didn't want to know how far he had to fall.

Persevering, Noah gritted his teeth and propelled himself upwards, stretching for a nearby groove with a quiet grunt of exertion. His legs were shaking, his bruised knees and aching calves protesting at holding his body in such a precarious position. Daring to turn his head and glance at the window just at his right, he nearly sobbed in relief at seeing the curtains drawn. As far as he knew, it was the window to one of the many guest rooms, and drawn curtains meant the occupant wasn't likely to see him if he chose to rest there for a few moments.

Practically throwing himself on to the stone ledge, Noah sucked in a deep gulp of air, shoulders heaving with the effort. At the sudden relaxation, some of his muscles began to cramp painfully, forcing him to squeeze his eyes shut and bite down on his sleeve to stop himself crying out. He couldn't have said how long he sat on the window sill, riding the cramps out. Crysta's window was diagonally to the right above him, only the next floor up, but those few feet looked like miles to the exhausted teen.

When he could finally stand without his legs giving out on him, he wiped clammy hands on his trousers, wincing when he realised that not all of the moisture was sweat. Hopefully he wasn't leaving bloody handprints on the wall up to the window.

Noah felt as if he might pass out with relief when he eventually swung himself up to crouch on Crysta's window sill. The curtains were half drawn, just the way she liked them, and he peered in through the glass, a smile on his face at seeing her sprawled out in bed fast asleep, her silky hair lying haphazardly across her pillow, highlighted by the glow of the moonlight. Part of him felt low for watching her sleep, but he pushed the feeling away, testing the window. He was there for a reason, not just to watch her.

The window was locked and it took a tricky bit of balance and recklessness to get it open without falling off the sill. Managing to create a gap big enough to fit through, he eased himself into the room, stepping down on to the desk beneath the window and flinching as it creaked under his weight. Hastily clambering down to the floor, he left the window open, edging closer to the bed. How would he wake her up without startling her?

He stood several feet from the bed, staring for a moment. His heart physically hurt at the sight of her after having parted on such bad terms. He wanted nothing more than to take her in his arms, to beg her to forgive him and let him explain himself. Crysta didn't stir as he moved in closer, her face completely relaxed in sleep. She was paler than usual, with dark circles under her eyes, and it looked like she'd been crying. Noah's chest ached.

'Crysta,' he murmured gently. 'Crysta, wake up.' She didn't move, so he stepped up to the edge of the bed. 'Crysta, it's me, wake up.' He reached out tentatively for her shoulder, intending to shake her awake, but before he could touch her there was a blur of movement, and the next thing he knew he had a knife aimed at his throat and piercing grey eyes were glaring at him without even a hint of sleep.

It took a few moments for Crysta to recognise him, and when she did, her eyes widened in surprise and her grip on the knife faltered. Noah took the opportunity to bring a hand up and relieve her of it, tossing it on the carpet behind him. Crysta was terrifying enough without a blade in her hand.

'Noah,' she breathed, stunned. 'What in storms are you doing here? How did you even get in?' she exclaimed in a hiss, pulling her quilt up to her chest as she sat up properly. 'What did you do to Damien?'

'Nothing, nothing,' he insisted quickly. 'Damien doesn't even know I'm in here.'

'Then how . . . ?'

'Window,' Noah supplied, jerking a thumb behind him. Crysta stared blankly.

'Noah, my bedroom is fifty feet above ground level.'

He nodded, gaze steady.

'I know.'

She blinked, then huffed, shaking her head. 'Reckless idiot. What are you doing here? I could've killed you just then,' she whispered angrily.

'I needed to talk to you.'

'I don't want to hear it,' she retorted immediately, her tone venomous. 'I don't think there's anything you could possibly say to fix what you've done.' Noah winced, but persevered. He could clear the air with Crysta when he knew she was safe, but he had more important things to tell her first.

'You need to listen to me, Crysta, it's important. Someone's trying to kill you.'

'Damien!' she called, and Noah's eyes went wide in alarm. He lurched forward, placing a hand over her mouth to silence her shout.

'I'm serious! I overheard it when I was in the lower city –'

'With your girlfriend?' she spat, voice muffled by his hand as she struggled away from him.

'*No*,' he said, flinching. 'Someone is planning to poison you at the opening ceremony, I don't know who or how, but you have to listen to me – your life is in serious danger!'

She wrestled him away from her, taking in a deep breath. 'DAMIEN!' she screamed, so loud Noah thought his eardrums might burst. Before he could move the door burst open and Damien came running in, stopping in his tracks when he saw Noah.

'What in the gods – how did you get in here? It's the middle of the blasted night!' He shut the door behind him to avoid drawing more guards to the room.

'He says he climbed in,' Crysta declared skeptically. 'Through the window.' Damien looked at Noah in absolute bewilderment, then over to the open window.

'He . . . right. Of course he did. Well, however you got here doesn't change the fact that you're trespassing in a princess's bedroom at one in the bloody morning! If you were anyone else I'd have shot you dead by now,' Damien growled, stepping forward to grab Noah by the shoulder and drag him further back from the bed.

'Listen, Damien, you need to let me speak. A man is going to try to assassinate Crysta at the festival, he wants to poison her. I heard him in the lower city the night before the court dinner.'

'If you heard before the dinner, why didn't you say anything then?' Crysta asked sharply.

'I should have. But I hesitated because I had no information and I didn't want to worry you! All I knew then was that a man wanted to assassinate you, and, well, then everything went a bit downhill.' Crysta snorted.

'The guards would have heard,' she said. 'You're lying, trying to scare me into keeping you close. Do you really think I'm that gullible?' Her words were harsh but her expression didn't match them, and Noah shrugged off Damien's grip to take a step forward.

'The guards are never in the lower city, they wouldn't know a thing. Do you really think I'd lie about something as important as your safety? Crysta, love, *please.*' He reached out to take her hand, squeezing it tightly. Her gaze met his, and he tried to express as much apology as he could without words, wanting nothing more than to hold her tight and hide her away from anyone who might do her harm. 'You need to trust me. You did before.'

'That's enough,' Damien interrupted, grabbing Noah once more, tighter this time. Crysta shook herself, face hardening. Noah cursed silently; if Damien hadn't been there she might have listened.

'You've caused enough problems around here, Noah. My men are the best Erova has to offer; if there was something going on, we'd know. Unless you've got proof? A name perhaps?'

Tearing his gaze away from Crysta, Noah clenched a hand in his hair. 'Not . . . exactly. I don't have a name, but I know that whoever it is bought velora from Tor Virtan's pharmacy in Fausia, and he sounded like a nobleman. It's not much, but you have to believe me, someone is planning to kill you, Crysta!'

'Just go!' she shouted, her voice cracking as a sob escaped. Tears gathered in her eyes, her hands clenched tight in her bedsheets. 'Haven't you done enough to hurt me already? I said I never wanted to see you again, and I meant it.' Her breath hitched as she tried to calm herself. 'I'm so *tired*, Noah. I've got the festival to deal with – I've got Rosa and my parents to deal with, thanks to what you made her do. I just want to sleep, and to forget you ever existed.' She visibly crumpled, flinching when he made to try and comfort her.

'You can't fix this, Noah. You betrayed my trust in the worst way possible, and there's no going back from that.' She looked utterly broken, her shoulders slumped and her knees tucked up to her chest like a small child after a nightmare. Noah felt his heart twist at seeing her like that. At knowing he and he alone had caused it. Did Rosa look the same? How had Leon and Sofie reacted? He had been thrown out before he could see that, and he felt nauseous just thinking about having caused such difficulties between Rosa and her parents. Maybe Crysta was right; maybe he couldn't fix what he'd done.

'I'm going,' he said, relaxing against Damien's restraint. 'But please, wear your armour at the opening ceremony. And the mask I made for you. I . . . I hope you like it. And tell Rosa I'm sorry, would you? I never meant to hurt her. I never wanted to make her feel ashamed of her feelings for Lena.' How he'd treated Rosa was one of many things he

238

truly hated himself for, and he wouldn't be surprised if the girl never spoke to him again.

'You should've thought about that before you did what you did,' Crysta spat, shaking her head. 'Go, Noah. And if you climb through my window again you'll find spiked wire on the sill.'

Damien began to march him from the room, and Noah craned his neck to look back at the woman on the bed, catching her gaze.

'I love you, Crysta. Through all else, that hasn't changed, and it never will,' he vowed. She turned away, and Damien dragged him out of the room, shutting the door quietly behind them.

'You've got some nerve, you know that?' the captain muttered under his breath, taking Noah down the servants' stairs so as to avoid drawing attention from anyone who might be wandering the corridors so late at night. 'Did you honestly climb to her window?'

'I think I left some blood on the walls,' Noah confirmed, looking down at his scraped hands. 'Check for yourself in the morning.' Damien shook his head in disbelief.

'You're a fool,' he declared. 'You could've killed yourself.'

'It would have been worth it, to make sure she's safe,' Noah replied without missing a beat. That made Damien falter, but the older man pretended he hadn't heard.

They reached the antechamber Noah always used when leaving the palace, and he felt a disorienting sense of déjà vu as Damien dragged him all the way across the courtyard to the guard station.

'I won't warn you again, Noah,' he said as he led him through the station towards the front door. 'Stay out of Crysta's way, and out of mine, or you'll end up in prison, or worse. You're lucky she didn't ask for you to be locked up.'

'I know,' he agreed; their patience with him was quickly wearing thin. 'But, Damien, listen to me about the assassin. I wouldn't make this up, not when it comes to Crysta. I'd never do anything to put her in danger. I know I don't have much right now, but I'm going to find out more, I swear it. I won't let Crysta get hurt. There's no risk in listening to me. Make sure she's well protected. Her food too.'

Noah watched Damien's face with bated breath. He prayed to the gods that Damien would take his advice and raid Virtan's pharmacy. At least then he might believe him about the assassin and start investigating for himself. Finally, the captain's jaw squared, his face hardening.

'The festival is only a few days away. I'm busy.' Noah winced at the man's words, but nodded in acceptance. He didn't blame Damien for hating him; he hated himself right now.

'Right. Of course. I'll just . . . go, then.' Shaking free of the captain's grip, he made for the door under his own power, not sure his knees would survive another toss to the ground outside. Damien didn't make any move to stop him, instead leaning on the end of a nearby desk and folding his arms as he watched him leave.

The air outside seemed bitterly cold now that his adrenalin rush had receded, and he huddled deeper into his jacket, picking up his pace for the walk home.

It was almost sunrise by the time Noah got in. He washed the grit from his cut hands and wiped them with antiseptic, cursing to himself in the silent bathroom. Despite the hour, he had to focus on the next part of his plan. He'd warned Damien, even if the man didn't want to listen. And he'd told Crysta he loved her, whether she believed it or not. It was finally time to face Diora.

24

It was a virtual reflex at this point: covering visible skin in pale make-up; shading his face to subtly alter its contours; hiding his natural dark hair with the blond wig. After three years of making the transition, he had it down to a science. But this time was different – if all went as planned, this time would be the last.

His hands shook as he raised them to put in his contacts, and he took a deep breath to steady himself. He could do this. One more stint as Daniel, and it would all be over. One way or another.

For someone who was walking into a situation knowing that he might not come out of it alive, he was surprisingly calm. His mind was clear and his pulse steady as he sank into his desk chair and dug around the drawer for his notebook, ripping out a clean page. Then, he began to write.

Dear Damien,
Please don't burn this in anger, at least not until after you've read it.

There's a lot I've been hiding from you over the last couple of years, though I hope once you know the truth you'll understand why I did so. I just wanted to help people. I just wanted to make things better.

I know you've heard of Daniel Novak, and that you're aware of what he does in the lower city. What you don't know is that he and I are one and the same. That disguise Rosa mentioned, when she saw me on the bridge with Emilie? That was Daniel. Emilie was an important source of information – she is the younger sister of one of the men who has been tormenting the lower city for far, far too long. I don't know how much you know of Diora, but he's cruel, he's dangerous, and he needs to be stopped. I have tried to do this myself, but if you're reading this letter, it means I didn't succeed. It means Diora won, and that his empire is bigger than I can handle.

I won't waste your time with the details, as all that will be in the papers sent along with this letter. Everything you need to know – everything Daniel knows – is in there, do with it what you can.

There's a more urgent matter at hand. I wasn't lying about the plot to assassinate Crysta. I told you about Tor Virtan, but his details are in the papers too if you need more convincing. Perhaps you'll be able to succeed in finding the assassin where I failed. I kept you in the dark until now because I feared that bringing in the guards would send Diora into hiding. That isn't my problem, now.

This is not some last-ditch attempt at trying to win Crysta back. If you're reading this, I'm dead, so it hardly matters anyway. Whatever Crysta thinks of me – whatever you think of me – I refuse to let anything happen to her if I can help it.

I hate goodbyes, so I'll make this brief. You have been a great friend to me, Damien, and I have appreciated that more than you shall ever know. You may not think much of me now, but I have always thought highly of you.

I would write how much Crysta means to me, how much I can't bear to be parted from her, but I doubt she wants to hear it. Please just tell her I love her more than words can describe, and I'm sorry for everything. I'm sorry to Rosa too; I will never forgive myself for how I treated her, but rest assured the Goddess will no doubt enact a suitable revenge once I am in her domain.

There is always more to be said, but time is running short. Please, my friend, look after Crysta for me now that I cannot. You have been doing so far longer than I, after all.

Love,
Noah

Blinking away the prickling sensation in his eyes, he dug an envelope from the assorted detritus on his desk, folding the letter away neatly. Before sealing it, however, he went through his notebook with military efficiency, ripping out any scrap of information related to his ongoing work, any titbit or note that had yet to be resolved. Every bit of it went in the envelope – if Daniel never made it back from his confrontation with Diora, he wanted Damien to know everything. Dead men had no use for secrets, after all.

Only when he was sure he had included everything did he seal the envelope, grabbing another piece of paper for a much briefer missive.

Da,

I've gone after Diora. If I have yet to return by noon, then I fear I shall not be returning at all, and I must then ask you to take this envelope to Damien as quickly as possible. Crysta's life depends on it.

I'm sorry — I'm sorry I won't be coming home, and I'm sorry for getting into this mess in the first place, and I'm sorry I couldn't be the son you deserve, the son you and Ma would have been proud of. I tried my best, but we both know there's no excusing clumsiness, and I have been nothing but clumsy in my handling of things these past few years. Please do not mourn me like you mourn Ma. You have too much joy in your heart to let it fade to darkness. And don't you dare take the blame for any of this. You have taught me so much about what it means to be a man, to be a good person. I only regret I wasn't a better student.

I love you,
Noah

Now there was no hiding the tears on his cheeks. He wiped them away furiously, folding the paper once the ink was dry. With any luck, his father would never read that note. But he didn't want to take any chances; it would destroy him if Noah just disappeared one day and never came back.

Setting the bulging envelope on his desk, the note propped on top of it, he prayed his father would stay in the workshop for most of the morning. He hadn't even seen the man in over a day, but it would be just his luck if Evander decided to greet his son with breakfast and start to worry before there was cause. Goddess willing, he'd be home before there was even time to miss him. He tried to convince himself of that, ignoring the tug in his chest that urged him to go and wake his father, hug him goodbye and tell him he loved him, just in case it was his last chance. He shook it off; he couldn't afford to think like that now.

Daniel left his satchel behind for once, then reached under his bed for a small wooden box. He smiled faintly as he did so, imagining a day when he no longer had to split his time between two identities; no more sleeping in alcoves to keep an eye on people; no more following suspects around the city for days on end; no more having to make excuses to Crysta as to why he couldn't see her that day. Of course, as things stood, she didn't want to see him anyway, but . . . he would work on that. He'd been so reluctant to give Daniel up at first, wanting to hold on to that feeling of power, but after all the trouble his alter ego had got him into recently he couldn't wait to be rid of him. All his affairs were in order, he'd tied up all the loose ends that mattered – except one. A few more hours, and then he'd be free.

Inside the box was a small pistol he'd built himself, resting in a discreet shoulder holster. Only those with registry forms could keep firearms on their person, and they couldn't be filed until the age of twenty, but Damien had bent some rules after discovering that Noah had built his own pistol in his free time, teaching him how to use it responsibly before allowing him to keep it.

He strapped on the holster underneath his jacket, the firearm hidden from view. He'd never used it before, except to practise his aim, and he hoped desperately he only had to fire it once. He wasn't even sure he'd have the courage to do that much.

Running through his mental checklist, he took a deep breath, turning for the door. He could do this. He had to.

Petria was in a part of the lower city Daniel hardly ever visited; it was inhabited mostly by families with moderate incomes, who never got into trouble and were so close to the upper city that they were practically part of it, but for lack of birthright. It was a residential area full of neat little houses with the smallest of gardens, all near identical in their rows. Some were decorated for the festival, festooned with bright ribbons or paper lanterns. Daniel's brow furrowed; had Adamas lied to him?

Finally, he reached a rooftop on Caria Street, and things began to make sense. The house he stopped in front of was larger than the ones around it, set apart by narrow stretches of grass and a tall steel perimeter fence. Nothing about it was particularly unusual or suspicious, but upon closer inspection Daniel noticed that the man across the road, sitting on a bench under a street lamp with a book open in his lap, had not turned his page in several minutes. The woman two doors down had been watering the same hanging basket for so long water was freely gushing from its bottom. And around the back of the house, visible only to Daniel from his raised viewpoint, were two men who seemed to be playing the slowest game of cards he had ever seen in his life. On their own none of them would have been particularly remarkable, even in the semi-dark. Some people had odd habits, and Daniel had definitely seen stranger things. But the gold ring glinting on each person's right middle finger told him he was right. They were guarding the house, there was no doubt about that.

It made sense, he supposed, for the man to live far removed from the majority of his business. Out here, where people were happy just to go about their own lives, was the perfect place to hide. Diora's men could come and go as often as they liked, and no one would have a clue.

Daniel found a good perch on the roof of the house next door, settling down to watch carefully, noting each guard as they became apparent. Getting in wasn't going to be easy. Still, he thought he had an advantage – his usual methods of breaking and entering weren't exactly common enough for Diora's guards to expect them. If he was clever enough, he could slip under their radar.

Removing Adamas's stolen ring from his pocket, he slid it on his right middle finger. It was a little loose, but not likely to slip off. That would make things easier, once he got inside. He kept low, scurrying across the roof to be in a better position when he got the chance to jump. The back of the house was the least guarded, and was also the shortest distance from the only window big enough for him to squeeze through – if he could get to the third floor and open it without being seen.

The stone of Diora's house was almost as smooth as the palace walls. Daniel knew that, much like the palace, if he *believed* he could climb it the chances were that he would. But if he doubted himself, even for a split second, he would fall. Climbing was an all-or-nothing kind of venture, which was half the reason he enjoyed it so much. The urge to push himself further, to challenge himself past what he'd thought were his limits, gave him a high like no other. He just wished he were still doing it purely for his own enjoyment.

The guards around the back of the house were standing close together discussing something in low voices. One of them was constantly checking his pocket watch, clearly impatient for his shift to end. The impatient guard gestured to his companion, slumping in relief and shaking his hand. The pair went their separate ways, leaving the back of the house unguarded – for now at least. Breath catching in his throat, Daniel stood up; he wouldn't get a better opportunity than this. He didn't know when the next shift of guards would arrive. He had to move fast.

Swinging himself over the edge of the rooftop, he carefully climbed down to the cobbled street below, eyeing the fence in front of him. It was a basic wrought-iron fence with barbed points on top, about nine or ten feet tall. He'd scaled worse. Gripping the smooth metal as best he could, Daniel slowly worked his way up by wedging his feet between the vertical bars, inching higher and higher. His hands ached with the effort of trying to get a firm hold on the round bars, but he pushed through, stretching up the last few inches to grab hold of the horizontal bar across the top of the fence. Just above it were the barbed protrusions, and Daniel winced at the sight of them. They would leave a nasty scar if he made a wrong move.

Hanging there for a few moments to get his breath back, he didn't dare check to see if the new guards had arrived. Heart racing, he brought his feet up high, bracing them between the bars and leaving him tucked in a ball. His next few movements had to be timed and placed perfectly.

'One, two, *three*!' he breathed, on the last count pushing up with his legs and letting go with his hands, rocketing upwards and straight towards the sharp twists of steel. Bringing one foot up, he stepped on the horizontal bar between two barbs, forcing himself the rest of the way up and over the fence without cutting himself. The grass helped soften the blow as he hit the ground, falling seamlessly into a forward roll to avoid breaking his ankles, and popping smoothly back up on to his feet.

His chest was heaving, his heart beating so fast it made him a little light-headed, but he didn't have time to dwell on it. He'd been quiet in his landing, but there was no guarantee the guard at the front gate hadn't heard him. Sprinting towards the wall below the third-floor window, Daniel shook the tension out of his shoulders and began to climb.

Compared to the palace walls this was a walk in the park, but it still required focus. Digging into the tiny grooves between the stone blocks with his fingertips, he used the edge of a window sill below as a foothold to propel himself up. Sometimes his height was detrimental to his climbing, his long limbs making it hard to tuck himself up for some of the closer-together holds, but in this case he was already halfway there, through virtue of his height and long reach. His pulse was like a ticking clock in his ears, reminding him that he didn't have long before his luck ran out and the guards spotted him.

The third-floor window had a narrow sill, barely enough to perch on as he tried to find a crack to pry the window open. There was no lock on it that he could see, but it fit fairly snugly into its frame.

Sliding one of his lock–picking tools into a small gap at the side where the window met its frame, he wiggled it, desperately hoping for something to catch. 'Come on, come on, please,' he muttered under his breath, trying to find the mechanism. He felt like he was far too exposed, sitting on the side of the building, as though any minute he would be spotted and shot down.

Finally, something clicked, and he managed to pry the window open just enough to fit his fingernails in the gap, wrenching it the rest of the way and diving through before he could lose his balance. Luckily the corridor was clear, and he scrambled to his feet, shutting the window behind him. He was in.

Pulling his hood up over his head, Daniel twisted the ring on his finger to reassure himself it was still there and started down the corridor. Diora was somewhere in this building, and Daniel was so close he could almost taste success. But getting in had been the easy part – now things would get a little tricky.

The inside of Diora's house wasn't quite what Daniel had expected; there were no blatant signs of the man's wealth, nor seedy back rooms filled with crates of illegal substances. In fact, there was very little in there at all. The walls were all painted pale grey, with dark wood panelling and furniture. There were a couple of paintings hung here and there, portraits of people Daniel didn't recognise, but other than that the house seemed fairly impersonal, like it was empty and waiting for a new owner. Had he not seen all the guards outside he would have been sure he was in the wrong house.

At the end of the corridor was the top of a narrow wooden staircase, spiralling down through the entire house. He had little clue which floor Diora's office might be on.

Hearing footsteps on the glossy oak floors, he tensed, keeping his head ducked and walking straight for the staircase. The last thing he wanted was someone stopping to talk to him.

The woman approaching from the corridor behind him didn't seem to question his presence and followed him downstairs, clearly more certain of her destination than Daniel was of his. She turned off on the second floor, and he stopped on the floor below, thinking. It was unlikely that Diora's office was on the ground floor – that would leave it open to far too many people coming and going. It was possible it was on the third floor, where Daniel had entered, but again that seemed unlikely; that floor was probably Diora's living quarters, furthest away from any of his employees who might be wandering around. He guessed it must be on the first or second floor.

Backing up the stairs to return to the now empty second floor, he eyed the many plain doors lining the corridor, wondering if any of them might be Diora's office. Before he could decide whether or not to look and find out, one of the doors opened and a bearded man stepped out. He froze when he spotted Daniel, eyeing him carefully. Daniel ducked his head to obscure his features with the hood of his jacket, feeling the blood drain from his face.

'Who are you?' the man asked, taking a step forward. 'And how did you get in?'

The man's hand moved to his hip, pushing back his jacket far enough for Daniel to see the holster strapped to his belt. That wasn't good.

25

Rushing forward, Daniel pushed the man back into the room he'd come from and shut the door behind them before the alarm could be raised. The man scowled in rage, tearing himself from Daniel's grip. 'I've seen you before,' he hissed, trying to pin him against the wall. Daniel, as usual, had the height advantage, and he flipped them around until it was Diora's man that was trapped.

'Hel—' The attempted cry for help was cut off as Daniel shoved a hand over his mouth, flinching as the short burst of sound echoed slightly within the room. Had anyone heard it?

'That wasn't nice, now, was it?' he muttered, giving the man an annoyed look. Finding Diora would be impossible if everyone in the house was hunting him down.

The man struggled against Daniel's vicelike grip, making stifled sounds against his palm and attempting to reach for his gun. Daniel grimaced before reeling back and snapping forward, slamming the man's head against the solid brick wall. He dropped like a stone, and Daniel dragged his unconscious body beneath a table, hoping no one had heard the muffled thud. He now had even less time to find Diora; the man wouldn't be unconscious forever.

The room he was in seemed to be a nondescript office full of files, and Daniel's fingers itched to search through them for more information on Diora's crimes. But if he did this right it wouldn't matter much longer, anyway.

Easing the door open, he let out a relieved breath at seeing the hallway was empty. Heart racing, he sprinted across the room to hit the staircase, praying to the Goddess for luck as he ran.

Sliding to a halt so suddenly he almost fell down the stairs, he retreated several paces at hearing footsteps descending. He ducked back into the corridor he'd come from, panic rising as the footsteps drew closer. He looked frantically around for a place to hide. The corridor was dimly lit and the ceilings were high. An idea was forming, and he lurched towards the very end door before he had time to think it through. Using the doorframe as a stepping stone, he hoisted himself up and made an awkward twisting manoeuvre on the way, pushing off with his legs to stretch across and then grip the top of the opposite door frame. Bracing his feet high on the wall and using the end wall to lean on, he kept himself tucked almost flush against the ceiling, stretched from one side of the hallway to the other. It wasn't comfortable, and he could already feel his forearms shaking with the effort. Gritting his teeth, he held on tight, trying not to breathe too loudly. So long as no one looked up, he'd be fine.

Footsteps echoed closer, and Daniel felt sweat trickling beneath his shirt collar. He held his breath as two women turned into his corridor, talking quietly between themselves. They didn't look his way, slipping into the room at the opposite end of the corridor without a moment of hesitation. Silence reigned once more, and Daniel let himself drop as quietly as he could, shaking out his aching arms. 'This is getting ridiculous,' he breathed to himself, jogging silently back towards the stairs.

His luck changed on the floor below, where a man stood guarding the door at the end of the corridor, his arms by his side and a pistol at his hip. There would be no reason to guard an office unless it contained something important. Or someone. Bingo.

The guard at the door looked up when Daniel started walking down the corridor towards him. 'I'm sorry, I'm afraid the Boss is in a meeting at the moment, you're going to have to wait if you want to talk to him.'

'No, I don't think I am,' he replied evenly, and before the guard could even blink Daniel punched him swiftly in the temple. For the second time in ten minutes he watched a man slump into unconsciousness, catching him before he could hit the ground. 'I seem to be making a habit of this.' He had Damien to thank for that move; the captain had taught him to incapacitate as quickly and painlessly as possible. The guard would have an absolute thunderstorm of a headache when he woke up, but should otherwise be fine.

Swallowing sharply as his throat grew dry, Daniel reached for the door, pushing it open. The room inside was large and was the only part of the house he'd seen so far that looked like it actually belonged to someone. The tall mahogany shelves were full of books and trinkets and even a few photographs, and the walls were a muted gold. In the centre of the room sat a large wooden desk with one chair behind it and one in front; both chairs were occupied.

It didn't surprise him to see Laurent sitting in the chair in front of the desk. What did surprise him, however, was the man behind the desk.

Diora was much older than Daniel had expected. He had thinning white hair and a deeply wrinkled face, his hands trembling around a mug of tea. He wasn't particularly large, and his clothes fit like he had once been a much broader man but had shrunk with age. For someone who ruled the lower city with an iron fist, he was a sorry sight.

Both men looked up at Daniel's entrance, startled, and Laurent immediately jumped to his feet. Daniel nudged the door shut behind him with his foot; he could do nothing about the unconscious guard outside, but he could at least attempt to be stealthy about his confrontation. 'Novak,' Laurent accused, making Daniel half smile.

'My reputation precedes me, I see,' he replied, lowering his hood.

'What in the name of the gods are you doing in here? How did you get in? The guards –'

'The one outside the door will be fine when he wakes up, and the others have no idea I'm here. Really, Diora, your security is a little lax, all things considered,' Daniel said, addressing the elderly man directly. Diora smirked, leaning back in his chair.

'So you're the infamous Daniel Novak,' he drawled, his voice hoarse. 'I must admit, I'm surprised we haven't met before. You've been quite the thorn in my side these past few years.'

'I try,' Daniel replied, striding further into the room. 'You're not what I expected.'

'Thought I'd be younger?' Diora presumed, chuckling. 'Most do. That's why Laurent here does most of the business on my behalf. He's much more intimidating, don't you think?' Diora set his mug down, clasping his hands in front of him. 'To what do I owe the pleasure, then?'

Daniel blinked, taken aback. The man was being far calmer about his intrusion than he'd expected. Diora was full of surprises it seemed.

'Sir, do you really think indulging him is a good idea?' Laurent said hesitantly. 'I can have him removed if you wish.'

'No, no. He's come all this way, let him say his piece. Though if that holster he's trying to hide is anything to go by, I know exactly what he's here for.' Daniel froze, and Laurent took a threatening step towards him. At Diora's raised hand, however, he halted. 'Calm down, Laurent. The day this brat has the guts to shoot an old man is the day I eat my own hat. Now, Mr Novak, come. What grief do you have with me? I protect this fair city where our dear friends the guards fall woefully short. People look up to me, they love me. What do you gain from destroying that?'

'They only look up to you because they don't know what you're truly doing to them,' Daniel argued. 'I know about everything, Diora. All the shady deals and side payments to anyone conducting illegal ventures, keeping them going so that your men can swoop in and "save" people from their clutches, taking payment in recompense. You're earning money from both sides! Tell me, where has that left you? Alone in a house that's far too big for one person, old and frail and surrounded by money you'll never be able to spend. Was it worth it? Hurting all those people?'

'Oh, absolutely,' Diora said, the facade of a harmless old man melting away into a vicious grin. 'I'd do it thrice over if I could. It's fascinating how gullible people are, how easily led. All I had to do was gather some young men and women who wanted to do good in the world but weren't too bright about it, have them help a few people in sticky situations, and suddenly I have a reputation. I can do anything I like! So long as I'm discreet, and pay people enough to keep them quiet, I can sell whatever I want to whoever I want and everyone in this stupid city believes me to be their virtuous saviour, keeping them from harm where the guards can't be bothered! The only one coming anywhere close to my reputation is you, you little upstart. I should've had you killed.'

'You tried, two years ago,' Daniel pointed out darkly, watching Diora's grin widen, his brown eyes flashing.

'If I'd tried my best you wouldn't be here, trust me, lad. I figured you'd get bored, or meet your own unfortunate demise sooner or later. You only had a handle on a fraction of my empire. It was like having a particularly persistent fly in my face – irritating, but not a threat.' The old man chuckled at the look on Daniel's face. 'Oh, you poor boy, I bet you thought you had me all figured out, didn't you? Thought you had your eyes on everything I did. How naive of you! You barely scratched the surface.'

Glaring, Daniel rounded the desk, smoothly unholstering his gun. 'It doesn't matter how much I know,' he spat. 'It's not like you'll be alive much longer to continue your business.'

'Look at me, brat, I haven't got many more years left in me anyway,' Diora retorted, looking unconcerned as Daniel pointed the firearm directly at his head. Laurent, still on the other side of the desk, had his own pistol in hand, pointing at Daniel. But he didn't shoot. 'My empire is strong enough to support itself without me leading the way! I have Laurent to take over when I'm gone, and plenty of other men willing to take his place should you kill us both today.'

Daniel kept the gun steady, his other hand slipping into his jacket pocket for a moment as he leaned one hip against the desk. 'I know enough to bring the guards swarming into the lower city like flies on a carcass, once the festival is over,' he said. 'I've already got people closing up shop just at the *threat* of my punishment. If you really think your little empire will survive once the truth gets out about what you've been doing, you've truly lost some sense in your old age. People will never trust the gold ring again. And all that money you've amassed will just sit and rot. Sooner or later your name will be barely a thought in people's memories, little more than a blemish on Talen's great history. You might have an empire now, but what good is that if everything you've worked so hard for stays underground? There will be more documentation on the king's sneezes than there will be on you.'

'I didn't do it for the legacy, lad,' Diora told him, looking almost senile in his smugness, eyes bright. 'I didn't even do it for the money. Though that was definitely an incentive. No, I did it because I *could*. With the guards too busy worrying about the upper city, the lower city was ripe for the taking. And the upper city's going the same way; all I need

260

is one poor harvest to get my foot in the door, and those arrogant upper-city types will be worshipping the very ground I walk on!'

'The upper city would never fall for your lies,' Daniel spat. He was surprised when Diora chuckled at that, leaning forward conspiratorially.

'Oh, and you'd know all about the upper city, wouldn't you?' There was something in his tone that made Daniel freeze uneasily. 'I let you run about and play the hero for long enough, but as you recently started sticking your nose a little *too* far into my business, I thought I'd best prepare to cut it off if necessary. The *mysterious* Daniel Novak – you're a hard man to find, for someone ever present. But as good as you might be at hiding, my men are better at finding. And wasn't it so very *interesting* to learn that when Daniel Novak leaves for the day, he retreats north of the river?'

Something must have shown on Daniel's face as Diora let out a quiet noise of triumph. 'Didn't think anyone saw you, did you, brat?' he taunted. 'Funny how you say you're all about the protection of the lower city, when you're one of those upper-class bastards who let it go to the dogs.'

'You know *nothing* about me,' Daniel hissed, making Diora tilt his head in consideration.

'I will do soon, though,' he replied. 'After all, every man comes from somewhere. Every man has a home ... parents.' Daniel flinched, and Diora smirked. 'There we go. I knew it couldn't be too hard to find your weak spot. Everybody has one, if you know where to look.' He leaned back in his chair, as if Daniel had merely popped in for tea and a chat.

Daniel's stomach turned at the thought of Diora's men following him home, finding his father – finding his true identity. He couldn't allow that to happen. 'If you were hoping to catch me off guard, I'm afraid warning me of your plans isn't the best way to go about it,' he said, trying to keep his voice calm and steady. Diora chuckled.

'I don't need you off guard, boy. I've got bigger problems than your sticky little fingers in my business. Though I'm sure if I asked, Laurent here would be all too happy to cut those fingers off,' he added with a bloodthirsty smirk. 'You won't leave this house alive, so it matters little to me. You'll be too dead to care when I bend your precious monarchy to my will, and put my own men in charge of this Goddess-forsaken city.'

Connections that Daniel had been too scared to make before started clicking into place in his mind. 'It *is* you who wants the princess dead,' he breathed, horrified. One of Diora's eyebrows rose.

'Oh, you know about that one, do you?' he mused, unconcerned. 'Well done you. Not that it matters. That older princess is rather ... headstrong, is she not? The young one spooks at the sound of her own voice – she'll be a much better fit for the sort of monarchy I want. Get rid of that little maid she's gone and fallen for, give her a husband who'll keep her in line, and Talen is mine for the taking. And, of course, with Talen comes the Talen trade agreements; the rest of the lords of Erova will fall in line, one by one, until the only name on their lips is mine. I don't even need to live to see the end of it – the wheels are already in motion, brat, and I'm afraid you're too late to stop them.'

'Over my dead body,' Daniel growled, fury boiling over so much that the hand holding the gun began to tremble.

'Yes, well, that's sort of the plan,' Diora agreed. 'Now don't you see why I do what I do? I can pull whatever strings I want and people will still look upon me as their saviour, their protector. Find the right idiots and pay them enough, you can even get them to do your bidding and think it's their idea.' He laughed, shaking his head. 'That poor brainless outlander thinks I'll promise him the younger princess if he kills her sister, he practically *begged* me for the job. Anything to get above his foolish brothers.'

Daniel latched on to the snippet of information, filing it away for later. 'And he's not a suitable candidate? Not easily manipulated enough?' he pressed, hoping against hope that he could get Diora to slip up, to mention a name. The old man smirked.

'That little snake is far too selfish to be of use to me. But he has access to the opening ceremony, which is what I need. It'll be quite the show, don't you think?' He chuckled. 'Little Princess Crysta, dropping dead in the middle of the biggest event of the year. No surer sign that the Goddess is displeased with the monarchy. People will be begging me to take over, once I've rescued them from starvation with my food stores.'

'You won't live that long,' Daniel vowed, his resolve strengthening. Any doubt he might have had about ending Diora's life was gone – if he let the man live everyone he cared about would suffer. His father, Crysta, Rosa and the king and queen; he couldn't let Diora and his gang get to them. And yet, he couldn't quite bring himself to pull the trigger.

'There's a reason the lower city looks up to me – it's because I step in and put a stop to things when people cause trouble.'

'And then you just blackmail them into behaving,' Diora finished for him in a conversational tone. 'That's how it works for you, right? Protect those who you think deserve it, threaten those who don't do what you want. Now why does *that* sound familiar?' He paused as if pretending to think. Daniel's mouth opened but nothing came out, all arguments dying in his throat.

Diora seemed aware he'd gained the upper hand, for his smirk widened almost comically. 'Truth hurts, doesn't it, brat? But if you embrace it, if you admit why you really love the work you do, you'll be better off. I know I was.' He reached for his tea, holding the mug between his hands as his gaze stayed steadily on Daniel. 'All that power, the feeling of being *needed* by those simpletons who had no idea I was the very evil they were paying me to protect them from. You must know some of what I'm talking about, lad. Doesn't it feel *wonderful* to have people rely on you for their safety? To know that you are all that stands between that person and certain tragedy? You and I aren't so dissimilar, after all.'

Daniel stepped closer, the muzzle of his pistol pressed against the centre of Diora's forehead. The man didn't even flinch. 'We are *nothing* alike,' Daniel growled. 'I protect people because they don't have the means to protect themselves, and I ask for nothing in return. You manipulate them into giving you their money to save them from the demons *you* created.'

'Yes, well, you're only young. There's still time,' Diora said with a shrug. He brought his mug to his lips, seemingly unconcerned that Daniel was standing right there with a gun to his head. 'Though perhaps we aren't too alike, after all. I know I, even at your age, would never have taken this long to kill someone. What's the matter, brat? Can't shoot a defenceless old man?' Taunting him, Diora drank deeply, emptying the cup and setting it back on the desk.

Daniel's hand began to shake again, more with rage than anything else, but he lowered his gun. 'You're right, I can't shoot an old man,' he agreed. 'And I don't think that's a bad thing.' Stepping away from the desk, a smirk came to his lips as Diora coughed. The elderly man coughed again, gnarled hand flying to his throat, his eyes bugging out as he began to choke. 'However . . .' Daniel opened his free hand, revealing an empty vial; the vial that had contained the poison he'd confiscated from Emilie's brother. 'I'm certainly not above poisoning one.' He already knew he was a coward – as long as the job got done, it hardly mattered any more.

Diora's face purpled as he struggled to breathe, his eyes turning bloodshot. Laurent rushed to his side, shaking his shoulders and calling out to him desperately, offering him a tankard of water. But it was too late; in less than a minute Diora stopped struggling and went lax in his chair, head lolling as his skin turned chalk white. 'Diora? Diora, sir, wake up!' Laurent urged, checking his pulse and finding nothing. With a muttered curse, he spun round, levelling his gun at Daniel once more.

'I wouldn't do that if I were you,' Daniel said hastily, holding his own gun up defensively. Not that it was much of a threat; he'd already proven he wasn't brave enough to use it.

'Why not?' Laurent spat. 'You killed him, I should kill you.'

'You owe me a life debt,' Daniel informed him. 'That poison? I took it off Adamas Laine. He was planning on using it to kill you. I discovered it while investigating a . . . personal matter. I almost let him keep it too – what did it matter to me if you died? One less person to take over Diora's empire. But he said he was doing it because you kept getting cold feet, and I thought that maybe you don't deserve to die. Besides, you've got a child now. '

Laurent abandoned the gun, surging forward to pin Daniel to the wall by the throat, shoving him so hard the trinkets on the bookshelf beside him rattled. 'You stay away from my family,' he breathed angrily. Daniel shook his head.

'I haven't touched them, and I won't!' he insisted. 'I have no interest in them. And I'll only have an interest in you if you do what Diora said you would and take his place. I just thought you might like to know that you would have died if not for me. And I doubt Adamas is the only one looking for power; just think how many more people might be interested in doing that should you take over from Diora. Are you really willing to risk your child growing up without a father?'

Laurent's grip loosened enough for Daniel to free himself from his hold. 'Adamas was going to kill me? And you stopped him?'

'Let's just say he'll sleep with one eye open now that I've had a word with him,' Daniel replied, smirking. 'Also, he's been cuffed to a wall bracket in his own home for the last day, so that should make him think twice. You should probably send someone to release him, but I'll leave that decision to you.' A small, vindictive part of him liked the idea of Adamas staying there for a while longer, helpless. But he was trying to rein in that part of himself now.

'He was all set to poison you and take your place at Diora's side.' Daniel paused, fixing Laurent with a hard look. 'If you really do want out, this is your only chance. Tell everyone Diora had a heart attack, claim as much of his money as you can, and let his empire fall when I bring the guards in after the festival. Run as far as you can, buy somewhere nice for your family to live, far, far away from this entire mess. Because I can promise you now, if you're still here when the guards come in, they won't give you the option. And I won't save your life a second time.'

'I thought you were leaving? Word in the courtyard is that you'll be gone by tomorrow night.'

'You heard Diora; I have a life in the upper city. Unfortunately, that life and this one no longer coexist quite so happily.' If he was abandoning Daniel, it couldn't hurt to tell Laurent the truth. Especially if it helped keep him in line. 'Just because Daniel Novak will be gone, doesn't mean I won't still have eyes on the place.'

267

Understanding dawned on Laurent's face, and he ran a hand through his hair in distress. 'The Goddess is already displeased with me, I'm sure; she would no doubt strike me dead where I stand if I were to ignore a life debt.' He growled under his breath, then met Daniel's gaze. 'Fine. You have my word. Diora's empire will have no leader if I can help it, and when the guards return to the lower city I will not be in their way.'

'Tell me who plans to kill the princess and we're even,' Daniel said. Laurent shook his head, looking apologetic.

'If I knew, I would tell you. But Diora had many secrets, even from me.'

Daniel cursed; there went his hope of an easy lead. He glanced back at the dead man still slumped over the desk. 'There's no way I'll get out of here without being seen, and if you don't raise the alarm before his body gets cold it'll look suspicious. Give me a distraction to get out, and I'll never darken your door again.'

The deal was sealed with a handshake, Laurent's grip a touch rougher than necessary. Daniel pulled his hood up. 'Good luck,' he murmured, pocketing the empty vial and making sure his jacket covered the holstered gun properly.

'And to you,' Laurent returned quietly. With one last look back at his handiwork, Daniel slipped out of the office, shutting the door behind him. The guard he'd knocked out was still on the floor, his breathing shallow.

Heart pounding, Daniel went up to the third floor. He glanced out the window, seeing the guards around the back were in place, when suddenly he heard the shout he'd been waiting for. 'Help! Help! I need a medic! Someone come quickly!' It was Laurent, standing in the stairwell of the floor below. 'The Boss has had a heart attack!'

Immediately, Daniel heard several sets of footsteps pounding up the stairs, rushing for Diora's office. He waited by his window, watching as someone ran out of the front door, shouting to the guard at the front gate. The man immediately called to the two men around the back of the fence, no doubt urging them to find a doctor. They both jumped to their feet and sprinted away, leaving the coast clear for Daniel. Not wasting a second of the opportunity Laurent had given him, he opened the window and swung himself over the ledge, dropping down to the ground with only a slight pain in his knees.

He could hear panicked conversation from the open window, and hurried around the corner in case anyone could see him. Mentally groaning at the thought of scaling the perimeter fence, he hauled himself up it anyway, using the momentum of his push off the top to reach for a nearby rooftop with his fingertips, hanging off the ledge rather than letting himself free-fall on to the stone ground.

Leaving Diora's house in chaos as the guards scrambled to revive their long-dead boss, Daniel didn't look back, waiting until he was several streets away before whooping in delight, praising all three gods. Diora was dead, and he was free. Daniel was needed no longer.

26

As much as he wanted to rip his disguise off there and then and throw it into the river, Daniel kept it on as he travelled home, his heart much lighter than it had been in a long time. Diora's death had by no means solved all his problems – he still had to find Crysta's assassin before the festival began, and then work on getting her to listen to his apologies – but it meant that for the first time in over three years, he only needed to be one person. He was Noah Hansen; Daniel Novak no longer existed. And the lower city was free of Diora's hold, or at least it soon would be. Things were finally starting to go in his favour.

'Da, I'm home!' he called, heading straight for the stairs down to the workshop. 'Storms, are you *still* in there?' There was no answer, even when he knocked on the workshop door, but it was unlocked.

Nudging the door open, his eyebrows shot up as soon as he saw the inside of the room. His own half of the workshop was just as messy as it always was, though he was relieved to see all the masks had been sent out to their respective owners. His heart clenched wistfully; he had so desperately wanted to see Crysta's face when she saw hers. He was more proud of it than anything else he'd ever made.

His father's side of the workshop, however, was spotless. No, not spotless – *empty*. The desk was bare, the shelves neatly organised and containing only the outstanding orders, and every trace of the project he'd been working on for the past few months seemed to have vanished. Evander sat at his desk, working on a small mechanical carousel. 'Good gods, man!' Noah exclaimed, startling his father into looking up. 'Where is everything? Where's your project?'

'What? Oh, that.' Evander looked flustered, and glanced aside with the air of a man about to lie. 'I took it up to my room, it was getting a little too large to keep in the workshop. Don't worry about it, lad. Where have you been?' Noah ignored him, heading up the stairs to his father's room. He burst through the door and froze, gaping.

Standing at the foot of the bed, dressed in a beautiful ivory gown that Noah recognised as his mother's, was . . . well, he wasn't quite sure what it was. It was the shape of a human woman – of Noah's mother, Alina – but made purely of metal. The craftwork was impossibly detailed, right down to green-painted metal fingernails on the automaton's hands. And the face . . .

The machine wore a full-face porcelain festival mask that had been painstakingly crafted and painted to replicate his mother's face, down to the last freckle. A wig sat on the machine's head, dark brown hair the same shade as Noah's falling in soft waves just past its shoulders. Unseeing green eyes made of glass stared at him, as familiar as his own behind the hazel lenses he still wore, and an ivory lace choker set with brass gears and heart-shaped rubies rested around the machine's neck: his mother's choker. It was like staring at a terrifying copy of his mother as she had been before she died; the same face, the same body and clothes, but ... cold. Metal skin and an empty gaze. It reminded him of the stuffed animals he'd seen about the palace, preserved after death for people to admire and study. There, but not present, not containing a soul.

'Noah, I can explain,' Evander said quietly, making him realise his father had followed him upstairs.

'Father, what have you done?' Noah breathed, feeling sick. It was like a physical blow to be staring at something so astonishingly identical to his mother, ten years past her death. As always, his father's work was flawless.

'I've brought her back,' Evander insisted earnestly, nudging past his son to get into the bedroom and crossing to the automaton's side. He took its hand in his, bringing it up to his lips. 'Look!' With his free hand he reached up to part the hair at the back of the machine's neck and flicked a switch. Noah jumped as the machine whirred to life. The eyes glowed with the purple-white light of a tyrium flame, tinted green by the painted glass, and the limbs moved to stand a little more naturally. Had he not been so horrified, he would have been impressed at how lifelike the machine's movements were.

Evander stared at the facsimile of his wife with adoration in his eyes, then turned back to his son. 'See? She's back, lad. Your mother is with us once more.'

'It is good to see you, my son, Noah.' Once again he jolted, not having expected the machine to speak. The words were completely flat, like they were being read from a script, making him wonder if his father had done exactly that. The lips didn't move like a person's would, the jaw just moving up and down to imitate speech, but the voice was close enough to his mother's that it made him want to cry. Only a tinny quality betrayed it, like the sound of someone speaking in a newscast.

'Da, this is insane. This is . . . this isn't right. This isn't Mother.'

'It's as good as I'm going to get!' Evander retorted, looking belatedly surprised at the harsh tone he'd taken with his son. 'I'm sorry, I . . . it's difficult for you to understand, lad. You were young when she passed, and now you've had more of your life without her than you did with her. I, on the other hand . . . I still don't feel like I'm *living*, without her around. I love you, gods know I love you more than my own life, but . . . I just *miss her so much*.' His voice cracked, and he clenched the metal hand tighter as a tear escaped to trickle down his cheek. Noah stepped forward, perturbed by the automaton but needing to comfort his father, and pulled the shorter man into a crushing hug.

'Oh, Da,' he breathed. 'If I'd known, if you'd told me – this isn't the answer, Da. You can't replace a person with a machine.'

'"*We create the unimaginable*," or had you forgotten?' Evander responded, quoting their business motto at his son. 'She's not perfect, not yet. But she'll get there, in time, once I've worked out the kinks. She's beautiful, don't you think? My greatest creation yet.'

'She's metal and porcelain and glass,' Noah argued gently. 'That's no match for flesh, blood and bone. Storms, Da. It's been a decade!'

'And every day still feels like the first day without her,' Evander sobbed, tears running freely on to his son's shirt. 'Especially with you around. Gods, you don't even know how much you look like her, do you? More and more each day, like a walking picture of everything I've lost! I've hated myself for not keeping a closer eye on you – not stopping you from being out all day and night, but it meant I didn't have to see her face every time I looked at you!' Noah recoiled as if hit, taking a step back.

'You think that's my fault? I can't help my genes, Father. But if I'm such a painful reminder, perhaps it would be best if I left you alone with your *greatest creation*. After all, I clearly don't measure up to that status any more.'

Evander's eyes widened in sudden grief and he opened his mouth to speak, but Noah didn't want to hear it.

Pulling away from the hand on his shoulder, he gave one last look of horror at the machine, which was now tilting its head at him inquisitively, and left the room. He heard the blood pumping in his ears as he ran down the stairs to his bedroom, and was surprised to find his cheeks wet with tears when he shut the door behind him, locking it.

Noah tore the wig from his head and tossed it hard against the wall above his bed, letting his natural hair fall loose as he pulled off the wig cap. He forced himself to steady his hands enough to remove the lenses from his eyes, not wanting to blind himself in his heightened emotion, but he didn't bother replacing them in their case. He wouldn't need them any more; didn't need Daniel any more.

Wishing he could shower, Noah grabbed the cloth and bowl of water and began scrubbing hard at every inch of make-up covered skin, watching the pale cream vanish to reveal his natural skin tone, the familiar angles of Noah's face emerging from behind the false ones of Daniel's. Even when it was all gone he kept scrubbing until his arms and face were pink, finally throwing the cloth against the back of his bedroom door. Free of his disguise, he turned to the mirror hanging on his wardrobe door, examining his face closely. All he could see when he looked at himself now was painted porcelain, glowing glass and bronze metal skin. He felt like he was going to be sick.

'Noah, please, let me in!' Evander called from the other side of the door, sounding desperately apologetic. 'We can talk about this! I should have told you sooner, but I knew you wouldn't approve; I knew you'd react this way! You don't understand, son, you've never been married!' Noah snorted; no, he hadn't, but he'd been in love. Was still in love. And even if Crysta were to die, he would never replace her with a piece of machinery. Machines couldn't make you smile when you were having a bad day, or hold you as you cried, or rest warm against your skin with your pulse in time with theirs.

Ignoring his father banging on his door, Noah grabbed the box of matches from the ledge above the small fireplace, quickly lighting the fire and prodding it with the poker until it got going. His room lit by the flickering light, he moved to his desk, throwing the note he'd written for his father into the flames. He wouldn't be needing that any more. He threw in the letter he'd left for Damien too, though he didn't touch the notebook pages in the envelope. Those were still useful.

Opening the desk drawer, he dug out the notebook, the pages sitting oddly now that so many had been ripped out. Page by page, he tore them out and tossed them in the fire, watching three years of his life go up in smoke. The information was obsolete now, the problems solved and the secrets no longer his right to know. Eventually there was nothing left but blank pages and a roaring fire. Noah reached for a pen, scrawling a messy note on one of the clean pages of the notebook.

He signed the note *Faithfully, Daniel Novak*, then tore the page out and stuffed it inside the envelope. The rest of the notebook went, leather binding and all, into the fire. He sealed the envelope with a blob of wax from a dark green candle on his desk, writing Damien's full name and title on the front. He'd pay someone a few silvers to drop it off at the guard station on his behalf that afternoon; he didn't want to be caught doing so himself. The last thing he wanted right now was Damien investigating Daniel; he needed the man's focus to be on Crysta.

Green eyes turned to land on the wig lying on his bed, and Noah's lips curled in a dark smirk. Finally, he could be rid of the disguise for good. He grabbed it from the bed and, hesitating only the barest moment, threw the wig on the fire. He dug out his pale make-up and sponges too, adding them to the blaze. The wig caught alight like dry straw, while the make-up bubbled and popped in the heat. Glancing down, he caught a flash of gold, seeing the ring he'd stolen still on his finger. He pulled it off, throwing that in as well, not wanting to keep the symbol of lies and greed. The symbol of what he could have ended up as had he been a little more cruel, a little more power hungry. Diora hadn't been entirely wrong when he'd said they were similar in some ways. But Noah was better than him; Noah had morals, and love, and dignity. Diora had none of those.

The acrid smell of it all burning made Noah gag, his eyes watering at the smoke drifting around his room. Still, he didn't look away, using the poker to keep everything going until all that was left was a pile of ash. Everything that made him Daniel. All of it, gone, forever.

'Nothing to stop you looking at my face now, Father,' he murmured to himself, wiping at his gritty eyes. His gaze moved to the picture of his mother. It was easy to pick out the similarities between her and himself. That machine paled in comparison to her beauty. In the light of the fire it almost looked like her painted smile had widened, a look of approval in her eyes. In the beginning Daniel had in some ways been about gaining his independence, claiming control over his life and his actions – control he hadn't had as his mother wasted away before his eyes, as he'd been sucked into the family business without his father even considering the possibility he might want to do something different. That control had long since disappeared as Diora's web over the lower city grew ever tangled, but for the first time in long years Noah felt like he was taking it back. He thought his mother would have been proud of him. He had hoped his father would be too, but . . .

Noah sighed. He could deal with his father's mad contraption later – right now he needed to go out and do whatever he could to prepare for the opening ceremony of the festival tomorrow. Crysta's life depended on it.

27

Noah warily unlocked the door, surprised when he didn't find his father on the other side of it. Leaving it wide open to air the room out, he went up to the kitchen. The machine was at the stove in front of a saucepan of something, one claw-like hand gripping the handle, while his father gazed on with adoring eyes.

'What's it doing?' Noah stared, aghast.

'Noah! Don't be so rude to your mother! She's taking the time to cook you brunch, isn't that lovely of her?' The machine was oblivious, not even looking towards him.

'That machine is not my mother! Gods, have you gone mad? Mother is dead, and no machine will replace her!'

Evander ran a hand through his hair, reaching for his mug and taking a long swig of coffee. 'Noah, please,' he begged. 'She's all I've got.'

'You've got me,' Noah retorted, hurt clear in his tone.

'Not for long!' Evander argued earnestly. 'You'll fix things once Daniel is out of the way, and you'll propose to Crysta, and then you'll move into the palace to be with her, and where will I be? Here, on my own.'

'No one would argue if you wanted to come with me, Da.'

'What on Tellus would I do in a palace?' Evander said wryly. 'I don't belong there, lad. I'm too old to up and move, and I need my workshop.'

'You could take on an apprentice,' Noah suggested, finally edging fully into the room to sit at the table, still eyeing the automaton. 'You won't be able to keep working forever.' He wouldn't be able to take over the business, not if he married Crysta.

'But that won't solve my problem of being alone,' the older man insisted. 'Ten years of emptiness . . . I'll take whatever comfort I can get.' The automaton thrust a bowl of soup in front of him, then set down a mug of coffee so hard that it slopped over the sides. Obviously there were still a few issues to work out. Still, Evander beamed at it before turning back to Noah. 'Leave it alone, lad. You wouldn't understand.'

'*I* wouldn't understand?' Noah repeated incredulously. 'No, *you* don't understand. You've been so wrapped up in this monstrosity you hardly noticed the world going on around you!'

'Why should I? It's not like it impacts me. The masks are done, the world will go on without my notice.' Noah felt his anger rise at the man's words; how selfish could he be, to just give up? He was so quick to dismiss the rest of the world – dismiss Noah – as no longer worth his attention.

'I killed a man this morning,' Noah declared without feeling or expression. Evander went pale.

'What?'

'Diora's dead. I poisoned him. He's dead, and I did it. I murdered a man, and you were too busy wallowing in your

279

own grief to even notice me leaving the bloody house to do it. I've barely been home in the last two *days*, Da.' It hadn't really sunk in until he'd said it aloud. He was responsible for taking a man's life. He wasn't sure how to feel about that.

'He's gone?' Evander asked, and Noah nodded in confirmation. 'Storms. I . . . I'll admit, I didn't think you'd actually go through with it.'

'Guess I'm not as good a man as you thought I was, hmm?' Noah said, earning a sharp look.

'Don't say that. Killing him doesn't make you a bad person,' Evander insisted.

'But you wouldn't have done it,' Noah said, watching the older man falter.

'Then perhaps that makes *me* the lesser man, not you,' he replied eventually. 'So that's it, then? Daniel's gone for good?'

'I burned it all,' Noah confirmed. 'You'll have to put up with me being a constant reminder of your dead wife. Sorry.' Evander's eyes went wide and he spluttered, but Noah talked over him. 'I'm going out again,' he said, getting to his feet. 'I don't know when I'll be back.'

'Noah, please,' Evander begged. 'We really need to talk about this.'

'Diora might be dead, but I'm not done yet. Crysta will *die* if I don't do something, Da. Talking about . . . whatever this is,' he waved his hand at the machine, 'can wait until after I know she's safe.' That was news to Evander, who froze in shock, hands clenching in his lap. Noah felt briefly guilty for keeping his father in the dark so far, but it wasn't as if the man had made himself available for updates.

'Storms,' Evander cursed. 'What – no, you can explain later. Go. If you need any help, you know where I am.' Noah nodded curtly, heading downstairs to shower and change. He suddenly felt filthy from the inside out as he remembered the life leaving Diora's eyes.

In the bathroom Noah stared at his face contemplatively. He'd be snooping about the upper city this time, and there were too many people who would recognise Noah Hansen lurking about. He grinned wryly. Perhaps he shouldn't have discarded Daniel and his theatrical paraphernalia so soon. He had nothing left to disguise himself with but he needed to look different somehow. The last thing he needed was someone mentioning his skulking in idle chit-chat at the palace and accidentally tipping off the assassin.

Noah pushed his hair back from his face to get a better look at himself. His hair *was* getting a little long lately. Crysta was forever on at him to cut it, but he'd always resisted, or pretended to forget. Maybe now was the time.

Reaching into the cabinet, he found a pair of sharp scissors. That would definitely be enough of a change to throw people off track.

The closer Noah got to the palace, the more deserted the streets were, everyone flocking to the lower city to celebrate and enjoy the festival. The only group to be seen in abundance was the guards in their leaf-green uniforms, setting out temporary metal barriers and blocking the many entrances to the main courtyard outside the palace.

For anyone else, it would have been an impossible task to climb up the back wall of the bank and roof-hop all the way along the street towards the buildings lining the court-yard. And for anyone else, it would have also been an impossible task to climb four storeys of the palace wall. At the mental reminder, Noah glanced towards the palace, eyes seeking the wall in question. He smirked. Sure enough, there were several small rust-brown smears on the stone below Crysta's window and the window sill itself. He wished he could have seen Damien's expression when he'd seen that.

He stopped on the roof of the fabric shop next to the temple, clinging to the smooth tiles of the slanted roof. That was one thing he hated about the upper-city buildings; they were far enough into Erova's dead zone that they didn't need to be squat and flat to brace against storms. Slanted roofs were far more difficult to climb and run across.

Getting on to the temple roof would be the most ideal vantage point, but despite his many years of experience in throwing himself off buildings and attempting to climb them again, this was one height he'd never managed to reach. The temple was an ornate building with elaborate twists of metal edging the roof, which would no doubt shred his hands if he tried to grab them. And it was too far from any surrounding building to jump on to; it was well and truly out of his reach. He sighed to himself, climbing to the peak of the roof he was on and sitting astride it, hidden from view by the chimney. The guards would soon have all the barriers locked in place, and then the palace servants would begin bringing the courtyard to life for the feast and ceremony.

Not for the first time, Noah wished he could be in two places at once; so many names were swimming around his head after what Diora had told him, but he couldn't waste his time investigating them individually. The only thing he could do now was survey the courtyard where the ceremony would take place, checking for any hideaways or weak spots a potential assassin could take advantage of. Besides, he needed to find his own route past the barrier, seeing as he was no longer welcome inside the palace gates.

Eyes to the horizon, Noah scanned the area, looking for anywhere with a good vantage point if the assassin's chosen method was poisoned dart. He couldn't be too far from his target or he'd risk the dart flying off course in the wind. That ruled out most of the rooftops in the area. Noah growled to himself, unable to see anywhere that would be out of sight and yet suitable to shoot from. No trees, no walkways, no ledges. If a dart wasn't possible, it left poison in Crysta's food as the most obvious option. That didn't sit well with Noah. He could find a sniper and stop them before they could fire, but it would be too late for him to do anything but watch if Crysta ate something laced with velora.

A familiar shock of jet black hair caught his eye, and he watched as Damien stepped out of the guard station within the barriers. Noah checked his pocket watch; if Damien was checking the perimeter already, it had to mean they were nearly at lock-in, and it wasn't yet six in the evening – earlier than usual. He didn't know if that was a good sign or not.

Several loud clangs of metal on metal rang through the empty courtyard; the sound of the barriers being bolted together – eight feet tall and topped with barbed wire, their bars thick and solid, an unmovable wall until the guards dismantled them. People would be able to see through them to watch the opening ceremony and the feast, but no one would be getting through without an official invitation.

Noah scanned the surrounding area, wondering if he was missing anything. He gritted his teeth, lowering himself over the edge of the building and into the alley below, intending to get a closer look before he had to call it a night – and, if he was completely honest, hoping to catch a glimpse of Crysta as the festival preparations began. The clock was ticking, and for the first time Noah began to wonder if he would be able to beat it.

Hurriedly ducking around the side of one building and towards a corner of the courtyard absent of guards, Noah kept his head low and his steps silent, his green eyes alert as they scanned the area. He resisted the urge to kick something in frustration. He felt helpless; how was he supposed to protect Crysta when he didn't know who or what he was protecting her from? During the ceremony, the assassin might be any one of the men sitting at the tables. They could get the poison in her food before the ball even started. There were so many ways the ceremony could play out, so many ways Noah would be unable to do anything but watch as Crysta died, that he was beginning to wonder if he might as well give up and head home. But even fruitlessly wandering the courtyard was better than sitting at home and imagining endless worst-case scenarios.

Running a hand through his new short hair, he shook his head, trying to regain focus. He had to stay on track. He couldn't give up now; he was running out of both time and options. He needed to find a way through the barrier before the crowds blocked his view.

Four guards, directed by Damien, began to open the palace gates. Noah stuck to the shadows and watched a small army's worth of servants emerge from the palace doors, carrying enormous round tables and ornate bronze chairs to the courtyard. It was like watching ants at work, all dressed in the same green uniforms, working as seamlessly as a machine to set out the tables as efficiently as possible.

In all the chaos he took the opportunity to make a break for the opposite side of the courtyard, ducking behind the decorative stone pillars and sprinting along the barricaded parade entrance. On the other side of the courtyard were yet more buildings, and the stairway up to the small plaza that overlooked the courtyard was also barricaded off.

Noah's gaze slid to the plaza. It stretched out above the roof of the café, its stone railing weathered with age. He wouldn't be able to climb the wall of the café without being noticed, but if he could get to the roof of the dressmaker's beside it, he should be able to jump across to the plaza, beyond the barriers. And more importantly, back into the courtyard come morning.

Noah eyed the wall he was about to climb with a critical gaze, looking for footholds and handholds in the rough stone. Just as he stepped up to it, reaching for a low groove, he felt a hand curl around his jacket collar and yank him backwards.

'Of course.'

Noah turned, offering Damien a faint half-smile, which faltered at the man's irritated look.

'Some of my men said they'd seen a suspicious figure sneaking about the courtyard, disappearing before they could get a proper look at him. I should have known it would be you.' The captain released Noah's collar, shaking his head in exasperation.

'The fact that they noticed me at all means I'm slipping,' Noah muttered, disgruntled. Damien gave him a pointed look.

'What are you doing here, Noah?' he sighed, sounding more weary than angered. He looked like he hadn't slept in days, and Noah felt guilt rise at the trouble he'd been causing the man.

'Checking the area, what else?' Noah replied evenly. 'I still don't know who is planning to assassinate Crysta, but I'm going to keep searching. I won't let anything happen to her.'

Damien sighed, leaning against the wall of the café. 'Have you ever thought you might have overheard those men incorrectly? There might not be a threat to Crysta's life at all. Your own life, however, when Crysta finds out what a nuisance you've been making of yourself, is debatable.'

'Crysta can do what she wishes with me, if it means she's survived the festival to do it,' Noah retorted. 'Trust me, the threat is real.' He couldn't tell Damien that Diora had been behind it, or admit to the connection between himself and Daniel Novak. Not yet, at least; there wasn't nearly enough time to explain himself properly. 'Besides, if there's even the slightest chance that someone wants to hurt Crysta, are you really going to let that go ignored?'

'There's always a threat to Princess Crysta's life,' Damien snapped in reply, clearly losing his patience. 'Every waking moment of every day, there is the potential for someone to make an attempt on her life – on any of the family's lives. I deal with that the best I can, Noah. And while I'm sure you think you're helping, I don't need to be worrying about what you're getting up to on top of everything else.' His voice grew progressively louder as he spoke, until he was almost shouting in the narrow alleyway. Noah went wide-eyed, taking a step back in shock. He'd never seen Damien lose his temper in such a way before. 'Especially when I don't even know if I can trust your word right now,' the captain added.

'My word is as good as it's ever been!' Noah argued, indignant. 'I'm not going to just sit here and let the worst happen, especially as I seem to be the only one actually doing something to try and prevent it!'

Damien bristled, glaring. 'Don't act like I'm not taking the threat seriously, Noah. Security has already been doubled, the seating has been rearranged – and believe me, that was no small feat – and the king himself is aware. He's also aware of how you treated both his daughters, which is reason enough for you to be as far from the palace as possible, if you know what's best for you.' Noah winced; King Leon would no doubt be absolutely furious.

'I'm sorry, Damien, I didn't think –'

'You never do, do you?' he cut him off harshly, rubbing at his temples. 'Storms, I forget how much of a child you are sometimes. Get out of here, Noah. And stay out of the way of my men, if you have any sense in that lump of flesh you like to call a brain. All they've been told is that someone has designs on Princess Crysta's life, and to shoot on sight if anyone looks suspicious. That could be you, if you keep meddling where you don't belong. I know you're only trying to help, but the best way you can do that is to keep your head down and let me do my job. Clear?'

Noah bit his lip, guilt warring with his insistence that he was helping, that he was far more skilled than Damien gave him credit for. If Damien knew the truth about Daniel, maybe he'd think a little differently. 'Perfectly,' he relented. 'I never meant to belittle your abilities, Damien, or those of your men. But you've hardly given any sign that you've been taking my word seriously. Would it have killed you to say "Yes, Noah, I hear you and will take your warning into consideration"?'

'Yes, Noah, I hear you and will take your warning into consideration,' Damien recited, rolling his eyes. 'Will you leave now? I have work to do.' Noah snorted; now who was the child?

'All right, all right, I'm leaving. But you should know, whoever the assassin is, he has brothers, at least two of them, probably older,' he added, remembering Diora's words. 'It's not much, but it's all I've found out to narrow it down.' Unfortunately, multiple sons weren't uncommon in noble families. Damien nodded to show he understood, and Noah took a step back. 'Good luck tomorrow, my friend. Stay safe. I know you'll do your job to the best of your ability.' The only problem was, Damien's job was to look out for everyone, not just Crysta. Noah had great confidence in Damien, but even the best of men had limits.

'Stay out of trouble, brat,' Damien said with a reluctant half-smile. Noah winked at him, then turned back to the wall, easily hoisting himself up and beginning his climb, swinging over the railing to land feet first in the plaza. It was empty, as he'd anticipated. As the street lamps flared to life in the quickly fading light, he took one last look at the courtyard bustling with activity, before turning away and heading home. He had to prepare himself for opening day; at least now he had a way inside the barriers. That was the first of his problems dealt with – if only the others could be so simple to solve.

28

When Noah returned home at a little past ten, he found his father in the workshop, catching up on some of their back orders. 'Where's that machine?' he asked, and Evander frowned at his wording.

'Upstairs in bed; she's had a long day.'

'Machines don't sleep, Da,' he replied, sighing.

The older man looked up, then his eyebrows rose. 'You cut your hair,' he observed. Noah shrugged, running fingers through the short strands.

'I needed to look different enough that people wouldn't immediately recognise me running about the upper city on the tail of some noble or another,' he replied. 'Besides, Crysta prefers it this way.'

'And how did today's excursion go, then?' Evander queried.

'Pretty dismally, to be honest,' Noah mused, sitting at his work desk and resting an elbow on the wood, propping his head in his hand. 'There are too many possibilities, too many people to search for in such a short time frame. I . . . I don't know what else I can do before tomorrow, Da. I haven't got enough to go on.'

Evander wheeled his chair over, resting a hand on his son's shoulder. 'You'll figure something out, lad, and catch the bastard who dares threaten Crysta's life. Then you'll stop him, and she'll have no choice but to fall to her knees in front of you and declare her everlasting love.' He winked at his son, and Noah couldn't help but snort.

'If you say so, Da. But I think it'll take more than stopping an assassin for her to love me again.'

'Dear boy, she hasn't *stopped* loving you!' Evander protested. 'She might have the unholy anger of the Goddess herself inside her, but that doesn't mean she doesn't still love you. Love like that, the feelings between the two of you . . . that doesn't go away in the blink of an eye. She'll hate herself for feeling the way she does, but she won't stop.' There was a wistfulness in his eyes that made Noah's heart clench, and he reached up to squeeze his father's hand, wondering if he'd judged him a little too harshly. Yes, the mechanical woman upstairs was a certifiably insane invention, but . . . his heart was in the right place. But he'd never get over his grief if he kept holding on to ghosts.

'Loving me doesn't mean she'll take me back, though,' Noah reasoned, shrugging.

'It will when you tell her about Diora and she realises what a big misunderstanding this has all been,' Evander said, sounding confident. 'Now, come on, show me what you've got. I may rarely leave this workshop, but I'm still well aware of what those in the court are getting up to! Maybe I can help you narrow down your list.' He looked expectantly at his son, and the teen reached into his satchel for his notebook, opening it to the most recent page, where he'd written down every name he could conceivably think of as a suspect. Every outland noble with multiple brothers, underlining the ones who might have reason to hate the monarchy. Evander let out a long whistle. 'That's quite the list.'

'Isn't it just,' Noah agreed, running a hand over his hair. 'It's going to be a long night.'

So caught up in planning for the day ahead both Hansen men started at the sound of the doorbell ringing. Noah jumped to his feet. 'If this is a last-minute order, I'm shutting the door in their face,' he muttered grouchily. Jogging up the stairs, he was all set to snap at whoever was at the door, but his words died in his throat as he wrenched it open and saw Lena. The handmaid was standing nervously on the doorstep, but when she saw Noah she met his gaze with confidence. 'Master Hansen,' she said. 'May I come in?'

'What are you doing here?' Noah blurted, stepping aside to let her through. She frowned, and panic gripped him, a dozen scenarios running through his head. 'Is everything all right at the palace? Is Crysta OK?'

'Crysta's fine, as is everyone else,' the handmaid assured him, voice soft, and he let out a breath he didn't know he'd been holding. 'I came to talk to you, but I don't have long. Rosa's asleep, but probably not for long. She hasn't been sleeping well lately.' Noah swallowed guiltily.

'Come on down to the workshop. Can I get you anything? Tea?' She shook her head, following him downstairs, where Evander was waiting with curious eyes. 'You've not met, have you? Lena, this is my father, Evander. Da, this is Lena, Rosa's handmaid.'

'You mean the one you blackmailed Rosa about?' he asked shrewdly, and Noah could feel the shame creeping up his cheeks.

'That would be the one, yes.'

'Lena, dear lady, it is a pleasure to meet you,' Evander said, bowing. 'And I apologise for my son's callous behaviour towards you and your paramour.'

'The pleasure is all mine, sir,' Lena replied shyly, giving a quick curtsey. 'But with all due respect, Master Noah is old enough to apologise for himself.' Noah blushed, ducking his head and offering her a seat.

'Noah's old enough for a lot of things he has yet to do,' Evander retorted ruefully. 'I'll give you some privacy. Shout if you need anything.' With that he left the workshop, and Noah claimed his chair, dragging it opposite Lena's. She pursed her lips, hands folded in her lap.

'I found something very interesting in Captain Conti's office this evening while I was tidying,' she said, getting straight to the point. The slight smile on her face suggested that it wasn't entirely within her duties to tidy Damien's office. Noah was sure he didn't want to know what she'd really been up to. 'Some scraps of paper on his desk, all from the same envelope.' Her amber gaze met Noah's steadily, and he knew where the conversation was going. 'Those scraps all had tip-offs for the guards written on them, things that should have been secret, things that only those who spend a lot of their hours lurking about the lower city could possibly find out. And they were all written in the same handwriting too. A very familiar hand; I really don't know how Captain Conti hasn't realised for himself.'

She paused, giving Noah a pointed look. 'But the strange part is, while those notes were all in your script, they did not bear your name. They were instead signed from a Mr Daniel Novak. Funny, isn't it?'

'Very odd,' he agreed evenly, wondering what she was getting at. Did she want him to admit to Damien that he was the mysterious informant?

'You forget, Master Noah, I may be a palace servant but I grew up in the lower city, and I still have plenty of family and friends there. I know who Daniel Novak is. What I don't know, sir, is why you and he share the exact same handwriting.'

With a sigh, Noah scratched at the faint stubble on his jaw. 'We share the same handwriting because we are the same person,' he admitted. 'I am – was – Daniel Novak. Daniel was a disguise.'

'The disguise you used when meeting that girl in the lower city, the one Rosa and I saw you with,' Lena presumed. Noah nodded his head, making a noise of frustration.

'I didn't invent Daniel to meet with Emilie,' he insisted. 'That happened later. I invented Daniel before I even met Crysta – because I was foolish, reckless and barely fifteen years old. And then things escalated, and I couldn't stop.' He paused, thinking for a moment. 'You say you know enough of the lower city to know of Daniel. I take it you also know of Diora?'

'Of course,' Lena said. 'Though I heard he passed away this morning. It's a shame, after everything he did to help people.' Noah couldn't stop the bitter snort that escaped him.

'Diora wasn't what he seemed.' Starting from the beginning, he told her what he knew about Diora's true business, and how he, as Daniel, had been involved. He kept talking until his voice was hoarse. 'So, you see, I needed Daniel to keep people safe, and I needed Emilie for information on Diora's business. I'm not saying it's an excuse, or that Crysta doesn't have the right to be angry over it. But my reasons are valid, and in my mind, I never truly cheated on Crysta. I never loved Emilie. My feelings for Crysta have never wavered for a moment. Everything I did as Daniel, I did for her and for Talen, and all I need is for her to let me explain that.'

Lena was silent for a long moment, fingers unconsciously clutching at her skirt. She seemed to be taking it all in, and Noah didn't blame her for being shocked. 'If all that is true, and I don't doubt it, then I refuse to believe you're as vindictive as you seemed when you threatened Rosa,' she eventually declared, before her expression softened. 'You . . . you could have told His Majesty about us ages ago, if you'd truly wanted to hurt Rosa. She said you told her you'd known almost from the start. If you had wanted to be cruel, as Rosa believes, you could have just said something regardless of whether Rosa knew one of your secrets. But you didn't. And the actions of Daniel Novak, especially after what you've just told me, are not the actions of a cruel man.'

'I never wanted to hurt Rosa, or you,' Noah said firmly. 'And I truly am sorry for the pain I caused both of you. I just . . . I panicked. I couldn't let Crysta find out about Emilie. I'd already begun the process of Daniel's disappearance by then. If Rosa hadn't found out, I could have killed Diora and got rid of Daniel, and Crysta would have been none the wiser and there wouldn't have been any problems.'

'And you think that best?' Lena asked, raising her thin eyebrows. 'You would have preferred for Princess Crysta never to know that you had been unfaithful? Or that you had done all those brave deeds? You wished to start a marriage with a foundation of lies?' Noah winced; when she put it like that, it made him sound awful.

'I would have preferred for Crysta to stay oblivious rather than worrying about something she has no cause to worry over. I sent that information to Damien in the hopes of encouraging the guards to police the area better, now that Diora's hold is released and Daniel is gone. Crysta has never needed to know. And Emilie was just a source of information. But it was duty, nothing more. Yes, it was wrong, but . . . I wasn't unfaithful.'

Lena stared at him for several long moments, incredulity in her eyes. 'You, sir,' she declared finally, 'have a *lot* to learn about women.' She shook her head, clearly exasperated. 'You may not have considered it a betrayal, but it was one all the same, and I don't blame Princess Crysta in the slightest for being rid of you. But in spite of that, you're not a bad man, and you've helped more people than you can imagine with your work as Daniel, as poor as your choices were. But it's not my place to judge members of the court.'

'Am I a member of the court, now that Crysta wants nothing to do with me?' he retorted drily. 'Judge away, Lena. Storms know I deserve it.'

'You'll be judged by someone far more suited to it than I, sir. The Goddess will make sure of it,' Lena vowed. 'But discussing Daniel Novak wasn't the only reason I came calling, though I am glad you told me. I overheard Princess Crysta and Captain Conti talking this morning, describing how you had intruded upon the princess's chambers.' Her wording made Noah grimace.

'Captain Conti was saying you were full of talk of assassins and poisonings,' Lena continued, sounding wary. Noah leaned forward in his chair a little, nodding. If he could get Lena to believe him and get her on his side, it would make his job ten times easier. Not only did she have unfettered access to the palace, but she could also come and go from the kitchen as she pleased, and would likely notice if anyone suspicious was lurking there.

'One of the noblemen is planning to poison Crysta at the opening ceremony tomorrow,' he told her without hesitation. The handmaid gasped, her amber eyes widening and her hand flying to her mouth.

'What? But, how do you know?' Noah told her of the night he'd overheard the men talking and everything he'd learned since. She listened intently, looking more and more horrified at every word.

'Damien and Crysta don't believe me,' he said once he'd told her everything. 'They think I'm making up stories just to get back in Crysta's good books. But I swear, Lena, on the Goddess herself, I would never lie or joke about something so important as Crysta's life. Someone wants to kill her, and I have only hours left until they try to do it.'

'Gods,' the brunette girl breathed, stunned. 'Surely Captain Conti knows you'd never lie about something like that! He may be angry, but he knows how much you love

Princess Crysta! Storms, he'd never forgive himself if he let something happen to her! None of us would.' Noah nodded, his mouth a grim line.

'Whether he believes me or not, he still won't talk about it,' he replied.

'I'll do what I can to help you, for Rosa's sake,' she agreed after a long silence. 'I think she would die if anything happened to her sister.'

'How . . . how is Rosa? Now, I mean?' he asked tentatively.

'Better,' Lena admitted. 'But still not back to her usual self. Some members of the court have been . . . exceptionally rude towards her. Princess Crysta and Captain Conti have been nothing but supportive, thank the gods. And her parents are . . . well, they're trying. I think my class is a bigger blow to them than my gender, to be honest, sir. You were difficult enough, but at least you're upper-city born. I don't think they know what to do about the whole situation. Her Majesty even invited me to have tea with her, to get to know me better.' She didn't look too thrilled about that, and Noah remembered vividly his own experience of tea with the queen when he'd first started courting Crysta.

'It's terrifying, isn't it?' he murmured sympathetically, making her nod.

'Completely,' she agreed, then gave a soft smile. 'But it's far better than the alternative. I don't think poor Rosa ever expected them to take it quite so well. The Goddess has truly blessed us.'

Noah smiled at the news, glad for the two girls. 'Would you tell Rosa how sorry I am? And explain to her about

Daniel, and Emilie? Even if she still hates me, at least she'd know the truth. I can't bear for her to think I was truly unfaithful to Crysta.'

'I'll talk to her, but I can't promise she'll listen,' Lena agreed. 'And I've got a hundred-odd duties tomorrow, but I'll do my best to keep an eye out for anything suspicious.'

'Will you keep an eye out in the kitchens too?' Noah requested. 'If it's poison this man is planning to use, then it's entirely likely he'll try and slip it into Crysta's meal at the opening ceremony. He did say he wanted it to have a big impact, after all.'

'I'll watch her food every second until it's in front of her,' Lena promised. She glanced up at the clock, frowning. 'I need to go; if Rosa wakes and I'm not there, she'll worry. Besides, I have to be up before dawn tomorrow. Storms, I can't wait for the festival to be over.'

'You and me both,' Noah agreed. He escorted her up to the hallway, hardly able to believe the turn of events. Surely it was all an elaborate dream, and he'd wake up having fallen asleep at his desk. 'Thank you for all this, Lena. To know there's someone inside the palace looking into this as well . . . it certainly makes me feel better.'

'I want Princess Crysta to be safe just as much as you do, sir.' Lena paused on the doorstep, looking hesitant. 'I apologise, for judging you so harshly. You thought your reasons were the right ones, and I can understand that. And, for what it's worth . . . Princess Crysta is dreadfully lonely without you. She hides it well, but Ana and I can tell. Everyone in the court has been told that your father has been taken ill, to explain your absence. Every time someone asks after you, she gets this look in her eyes. She misses you.'

With that, she left, hurrying away into the darkness. Noah shut the door and made for the kitchen. The door was ajar, and he rolled his eyes; his father was so predictable.

'Well, how did it go?' Evander asked as his son entered, earning a raised eyebrow in response.

'We both know you were eavesdropping on the entire conversation, Da,' Noah retorted. 'Who do you think I inherited that particular skill from?'

Evander shook his head, smiling ruefully. 'You caught me. I think it went far better than you could've hoped for. And now you've got eyes on the inside too. Crysta is safe as houses.' Noah frowned, wishing he could be as optimistic as his father.

Retiring to his room, Noah prepared himself for a night of tossing and turning; every time he closed his eyes all he could see was Crysta's face, his brain providing image after image of her beautiful tawny skin paling in death. He tried to direct his thoughts to a happier place, imagining Crysta seeing her mask for the first time in the morning. Would she even want it, knowing he had made it for her? It wasn't like she'd have much choice. There weren't any other mask-makers of royal standard in Talen.

That train of thought wasn't helping matters, so he buried his face in his pillow, trying to ignore his stomach churning with anxiety, his throat tight at the thought of losing Crysta for good. He'd done all he could, for now. He just had to hope it was enough.

29

Even if Noah had been able to have a lie-in, the noise of the city outside would have made it impossible. Even in their little house, far from the river between the upper and lower city, the sound of the festival was near deafening. A series of quick explosions jolted him from a doze it felt like he had only just fallen into. He groaned, burying his face in his pillow before reluctantly sitting up and looking at his clock. '*Gods*, who lights fireworks at six in the morning?' He'd forgotten about that part of the festival; for the past two years he'd been in a guest chamber in the palace, too far away to hear the fireworks go off early. All he'd had to worry about was getting up in time to take the tram down to the shipyard with Crysta, ready to start the parade.

He sighed to himself at the thought of Crysta, imagining her going about her opening day routine without him. She'd probably be just about to get the tram, where she'd get fully dressed and made-up on the journey down to the lower city. Then she'd put her mask on – since Noah wasn't there to do it for her – and they'd join the royal carriage. He wouldn't get to be there for that either. He wouldn't get to see her eyes light up in awe at the sight of her mask, feel her kiss him in thanks for creating such a beautiful adornment.

Still, he was awake now, and there was no point in trying to go back to sleep. The parade would be starting down in the shipyard in an hour, and he had to get ready. Still in his sleep clothes, Noah wandered upstairs, surprised to see his father up and about already. 'Fireworks get you too?' he asked.

'Every bloody year,' Evander muttered, running a hand through sleep-rumpled hair. 'I've got the coffee on, sit down, lad. You'll be leaving soon I expect?'

Noah nodded, sliding into a chair. 'I'll set up in the clock tower while the parade's starting up,' he said, gratefully accepting the coffee passed to him. 'No point in me trying to get down to the port and follow the parade up.' Nothing would happen in either the shipyard or the lower city; Crysta would be far too well guarded there, where the chance of something going wrong was greatest. It was the upper city he had to watch out for. He'd wait for the parade to get closer to the courtyard, keep an eye on it as it passed through, and then head for a better vantage point once it was closer to the palace. If he could see every inch of the opening ceremony feast, he'd be in the best position possible to stop anything happening. In theory. 'Will you be emerging to watch the parade at any point, Da?'

'I suppose, at some point,' Evander sighed. 'It would be nice to see the festival begin. And it'll do me no good to sit here worrying about poor Princess Crysta.'

'That's the spirit.' Noah wolfed down two pastries and drained his mug, getting to his feet. 'I need to shower and get dressed.'

Once clean, he padded through to his bedroom and flung the wardrobe open, staring at the clothes inside with indecision. He had carefully laid out soft, unrestrictive clothes in dark bronze and silver to wear today, appropriate for the festival but not eye-catching. But his gaze kept straying to the outfit that had been made for him for this year's festival, the one that went specifically with the dress Crysta would be wearing. It was in a protective bag at the end of the rail.

He couldn't wear it, he knew that; not only would it give him away a mile off, it was far too restricting for the amount of climbing he planned to do. But he wanted to. Gods, he wanted to. In his mind he had images of swooping in to save the day at the very last minute, saving Crysta's life in front of the entire country, and Crysta being so grateful she immediately invited him to the head table to sit with her and the family, like he should have been, the pair of them looking stunning as they stood side by side in their matching outfits.

He shook his head to rid himself of his foolish fantasies, mentally berating himself. 'Mind on the task at hand, Hansen,' he muttered under his breath. Combing his damp hair into place, he bent to lace his knee-high brown boots, then reached beneath his bed for the small wooden box containing his mask for this year's festival. That too would match Crysta's, but he wasn't willing to dig out one of his old masks. It was bad luck to wear the same mask to two different festivals, and besides, he'd put so much work into it, it would be a shame to let it go unworn.

Another barrage of fireworks and several loud gongs from the clock tower informed him that the parade had officially begun, and he stared down at the closed box, sighing to himself. Crysta would have her mask on by now. Would she hate it, the craftsmanship tainted by her thoughts of him? Or would she realise that he couldn't have made such a beautiful gift for her without being truly, embarrassingly in love with her? He wouldn't get to see it properly until the opening ceremony, and even then it would be from a distance.

Leaving his mask in its cushioned box for now, he put it carefully in his satchel and reached underneath his bed for his shoulder holster. He couldn't help but think of the last time he'd worn it, but pushed the thought away. Now wasn't the time to dwell on such things.

With the holster hidden beneath his jacket, Noah shouldered his satchel and left the room, his expression grim. If he could just get through the opening day with everyone alive, he resolved to spend the rest of the festival locked in the workshop ignoring the rest of the world, ritual be damned.

Evander was dressed in his festival clothes when Noah knocked on his bedroom door, though the clothes were clearly several years old. Still, he looked respectable enough, his mask in its box on the bed. He almost hadn't made himself a mask; it had only been with Noah's insistence that he'd bothered. If it was bad luck to wear the same mask twice, it was worse not to wear one at all. The Goddess was pleased by beautiful things, and going plain-faced on a day designed to please her was just asking for trouble.

Noah sighed at seeing the automaton dressed in one of his mother's old festival outfits, its lit eyes swivelling to gaze in his direction when he entered. He couldn't say it was staring *at* him – there was no focus, no intent – more . . . staring *through* him. 'You're not taking it with you, are you?' he asked incredulously. Confusion clouded Evander's face before he deciphered his son's sentence and glanced at the automaton.

'What? No, no, she's far too delicate. I wouldn't want her getting hurt!' he said, taking the machine's hand in a loving grasp. It didn't move. 'She was just helping me with my buttons. Like . . . like she used to.' His gaze grew forlorn, and Noah resisted the urge to sigh once more. He didn't have time for this.

'Well, I'm going to leave now, if you wanted to come with me as far as the Tolia pavilion.' If he left his father there, he was unlikely to get swept up in the crowd and start to panic, but he would still be able to see the parade pass through. Far better than taking him to either of the court-yards or the smaller plazas in the area.

'I . . . yes . . . well, I was hoping to have just an hour or two in the workshop, you understand?' Evander stuttered, eyes widening at the prospect of leaving the house. Noah opened his mouth to point out that if he left him to make his own way to the festival he would never get there, but before he could do so there was a knock on the door. He paused, frowning.

'You need to get that,' he said. 'I'm not supposed to be here.' Evander nodded, nudging past his son and shutting the bedroom door behind him. Noah turned, now alone in the room with the automaton, and eyed the terrifyingly realistic porcelain face. 'You can understand me, can't you?' he asked tentatively, and the machine's head jerked in a nod.

'I can, my son,' it replied, making him wince.

'I'm not your son. Storms, Da's truly gone mad,' he murmured, wishing the machine's construction wasn't covered by fabric and sheets of metal. He wanted to break the thing apart, to figure out what made it function, and destroy it, but he didn't think his father would recover from the shock.

Edging closer to the door, Noah leaned against the wood to listen, wondering who was in the hallway.

'Oh, Mr Hansen! You're looking very dashing there. Not got your mask on yet?' Noah grinned to himself. Of course. Marie Reyes, bless her soul.

'Oh, I, uh, no. Not yet. You look very lovely, madam,' Evander added, flustered. Noah chuckled under his breath, shaking his head. That solved his problem about dragging his father out of the house.

'Tell Da I've gone already, and tell him to have fun with Marie,' he said to the automaton as he moved around the bed towards the window. He didn't know if the machine could pass on messages, or even had the memory to retain them, but it was no matter. Evander would realise what had happened when he came back to the bedroom and saw Noah gone.

Slipping out of the small window, he dropped down to the street below, turning to jog towards the clock tower. If he made it fast, he might even get there before the area around it became too crowded. The parade would barely be out of the shipyard yet, but that didn't stop people from setting up camp at the parade barriers hours before it was due to arrive, eager to get a good view.

Everyone around him was full of good cheer, calling the Goddess' blessings to anyone who passed by. Noah wished he could share their enthusiasm, but his thoughts were focused on the princess standing in a carriage in the middle of the parade, wondering if today would be her last.

Not if he could help it.

30

Noah had to wrestle his way through crowds of people as he drew closer to the base of the clock tower, and he grimaced at seeing the large stone structure wrapped in strings of brightly coloured paper lanterns, each glowing vibrantly. That would make getting up there a little more difficult than usual; the last thing he wanted to do was knock a lantern and set something on fire.

Standing at the base of the tower and facing away from the parade route, he plotted out the best way to reach the clock face. He started climbing, making sure to be extra careful with the lanterns. Eventually he made it to the top, and edged his way around the large bell to get to the side that gave him the best view of the parade. He'd set up closer to the palace later, as he knew the assassin wouldn't strike until the ceremony, but he still wanted to watch the whole parade. Just to be safe.

He could see right down to the skyship port from the clock tower, and he smiled at seeing the parade slowly snaking its way up, the royal carriage at the very head of the procession, palomino horses gleaming in the sun as they walked elegantly. The parade seemed almost endless, full of marching musicians and dancers, and acrobats flinging themselves in the air, staying in perfect time with each other as they went. Spaced throughout the parade were large steam-powered carriages, almost like trams without tracks, which were covered in vibrant flowers and swathes of fabric, some of them painted with huge murals of the Goddess and her taming of the gods.

The watching crowds cheered and clapped as the parade passed them, children on their parents' shoulders to get a better look at the spectacle. The court members would all be mingled among the city's crowds, sticking with the masses until it was time for the ceremony. That was half the aim of the festival; to have the upper and lower classes interact, to remind them that there was little difference between them. The masks everyone was wearing only emphasised that. The level of anonymity put the court members and upper classes on a more even footing with those from the lower city, and broke down the barriers between them.

Noah let his gaze drop to the royal carriage, trying to see who was standing on the balcony at the back. Damien was there, of course, looking resplendent in his emerald dress uniform, his filigree mask just as spectacular as Noah had envisioned it. His heart warmed to see his friend wearing the mask he had made him, despite everything. Perhaps not all was lost, after all.

Still searching, Noah sighed when he realised he couldn't see Crysta anywhere. She must be inside the carriage. He so desperately wanted to see her; just as he hadn't let her see her mask, she had refused to let him see her dress for the opening ceremony. He'd only been given a colour scheme and a vague idea when he'd asked for details to help match the mask to it.

Rosa, however, was standing out on the balcony, waving to the crowd with barely any hesitance. Noah would bet money that Lena was right behind her, just out of sight in the doorway to the balcony, murmuring words of assurance. The younger of the two princesses looked radiant, her dark hair hanging in a long braid threaded with bronze ribbon and bright green feathers, to match the feathered design of her mask. Her dress was long and flowing, fluttering in the faint breeze created by the parade's movement, the pale bronze material shimmering like spun metal and accentuating her darker skin. He was glad to see her arms covered from shoulder to wrist in gleaming bronze filigree armour, looking like it was part of the dress itself. Most people probably didn't even realise it was armour. He wondered if it had been Lena or Damien who had insisted on the extra protection, and hoped desperately that Crysta was wearing some form of armour as well.

As the parade crossed the bridge into the lower city raucous cheering filled the air. There was a pang of regret in his chest as he watched the parade from above, and he wished he could be down there. He felt restless, here on the outskirts. Though the responsibility he'd shouldered as Crysta's suitor during the festival had seemed heavy, he would now happily take it if it came with the excitement of being at the heart of things – at Crysta's side. That kind of adrenalin rush was what Daniel had thrived on, but Noah . . . well, without Crysta he felt like he barely had more soul than the monstrous automaton taking up residence in his father's bedroom.

It took almost three hours for the parade to cross the entire lower city, and more fireworks coloured the skies as it crossed over the bridge into the upper city. From there it would only last another hour before finishing outside the palace, with perhaps half an hour for the parade to disperse and the barriers close again. Then the opening ceremony would begin. If Noah wanted to get to the palace courtyard before the ceremony started, he had to move now.

With one last wistful glance at the royal carriage, out of which Crysta had still not appeared, he lowered himself over the edge of the clock tower, preparing for the climb down. Keeping his satchel from bumping into the wall, mindful of his mask inside, he eased himself down and away from the crowd of people pushing and shoving their way towards the upper courtyard. Finding a quiet spot in an alcove with a bench, he opened his satchel and carefully pulled out the box, flicking the catch and opening it. He grinned, seeing his mask lying inside.

The base was solid bronze and covered the top half of his face. The entire mask was covered in gears and cogs, with a small jewel-studded bronze lizard resting just above the right eyebrow. There was a tiny switch above the strap on one side, and when he turned it on the gears on the mask would spring to life and the little clockwork lizard would scurry across the mask to the other side, turn around and scurry back, green and white stones glittering. He'd always liked lizards; their ability to hide in places that should have been physically impossible was something he admired.

Carefully, he lifted the mask to his face and set it in place with a gentle hand, using his other to fasten the strap above

311

his ears. It sat far better now that his hair was short. Mask firmly in place, he jumped to stand on the plaza railing, pushing off from there to climb on to an overhead walkway that ran towards the West.

Wishing he'd brought some earplugs to block out the crowd's roar, he jogged across the tops of the houses. The palace rose on the horizon like a great shining beacon, the metal on the building gleaming in the sunlight, and Noah's pulse picked up as he grew closer to it. He'd overtaken the parade now, and if he got to a good hiding spot he'd be able to see it arrive in the courtyard.

Finally, he reached the end of the residential district and stopped on the roof of the house at the very end of a row. The courtyard was so close he could almost taste it, but there was still the matter of the barriers to get around. Now everything was in full swing, there were green-clad guards wherever he looked. He cursed as he saw that the route he'd used the night before was swarming with guards, and the railing had been barbed; damn Damien! He knew rationally that the captain had sound reasoning – if Noah could use that route, then someone else could do the same – but still, damn him!

His eyes drifted over the buildings in front of him, looking for an alternative route. Everything seemed to be blocked off tightly, or packed with guards. For the first time in his life Noah had the sudden thought that he might be unable to access where he needed to go. That wasn't part of the plan!

Heart hammering against his ribcage, his gaze flicked from place to place, searching for alternative routes. Blocked; too crowded; too guarded – every possible way was barred.

Aware that every wasted second was one step closer to losing Crysta, he wracked his brain, panic rising. Suddenly, it struck him: the temple. If all possible routes were unavailable, then maybe it was time to try something a little impossible.

The temple was on the opposite side of the courtyard from where he was perching, so he scrambled down the side of the building and reluctantly dived into the flow of the crowd. He wouldn't be able to walk straight across to the other side – the parade barriers were in the way, and trying to cross the barricade would do nothing but get him arrested – but he could head further towards the courtyard and slip around the back of the palace. It would take time, time he wasn't entirely sure he had, but it was his only option.

Trying to get anywhere with haste in the festival crowd was like trying to swim through treacle, and Noah found himself glancing obsessively at his pocket watch, trying not to push past people so rudely that he got noticed. Only a few yelps as he slipped through the crowd betrayed the many feet he'd accidentally trodden on. The nearer he got to the palace courtyard, the thicker the crowd became, and the more it was full of Talen's upper-class citizens, who were more likely to take offence at his audacity in asking them to move aside. His expression was set in a near permanent glare behind his mask, and more often than he cared for he was brought to a standstill. He had no idea where the parade was, but hoped that since the crowd hadn't started whooping and screaming it was still a fair way off.

Reaching a less crowded area as he edged around the side of the palace gates was like a gasp of air to a half-drowned man, and Noah revelled in the fact that he could move his limbs more than an inch in each direction. He sprinted towards the steps that would lead him to the next overhead walkway, and took them three at a time. If he wanted to make it right around the palace gates to the other side of the courtyard, he'd have to hurry.

He felt like he was flying as he raced across walkways and over rooftops, hardly ever dropping down to street level. But it still didn't feel fast enough; the parade surely had to be nearly there!

All he had to go on was the noise of the crowd, which had increased to an ear-splitting but uniform roar that told him nothing. What if the parade was nearly over, and the assassin planned to strike before the opening feast even began? There was no way Noah would get there in time!

His world had narrowed to nothing but the rush of blood in his ears and the rhythmic pounding of his feet on stone. He kept running, then jumped on to the railing of the walkway he was using, eyes on the grocer's roof several feet away. As he pushed off, his arms outstretched, he heard a loud cracking noise, his eyes widening as he felt the stone beneath the railing slide away. The railing was crumbling under his weight, a whole section of it landing on the walkway with a smash, and instead of propelling forward on to the roof opposite Noah found himself free-falling down the gap between the walkway and the building.

Crying out on instinct, he twisted in the air and reached up with one long arm, wrapping his hand around the metal support strut of the walkway's railing, sweaty palm struggling to keep his grip. He managed to grab it just before he fell out of reach, jerking to an abrupt halt that wrenched his shoulder so hard his eyes watered, and he thought he heard a snap. He gritted his teeth, swinging up to reach for another support strut with his other hand, his fingers brushing the metal several times before he was able to grip it firmly. His left shoulder still searing with pain, Noah forced himself to ignore it and focus on pulling himself up to the walkway. Tucking his knee up as far as he could manage, he tried to stretch his leg up and hook his foot through the railing. His first attempt failed, causing him to swing back hard and jar his shoulder again, and he swore softly at the pain.

On his second try he managed to hoist himself up high enough to throw an arm over the stone top of the railing, rolling over and landing sprawled on the paved walkway. Chest heaving, Noah lay there on his back for a minute or two, wondering if he was capable of moving. His pistol was jabbing him in the spine, and while he was at least eighty per cent certain his shoulder wasn't dislocated – he knew how that felt from experience – he'd probably wrenched at least one muscle. That was going to make climbing the temple a hundred times more difficult.

A series of loud bangs went off, and he jumped, groaning at the new jolt of pain it caused. Above him in the sky he could just about make out showers of coloured sparks, and his heart sank; more fireworks. That meant the parade had reached the palace courtyard. He was almost out of time.

Ignoring the pain and the tears running from his eyes behind his mask, Noah dragged himself to his feet, readjusted his pistol and satchel and gingerly flexed his shoulder, hissing in a sharp breath. Yes, climbing the temple was going to be *fun*.

31

It took a little while for Noah to regain his momentum, but gradually the adrenalin coursing through his veins made the pain in his shoulder barely an afterthought. He would probably hate himself in the morning – and probably for several weeks after that – but as long as Crysta was alive, he didn't care. Time was ticking down until the opening ceremony began, and he needed to be on top of the temple before then.

As he came around the other side of the palace he could just about make out the lights and streamers decorating the courtyard, and heard the swell of festival music grow louder. He could see the temple in the distance now, with its elegant yet deadly metal spirals on the roof and its flat stone walls, and he laughed breathlessly. He truly had gone mad to think he could climb it.

He stopped on the roof of one of the taller buildings to look towards the palace courtyard, his breath catching in his throat at the beauty of it. It was a riot of green and bronze, intermixed with earthy browns and pale greys. Metal-wrought statues of animals stood everywhere, looking so lifelike Noah half expected them to begin moving. The tables were immaculately laid out, awaiting the members of the court, and the head table was truly fit for royalty with its emerald green cloth and wreaths of bright flowers.

No one was out there yet, and there were still several troupes of dancers and acrobats from the tail end of the parade making their way towards the courtyard, but Noah could tell he had maybe ten minutes before the monarchs came out to open the festival. Ten minutes in which to get on to the roof of the temple and start looking out for anyone suspicious. He could only hope Lena, wherever she was, was watching the food with eagle eyes.

Reluctantly joining the crowd below, Noah fought his way past people of all ages and sizes in his journey towards the temple, eyes fixed on the imposing building. No one in the crowd noticed him as he crept around to the back of the tall building, eyeing the smooth wall for a crack or crevice so he could start his ascent. The barricades were flush against the wall of the temple at the front, and he wished they weren't so visible or he could have used them instead. There was only one guard at the smaller back door of the temple, and Noah carefully avoided his line of sight, eventually deciding to jump for the lowest window sill.

It was several feet above even his long reach, but after a decent run-up he managed to propel himself high enough to grab it with the tips of his fingers, holding on for dear life and trying to dig his toes into the barely there joins between the stones. If he could get a little higher, he'd reach the part of the wall that was decoratively cobbled – a far easier prospect.

Securing his grip on the rough stone and walking himself up the wall enough to hook a heel over the window sill, Noah hoisted himself up, perching on his toes on the narrow ledge. The window was far too tall for him to reach for the wall above it, but at least he was off the ground. He needed to move fast; the longer he was visible on the wall of the temple, the more chance he had of being spotted.

'Come on, Hansen,' he muttered to himself, shuffling to the very edge of the sill and having to turn his head at an awkward angle to see all his available options from behind his mask. With one foot still on the sill, he moved the other up to squeeze his toes between two slabs of stone, glad for the give in the leather of his soft-soled boots. Thank the Goddess he hadn't given in to the temptation to wear his royal festival garments.

Slowly, steadily, Noah made his way up the wall of the temple, attempting to climb diagonally to get further towards the front of the building. He couldn't see what was going on in the courtyard, and it made him nervous. After what felt like an age, he reached the cobbled part of the wall and gripped two protruding rocks to give himself a breather, shaking out his limbs and rotating his aching shoulder as best he could without losing balance. Storms, he was going to get himself killed with his reckless stunts one day; he wasn't entirely confident that day wouldn't be today.

While he had the advantage of the cobbles, Noah made his way around the circular tower to get a view of the courtyard. As he craned his neck to get a better look his heart sped up at the sight of the tables beginning to fill with nobles. Once the entire court had sat down, the monarchs would take their places and the ceremony would begin.

He still had at least twenty feet to go before he would reach a point high enough to cross over to the roof of the bank, and only ten more feet of it was cobbled. After that was the first row of lethal-looking metalwork, and it only got more difficult from there.

The cobbles felt like a glorious respite after the flat wall and he scaled them quickly, pausing in front of the wrought-iron decoration on the edge of the lower roof. Worn dull in some places but razor-sharp in others, Noah couldn't see a way of climbing over them without causing himself serious injury. Fantastic.

Edging further around the wall until he reached a small section that looked slightly less deadly than the rest, he shrugged his sleeves down to cover his palms, hoping a layer of fabric between skin and metal might protect him. It was a dangerous way to climb, but it would be worse to climb with shredded hands.

Tentatively grabbing at a thick twist of smoothed metal, Noah hissed as a sharp piece nicked his knuckles. Pulling himself higher with his better arm, he reached his injured one over the top of the metalwork, looking for something safe to hold. His sleeve was well and truly mangled as he used it as a barrier between his forearm and the top of the iron edging, and the other sleeve soon reached a similar state as he shifted his hand next to its partner, ready to swing himself over the top. With his toes still on the cobbled part of the wall, he was about as balanced as he could be, and slowly began to slide himself up the wall one step at a time, searching blindly for good footholds.

Finally, his feet were up high enough that when he straightened his legs it sent him leaning over the top of the metal structure, balanced by his hands. The next part was possibly the most difficult of the entire manoeuvre, getting his legs over the metal and on to the two-foot wide ledge that ringed the protruding tower of the temple. One wrong move and he could be dead. His heart was racing, clothes starting to stick to his skin with sweat, but he forged on. Lifting one leg, he felt the metal cut through his trousers and into his knee like a knife through butter.

He nearly cried in relief when he got a foot firmly on the ledge, allowing him to lever the rest of his body over the intricate metal caging and on to the stone. Bleeding from more places than he cared to count and feeling like every cell in his body was on fire, Noah dropped into a sitting position with his back against the tower wall, letting his head fall against the stone just hard enough to return him to focus. 'I'm crazy,' he declared softly, shaking his head. 'I've completely lost my mind. Storms, what am I *doing*?' Saving Crysta. It was too late to be second-guessing himself; he wouldn't be able to get down alive if he did. The only way was up, and then across to the bank.

Allowing himself only a minute to rest, he faced the wall he had to climb next. Fifteen feet of near flat stone, with another row of metalwork and some decorative metal fish before he reached a ledge high enough to jump to the bank. He was amazed he hadn't been spotted yet; thank the Goddess his clothing blended in with the stone, and that the crowd's focus was elsewhere.

Reaching up for a handhold, Noah prepared to start the next leg of his climb, only to freeze when the crowd went completely crazy, cheering and screaming wildly. That could only mean one thing. He turned and his jaw dropped slightly, his eyes widening as he took in the sight in front of him. The king and queen were walking up to the head table, looking exquisite in Erova's royal colours, but his eyes were fixed on Crysta several paces behind them. For a moment he forgot to breathe.

She looked like the Goddess herself had taken human form, her jet black braid shining in the sunlight. Her skirt was made of an opulent green fabric, sheer from just above her knees to the ground, showing off knee-high brown leather boots, their bronze detailing sparkling. From there upwards was an underskirt in a rich emerald green silk and a bright bronze satin bodice, both embroidered with what looked like leaves studded with emeralds. He was relieved to see equally bright bronze silk armour covering her arms.

But it was the mask that took his breath away. It covered almost the entirety of her face, only her eyes, lips and chin bare, and stretched down to meet the wide green taffeta choker around her neck. The choker was covered in gears, with a large teardrop-shaped emerald on delicate bronze chains resting on her chest, and with her hair pulled back and threaded with bright green ribbon it was easy to see how the gears intertwined with those on the mask, allowing the small green-jewelled metal fish to swim around the choker and up over her nose, then back down to her neck. She looked like a warrior queen; all she needed was a blazing sword in her hand.

He was glad to be sitting on the ledge at this moment, for he surely would have fallen if he'd been climbing. The mask looked even better than he'd imagined. Even from this distance, he could see Crysta's grey eyes shining happily through the eyeholes of the mask, and the gap in its lower half showed her beaming smile. The opening ceremony and masquerade ball were her favourite parts of the entire festival. Noah just wished he could be there to enjoy it with her.

A green-clad servant hurried up to hand a loudspeaker to Crysta. A hush fell over the crowd, and he could feel his heartbeat in his ears; it had begun.

There was total silence as everyone waited for the princess to speak, as was her right as the eldest daughter of the Goddess. She was to lead the country in prayer, and bless the land for the year to come.

'Ladies, gentlemen and children,' she started, her voice confident and even, loudspeaker held firmly in one lace-gloved hand. 'Thank you for joining together to celebrate this past year, and for offering your hearts and your souls to the Goddess in plea for a year of prosperity to come.' Noah shook his head, forcing himself to ignore the sound of Crysta's voice; he knew her speech almost off by heart, having listened as she practised. He had to climb while everyone was distracted; surely no one would anger the Goddess so badly as to kill the princess before she could recite the prayer.

Knowing how long Crysta's speech was, and how long the prayer would take her, Noah knew exactly how much time he had to get on to the roof of the bank. It wasn't nearly as long as he needed. Reaching for the handhold he'd been about to grab before the monarchs arrived, he tried to block Crysta from his mind. He needed to concentrate on nothing but the wall in front of him if he wanted to make it to the top in time.

Climbing over the second row of metalwork was infinitely more difficult than the first; there was no ledge to throw himself on to at the other side. One of his sleeves was almost ripped clean off about five inches from the cuff, and the shins of his boots were near shredded from the sharp metal, but at least when he got to the other side he was able to stand on the sturdier strips of solid metal, finding a section smooth enough that it wouldn't cut through the soles of his boots. Seeing the last stretch of wall decorated with gleaming metal fish leaping through waves, he studied them closer, eyeing the way they were bolted into the wall; they would make far better hand and footholds than the wall itself.

A grin on his face as he used a protruding fish fin to hoist himself up further, Noah finally felt like he'd actually make it; he was so close to the last ledge before the tower narrowed into a spire. He could use the ledge to jump over to the roof of the bank, where he'd have easy access to almost every building on that side of the courtyard.

A murmured prayer escaped his lips the moment he pulled himself up to crouch on the ledge, but he didn't have time to stand and celebrate his achievements. His gaze moved to the bank, about eight feet away and several feet below the ledge he was on; the perfect distance to jump without injuring himself more than he already was. His entire left arm and a good section of his torso were numb from the pain by now, but he was glad of it; his left shoulder was his landing shoulder. Standing with his toes just hanging over the edge of the roof, Noah refused to look down at Crysta as she spoke the requisite words of prayer, keeping his eyes focused on the flat roof in front of him and judging how much power he'd need for such a jump.

He flung himself from the ledge, eyes wide open as he jumped out into the gap, free-falling towards the bank roof. For a moment, he was terrifyingly certain he'd misjudged and was about to slam face first into the bank's wall, but he landed with an awkward roll that became more of a sprawling skid when his shoulder collapsed beneath him. It wasn't quiet, and Noah felt dread curl in his stomach as he waited for someone to call him out. Nothing happened – evidently the crowd were so immersed in prayer they hadn't noticed – and he let out a silent breath of relief.

He immediately dragged himself up again, crawling over to the raised ledge at the front of the building and leaning on it to watch as Crysta finished her prayer, closing with a short speech. Applause thundered from every direction as she sat down, and Noah felt a proud grin lighting up his face behind his mask even as he scoured the courtyard for anything unusual. It was only Crysta's second festival leading the opening ceremony, and she was already a pro. She would make a fantastic queen.

Applause fading, several servants rushed out with plates of food and goblets of wine, depositing them in front of the two princesses. Noah's heart was in his throat; the food must be eaten as an offering to the Goddess. If the poison was going to be in anything edible, it would be that.

Standing several paces behind Rosa's chair, dressed in her best uniform, was Lena, and he wished he had some way of signalling her to ask if the food was safe.

Noah was torn between watching the nobles and watching Crysta as she cut a piece of meat and raised her fork to her lips.

Nothing happened.

She swallowed, going for her next bite, and still nothing happened. Rosa too seemed perfectly fine.

His gaze scanned the gathered nobles, picking out the men who had been on his list of suspects, trying to see if anyone looked a little too eager for Crysta to keep eating. They were easy for him to spot, even in their masks – every court mask had been made by himself or his father, and he had each owner ingrained in his mind. Suddenly, he froze, a whisper of Diora's words coming into his head. *That little snake is far too selfish.*

He scanned the tables hurriedly, heart racing as he looked for the hideous serpent-faced mask he'd been commissioned to make. His gaze landed on an empty seat at one of the tables, and he swore quietly as he recognised the masks on the people sitting either side. Fabian Silva was nowhere to be seen.

32

Trying not to let his panic overwhelm him, Noah tried to work out where the young nobleman could be. He looked around to check he hadn't made a mistake, even as his instincts told him he was right. It all added up; Fabian was a minor member of the court, not due to inherit a title unless all three of his older brothers perished, and he was incredibly bitter about it. The spineless little worm of a man was constantly looking for ways to increase his standing. He was exactly the sort of man to seek Diora's help for a price.

Shifting to a crouched position, still hidden behind the ledge, Noah wished he'd brought some binoculars as he peered across to the other side of the courtyard, wanting to check the side he couldn't reach first, just to be sure. The only people he could see were green-clad guards, the bronze sashes and epaulettes of their dress uniforms shining like beacons. There were far too many of them for someone like Silva to get past. Turning, Noah focused his gaze on the courtyard itself, first studying the area directly around Crysta. Surely Silva wouldn't be so stupid as to try attacking her directly? Damien was sitting on her right; the man wouldn't get within fifteen feet of the table before being stopped.

'Think, think,' he murmured, rubbing at his temples behind his mask. He forced the thought of poison from his mind, imagining what he'd do if he wasn't aware of the method of assassination. For all he knew, the poison could have been a back-up plan, or even a red herring. It had already led him astray once. Might Silva use a gun of some sort? He shuffled further towards the other end of the roof to get a better look at all the buildings on that side of the bank. He froze.

There was a window open on the top floor of the lecture hall four buildings away, and a short rope ladder was clearly anchored in place. The roof had a high ledge that he couldn't see over, but he would bet any money that Silva was on that ledge. Gods only knew how long he'd been missing from the dinner before Noah had noticed; he could be preparing to shoot at any moment.

With not a second to spare, he got to his feet and hurled himself off the edge of the bank, stumbling a little in his exhaustion as he landed on the building beside it. He straightened up and made for the next building, which was slightly taller. Then the next. And the next.

Finally, Noah stood on the roof of the building adjacent to the lecture hall, making sure he was completely silent as he crept closer to the edge. He could hear quiet shuffling and the occasional mutter, and it was easy to place the nasal voice as Silva's.

Noah jumped down to a window sill on the lecture hall's second floor, landing with the slightest tap of soft boots on stone. He froze, just in case Silva had heard him. Waiting for as long as he dared, he began to climb as quietly as possible, taking it slowly once he reached the top of the wall, every inch of his body protesting. Still flat against the stone, he peered over the ledge on to the roof, biting his lip to stop himself making any noise. Sure enough Silva was there, crouched on one knee facing the courtyard, a crossbow mounted on his shoulder, his snakeskin-patterned mask tossed aside. Heart pounding as he saw the man lining up his shot, Noah clambered over the edge of the wall to stand on the roof, his footsteps loud enough to startle Silva. The nobleman turned, brown eyes wide in alarm when he caught sight of Noah. 'What? How – who are you? How did you know I was here?' Silva spluttered in a hiss, aiming his crossbow at Noah instead.

'Let's just say a little birdie told me . . . or perhaps a mean old spider is closer to the mark,' Noah retorted, taking a step closer. Anything to keep Silva's attention off Crysta for as long as possible.

The noble scowled. 'I knew the old man couldn't be trusted. He promised me the kingdom for this!'

'He's dead,' Noah informed him. 'Sorry, my fault. He can't give you anything – your little deal is void. So put the crossbow down, before you do something you regret.'

'I don't need him! All his death means to me is that I don't need to repay his favour. Now, I don't know who you are, but I have no issue with killing you too, so if you want to survive I'd suggest you run now.'

'I'm insulted, Fabian,' Noah responded. 'You don't recognise me?' He lifted his mask just long enough for him to glimpse his face. Shock entered Silva's eyes, and in the split second it took for his finger to start moving towards the trigger, Noah made what was quite possibly his most impulsive decision of the day – which was saying something. Praying his luck would hold for one more reckless venture, he sprinted directly at the noble, grabbing him in a tackle, sending both of them careening off the roof of the lecture hall.

Noah released Silva and focused on his own landing, tucking himself into a ball and rolling as smoothly as he could with his injured shoulder as he silently hit the ground. Silva, on the other hand, spent the entire two-storey descent screaming, and landed on his hip on the cobbled street. He groaned, and Noah quickly moved to stand over him, placing one foot on the man's throat. Not hard enough to hurt, but enough to make him think twice about attempting to get up. Silva whimpered.

'You're supposed to be tending to your dying father, or something,' the noble said, voice a little breathless from his fall. His crossbow was still in his hand, though it appeared to be broken, the bolt lying on the ground beside him.

'Clearly I'm not,' Noah said, shrugging the one shoulder he could still actually move. He looked up at the courtyard, flushing beneath his mask when he saw that every single person's attention was fixed on him. Several people were out of their seats, including the royal family and Damien, and Noah saw the shock in Crysta's eyes when she realised who he was.

'Do you believe me now, Damien?' he called across the courtyard, the tiniest hint of smugness in his voice. He was almost disappointed that Damien was wearing a full-face mask; it made it impossible to see his no doubt gobsmacked expression.

A moment's distraction was all Silva needed, and he shoved Noah's leg and struggled free. He was on his feet in a blink, crossbow abandoned on the ground. He threw a punch, but Noah ducked. 'I could have had it all,' Silva growled, grabbing him by the jacket and twisting. Noah easily escaped the grip, kicking at the nobleman's knee, ever thankful for Damien's combat lessons.

'Noah, what on *Tellus*?' Damien yelled, running towards them. Noah dodged another punch, matching Silva blow for blow.

'Here's your assassin,' he snapped, his attention focused on trying to subdue Silva. 'You're welcome.' If he hadn't been able to climb the temple, or hadn't spotted Silva in time, Crysta would be dead.

With a surge of anger, Noah got the upper hand before Damien reached him, grappling with Silva until he was pinned once more, this time by Noah's entire body. From the searing pain in his chest, Noah was fairly sure he'd cracked a collarbone, to go along with his ruined shoulder, and his vision turned a little white around the edges. Out of the corner of his eye he noticed Crysta. He felt light-headed just looking at her, though the pain probably had a hand in it. After not seeing her for days on end, missing her every minute, it took all his remaining strength to focus on Silva.

He turned to the man pinned beneath him, fixing him with a cold stare. 'You'd best explain yourself to your princess and your country before I allow the good captain here to take your pitiful carcass away.'

Silva merely glared at him, and Noah increased the pressure on his throat until he finally cried out. 'All right! All right!' He took in a deep, wheezing breath, making Noah wonder if the fall had cracked some of his ribs. He hoped it had.

'I did it for Rosa.'

'What?' The shaky voice was Rosa's, peering out from behind her sister, her face pale where the mask didn't cover it. 'I would never want my sister dead! I love her!'

'With her in the way, you could never be queen as you deserve to be!' Silva protested, breaking into hacking coughs after his exclamation. When he'd regained his breath, he looked back at Rosa, eyes shining deliriously. 'I knew that if I could just make Princess Crysta obsolete, you would have the throne in your grasp, and it wouldn't take long for me to make you fall in love with me. We would have married, and become the most powerful ruling couple Erova has ever seen!'

Dead silence greeted his words, before Noah snorted quietly. 'You, uh, missed Princess Rosa's rather vehement declaration of love for her handmaid, then?' No wonder Diora had chosen to work with Silva, if he was delusional enough to think that would ever happen. A crowd had gathered now, half the court out of their seats and close enough to hear Silva's words.

'A foolish childhood fancy – everyone has them,' Silva dismissed with a wave of his hand. 'She would have grown bored of the girl soon enough, and realised she needed a man to satisfy her.'

Rosa laughed, half incredulous, half hysterical. 'How *dare* you claim to know what I want? And how dare you pretend your delusional, power-hungry plans are on my behalf! You are *nothing* to me.'

'I was so close! We could have had everything, my lady. You'll never know what you've given up by letting this *low-class scum* stop me,' Silva spat in reply, anger growing in his dark eyes.

'That's enough,' Damien cut him off with a growl. 'Noah, let the bastard get up so I can arrest him.' Noah did as he was asked, reaching gingerly for the broken crossbow. Damien dragged Silva to his feet by the front of his jacket, patting him down in search of any other weapons while two guards held him by the arms. Silva grunted in pain several times, but no one seemed to care. Noah turned at the tap on his shoulder, seeing Crysta standing behind him, her eyes apologetic.

'Noah, I'm sorry,' she began softly. 'I should have trusted you about the assassin. I just . . . I was hurt. Because of Emilie.'

'I didn't think I was being unfaithful, truly,' he insisted. 'Now that you're safe I can explain –' At the sound of a throat being cleared he glanced at Damien, who was frowning.

'I thought you said the method would be poison?' the captain asked. 'There's nothing on him to indicate that, not unless he's hiding it *very* well.'

Noah shrugged. 'I thought it was,' he said, glancing down at the crossbow in his hands. 'But maybe that was a decoy.' Silva snorted, but Damien ignored him, gesturing for his two colleagues to start walking him towards the guard station. After two steps, Silva suddenly shoved an elbow into one guard's stomach and pulled away from the second. The guard doubled over, loosening his hold just enough for Silva to break free. Instantly he snatched the crossbow bolt off the ground and snarled at Crysta with a vicious grin.

'You didn't think I'd give up so easily, did you?' he hissed, launching himself at the princess. Noah dropped the broken crossbow and threw himself directly between Crysta and her assailant, but Silva, moving like the serpent on his discarded mask, ducked under his arm and lunged, the crossbow bolt in his hand headed tip-first for Crysta's chest.

Crysta screamed, and Noah's uninjured arm reached out to shield her, his hand wrapping around the pointed head of the bolt, forcing it out of Silva's grasp. His hand stung as the sharp point bit into his skin, but he didn't care, watching as Damien grabbed Silva around the waist and lifted him off the ground, handing him over to two of his strongest guards. To Noah's surprise, the noble gave him a look of triumph. His hand still stung from the crossbow bolt, and it took a few moments to realise this was where Silva's gaze was directed. Not at Crysta, or Rosa, or even Damien, but straight at Noah's hand. The teen looked down at his hand, the stinging sensation becoming more and more intense. His fingers were stiff as he unclenched them.

Almost immediately his entire hand began to burn, and his eyes widened. The head of the bolt was glistening, but not with blood, and Noah felt an overwhelming sense of dread as the burn raced up his arm, his heart pounding dangerously fast in his chest. Ten minutes, he remembered. From contact to death.

He staggered, the bolt falling to the ground with a clatter, and looked up at Crysta. The terrible word formed on his lips. 'Velora.'

Horror dawned in her eyes. 'Noah, no!' she breathed, rushing towards him. His skin began to feel as if it was melting, his muscles spasming as agony flooded through him. Crysta dropped down to him, and he cried out when she grabbed his shoulder. 'Please, no – Damien, help!'

Her scream echoed in Noah's head, sounding distorted and faint, the pressure rising behind his eyes. He felt like his brain was going to explode in his skull.

'Found the poison,' he choked out, tongue feeling twice the size it should. 'Crysta –' He coughed, tasting copper. His vision began to blur. He couldn't fight it as the world began to spin around him, his senses nothing but fire and pain as everything went black.

33

His entire body felt like it had been dipped in acid and left to dry directly over a roaring fire. His eyelids felt like lead as he tried to open them. Everything about him felt like lead, now he thought about it, and he tried to remember what had brought him to such a state. He remembered climbing; lots of climbing. And a fair amount of falling too. And . . . Crysta? Looking like a gift from the gods in a beautiful green dress. There had been a great deal of panic, and pain, but Noah's brain hurt when he tried to focus.

Still with his eyes closed, he tried to figure out where he was; he was lying down, he knew. It was a fairly comfortable place to be lying down, even if he did feel like the storms had decided to have their fun with him. He tried to listen for any sort of noise, but he felt as though his ears were plugged with cotton. Was he dead? He'd thought death was supposed to ease pain, not prolong it.

Noah managed to force his eyes open, but his vision blurred. The room was light and large, but all he could see were vague blobs of colour, and he didn't recognise anything. Several seconds later his eyes focused, and understanding dawned on him: the palace medical wing. Why was he there?

'Oh, thank the gods you're awake!' Crysta breathed, and he turned to see her sitting in a chair at his bedside. How long had she been there?

'What . . . what happened?' he croaked, surprised at how hoarse his voice was. His tongue felt wrong in his mouth and his lips were bone dry.

'You don't remember?' she asked, brow furrowing. She reached over to a small table at her side for a cup, and was soon spooning small chips of ice past his lips. He relished the cool moisture, trying to think back a little further now that his eyes were open. He'd been separated from Crysta, he remembered that much. And he remembered worrying for her safety. His brow furrowed, his head aching as he desperately tried to figure out what was going on. He searched inside his head for any solid memory of the past week.

It all came rushing back abruptly: the argument, breaking into the palace, the festival, Silva, everything. Even his father's disturbing automaton. 'Silva,' he murmured, voice a little stronger. 'Tried to kill you. Fell off a building. Then . . . ?' He trailed off, not remembering anything past that.

'You grabbed one of his poison-tipped crossbow bolts, remember?' Crysta explained, reaching to stroke his clammy forehead. 'To protect me. You almost *died*, Noah.' She choked on a sob, and he wished he could reach out and comfort her, but he couldn't feel his arms.

'It was velora,' he murmured, the question clear in his eyes. People didn't survive velora.

'Damien had the antidote on him,' Crysta answered. 'Thank the Goddess. But . . . there was a slight problem.' His frown deepened at the tone of her voice.

'What?' he asked apprehensively, dreading the answer.

'The doctors had to . . . they had to take some of your arm, Noah. It was too badly damaged by the poison. I'm so sorry.' Tears slid down her cheeks, and Noah froze, wide-eyed. Ignoring Crysta's protests, he craned his neck, trying to sit up. His left arm was bound tightly to his chest, and at the searing pain in his shoulder he remembered why, but his right arm lay limp at his side, and there were thick bandages wound tightly around his bicep. Below that, his arm was definitely a lot shorter than he remembered. It seemed to end at the elbow. He stared blankly, stunned. Half his arm was . . . gone?

'There was no other way?' he asked roughly, and Crysta shuffled her chair closer, stroking his hair as she shook her head.

'I'm sorry. It was your arm or your life, and I would much prefer to keep you alive,' she added with a weak smile.

'I thought you'd rather I leave and never come back?' he returned, remembering their arguments. Crysta sighed, looking apologetic.

'Near-death of a loved one tends to result in a change of perspective,' she replied. 'Besides, Lena told us everything – Rosa and Damien and me. She told us about Diora, and Emilie, all the things you did as Daniel.'

'I'm sorry for hiding it from you,' Noah said instantly, lying back down and turning his head towards her. 'I thought I was helping, but I've learned now that I was wrong. I've learned a lot of things this last week.' A lot of things he should have learned years ago. Better late than never, he supposed.

'You *were* helping,' Crysta insisted. 'Damien and his guards had no idea what was going on in the lower city; you're a hero over there. You saved lives. But I'm sorry too; I should have let you explain before judging you. I shouldn't have been so impulsive. Forgive me?'

'There's nothing to forgive,' he said weakly, relieved that she didn't seem to be angry at him any more. 'Wait. Festival. Shouldn't you be in prayer?' He didn't want her ignoring her duties to the country and the Goddess just because he was injured. She laughed lightly, leaning down to kiss his forehead.

'Noah, the festival is almost over. The closing ceremony is tonight; you've been unconscious for days. The doctors weren't certain you'd ever wake up.' Her face was pinched, and his chest clenched at the thought of her having to go through almost the entire festival thinking he might be gone for good.

'Help me sit up,' he urged, trying to wriggle further up the bed.

'Stop it, you'll hurt yourself!' Crysta fussed, grabbing some pillows from the empty bed next to Noah's and piling them up behind him. 'Happy now?'

Not looking too long at the bandages, he gingerly raised his aching right arm, stretching it out towards Crysta. 'I will be when you come here and let me hug you as well as I can right now,' he replied, voice solemn. Crysta choked back another sob, wasting no time surging forward and gently wrapping one arm around his neck, burying her face in his chest. He was shirtless, he noticed for the first time. Uncaring, he settled what was left of his right arm around

338

her, dropping his head to press his nose to her hair, inhaling deeply. Gods, he'd missed her. 'I'm alive,' he murmured soothingly. 'I'm alive, and awake, and I'm *fine*.'

'You're far from fine,' she scoffed, and his gaze dropped to his bandaged elbow. Storms, why did it have to be his right arm? He'd have to relearn everything left-handed. Fencing, painting, writing . . . he'd never climb again. Not without severe difficulty, at least. And especially not considering how much he'd no doubt damaged his left shoulder. He was going to be useless for months.

'Does this mean I don't have to learn piano any more?' he asked instead, forcing a smile on to his lips. He could mourn his arm later; he needed to be strong for Crysta now. She let out a giggle, looking up from his chest.

'I love you,' she declared softly, cupping his cheek. 'And I want to marry you. As soon as possible.'

'Isn't it supposed to be me who asks that question?' he said with raised eyebrows. She smirked, thumb gently brushing his cheekbone.

They both turned at the sound of footsteps, and Noah's breath caught in his throat as his father entered the room. Evander did a double take at seeing his son awake, letting Noah get a good look at him; the man looked like he'd aged thirty years in the last five days. 'Oh, my boy,' he breathed, rushing forward to Noah's bedside. Crysta barely managed to back up in time to avoid being grabbed in the hug, and Noah choked back a sob at his father's crushing embrace. 'My dear, dear boy. I thought I'd lost you too.'

Tears stinging at his eyes, Noah hugged back as best he could with his injuries, shaking his head fiercely. 'Still here,

Da. Promise. Not quite in one piece, but here all the same.'
Evander pulled back, looking at the place where his son's
right forearm used to be.

'At least this means I won't have to worry about you falling
off a rooftop any more,' he muttered, and Noah let out a bark
of surprised laughter. Trust his da not to sugar-coat things.

'Been there, done that,' he replied with a grin. 'Suppose
it's time for me to grow up.' Evander chuckled, ruffling his
son's hair.

'I've been telling you that for years,' he teased, then
leaned in to kiss the teen's forehead. 'I'm proud of you, lad.
But by the gods, if you ever do anything so reckless again
I'll kill you myself.'

'I think we're all proud.' Noah startled at the new voice,
seeing Damien approaching with Rosa at his side. The
captain was out of uniform for once, and more unshaven
than usual. 'And I owe you an apology or two, Noah. Or
should I say Daniel?' Evander looked surprised at the reference, and Noah's smile became more of a grimace.

'Just Noah is fine,' he said firmly. 'Daniel Novak is gone
for good, don't worry. And you don't need to apologise; like
you told me, you were just trying to do your job.'

'Clearly not well enough.' Damien ran a hand through
his hair, a wry smile at his lips. 'You caused quite the scene,
you know,' he informed Noah. 'Diving off the lecture hall
with Fabian Silva like that. Everyone's still talking about it,
even as far as the shipyard.'

'Where's Silva now?'

'Prison, where he belongs, awaiting trial. It won't be
pretty,' Damien replied, sounding darkly satisfied. 'I won't

be surprised if the court wants him dead.' Noah couldn't find it in himself to feel bad about that. 'If you'd not been there, Crysta would be dead by now. I'll never be able to thank you enough for that; I don't think any of us will.'

'Don't be ridiculous,' Noah said. 'If anything, I should be thanking you for saving my life with that antidote.'

'I think we all have things to apologise for, and things to be grateful for,' Rosa said quietly. 'Maybe it would be best to just draw a line under everything and move on, or we'll all be indebted for years.' Her eyes met Noah's directly as she spoke, and he felt a lump rise in his throat at the clear gesture of forgiveness. He would never forgive himself for what he'd done to her, not completely, but at least it was looking like she wouldn't hate him forever.

'That . . . that sounds like a good idea,' he agreed, voice thick. A silence fell between them, and Noah found his eyes straying to his missing hand, still unable to believe it had actually happened. How long would it take him to get used to it? He could see a lot of broken plates and mugs in his near future. Part of him wanted the bandages to come off, needing to see proof that his forearm was truly no longer there, while another part of him didn't ever want to see the stump of his elbow.

'So when can I get out of here?' he asked, breaking the silence. As overjoyed as he was to be back on Crysta's good side, he just wanted to go home. Trying to act like he was fine was exhausting, and he wanted privacy before he let himself fall to pieces.

'Matron Karoline said you're free to go whenever you feel up to it,' the captain told him. 'The poison is out of your system, so other than your previous injuries, you're fine. Speaking of which, storms, lad, what did you do to your arms and legs? You look like you've slept on a bed of razors!'

'Climbed the temple to get over the barrier,' Noah explained, watching as Damien's jaw dropped. 'I wouldn't recommend it.'

'By the Goddess; first the palace, now the temple. It's probably a damn good thing you're no longer able to go crawling up the walls – we'd never get any peace!' He shook his head, astonished.

'I won't be doing it again, I can promise you,' Noah muttered wryly. 'Da, will you help me dress? Then we can head out.'

'You can have a room in the palace, if you'd like?' Crysta offered. 'Both of you, of course. You don't have to leave straight away.'

'You won't want me underfoot while you're trying to close the festival,' Noah said with a shake of his head. 'I'll be back tomorrow, though, and maybe I'll stay a while after that.' He didn't want Crysta to spend the entire evening fretting over him and apologising. He just wanted peace.

'You'd better,' Crysta murmured, understanding in her grey eyes. 'We'll leave you to get dressed, then.' She leaned over to kiss him on the cheek. 'And Mother and Father will want to see you before you go. They've been awfully worried about you.' Noah smiled, nodding, and everyone except for Evander left the room, the older man getting to his feet.

'You all right?' he asked his son, a knowing look in his eyes. If it had been anyone else Noah would have put on a brave face, insisting a little thing like a missing hand couldn't slow him down. He sighed, his right arm moving reflexively to run his fingers through his hair, before he realised what he was doing and aborted the movement, letting the half-limb fall to his side.

'I will be,' he replied, not sure who he was trying to convince, himself or his father. 'I just . . . need some time to adjust. Come on, let's get me dressed, then we can go home.'

Waving off the many offers of an escort home, Noah and his father headed across the courtyard. Stepping inside the guard station, Noah's eyes widened; as soon as they spotted him, every single man and woman in the room stopped what they were doing, stood, and saluted him. 'What on Tellus?' he murmured to himself.

Felix beamed at him. 'We wanted to thank you, sir, for putting your life on the line for the princess. You showed bravery that any guard of Erova would envy. We appreciate that. And,' he added with a grin, 'if you're ever in the market for a new profession, you only have to ask.' Noah snorted at that, glancing around to see that everyone had gone back to work, then he leaned in closer to Felix.

'Between you and me, I may already have that covered,' he murmured. 'If a certain question is received well.' It took several seconds for his meaning to click, then Felix beamed again.

'You're going to do it, then, sir? Finally?' he asked quietly, looking eager. Noah nodded; the more people he told, the less likely he was to lose his nerve at the last minute.

'I think it's about time, don't you?' he said, a smile creeping across his lips. It was long past time, truthfully.

Leaving Felix to get back to work, Noah and Evander walked to the courtyard outside. It was just as much a riot of colour and activity as he remembered it being from the opening ceremony, servants all working to set the tables and finish off the new decorations.

His gaze flicked involuntarily to the paved area outside the lecture hall, where he'd almost died. There was no trace of anything amiss. Noah didn't know what he'd been expecting – blood spatter, a mark on the paving stones, he wasn't sure. It had been a remarkably bloodless confrontation.

Tearing his gaze away, he forced himself to keep walking. As he stepped up to the gate he was greeted with a veritable wave of noise. The entire crowd were applauding and cheering, and it took him several moments to realise they were doing so for *him*.

Noah hung back as the guard unlocked the gate, and was surprised when the crowd hurried to part respectfully, still applauding him.

He leaned heavily on his father as they walked home, keeping his head down and his bandaged arm as hidden as possible. He felt a pang of sadness, thinking of the usual route he'd take, climbing walls and running across rooftops. He wouldn't be able to do that any more.

Despite having to take what he considered the long way home, he was surprised at how quickly they seemed to arrive at their front door.

'Oh, it's good to be home,' Evander murmured, and Noah eyed him in confusion.

'Have you not been home recently?'

'Of course not, lad! I've been at the palace, waiting for you to wake up. You didn't expect me to just leave you there when we didn't know if you'd make it?' Noah flushed, and Evander swatted him lightly over the head. 'Daft boy. Go on, let's get some food in you and set you up in bed, you need more rest. Get yourself settled in the kitchen, I'm just going to go check on a few things.' He smoothed Noah's hair fondly, then turned away. With a sigh Noah continued into the kitchen, knowing he had little choice.

He stared at his right elbow, trying to drill into his mind that his forearm was no longer at the end of it. Now that the pain medication was beginning to wear off, he could *feel* his hand, feel his fingers clenched tight into a fist, but it was no longer there. It made his elbow ache.

His eyes drooped half closed as he waited, the exhaustion setting in once more. Wondering if he'd be able to stay awake long enough to eat anything, he nearly fell out of his chair at a loud cry of anguish from the room next door; his father's bedroom. He raced out of the kitchen and around the corner, stopping in his tracks in the doorway. His father was on his knees on the floor, moaning in distress, holding something tight in his arms. At a glimpse of metal and dark brown synthetic hair, it clicked in Noah's mind: the automaton.

'Da, what's wrong? What is it?' he asked, concerned. Evander looked up, tears in his eyes.

'I've lost her,' he wailed. 'I've lost her, she's gone. All over again.' Noah frowned at his sobbed words, stepping closer and dropping to one knee at his father's side.

'What's happened, Da?' he asked, voice calmer. Evander loosened his grip on the automaton, enough to show Noah the blackened, charred hole in the abdomen of the dress she was wearing. Through the burned fabric he could make out a melted, twisted mess of metal, and his heart sank in realisation.

'I left her on when I went to the festival; Marie was here and I didn't want to look like a madman by having to double back. I thought she'd be fine, I thought I'd only be a few hours! There must have been something off in my calculations, and when I didn't come back and she was left on too long she just . . .'

'Overloaded,' Noah finished softly. 'Oh, Da.' He hadn't liked the machine, and had wanted it gone, but . . . not like this.

'I've lost her all over again, Noah,' Evander sobbed, staring down at the automaton's blank porcelain face, its eyes empty of tyrium light. 'Storms, I barely just got her back! What do I do?'

'Let her go,' Noah murmured, glancing down at his useless arms in frustration. All he wanted was to rest an assuring hand on his father's shoulder, but he couldn't even do that any more. 'She died years ago, Da. I know it hurts, but you have to let her go.'

'I don't know how, lad,' Evander whimpered, leaning his head against his son's chest as Noah shuffled closer. 'I lost her, and I almost lost you – I can't function on my own!'

'You're not on your own,' Noah reminded gently. 'I'm still here. And by the looks of things, I'm going to need you more than you'll need me.' He held up his stump pointedly, and Evander scoffed.

'Give it a few months, you and Crysta will be married; you'll have an army of servants to cater to your every need,' he retorted.

'Do you really think I want servants butting in on my life like that?' he asked incredulously. Evander frowned, and Noah ducked his head to lean his chin on his father's hair. 'I'll always need you, Da. I know it's hard for you, with Ma gone, and I wish I knew how to make that easier for you. But maybe this is a sign that trying to replace her isn't the way to go about it?'

Evander sighed in defeat. 'I suppose,' he agreed, still sounding upset. 'But, gods, Noah, I want her back.'

'You and me both,' Noah murmured, remembering warm hugs and a loving smile. 'But the world doesn't work that way, Da. You have to live with what you're given. Sometimes it can take a while to adjust.'

He looked down at his bandaged stump, biting his lip. It was going to take more than a little while to adjust to that, but he'd get there. 'The concept is brilliant, Da. But . . . maybe if you just build it as its own identity, you might get a little less attached if it has some technical faults.'

'Yes, maybe,' Evander said slowly, his mind clearly already caught up in the mechanics.

'Come on,' Noah urged, before the man disappeared to his workshop and forgot about the rest of the world once more. 'Food and bed, for both of us, I think.' All he wanted was to sleep, and start looking forward to a life at Crysta's side with no more secrets between them.

He paused as a thought crossed his mind, and he was again faced with his own uselessness, thanks to his injuries. 'Though, Da, would you do me a favour first?'

'Anything,' his father replied without hesitation.

'Would you send a quick note to the palace, asking Crysta to spare some time for me in the morning? I have something I need to ask her.'

It took a moment for the gears to click in Evander's mind, and his eyes widened. 'Truly?' he murmured. Noah nodded decisively. Tomorrow morning he'd go back to the palace, ring in hand, and drop to one knee the best he could in his current state, formally asking what had already been answered.

'It's about time, don't you think?'

He was out of obstacles; finally, there was nothing holding him back. It wasn't quite the way he'd imagined it, and he didn't doubt things would be difficult in the coming months – but they would be infinitely better with Crysta at his side. He needed to focus on the positives.

Everything else could wait.

Don't miss out on the first
Tellus adventure!

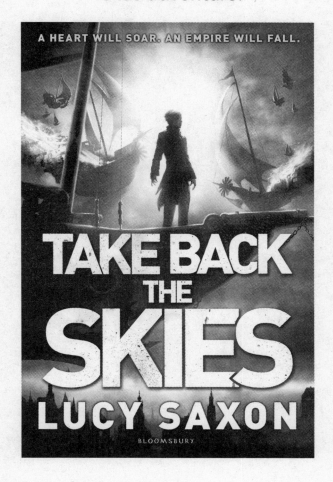

1

Rain fell lazily from charcoal-coloured clouds as Catherine Hunter sprinted through darkening streets, her long hair tied in a tight braid and tucked beneath a black knitted cap. Her thick woollen coat and black work trousers disguised her gender quite nicely. She was practically unrecognisable; only the people who knew her well would have been able to tell who she was.

A faint smile tugged at her lips as she reached the familiar tree beside the high stone wall that surrounded the area in which she lived. It took barely any effort to swing herself up into its branches, the knots worn into footholds by constant use. With practised ease, she scrambled up as high as she could manage, edging on to an outstretched branch that just brushed the wall's peak. From there it was just a short jump over the wall, her thud upon landing muffled by the grass. Taking no longer than a second to regain her balance, she resumed running, diving into a gap at the base of a bush. The fence panel behind it was open, as she'd left it, and she crawled through without a care for the mud on her clothes. Her father would never see them.

Flitting across the garden to the back door, she pulled a pin from her hair and slid it into the lock, opening it effortlessly. Leaving her boots at the very back of the hall closet, she shut the door soundlessly behind her, hurrying in socked feet towards the stairs. It was her habit to be silent, though she knew she was unlikely to draw her father from his office. Catherine would rather not risk it; the punishment for sneaking out was one she didn't like to think about.

After a brief detour to her bedroom to change into more appropriate clothing, Catherine wandered down to the living room, pulling her hair loose as she did so. She was unsurprised to see the newscast screen on in the corner; rarely did her father turn it off, even if he was nowhere near it. She sank on to the plush grey carpet, pulling her knees up to her chest and trying to regulate her breathing. Her father probably wouldn't want her to join him for dinner, but if he did decide to summon her and she gave herself away by looking out of breath, she could expect to be unable to sit down for at least a week.

She sighed to herself as upbeat music began to blare from the newscast screen and another recruitment broadcast played out. She wished that, just once, they might show something other than the war. Yes, she understood that the war with Mericus was important and people wanted to know what was going on – but didn't people also want to know what was going on in Siberene, or how the storms were in the East?

'Your child will be one of many, expertly trained to protect their country,' the cast told her in a proud, tinny voice. She sighed once more, tightly hugging her knees. Had she been a common child she would have been one of those sent to fight so the adults could stay behind and keep the country from crumbling. She wasn't sure whether to be thankful for her birth, or dismayed by it. Surely even war was better than the life of pseudo-freedom she had now. No amount of sneaking out to roam the streets could change the fact that she was trapped by her father's demands and expectations.

Gears whirred and she looked up to see the family servant – a mecha she had affectionately named Samuel – walking jerkily into the room, a tray of food in his claw-like hand.

'Is Father not eating dinner with me, Sam?' she asked, standing to accept the tray. The purple-white glow in Sam's eyes dimmed.

'No, Miss Catherine. Master Nathaniel is working,' he answered in his gravelly voice. Nathaniel was *always* working. Not that Catherine minded, as she liked being able to eat without being interrogated or insulted.

Sam reached out a thick bronze arm to straighten the silk throw over the back of the sofa, puffs of pale purple steam spilling from the thin chimney on his shoulder in time with the mechanical tick of his metal insides.

'And Mother?' she asked, setting her plate on the low table and sitting on the floor to eat.

'Mistress Elizabeth is sleeping.'

Her mother was always sleeping these days. Sleeping, crying or having a shaking fit. Her father kept telling her that the doctors were doing their best, but she couldn't remember the last time she'd seen a doctor at the house.

They had probably given up, just like her father, and were waiting for Elizabeth Hunter to die.

'Thank you, Samuel. You may leave.'

Catherine half-heartedly forked potatoes into her mouth. From the living room, there was a very good view of the shipyard, second only to the view from her bedroom. She spent a lot of time staring at the shipyard, watching skyships lifting gracefully into the air with canvas wings outstretched, the propellers beneath giving enough momentum for the ships to quickly latch on to the fierce updraughts that wound through the docks. How she wished to fly in a skyship: the freedom, the boundless space, with no expectations from anyone but herself and her crew. The ability to travel to countries she only dreamed of seeing, meeting new people and immersing herself in different cultures . . .

But that was all a fantasy.

She was destined – as her father had reminded her many times – to marry a high-born man, and produce many strong, healthy little boys and beautiful, gentle little girls to continue the family line. Though her father educated her like he would a son, that didn't extend to learning about the family business as a proper heir should. She was to serve her husband in every way, obey his orders, and swear fealty to the Anglyan government – just as her mother had. No one asked *her* whether she wanted to swear fealty, or raise lots of children, or even marry a respectable man, she thought resentfully. What if she wanted to marry a scoundrel? Gods, how she wished she could be a commoner! She would give up some luxuries for freedom of choice –

'Are you watching those silly ships again, Catherine?'

She jumped at the familiar sharp voice, almost spilling gravy down her blouse. Turning, Catherine tried not to grimace upon seeing her father's tall, imposing form in the doorway, his jaw set and his dark blue eyes stern.

'Yes, Father. And they're not silly! They're beautiful,' she insisted petulantly, for once, sounding much younger than her fourteen years.

Her father laughed coldly.

'Rusting piles of gears and timber, that's all they are. You'd best remove all that fanciful dreaming from your head now. It won't get you very far.'

Catherine didn't say anything; she knew better than to argue by now.

'I need to tell you something,' Nathaniel declared, and she refrained from rolling her eyes. Storms forbid her father talk to her just because he wanted to.

'You will be accompanying me to the dockside office tomorrow morning. I have a meeting with Thomas to discuss cutting rations, and he wishes you to be present.'

'Of course, Father,' she agreed, trying to hide her distaste. The only reason Thomas Gale wanted her there was to discuss her betrothal to his loathsome son Marcus. He was an arrogant, bull-headed boy whom she despised with every fibre of her being, but her opinion mattered little. It was a good match from a political perspective and her own feelings were irrelevant.

'Good. Wear your best dress, I want you presentable,' her father instructed, eyeing with distaste her plain white blouse and tatty leather breeches. 'I intend to formally offer the betrothal contract, though I can't submit it as you're not yet a woman.'

Catherine nodded dutifully, thanking her lucky stars for her late development, and Nathaniel left the room, no doubt to go back to his office and continue working. Sometimes she wondered if he ever actually slept.

On the screen, a war report followed yet another recruitment cast, and she paused to listen.

'*Massacre by Merican soldiers at an Erovan medical centre, no survivors. Five hundred dead.*'

She felt suddenly nauseous. How could things like this be happening to Erovan civilians? There were only a few leagues of raging ocean and a single small storm barrier between Anglya and Erova, and the barrier had been there for as long as anyone could remember. Navigating the thicker clouds and tightly grouped whirlwinds was child's play to most pilots. Erova was closer than any other country, and took two days of flight at the most to reach, yet Catherine seemed so far removed from the troubles there. Not for the first time, she felt helpless. She wished that she were older, that she were stronger, that she could get out from under her father's thumb and do something to help. All too often she saw people gathering at the shipyard, dressed in combat uniform and boarding a military skyship. Boys and girls as young as thirteen stood shoulder to shoulder, led by stern guards who looked to be older than fifty. She yearned to be among them. Those brave soldiers were the only reason Anglya was safe from Merican attack.

She turned the newscast screen off and left the room, wandering to her mother's bedroom. Knocking, she nudged the heavy door open, her eyes adjusting to the darkened room. A lamp flickered at the bedside table.

'Mother?' she called softly.

'Catherine, dear,' a feeble, whispery voice breathed in reply, surprising Catherine. It wasn't often she found her mother awake and coherent. She smiled, crossing to the bed.

'How are you feeling?' she asked quietly, clambering up on to the soft bed and peering into the cocoon of quilts to see her mother's small face, clouded eyes staring dazedly up at her. Elizabeth's skin was pale and papery, and her once shining golden hair was dull and prematurely grey, but the barest hint of a smile tugged at her colourless lips as she looked up at her only child.

'No better or worse than usual,' said Elizabeth, and Catherine bit her lip. That was always her mother's answer. 'How are *you*, dearest?'

'Father wants to betroth me to Marcus Gale,' she announced, scowling.

Elizabeth's smile faded.

'When you were but a baby, and I was in better health, I used to talk of betrothing you to a beautiful little boy who would grow up to be a great man. But alas, he's gone, as is his mother . . .' Her voice trailed off and she stared wistfully at the familiar photo on the nightstand. It showed Elizabeth as a younger, healthier woman, with a beautiful blonde woman at her side. Both were dressed in exquisite gowns. The other woman was Queen Mary Latham, and the picture had been taken at the ball celebrating her son's seventh birthday. It was one of the last photographs taken of the woman before the entire royal family disappeared.

Before the war escalated and everything started to go downhill.

As Catherine was about to leave Elizabeth to rest, her mother spoke again with unexpected force. 'Don't let your father decide your future, Catherine! I let my father decide mine, and while I got a lovely daughter out of it . . .' She didn't need to finish her sentence. 'Your heart is yours and yours only to give away, and one day, you will find the man you wish to have it, and he will give you his. That man does not have to be Marcus Gale.'

Was her mother telling her to defy her father? How could she? She was the sole heir to the Hunter fortune — she might as well burn herself from the family tree.

'You are a brave girl, Catherine, and destined for greater things than becoming Marcus Gale's wife,' her mother said, her grey eyes clear for once. 'Your father is . . . a difficult man. He doesn't always understand how his actions affect others. And he certainly doesn't expect a woman to have a mind of her own, especially his daughter. Stand up for yourself, sweetheart, and make your own way in the world. Perhaps a shock like that would teach him an important lesson.'

Catherine's own eyes sparkled with understanding and excitement.

'But what about you?' she asked, drawing a faint smile to her mother's lips.

'It is a parent's job to look after their child, not the other way around. Don't worry about me, dear.'

'Mother, you do know how much I love you, don't you? More than anything,' Catherine told her firmly, leaning in to press a gentle kiss to her mother's brow and swallowing back the lump in her throat.

'And I love you, my dear one. But you're almost a young woman now, and you're beginning to need your mother less and less. Just . . . teach that father of yours that he's not lord of the storms, would you?' Elizabeth replied with a look of fierce determination, which Catherine matched, rendering the family resemblance astonishing.

'Oh, trust me. He won't know what hit him.'